RUN

From the back streets of Manchester to the nightclubs and penthouses of the beautiful people, Mandasue Heller knows the world she writes. Born in Warrington, she moved to Manchester, where she found the inspiration for her novels, in the 1980s: she spent ten years living in the infamous Hulme Crescents and was a professional singer for many years before turning her hand to writing.

She has three children, three grandchildren, and still writes and records songs with her musician partner, Wingrove, between books.

By Mandasue Heller

RUN

Mandasue Heller

MACMILLAN

First published in 2017 by Macmillan
an imprint of Pan Macmillan
20 New Wharf Road, London N1 9RR
Associated companies throughout the world
www.panmacmillan.com

ISBN 978-1-4472-8833-6

1 3 5 7 9 8 6 4 2

A CIP catalogue record for this book is available from the British Library.

Typeset by Ellipsis Digital Limited, Glasgow
Printed and bound by CPI Group (UK) Ltd, Croydon, CR0 4YY

Visit **www.panmacmillan.com** to read more about all our books
and to buy them. You will also find features, author interviews and
news of any author events, and you can sign up for e-newsletters
so that you're always first to hear about our new releases.

For my precious mum, Jean Heller
You were, and always will be, my idol

Acknowledgements

All my love, as always, to Win, Michael, Andrew, Azzura, Marissa, Lariah, Antonio, Ava, Amber, Martin, Jade, Reece, Kyro, Diaz, Nats, Dan, Toni, Auntie Doreen, Lorna, Cliff, Chris, Glen, and Win's family.

Love also to Norman, Kimberley, Betty and Ronnie, Rowetta, Katy and John, Martina, Jac and Brian, Ann, Hilary and Carolyn.

Massive thanks to Sheila Crowley, Wayne Brookes, and the team at Pan Mac.

And a very special thank you to Liz, Dr Sue Burke, Judith, Sue, Dawn, Chris, Ann, Sylvia, Barbara, Rick, Fleur, the Bass's, the staff at St Rocco's, and my mum's church family. You were all amazing during Mum's illness, and I can't thank you enough.

Lastly, thanks to my friends and readers on FB and T. Your lovely messages always brighten my day.

Prologue

She shivered when the moon disappeared behind a thick bank of clouds, plunging them into inky darkness. Rain began to spatter the windscreen as the car tyres bounced slowly over the cobbles, and the sudden swish of the automatic wipers made her jump. Hugging herself, she gazed up at the rear windows of the derelict row of shops to her left and the uninhabited terraced houses to the right. Most were concealed behind metal sheeting or smashed, and they were all as dark as the alleyway they were driving into, which told her that there was no one around to help her.

He eased to a stop alongside a padlocked gate halfway along the alley and cut the engine before jumping out and walking quickly around to her side. An icy blast of wind whipped her cheeks when he opened her door, and her legs felt like jelly as she unhooked her seat belt and climbed out.

'Don't even think about it,' he warned, gripping her tightly by the arm when he caught her casting a surreptitious glance back down the alley in search of an escape route. 'I don't want to hurt you, but I will if I have to.'

'You already are,' she replied shakily, wincing at the pain of his fingertips digging into her flesh.

He let go after a moment, and she rubbed at the sore spot as he turned and slotted a key into the padlock. The gate opened on to a rubble-filled yard at the rear of an empty shop unit, and he waved for her to go in ahead of him.

'I can't,' she croaked, taking a stumbling step back. 'It's too dark. There could be rats.'

A squeal of fear escaped her lips when he seized her by the wrist and hauled her into the yard, and tears flooded her eyes when her ankle twisted painfully as he marched her across the debris. He stopped at the steel back door and unlocked it with a mortice key before shoving her into a tiny, pitch-dark hallway. A steep flight of stairs faced them, at the top of which was another door.

The hallway reeked of mildew and rotten food, but when they reached the top of the stairs and he opened the door, an even fouler smell hit her in the face. Covering her nose with her hand, she stumbled over the threshold into the flat above the shop.

The front room was dark, but the moon had emerged from behind the clouds and tiny pinpricks of light were leaking in through the holes in the metal covering the window. As her eyes began to adjust, she was able to make out the outlines of a sofa, a single bed, a cluttered coffee table, and what appeared to be an upturned cardboard box holding a portable TV.

Behind her, he locked the door and then slid his hand along the wall in search of the light switch. Squinting in the unexpected brightness, she inhaled sharply when her gaze landed on the origin of the putrid smell.

'Oh, my God!' she cried, staring in horror at the battered body sprawled on the floor between the sofa and the window. 'Is she . . .'

'Dead?' he finished for her. 'I'd say so, judging by the stench she's giving off. Not that she was too bothered about hygiene when she was alive,' he went on, a glint of disgust flaring in his eyes as he gazed down at the body. 'And she actually thought I'd be interested in a skank like her. What a joke!'

'I don't understand.' She stared at him as if she'd never seen him before. 'What did she do to deserve this?'

'She couldn't keep her big mouth shut,' he replied, gazing coolly back at her. 'And the other one's lucky she was out when I called round there, or she'd have got the same.'

'Is that why you've brought me here?' she asked. 'Are you going to kill me, too?'

He opened his mouth to speak, but the sound of a brick knocking against another in the yard below made him snap his head around.

'What are you doing?' she gasped, her voice rising to a squeak when he yanked a gun out of his pocket.

'Shut your mouth!' he hissed, pushing her out of the way

and rushing over to the window. Straddling the body, he pressed his face up against the glass and peered through a hole in the metal sheeting. Several shadowy figures were moving through the darkness below, heading towards the door. A bright light suddenly flared, causing him to wince as it hit his eyes.

'Armed police . . .' a voice boomed. 'Come out with your hands in the air!'

'We've got to do as they say,' she sobbed, her legs shaking wildly as she backed towards the door. 'They'll shoot us both if you make them come in! *Please* . . . I'm begging you!'

The vibration of a battering ram being repeatedly smashed into the steel door shook the floor beneath their feet, and she almost wet herself with terror when, seconds later, footsteps began to thunder up the stairs.

PART ONE

1

Manny's nightclub had been a dive when Leanne Riley and Chrissie O'Brien used to go there in their teens, but it had changed beyond recognition. The tacky carpets, graffiti-covered walls, and ever-present stench of puke and piss were all gone; as was the filthy red-velvet bench seat where Leanne had shared her very first snog with some boy whose name she had long ago forgotten. Now ultra-chic and buzzing with pretty young things, the club had a completely different vibe – and Leanne wasn't sure she liked it.

'Not quite what I expected,' Chrissie remarked as she gazed around. 'Bit posh, isn't it?'

'And we're a bit old,' said Leanne. 'I feel like a teacher at the school disco.'

'Oh, well, we're here now, so we might as well stay for a drink,' Chrissie said, pushing Leanne towards the empty table she'd just spotted between the stage and the gents' toilets. 'Grab those seats while I go to the bar.'

Leanne quickly made her way to the table. Glad that it was

tucked away in the corner because she felt so out of place, she pulled her phone out of her bag to check the time as she sat down. Nine o'clock. If Chrissie hadn't bullied her into coming out tonight she'd be safely tucked up in bed watching TV by now. And she knew where she'd rather be.

Glancing up when a shadow fell over her a couple of minutes later, she assumed that the man who was smiling down at her was about to ask if he could take the empty chair.

'Sorry, it's taken,' she said, quickly placing her hand on it. 'My friend's sitting here.'

Instead of walking away as she'd expected, the man's smile widened. 'It *is* you! I thought so, but your hair's longer than I remembered, so I wasn't sure. But there's no mistaking those eyes.'

Intrigued, Leanne peered at his face. He was very good-looking, with short black hair, soft brown eyes, and a sexy smile; and his tight shirt showed off his muscular arms to such great effect she almost wished she *did* know him. But she was sure she'd never seen him before.

'I think you're mistaking me for someone else,' she said, trying not to sound too disappointed.

'No, I'm not.' He shook his head. 'I never forget a beautiful face. It's Leanne, isn't it?' Amused when she gave a cautious nod, he said, 'It's Jake . . . Jake Pearce? We were at school together.'

Leanne tried to place his name, but she didn't remember any lads at school called Jake – *or* any who had been anywhere near as gorgeous as him.

8

'Maybe this will help.' He placed his glass on the table, squatted down beside her, and cleared his throat before saying in a high-pitched voice, 'Leanne . . . will you go t' pictures wiv us?'

'Oh, my God!' She clapped a hand over her mouth when a long-forgotten memory leapt into her mind. '*Pissy* Pearce?'

'Ouch!' Jake winced. 'Cheers for remembering *that*. It took me years to shake that one off.'

'Sorry,' she apologized, staring at him in wonder. 'But you've changed so much.'

'Well, it has been twenty-odd years,' he pointed out, resting his elbow on the edge of her seat. 'I must have only been thirteen last time I saw you.'

Shivering when the heat from his arm warmed her thigh, Leanne shyly crossed her legs and stared at him again. Pissy Pearce, as they had all called him back then, had been a skinny boy with a scruffy uniform and wild hair that everyone had said was crawling with nits. The other kids had bullied him mercilessly, but Leanne had never joined in because she'd secretly felt a bit sorry for him – which was probably why he had taken a shine to her and asked her out that time. To her shame, instead of taking him aside to turn him down gently, she had told him to get lost in front of the whole school.

'I'm so sorry about what happened,' she said guiltily. 'I felt really bad about it and wanted to apologize, but you moved before I—'

'Forget it.' Jake gave her a forgiving smile. 'It was only

9

kids' stuff. Anyway, it was my own fault for thinking I stood a chance with someone like you.'

'Don't be daft.' Leanne blushed, still struggling to believe that this handsome, self-assured man had once been *that* boy.

Jake suddenly reached for her left hand and raised an eyebrow when he saw that her ring finger was bare. 'Not married?'

Already flustered, Leanne shook her head and slipped her hand free.

'Still young, free and single, like me, eh?' Jake grinned.

Secretly pleased to hear that there was no Mrs Pearce, Leanne said, 'So, have you moved back to England now, or is this just a visit?'

'Moved back?' Jake gave her a questioning look. 'I never left.'

'Really? I heard you'd emigrated to Australia.'

'Nah, we only went to Liverpool. My old man took off a couple of months after we got there, and my mum wasn't coping too well, so we . . .' Jake tailed off and shrugged, before adding, 'Let's just say we didn't stay in one place too long after that. What about you?' He smoothly changed the subject. 'Where are you living these days?'

'Not too far from where I used to live,' Leanne said evasively, hoping that he wouldn't ask for her address. He was clearly doing okay for himself if his expensive-looking watch and clothes were anything to go by, and she would be ashamed to let him see the state of the bedsit she'd been living in since splitting up with her ex, Dean, the previous year.

'Are you okay?' Jake asked when he saw a frown flicker across her brow.

'Yeah, I'm fine,' she lied, determinedly pushing Dean out of her mind. 'I've just got a bit of a headache.'

'This music can't be helping.' Jake cast a pained glance at the DJ's booth. 'I've been here for an hour, and I haven't recognized a single tune yet. The joys of getting old, eh?' He grinned. 'I bet our folks used to say the exact same thing about the music *we* listened to.'

'Mine definitely did,' Leanne agreed, smiling at the memory of her dad plugging his ears with cotton wool whenever she played her Oasis CDs, because he claimed Liam Gallagher's voice made him feel suicidal.

'Ours was way better than the shit they were into,' said Jake. 'I mean, come on . . . *Elvis*?'

'I quite liked Elvis,' Leanne admitted. 'It was Status Quo I couldn't stand, but my dad was mad about them.'

'Yeah, my old man used to rave about them, too. And my mum was into Robson and Jerome.' Jake shook his head and reached for his glass to take a swig of beer. Narrowing his eyes when he spotted a familiar face on the crowded dance floor, he nudged Leanne's leg with his elbow. 'Is that Carl Bates?'

Leanne followed his gaze. 'No, it's his son.'

'*Seriously*?' Jake was shocked. 'Christ, Carl was half that kid's size last time I saw him.'

'Well, like you said, it's been a long time,' Leanne reminded him, amused. 'A lot's changed round here since then.'

'You're telling me,' Jake agreed. 'I didn't recognize the place when I moved back a couple of months ago. I knew they'd demolished the old flats, but I hadn't expected the new estate to be so big. I nearly got lost when I took a walk round there.'

'Terrible, isn't it?' Leanne laughed softly. 'We call it the maze, it's that bad.'

Jake had been staring at her as she spoke. He smiled when she noticed and gave him a curious look, and said, 'I'm glad to see *some* things haven't changed. *You're* still as gorgeous as ever, and I'd recognize that laugh anywhere.'

Leanne shyly dipped her gaze when a thrill of excitement rippled through her body. What the hell was happening to her? She had sworn off men for life after catching Dean in bed with another woman, and had refused to entertain the idea of 'putting herself back on the market' – Chrissie's words, not hers. Yet here she was, getting all hot and bothered about a man she hadn't seen in twenty-odd years. And not just *any* man, but the one she had cruelly humiliated the last time she'd seen him.

'Sorry,' Jake apologized, thinking that he'd embarrassed her by coming on too strong. 'I wasn't trying to hit on you, I just meant . . .' Unsure what else to say, he gave a guilty smile. 'Well, I suppose I'd best leave you in peace and get back to the lads before they think I've done a runner.'

Dismayed, because she hadn't meant to make him feel bad, Leanne was about to tell him that he hadn't upset her when Chrissie arrived with their drinks.

'Oi, Casanova, shift,' Chrissie barked, nudging Jake with her knee. 'You're in my way, and she ain't interested, so do one.'

A sly smile came on to Jake's lips as he stood up and turned to face her. 'Well, well, if it isn't Christine O'Brien . . . Larger than life, and twice as bolshie.'

'You what?' Chrissie flashed him a withering look as she flopped into her seat.

Still grinning, Jake turned to Leanne and winked at her. 'It was really nice to see you again, Lee. Take care.'

'You too,' she replied quietly, wishing that Chrissie hadn't come back so soon.

'Who the hell was that?' Chrissie demanded when he turned and walked away.

'Jake Pearce,' Leanne said, sighing as she watched him go.

Chrissie's expression was as blank as Leanne's had been when Jake had first introduced himself. But then her eyes widened, and she said, 'You don't mean *Pissy* Pearce?'

'Yep.'

'But he's drop-dead gorgeous! How the hell did *that* happen?'

'I guess he grew up.' Leanne reached for her wine.

'Wow.' Chrissie shook her head. 'Who'd have guessed he'd turn out like *that*? How did you even know it was him? I wouldn't have recognized him in a million years.'

'I didn't,' Leanne admitted. 'He recognized me and came over. I didn't have a clue who he was until he reminded me about that time when he asked me out and I told him to get lost.'

'Oh, yeah, I remember that. I thought it was hilarious at the time, but I suppose it was a bit brutal really, wasn't it?'

'More than a bit. I can't believe I was such a bitch.'

'Ah, you weren't that bad. And, to be fair, he should have known you wouldn't give him the time of day back then. You were the prettiest girl in school and he was an ugly little sod.'

'He's not ugly now, though, is he?' Leanne murmured, shivering as she recalled the intensity of Jake's gaze.

'He certainly isn't,' Chrissie agreed. 'Although, I can't say I was too impressed by that larger-than-life crack he came out with. If that was his roundabout way of calling me fat, I'll give him what for, next time I see him.'

'He was obviously talking about your personality, or he wouldn't have mentioned you being bolshie,' Leanne assured her.

'Suppose not,' Chrissie conceded, sniffing huffily. 'Although, that's just as bad.'

'But true.' Leanne grinned.

Unable to deny this, Chrissie took a sip of her wine before asking, 'So what's he doing here? I thought he'd emigrated?'

'So did I, but they'd only gone to Liverpool,' Leanne told her. 'Apparently, his dad walked out on them not long after they got there, so him and his mum moved around for a while. But he's back in Manchester now.' Pausing when Chrissie gave her a knowing look, she frowned. '*What?*'

'Nothing.' Chrissie smirked. 'Just, somebody seems to know an awful lot about somebody, considering they haven't seen them in years. And I'm betting they wouldn't be so quick to say no if that somebody were to ask them out again.'

'Don't be ridiculous!' Leanne spluttered. 'We were only talking.'

'Jakey and Lee-Lee sitting in a tree,' Chrissie teased. 'K-I-S-S—'

Conscious that the young girls on the next table could hear every word, Leanne hissed, 'It wasn't like that. Anyway, he's obviously not interested in me.' She nodded towards the bar where she'd spotted Jake talking to a blonde in a red dress. 'Look who he's with.'

Chrissie glanced over and rolled her eyes in disgust. 'Trust *her* to get her hooks into him!'

'Do you know her?' Leanne asked, watching as the woman pressed her breasts up against Jake's chest and whispered into his ear.

'We both do,' said Chrissie. 'It's Sally Walker.'

'*Really?*' Leanne narrowed her eyes and peered at the woman's face. 'Didn't she used to have brown hair?'

'Yeah, *and* tiny tits,' Chrissie sniped. 'Wonder who paid for those bazookas, 'cos *she* sure as hell hasn't done a day's work in her pampered little life.'

Leanne sighed as an uncomfortable feeling of envy settled over her. She hadn't run in the same circles as Sally when they were younger, so she'd never actually spoken to her, but she remembered seeing her around and thinking that her parents must be mega-rich, because she always had the latest trainers and the trendiest clothes. In stark contrast, Leanne's mum and dad had worked their backsides off just to keep a roof over their heads, so she'd had to make do with whatever they could afford. And twenty years on, she was no better off.

'Well, Pissy might look hot, but he's obviously a bit thick if he prefers *her* over you,' Chrissie said loyally. 'But sack him. We can still have a good time, so drink up and I'll get another round in.'

'To be honest, I'd rather go home,' Leanne admitted. 'The music's awful and, apart from us and *them*,' she nodded in Jake and Sally's direction, 'everyone looks about twelve.'

'Oi, we'll have less of that,' Chrissie scolded. 'It's not healthy to stay locked away in your room all the time. You've not been out in ages, so you're bound to feel a bit weird, but you've got to let go of the past and start thinking about the future.'

'What future?' Leanne asked dejectedly. 'I'm thirty-three and I live in a shithole. I've got no job, no money, and the man I thought I was going to spend the rest of my life with cheated on me and ripped me off. How am I supposed to come back from that?'

Chrissie saw the despair in her friend's eyes and squeezed her hand. 'I know it's tough, but you *will* get past this. And you're already halfway there,' she added with a sly grin. 'On the way here you reckoned you were never going to *look* at another bloke, and now look at you ... getting all excited over Pissy Pearce.'

16

'Don't call him that,' Leanne chided, still feeling guilty about the way she had treated him in the past.

'Whatever you want to call him, it's a good sign,' said Chrissie. 'Trust me, this time next year you'll be all loved up with a new man who treats you like a princess, and all that shit you went through with Dean will feel like a bad dream.'

'I doubt that very much,' said Leanne. 'But thanks for trying to cheer me up. I don't know what I'd do without you sometimes.'

'Ah, shut up before you have me in tears, you soppy mare,' Chrissie scoffed. 'And drink up, 'cos this music's doing my head in.'

Leanne didn't need telling twice. Downing her wine, she grabbed her handbag and jumped to her feet. As they made their way to the door, she cast one last sneaky glance in the direction of the bar. Sally seemed to be in mega-flirt mode, judging by the way she was pouting her glossy lips and flicking her platinum hair extensions around like some kind of animated Barbie doll. Jake's back was turned, so Leanne couldn't tell if he was enjoying the attention. But he was a man, so she figured it was a fair bet that he was.

Out on the pavement a few seconds later, Leanne thought about what had just happened as she and Chrissie made their way to the bus stop – and, more importantly, what it signified. She had built a massive wall around her heart after Dean, and no man had even come close to scaling it, so the fact that Jake had excited her was a definite sign that she was healing. And that was a welcome glimmer of light at the end of the long, dark tunnel she'd been stuck in all year.

*

Jake hadn't seen Leanne leave, so he was disappointed when he stole a glance at her table only to see that she'd gone. Pissed off with himself for not thinking to ask for her number when he'd had the chance, he swallowed the rest of his pint and summoned the barman to order something stronger.

He'd never been to Manny's before, and was only here now because it was the designated meeting point for the stag party he'd been invited to. The plan had been to have one drink here, and then go on a bar crawl around town. But the groom had already been pissed when they got here, and none of the other lads seemed in any hurry to leave, so it looked like they'd be staying put for the rest of the night.

'So what do you think?' Sally asked.

'Eh?' Frowning, because he hadn't listened to a word she'd been saying for the last fifteen minutes, Jake gazed down at her. 'About what?'

'The party?' She batted her false eyelashes at him – one of which, he noticed, was coming unstuck. 'It's not too far from here, so we could easily walk there. Unless you'd rather take a cab?'

'Sorry, I can't,' he said. 'I'm on a stag do.'

'Aw, don't say that,' Sally moaned. 'I told my friends to go on ahead because I'd be coming with you. Your mates could always come with us, if you don't want to leave them,' she persisted, determined not to lose her grip on him. 'There'll be loads of booze and sniff, so they'll have a great time. But they'd have to ditch the bimbos first,' she added with a hint of disapproval. 'I don't think my friend would be too happy if we turned up with a load of underage girls in tow.'

Jake glanced over at the tables in the corner where the lads were sitting, and saw that they had managed to persuade some girls to join them while he'd been away. A stick-thin redhead in a lime-green dress that consisted of little more than a few strategically placed straps was perched on Ben's knee. When the girl turned her head at that exact moment and stared straight at him, he instinctively knew that she would ditch Ben and attach herself to him if he went back over there.

Sighing, he turned back to Sally. He'd have preferred to be taking Leanne home tonight, but that ship had already sailed, so he had two choices: go with Sally and have a bit of fun; or stay here and risk upsetting Ben if the redhead made a play for him.

Decided, he downed the double brandy the barman had just served him, and jerked his head at Sally. 'Come on, then; let's go check out this party of yours.'

2

Leanne and Chrissie had called in at the local pub on the way home. More at ease there than they had been at Manny's, they'd had a few drinks and a sing-song with the old-timer regulars before staggering merrily back to Leanne's house.

They had been laughing at the antics of one of the old men in the pub as they rounded the corner, but the laughter abruptly stopped when they reached Leanne's front door and a foul smell hit them.

'What the hell is that?' Chrissie asked, wrinkling her nose in disgust.

'The drain in the backyard must be blocked again,' Leanne said as she slotted her key into the lock. 'And it'll be worse inside, so you'd best hold your breath.'

'Actually, I think I'd best give that nightcap a miss,' Chrissie said, wafting a hand in front of her face. 'I didn't realize it was so late, and I've got to go in early to open the shop in the morning, so I can't risk sleeping through my alarm.'

Guessing that it was the smell rather than the time that had changed her friend's mind, Leanne said, 'Go on, then. Get yourself off home.'

'I'll call round for a brew after work tomorrow,' Chrissie promised, taking a step back to distance herself from the stench when Leanne opened the door. 'But I'll be drinking it on the corner if that hasn't been sorted by the time I get here,' she added with a grimace. 'When I think how you used to live before that swine—'

'Don't!' Leanne held up a hand to silence her. 'I'll end up slitting my wrists if I let myself go there tonight. Anyway, the smell doesn't really reach the top floor, so I hardly notice it.'

'I suppose it can't be any worse than shitty nappies,' Chrissie grunted. 'Dylan's got diarrhoea again, and the house reeks of it. But our Tina doesn't seem to think there's a problem. Not that she's seen much of him since she moved back in, mind; she just dumps him on my mum and pisses off out with whatever man is stupid enough to buy her drinks. If she wasn't my sister I'd report her to social services, she gets me that mad. But my mum would never forgive me if they took Dylan away, so what can I do?'

'There's no point letting it get to you,' Leanne counselled. 'Just keep reminding yourself that she'll have her own place soon.'

'Like *that's* ever gonna happen,' Chrissie snorted. 'It's been two months now, and she hasn't even started looking yet. Still, I suppose it keeps Mum off my back, 'cos she's too busy fussing over the baby to nag me about my weight.'

'There's nothing wrong with your weight,' Leanne said loyally. 'You always look gorgeous to me.'

'I think someone needs new glasses,' Chrissie chuckled as she started walking backwards. 'See ya later, *Specky*.'

Leanne stuck two fingers up at her before heading inside. Plunged into darkness as soon as she'd closed the door, she flicked the light switch and tutted when nothing happened. Forced to feel her way down the narrow passageway, she cried out in pain when the pedal of a bicycle she hadn't seen dug into her shin.

'Damn it!' she cursed, hopping back just in time to avoid being hit when the bike toppled over.

'Oi, watch it!' her neighbour, Speedy, barked, trotting down the stairs with a torch in his hand. 'It's worth a bomb, that.'

'I'm guessing it's not yours, then?' She glared at him as she rubbed her injured leg. 'Been out on the rob again, have you?'

'I ain't robbed nothing,' Speedy retorted, his eyes glinting in the torchlight as he stood the bike up against the wall and examined it for signs of damage. 'It's me mate's, if you must know.'

'Then it definitely shouldn't be here,' Leanne said tartly. 'It's bad enough that I'm always tripping over *your* stuff without hurting myself on your mate's stuff as well.'

'Don't you ever stop moaning, you?' Speedy jeered. 'You wanna buy a dildo and give y'self a seeing to, you uptight cunt.'

Leanne opened her mouth to give him a piece of her mind, but clamped it shut again when Mad Maggie, the old lady who lived in the ground-floor flat, yanked her door open and demanded to know what was going on.

'Nothing.' She pressed herself up against the wall to squeeze past Speedy. 'Just *him* being his usual inconsiderate self.'

'Least I don't walk round with me nose in the air thinkin' I'm better than every other bastard,' he yelled after her as she set off up the stairs. 'And it's got nowt to do with you where I get my shit from, so stay out of my business in future!'

Leanne continued on up to the top floor without answering. Speedy couldn't have been nicer when she'd first moved in, and she had been grateful for his help when he'd insisted on lugging her boxes up the two steep flights of stairs. But that was before she'd realized he was only ingratiating himself so he'd have an excuse to call round whenever he felt like it and help himself to whatever she'd been careless enough to leave on show. He'd acted so hurt when she had confronted him about some missing DVDs, she had actually felt guilty. Until she'd caught him passing them on to his dealer in exchange for drugs the next day. The atmosphere between them had been icy ever since, and she would happily move out if it meant never having to see his ugly face again. But she could barely afford *this* dump, so a move was totally out of the question.

It was even colder inside her bedsit than it had been outside, and Leanne shivered as she slipped out of her jacket and pulled off her boots. It had rained earlier in the day, and as she walked into the kitchenette she could hear water dripping into the pans she had positioned around the floor. Already depressed, her heart sank when she switched the light on and saw a soggy chunk of plaster sitting on the ledge.

'Oh, that's just bloody great,' she muttered as she spotted a gaping hole in the ceiling above. 'So much for light at the end of the flaming tunnel!'

Too fed up to be bothered clearing the mess tonight, she took the half bottle of white wine she'd been saving out of the fridge and, grabbing a mug off the drainer, carried them to bed.

*

Woken by the monotonous *thud-thud-thud!* of garage music blasting up through the floorboards the next morning, Leanne groaned when her head immediately began to pound in synch with the bass kick. Peeling an eye open, she squinted at the bedside clock and cursed Speedy under her breath when she saw that it was only 9 a.m. He never got up before noon, so he was either doing this to spite her for having a go at him about that stupid bike last night, or he was due up in court today. And she sincerely hoped it was the latter and that the judge would throw the book at him.

Disgusted to find that she was still dressed, she winced when the empty wine bottle rolled off the bed and hit the floor. Kicking it aside, she stumbled, shivering, to the bathroom.

Almost jumping out of her skin when someone pounded on the front door just seconds after she'd parked her backside on the icy toilet seat, she leapt to her feet and, yanking her jeans up, went to see who it was.

Her landlord, Roger, was standing on the landing, and her stomach churned when she picked up the scent of wet dog coming from the revolting sheepskin jacket he never seemed to take off.

'Well?' he demanded brusquely.

'Well what?' She was confused.

'What's the emergency? You rang me last night and left a message.'

'Did I?' Leanne frowned, unable to remember making any calls last night.

'Yes, you did,' Roger snapped. 'And I don't appreciate being disturbed in the middle of the night, so ring me in office hours in future.'

Irritated by his lecturing tone, her head still pounding, Leanne snapped back: 'Well I don't appreciate you hammering on my door at this time of the morning, so wait till afternoon in future. And you're not supposed to just let yourself in, so ring the bell next time.'

'This is my house,' Roger reminded her. 'And if there's an emergency I have the right to enter at will. So what is it?'

Leanne had already had enough of him, and she didn't want him stinking her flat out with his mangy coat. But she needed the roof to be fixed, and she knew from experience that she might not see him again for weeks if she let him go now.

'In there.' She stepped aside and jerked her head in the direction of the kitchenette.

Roger brushed past her and walked into the tiny room.

When he saw the plaster on the ledge, and then the hole above it, he turned to Leanne with a furious look on his face.

'Why the hell didn't you tell me about this before it got this bad? It's going to cost an absolute fortune to repair that.'

'Don't blame me,' she protested. 'I told you the roof was leaking ages ago, and you said you were going to send someone to look at it. It's not my fault you couldn't be bothered.'

'I'm a busy man, you should have reminded me.'

'I tried to, but you never answer your phone.'

'You could have left a message.'

'You don't usually answer them either. I'm actually shocked that you're here *now*, considering I only rang you last night.'

'You should be ashamed of yourself, living like this at your age,' Roger sniped, casting a disapproving look at the water-filled pans on the floor and the dirty crockery in the sink. 'This flat was in perfect condition before you moved in, and *now* look at it.'

'Ex*cuse* me?' Leanne screwed up her face in disbelief. 'It was an absolute dump when I moved in, and it's been getting steadily worse because *you* refuse to spend money on it. You're lucky I haven't reported you to Environmental Health.'

'Is that right?' Roger narrowed his eyes.

'Yes, it is,' Leanne retorted, refusing to be intimidated. 'And that hole's just the latest thing I could complain about. Look at this . . .' She turned on her heel, marched into the living area, and pointed at the corner above the window where the faded flock wallpaper had turned black and was peeling away from

26

the wall. 'That's got to be a health hazard. *And* this.' She yanked the thin curtain aside to reveal a puddle on the windowsill. 'And don't even get me started on *that*,' she jabbed her finger in the direction of the ancient electric fire, 'because it's an absolute deathtrap!'

'No one's ever had any problems with it before.'

'Well, *I'm* never going to use it, so feel free to take it with you when you leave. I'm sure you won't mind letting your wife and kids use it if you think it's that safe.'

'Typical woman, blowing things out of proportion,' Roger sneered as he walked into the room and prodded the fire with the toe of his boot. 'It's got years left in it, that.'

'My dad was an electrician, so I think I know dangerous wiring when I see it,' Leanne argued. 'And while we're on the subject of electrics, the hall light's blown again and I nearly broke my neck tripping over something in the dark last night. Oh, and the drain's blocked.'

'And how would you know that? Daddy a plumber as well, was he?'

'I can *smell* it,' Leanne snarled. 'And I'd hurry up and get it fixed if I was you, because the neighbours weren't too happy about how long it took you last time.'

'They'll live,' Roger said dismissively as he leaned down to retrieve the empty wine bottle he'd just spotted poking out from beneath the shabby armchair. Tipping it upside down, he arched an eyebrow. 'Oh dear . . . Does someone have a little problem?'

'How dare you!' Infuriated, Leanne snatched it out of his hand and slammed it down on the bedside table. 'It's none of your business what I do in the privacy of my own room!'

'It won't be your room for much longer if you don't get your rent arrears sorted,' Roger drawled, giving her another blast of wet dog mingled with BO as he strolled out into the hall.

'What are you talking about?' Leanne demanded, following him to the front door. 'My rent gets paid straight into your account, so I can't be in arrears.'

'This month's payment hasn't gone in,' Roger informed her as he stepped out on to the landing. 'You've got two weeks to get it sorted, then you're out. And just so we're clear' – he wedged his foot in the door to prevent her from closing it – 'if I *do* have to evict you, I won't be bothering to go through the courts.'

'Don't threaten me,' Leanne said indignantly. 'You'll get your money. Now move your foot before I call the police and have you arrested for harassment.'

Slamming the door shut when Roger withdrew his foot, Leanne rested her throbbing forehead against the wood as she listened to him make his way down the stairs. When the front door had opened and closed, she went back into her room and sank down on to the bed. This was the last thing she needed, but there was no point sitting here thinking about it. As disgusting as this place was, it was better than being out on the street – which was exactly where she'd end up if Roger had his way.

3

Jake heard his phone ringing and rolled over in bed to blindly grope for it. It stopped before he got to it, and his eyes snapped open when he heard an unfamiliar voice whisper: 'Sorry, he's asleep; you'll have to try again later.'

Pushing himself up on his elbows, he squinted at the naked girl who was standing by the window with her back to him.

'Oops, sorry!' Sally gave a sheepish little grin when she turned round and saw him staring at her. 'Didn't mean to wake you.'

'Who was it?' Jake asked, averting his gaze from her breasts.

'Someone called Ben.' She walked around the bed and handed the phone to him before taking a short, black satin dressing gown off a hook on the door. Slipping it on, she leaned over and kissed Jake on the lips. 'Stay right there, lover. I'll only be a minute.'

Jake wiped his mouth on the back of his hand as soon as she'd left the room, and dialled Ben's number as he jumped out of bed and looked around for his clothes. His cock wasn't fussy

29

where it ended up after a night on the bottle, but a repeat performance in the morning was determined by his eyes. And while Sally might have looked all right last night, now, with her make-up smeared and her hair extensions matted, she looked ropey as hell.

'Well, good morning, Mister *I've only been back in town a few weeks and I've already had more leg-overs than your average rock star*,' Ben teased when he answered. 'Who's the lucky lady this time?'

'Sally Walker,' Jake told him as he snatched his jeans off the chair by the window.

'What, *the* Sally Walker?' Ben sounded surprised. 'The one who told Pete King you were spying on her in the leisure centre changing rooms that time and got him to kick ten shades of shit out of you?'

'That's the one,' Jake muttered, quickly zipping his fly before reaching for his shirt. 'I don't think she's realized who I am, and I'm not going to enlighten her. I just want out of here. Can you pick me up?'

'What's the rush?' Ben asked slyly. 'Now you're there, you might as well stay for breakfast.'

'I wouldn't even be here if you hadn't copped off with that little tart last night,' Jake grunted as he fumbled with his shirt buttons. 'So quit taking the piss and get moving.'

'Keep your hair on, I'm only messing. Where are you?'

Realizing that he had no idea, Jake walked over to the window and peered out through the net curtain, but the road below held no clues.

'No idea. I'll have to ask her and text it to you. Now get in the car and be ready.'

As he ended the call, Sally came in carrying two cups of coffee. 'You're not going already, are you?' she pouted, handing one of the cups to him. 'My mum and dad have gone out, so we've got the house to ourselves. I thought we might spend the day in bed.'

'I've got things to do,' Jake muttered, placing the cup on the bedside table and sitting down to pull his shoes on.

'Aw, don't go,' Sally moaned, perching beside him and resting her head on his shoulder. 'I was really looking forward to picking up where we left off last night. Or should I say this morning,' she corrected herself, giggling softly as she walked her fingers up his arm. 'You're a bit of a beast when you get going, aren't you? I thought you were never going to stop.'

Jake was starting to feel queasy. There was a gaping hole in his memory between arriving at the party last night and waking up, and he was pissed off that he'd let himself get into such a state. Sally was obviously satisfied, so the booze clearly hadn't affected his performance. But he didn't remember a single thing about it. He only hoped she hadn't given him a dose, because he could do without the hassle of having to book himself into an STI clinic.

Sighing when he didn't answer, Sally said, 'Okay, if you really *have* to go, I suppose I'll let you – but only if you promise to take me out tonight. I thought we could go for a meal, then hit a couple of clubs. What do you think?'

'I've got a lot on,' Jake said off-handedly, standing up so abruptly she fell flat down on to the mattress. 'What's your address? I need to let my mate know where to pick me up.'

Sitting up, Sally sulkily told him the address and smoothed her hair as she watched him text it to Ben. 'So when *am* I going to see you again?' she demanded when he was done.

'I'll ring you,' he lied, taking a swig of the hot coffee to ease the pounding in his head before snatching his jacket up off the chair and heading for the door. 'Cheers for last night.'

'Wait, you haven't got my number.' Sally jumped up and rushed to get her phone from the other side of the bed.

Jake had absolutely no intention of calling her, but he pretended to type her number into his phone to keep her quiet, and then tried again to leave. Sally pounced before he reached the door, and it was all he could do not to shove her off when she wrapped her arms around his waist and laid her head on his chest.

'I'm so glad I met you,' she purred, confirming his suspicions: she hadn't recognized him. 'I don't usually bring men home on the first date – and, believe me, they *always* ask,' she went on. 'But I'm not that kind of girl. I only go with men who are really special – like you.'

Above her head, Jake's eyebrows shot up. Who did she think she was kidding? Back in the day, she'd had a massive reputation for putting out at the drop of a hat, which was why Pete King and his idiot mates from the Year 10 footie team had sniffed around her like dogs on heat. So, unless she'd become some kind of born-again virgin since he'd left town, she was lying through her teeth.

'You are going to ring, aren't you?' she asked now, her needy tone telling Jake that she probably didn't get too many call-backs.

'Yeah, course,' he lied, quickly disentangling himself when he heard a car horn beeping outside. 'That'll be my mate. Best go.'

'I'll see you out,' Sally offered, following him out on to the landing.

'There's no need,' he said, quickly setting off down the stairs. 'Go back to bed and finish your coffee.'

'I want to wave you off,' she insisted, sticking on his heel. 'Anyway, I can't let you go without a goodbye kiss.'

'Probably best if we don't,' he mumbled. 'I've got wicked morning breath.'

'I don't mind,' she trilled.

No, but I do, he thought, wondering why tarts like her could never take a hint.

Determined not to let her lips come near his again, Jake yanked the front door open when they reached the foot of the stairs and lurched out on to the path, sure that she wouldn't follow him out in that slip of a dressing gown. Nodding good-bye, he rushed to Ben's car and leapt into the passenger seat.

Craning his neck to look Sally over when she came out on

to the doorstep, Ben muttered, 'Oh, my!' when he saw her nipples jutting out through the thin satin.

'They're fake, like the rest of her,' Jake said scathingly. 'Now, if you've finished gawping, drive.'

'Rough night?' Ben asked, glancing round at him as he set off.

'I wouldn't know.' Jake let out a weary breath and sank into his seat. 'She took me to a party in the Moss, and I can't remember a thing after that.'

'Head fuck,' Ben chuckled, guessing from the location that the party would have involved copious amounts of weed and over-proof Jamaican rum.

'Head*ache*,' Jake muttered, lighting a couple of cigarettes and passing one to Ben. 'How did you get on?' he asked as he rolled his window down. 'You looked like you were well on your way to a happy ending when I left the club.'

'Well I didn't get one,' Ben admitted, squinting as he took a drag on his fag. 'Some rugby-player types turned up, and I didn't see her for dust. Probably just as well, though,' he added philosophically. 'I think she might have been a bit young.'

'A *bit*?' Jake snorted.

'Yeah, well, I won't be going back there in a hurry,' Ben sighed. 'Our Glen had a good time, though.'

'Glen?' Jake frowned.

'My cousin,' Ben reminded him. 'The stag? Jesus, you've got a bad memory.'

'Getting old.' Jake shrugged.

'Yeah, I know,' Ben agreed with a smirk. 'So old, you don't even remember what you got up to last night. Sally Walker, though, eh?' He shook his head. 'Never saw that one coming.'

'All right, drop it,' Jake muttered, pulling his phone out of his pocket. 'I've got more important things to think about.'

'Like what?' Ben asked.

'This and that,' Jake said evasively as he flicked through his emails. 'Have you got a charger for this?' he asked when the 'low battery' alert popped up on the screen.

Ben glanced at the phone, and then nodded at the glove compartment. 'In there.'

Jake took out the charger and plugged one end into the cig-arette lighter and the other into the phone, then settled back to finish his smoke.

When they pulled up outside Ben's house a short time later, a figure at the other end of the road caught Jake's eye, and he quickly unbuckled his seat belt.

'What's up?' Ben asked when he leapt out of the car. 'Do you need the loo, or something?'

'Just someone I need to talk to,' Jake called over his shoul-der. 'Go in and put the kettle on. I'll be up in a minute.'

*

Deep in thought, Leanne had been staring at the ground as she made her way home. As if her day hadn't started off badly enough with the visit from her obnoxious landlord, it had got a whole lot worse when she'd called into the job centre to ask why her rent hadn't been paid, only to learn that her benefits had been stopped because she'd been placed on a six-week sanction for missing an appointment.

She hadn't received either of the letters they claimed to have sent out: the first calling her in for the appointment, the second informing her of the sanction. But the woman she'd spoken to clearly hadn't believed her – or cared – so she was now facing the prospect of trying to survive without money for the next six weeks.

Still reeling about her bad fortune, she muttered an apology when she bumped into somebody, and stepped aside to go around them. Irritated when they did the same and blocked her path, she looked up at last and was shocked to see Jake smiling down at her.

She hadn't been able to see him clearly in the club, but he was even more handsome than she'd thought, and her stomach did a flip when she noticed the gold flecks in his chocolate-brown eyes.

'Oh, hi,' she murmured, acutely conscious of the fact that she was still wearing the same clothes she'd had on last night, and hadn't even brushed her hair before rushing out of the bedsit this morning, never mind her teeth. 'Sorry, I was miles away.'

'No kidding.' Jake grinned. 'Anyway, I'm glad I bumped into you. I looked for you last night, but you'd already gone, so I didn't get the chance to ask if you fancied meeting up some-time – for a coffee, or whatever?'

'With or without Sally?' The words slipped out before

Leanne could stop them, and she gave herself a mental slap across the face as her cheeks burned.

'*Sally?*' Jake drew his head back and gave her a questioning look.

'She's your girlfriend, isn't she?' Leanne said uncertainly, wondering if she'd got the wrong end of the stick – *hoping that she had.*

'No, she's not!' Jake exclaimed, as if the very thought disgusted him. Then, frowning when it occurred to him that she might actually be friends with Sally and could already have heard it from the horse's mouth, he asked, 'What made you think that?'

'I just assumed you were together when I saw you with her last night,' Leanne admitted, her blush deepening, because now she'd let him know that she had checked him out before leaving the club.

'Well, we're not,' Jake said, smiling again as he added, 'And now we've cleared that up, what are you doing tonight?'

As stupidly pleased as she was to hear that he and Sally weren't an item, Leanne didn't want to appear too eager, so she gave a nonchalant shrug. 'Nothing much. Chrissie said she might call round for a brew on her way home from work, but that's all I've got planned.'

'How about we meet up after that, then?' Jake suggested. 'I've got some stuff to do this afternoon, but if you give me your number I'll ring you when I'm done.'

'Okay,' Leanne agreed simply, still playing it cool.

'Great!' Jake grinned. 'My phone's in the car,' he said then, taking a step back. 'Wait there a sec while I—'

Before he could finish, Ben called his name, and he turned to see his friend waving his phone in the air.

'It's Sally. I told her to ring back, but she says it's urgent.'

Furious, because he hadn't given Sally his number and could only assume that she'd gone through his phone and copied it down before Ben rang this morning, Jake gritted his teeth before turning to Leanne.

'I'm really sorry about this. Give me a minute to get rid of her and I'll be right back.'

'Don't bother,' Leanne said coolly.

'Hey, wait!' Jake spluttered when she turned and started walking hurriedly away in the direction she'd come from. 'It's not what you think. I can explain.'

Forced to stop when he caught up with her at the corner, Leanne raised her chin proudly. 'I really haven't got time for this, Jake. I'm busy, and your girlfriend's waiting to talk to you, so let's leave it at that, shall we?'

'But she's *not* my girlfriend,' Jake insisted. 'Last night was the first time I've seen her in years, and I didn't even want to talk to her, but I couldn't get rid of her.'

'So why did you give her your number?'

'I didn't.'

Leanne released a weary breath. He looked and sounded sincere, and she really wished she could believe him. But she'd been down this road with Dean, who would argue that black was white and night was day, and she had no intention of being taken for a ride again – by Jake, or *any* man.

'Mate, are you coming to take this?' Ben shouted. 'She's getting impatient.'

Leanne looked at Jake with disappointment in her eyes, then shook her head and walked away.

Sensing that it would be futile to follow her again, Jake marched back to Ben and snatched the phone out of his hand.

'*What?*'

'I only wanted to say hello,' Sally replied warily, thrown by his angry tone. 'I know you said you were going to be busy, but I didn't think you'd mind if I caught you before you got started. I really enjoyed last night, and I know you enjoyed it too, so I thought—'

'Let me stop you right there,' Jake interrupted sharply. 'I've tried to be nice about it, but you obviously can't take a hint, so let me spell it out for you. You're not my type – never were, never will be – and last night was a mistake I won't be repeating, so don't ring me again. In fact, delete my number, 'cos if I'd wanted you to have it I'd have given it to you!'

Ben sucked in a sharp breath when Jake abruptly disconnected the call. 'Bloody hell, man. I know they say revenge is best served cold, but that was pure *ice*.'

'It had nothing to do with revenge,' Jake replied tersely. 'She needed telling. Oh, and cheers for yelling her name out like that, by the way. I'd just convinced Leanne that I'm not seeing her, but now she thinks I was lying, she'll probably never talk to me again.'

'That was Leanne?' Ben frowned. 'Aw, mate, I'm sorry, I didn't recognize her. I would never have said anything if I'd known.'

'Forget it.' Jake sighed, raking a hand through his hair. 'You weren't to know. Hurry up and open the door, 'cos I really need a coffee.'

Ben unlocked his front door, but didn't follow when Jake stepped inside. It had taken Jake a long time to get over Leanne, but it was clear that he was still holding a torch for her if the gutted look on his face right now was anything to go by, and Ben felt guilty for ruining his chances. Determined to make up for his gaffe, he took his spare key out of his wallet and tossed it to Jake.

'Go on up and put the kettle on. I just remembered I need cigs.'

'Get me some while you're there,' Jake said, reaching into his pocket.

'My treat.' Ben was already heading back to the car.

4

Leanne was furious with Jake for lying to her – and even more furious with herself for being gullible enough to almost fall for it. *But that's men for you,* she thought bitterly. *They'll say anything to get a leg-over – and to hell with the girls whose hearts they're breaking in the process.*

Determined to forget about him and concentrate on looking for somewhere else to live before Roger turfed her out, she called in at the newsagent's on her way home and picked up a copy of the local paper. She'd come out and was about to cross the road, when a car suddenly swerved in towards the kerb and screeched to a halt, forcing her to jump back on to the pavement.

'You stupid idiot!' she blasted the driver through the windscreen. 'Why don't you watch where you're going?'

'I'm really sorry,' Ben apologized, climbing out and walking quickly round to her. 'I just spotted you at the last minute and had to slam the brakes on. Can we talk?'

Leanne's chest tightened when she recognized him as the

man who'd told Jake that Sally was on the phone. 'About what?' she snapped – as if she didn't already know.

'Jake.'

'Not interested.'

'Please?' Ben pleaded. 'I know you didn't believe him about Sally, but he was telling the truth.'

'It's none of my business either way,' Leanne said curtly. 'And I'm supposed to be somewhere, so if you'll excuse me . . .'

'You know you broke his heart, don't you?' Ben blurted out when she started to walk away. 'He was completely besotted with you. I've never seen him so cut up.'

Hesitating, Leanne said, 'That was years ago. And I apologized for it last night, so you're wasting your time if you're trying to make me feel guilty.'

'I'm honestly not,' Ben assured her. 'I just wanted you to know that he still likes you – a lot. And if you'd heard the way he spoke to Sally after you left, you'd know he's not interested in her.'

'He was interested enough to give her his number,' Leanne pointed out. 'And don't bother saying he didn't, because *he's* already tried that one.'

Eager to get off the subject of Sally before he tripped himself up and let slip where his friend had spent the night, Ben said, 'Look, I've no idea how she got hold of his number, but Jake said he didn't give it to her, and I believe him. He's a good man, and I'm asking you to give him a chance to explain, that's all. And if you won't do it for *him*, do it for *me*,' he added

42

cheekily. 'I don't think I can cope with him moping about like a sad-sack again. He was bad enough the first time round.'

Leanne folded her arms and peered at him thoughtfully. Chubby, with out-of-control curls, a soppy grin, and corduroy trousers that even her dad wouldn't be seen dead in, he was the complete opposite of handsome, well-groomed Jake, and she would never have put them together as friends. But he had a genuine smile, and she respected him for going out of his way to help Jake out.

Taking her hesitation as a sign that he was winning her over, Ben tipped his head to one side and gave her his best puppy-dog eyes. 'Have my powers of persuasion worked, or do I have to go back empty-handed and suffer the mighty sulk?'

'Okay, fine, I'll hear him out,' Leanne agreed. 'But if I find out that he *was* lying, that'll be the end of it.'

'*Yes!*' Ben punched the air in jubilation and backed towards the car. 'Oops, sorry, where are my manners?' he said, pausing after opening the door. 'Can I give you a lift somewhere?'

'No, it's all right.' Leanne smiled. 'I only live round the corner.'

'Me too! Leighton Avenue. Oh, but of course you already know that, don't you, seeing as you've just seen me there. *Duh!*' Ben gave a self-deprecating grin and slapped himself on the forehead. 'Right, well, I'd best stop waffling and let you go. Oh, but I should probably take your number first, so Jake can get hold of you.'

Laughing, because he had to be one of the ditziest men

she'd ever met, Leanne gave him her number, and then watched as he jumped into his car and drove away, almost colliding with a bus in his haste to get back to Jake.

Desperate to tell Chrissie what had happened, but conscious that her friend wasn't allowed to take personal calls during work hours, Leanne sent her a text message as she let herself into the bedsit a few minutes later, asking her to call ASAP.

Assuming that Chrissie must be on a break when, almost immediately, her phone started ringing, she answered it without checking the screen.

'You'll never guess what just happened . . . I only bumped into Jake Pearce on my way home from the job centre!'

'I know. I was there.'

Mortified when she realized it was Jake, Leanne held the phone away from her mouth and let out a silent scream.

'Leanne . . . ?' His voice floated up to her. 'Are you there?'

'Yes, I'm here,' she said, her cheeks blazing as she dropped the newspaper on to the bed and shrugged out of her jacket. 'Sorry, I thought you were Chrissie.'

'I kind of guessed that. So, Ben tells me he bumped into you at the shops?'

'Almost literally.' Leanne sat down to pull off her boots. 'He practically ran me over, and then nearly crashed into a bus.'

'He's a disaster waiting to happen, that one.' Jake chuckled. 'Thanks for giving him your number, though. Does this mean we can forget about earlier and start again?'

'I suppose so,' she agreed. 'But, like I said to your friend, if I find out you were lying about Sally, I'll—'

'I wasn't,' Jake cut in. 'And I swear I didn't give her my number. You're the only girl I'm interested in, and I'll prove it if you give me the chance.'

Leanne breathed in deeply when her stomach fluttered. 'Okay, I suppose I'm willing to give you the benefit of the doubt.'

'Great!' Jake sounded relieved. 'So are we still on for tonight? Only there's a restaurant in town that I thought we could try. Ben took his mum there for her birthday, and he reckons the food's really good.'

'Oh . . .' Leanne's heart sank. 'I didn't realize you wanted to go to a restaurant. I thought we were just going for a coffee?'

'In case you hadn't heard, they sell coffee at restaurants these days,' Jake quipped. 'But I'm easy if you'd rather go to a cafe or something.'

Leanne caught a hint of disappointment in his voice, and said, 'No, the restaurant will be fine. But I'll pay my share,' she added, praying as she said it that Chrissie would lend her some money.

'Behave!' Jake said sternly. 'I invited you, so I'm paying – and don't insult me by arguing about it. I'll pick you up at eight, if that's okay? What's your address?'

Too embarrassed to let him come within sniffing distance of the house, Leanne said, 'Eight's fine, but I've got to nip round to drop something off at a friend's place later, so why don't I meet you on the corner where I saw you earlier.'

'I'll see you there, then,' Jake agreed.

After saying goodbye, Leanne tossed the phone on to the bed and, rushing over to the wardrobe, yanked the door open. The drab collection of clothes that faced her killed her excitement stone dead. She'd had some lovely dresses when she was living with Dean, but she'd made the mistake of leaving everything behind when she stormed out after catching him screwing another woman in their bed, and by the time she'd felt able to confront him, the bastard had done a flit and the landlord had cleared the place out. And, just to add insult to injury, when Leanne had gone to the bank to withdraw her half of their joint savings, she'd found out that Dean had already emptied their account – and there hadn't been a damn thing she could do about it.

Time was supposed to be a healer, but the hurt and anger were never too far from the surface, and Leanne doubted that she would ever truly get over it.

Which made her wonder if she'd made the right decision in agreeing to go out with Jake tonight.

As gorgeous as he was, and as undeniably flattering as it was to know that he still liked her after all these years, she didn't know the first thing about him, and she wasn't sure she could take it if he turned out to be another Dean.

Thinking that it would probably be better if she put a stop to this before it went any further and she ended up getting hurt again, Leanne reached for her phone to call Jake and tell him she'd changed her mind. But it started ringing before she had the chance, and this time it *was* Chrissie.

'I'm rushed off my feet, so this will have to be quick. What's up?'

'It doesn't matter.' Leanne slumped down on the bed and flopped back against the pillows. 'I was only going to tell you that I bumped into Jake Pearce this morning and ended up agreeing to go out for dinner with him tonight. But—'

'Whoa! Back up there a minute, lady! You agreed to do *what*?'

'Go out for dinner with Jake.'

'*Really*? And Sally's okay with that is she?'

'That was a misunderstanding. He told me he's not seeing her.'

'Oh, well, if he's told you, then it *must* be true,' Chrissie said sarcastically. 'It's not like he'd be stupid enough to admit he's seeing another woman when he's trying to get into *your* knickers, is it? And we obviously imagined they were all over each other last night.'

'That wasn't what it looked like,' Leanne said defensively. 'Sally approached him, and he was only being polite.'

'Mmmm . . .' Chrissie didn't sound convinced. 'Well, I hope that's the truth, because I'd hate you to get messed about again. Just promise you won't rush into anything, 'cos—'

'If you'd let me speak, I *was* going to tell you that I'm not going,' Leanne interrupted. 'I was about to ring him when you called.'

'Why?'

'Because it's not worth the risk.'

'Don't be daft,' Chrissie argued. 'I know you loved Dean and it broke your heart when he turned out to be the world's biggest prick, but you can't tar every man with the same brush, babe.'

'Bloody hell, you've changed your tune, haven't you?' Leanne snorted. 'A minute ago you were making out like I was an idiot for agreeing to go out with him, and now you're trying to *persuade* me to go. Make your mind up.'

'I don't know him well him enough to have an opinion either way,' Chrissie admitted. 'But you spoke to him, and if you believed him, that's fine by me.'

'I actually did,' Leanne said truthfully. 'And I do really like him. I'm just not sure I'm ready to start dating again.'

'Well, you'd best hurry up and *get* ready,' Chrissie said bluntly. 'You ain't no spring chicken, baby.'

'Thanks!' Leanne spluttered. 'I thought you were supposed to be making me feel better, not worse.'

'Only trying to help.' Chrissie was unapologetic. 'Look at it this way: if you go out with Jake and it doesn't work out, you won't have lost anything, but you *will* have had a laugh and a nice dinner. And if you're really lucky, you might even get a bit of *dessert*,' she added with a sly chuckle.

'I don't think so!' said Leanne. 'This isn't a *date* date, so there'll be none of that, thank you very much.'

'If you say so,' Chrissie scoffed. Then, more seriously, 'Just promise you'll get him to walk you to the door if it's late when you get home, 'cos there were a couple of shifty-looking blokes hanging about round the corner from yours last night. They didn't do anything, but I could feel them watching me all the way down the street, and it really creeped me out.'

Unnerved by the sound of that, Leanne got up and wandered over to the window. There was nobody outside, apart from Speedy, who was kneeling on the pavement below fiddling with the bike that supposedly belonged to his friend. Afraid that he might spot her and accuse her of spying on him, she stepped back and gazed into her wardrobe again.

'Jake wants to take me to a restaurant, but I've got nothing decent to wear. Do you think your Tina would lend me something? She's around the same size as me, and she always looks good.'

'She *should* look good, the amount she spends on clothes,' Chrissie said scathingly. 'Or, should I say, the amount the idiot men she goes out with spend on them. I swear she's a prostitute on the sly.'

'Don't be wicked. She's not that bad.'

'Oh, she is, believe me.'

'Will you ask her?'

'No.'

'Aw, *please*, Chrissie. I'm desperate.'

'I said I'm not asking her, but I didn't say I wouldn't get you anything,' Chrissie said slyly. 'What kind of look are you going for?'

'Something classy,' said Leanne. 'You know what suits me.'

'Okay, leave it with me. I'll nip home after work and grab something. What time's Jake coming for you?'

'I said I'd meet him on the corner of Leighton Ave at eight.'

'How very romantic,' Chrissie teased. 'Are you sure he's taking you to a restaurant and not down the park with a bottle of cider?'

'Oh, ha ha, very funny,' Leanne drawled. 'It was my idea to meet him there, actually. I can't let him come here while it stinks of drain, can I?'

'Ah, I'd forgotten about that. Have you spoken to your landlord yet?'

'Yeah, he came round this morning. Apparently, I called him last night when I was drunk and left a message. I haven't got a clue what I said, but it did the trick, so it should get sorted in a month or so.'

'A *month*?' Chrissie was outraged. 'He can't leave it that long. Tell him you're going to report him if he doesn't do it sooner.'

'I can't,' Leanne admitted sheepishly. 'There's a problem with my rent, and he's already threatening to evict me.'

'What problem?'

Reluctant to go into it now, Leanne said, 'I'll tell you when I see you. You've got to get back to work, and I need to start getting ready.'

'It's not even lunchtime yet,' Chrissie pointed out. 'I thought you weren't going out till eight?'

'I'm not. But I need to take a shower, and you know how long my hair takes to dry. And then I'll have to do my make-up. And it's been a while since I wore any, so I'll probably need a few goes at it before I get it right.'

'God, you're hopeless.' Chrissie tutted. 'Leave it till I get there. I'll do it for you.'

'Thanks,' Leanne said gratefully. 'But no red lipstick.'

'And what's wrong with red?'

'Nothing – on *you*. But it makes *me* look like a super slut.'

'Don't be ridiculous,' Chrissie argued. 'I've seen you in red and you look amazing. You're just scared because you've forgotten what it feels like to have a man think you're sexy.'

Leanne couldn't deny that. She *was* scared. She hadn't been intimate with a man since Dean, and she was scared of giving off the wrong signals: too tarty, and Jake would think she was up for instant sex; too conservative, he'd think he was on a date with his aunt. It was a minefield of uncertainties and, once again, she thought about calling it off.

After saying goodbye to Chrissie, Leanne went to the bathroom to check if the temperamental shower was running hot or cold today. Relieved when it started to heat up, she went back into the bedroom to get undressed. She would make a firm decision about Jake later, but there was no harm in getting ready in the meantime.

5

Excited about her friend's impending date, because neither of them had had a whiff of male action in over a year – *three*, in her case – Chrissie rushed straight home after leaving work. Glad to find that Tina was out when she got there, she ran up to her bedroom to root out some decent clothes for Leanne from her sister's vast collection.

Annoyed to find the room in a complete mess, with clothes strewn all over the floor and make-up and dirty cotton wool balls littering the dressing table, Chrissie cursed Tina under her breath. They had shared this room when they were growing up, but it had been Chrissie's alone since she'd moved back home after losing her dad and her fiancé in quick succession three years earlier. This room had been her sanctuary, and she had relished the peace and order she'd managed to create. But that had all changed when Tina had turned up like the proverbial bad penny a few months ago, and it was now a constant battle to keep the room tidy.

At the sound of the front door opening, Chrissie cocked an

ear when she heard Tina yell: 'No, Jimmy, it is *not* okay. You promised to take me out tonight, and now you're telling me you can't, because your stupid girlfriend's having her stupid friends round for stupid fucking dinner? Well, I hope it fucking chokes you! And don't think I'll be sitting around waiting for you, 'cos I won't. There are plenty of men who'd jump at the chance to take me out, and they've *all* got bigger dicks than *you*!'

When Tina abruptly cut the call and started stomping up the stairs, Chrissie snatched a handful of clothes from the heap on her bed and stuffed them into a plastic bag. Hiding it inside her coat, she walked out of the bedroom just as Tina reached the landing.

'Everything okay?'

'Mind your own fucking business!' Tina snarled, pushing past her and going into the bathroom.

Smirking when Tina slammed the door in her face, Chrissie went downstairs and popped her head around the living room door to say hello. When she saw that her mum was fast asleep on the sofa with Tina's two-year-old son, Dylan, in her arms, she quietly backed out again and set off for Leanne's place.

*

Leanne hadn't been joking when she'd told Chrissie that it was going to take a long time to get ready. Her dad had always joked that her mum must have had an affair with a gypsy, because her hair was so much darker and thicker than either of theirs. But that thickness made it an absolute nightmare to style, and it was even harder to manage since she'd let it grow so long.

She hadn't been able to afford a trip to the hairdresser's in months, and didn't trust herself to go near it with scissors, so it was almost down to her waist by now. She usually kept it tied up in a pony or plait, but she wanted to make a special effort for Jake, so she'd spent the afternoon laboriously curling it one section at a time with her ancient heated rollers. It was hanging down her back in glossy waves now, and she'd pinned it up at the sides, leaving just two long tendrils loose to frame her face.

It had taken the better part of the day to achieve, and her arms were aching from lifting, rolling, unrolling, and rolling again, but she was pleased with the result. Now all she needed was for Chrissie to hurry up and get here, to finish the job and turn her into a restaurant-worthy date.

Still in her dressing gown when Chrissie arrived at last, Leanne was dismayed to see that her friend was still dressed in her smart work clothes.

'Haven't you been home yet?' she asked as Chrissie flopped into the armchair and kicked off her stiletto-heeled shoes. 'I've only got half an hour.'

'Don't panic, I've got the clothes.' Chrissie pulled the bag out from under her coat and tossed it to her. 'I'm not sure what's in there, though, 'cos our Tina came home and I just had to grab whatever was closest to hand.'

'I wish you'd just asked her,' Leanne said guiltily as she

pulled two dresses and a skirt and blouse out of the bag and laid them on the bed. 'I'll be looking over my shoulder all night in case she sees me and recognizes them.'

'Don't worry, I heard her having a row with her latest wallet, so she won't be going anywhere near any restaurants tonight,' Chrissie assured her. 'She's broke, so she'll probably just go to the pub and cadge drinks.'

Relieved to hear that, because she could just imagine Tina yelling, *'Hey, bitch, get my clothes off!'* in the middle of the restaurant, Leanne held one of the dresses up against herself and turned to Chrissie.

'I'm not sure about that colour on you,' Chrissie said thoughtfully. 'Try the other one.'

Leanne reached for the second dress, and Chrissie pursed her lips. 'Not bad. Now try the blouse.'

Leanne held up the blouse and raised an eyebrow.

'The colour's better, but I'm not sure about the frilly neck,' Chrissie mused. 'I think I'm too used to seeing you in your goth gear.'

'*Goth* gear?' Leanne gave her a bemused look. 'Since when have I been goth?'

'Since you apparently decided it was illegal to wear anything except black and grey,' Chrissie teased, getting up and hobbling into the kitchenette. 'Try the second dress on while I make a brew,' she called over her shoulder as she filled the kettle. 'Then I'll do your make-up.'

Leanne cast a worried glance at the clock as she slipped out of the dressing gown and stepped into the dress, muttering, 'God, I'm never going to be ready on time.'

'If you're late, he'll just have to wait,' Chrissie said as she reached into the cupboard for cups. Frowning when she noticed the debris on the ledge, she said, 'What the hell have you been doing in here? It looks like a building site.'

'Look up,' Leanne said, struggling to zip the dress.

Chrissie gazed up and muttered, 'Shit!' when she saw the hole in the ceiling. 'When did that happen?'

'It was like that when I got home last night. Roger tried to blame me for not telling him the roof was leaking, but I *have* told him. He just doesn't listen.'

'Typical!' Chrissie tutted as she dropped teabags into the cups. 'He's fast enough to take your money, but you don't see him for dust when something needs fixing. Subject of money . . .' She wandered into the doorway. 'What did you mean earlier about a problem with your rent?'

'My benefits got sanctioned, so it hasn't been paid this month,' Leanne explained. 'Roger told me this morning. Said I've got two weeks to get it sorted or he's going to evict me.'

'You're kidding? Why have they sanctioned you?'

'They said I missed an appointment, but I didn't get the letters they reckon they sent out, so I didn't even know about it.'

'God, that's awful. What are you going to do?'

'Nothing I *can* do, apart from tighten my belt and pray my numbers come up on the lottery.'

'I can always lend you some money if you need it?' Chrissie offered.

'Thanks, but I'll manage.' Leanne gave her a grateful smile. 'If worse comes to worst and I get evicted, I'll just have to go into a hostel. Which might not be so bad, actually,' she added philosophically. 'The council would have to give me a place if I was homeless, and I wouldn't have to deal with any more creepy private landlords.'

'I thought you'd already applied to the council?' Chrissie asked, going back into the kitchenette when the kettle switched itself off.

'I did, but then I got this place and lost my points.' Leanne sighed, then shrugged. 'Oh, well, there's nothing I can do about it, so there's no point worrying about it tonight. I'll only end up on a downer and ruin my date.'

'Ah *ha*!' Chrissie said victoriously. 'So you're finally admitting it's a date! I can read you like a flaming book, lady.'

'Think what you like,' Leanne shot back. 'But it's completely innocent as far as I'm concerned. Just two old friends having a chat and a bite to eat.'

'I'd be more inclined to believe that if you ever actually *were* friends,' Chrissie scoffed as she carried their brews in. 'The way *I* remember it, you hated his guts.'

'I didn't hate him. I just didn't really like him. But I *might* have, if I'd given him a chance.'

'Well, you certainly seem to like him now,' Chrissie said as she placed the cups on the table and took her make-up bag out of her handbag. 'Come on, then . . .' She sat on the bed and patted the space beside her. 'Let's get that face sorted.'

'Not too much,' Leanne cautioned as she perched on the edge of the mattress. 'I don't want it caked on.'

'You mean like Sally Walker doing her Coco the Clown impression last night?' Chrissie snorted, narrowing her eyes as she squeezed a blob of foundation on to the back of her hand. 'I was looking for the cameras when I saw the state of her; thought they must be filming *TOWIE* or something.'

'I thought she looked all right,' said Leanne, trying not to squirm when Chrissie smeared the liquid over her face.

'From a distance, maybe. But I bet she looked like a right slapper up close. No wonder Jake denied he's seeing her. He must be ashamed.'

'Well, if he is seeing her, I'll soon find out,' said Leanne. 'And that'll be that.'

'We'll see,' Chrissie said knowingly. 'Close your eyes.'

Leanne did as she'd been told and squeezed her eyes shut. She didn't wear much make-up as a rule; just a bit of lip gloss, and maybe a touch of mascara if she was going somewhere special. But Chrissie had to wear it every day for work, so she was much better at applying it.

'There you go,' Chrissie said when she'd finished. 'Take a look and see what you think.'

Leanne stood up and gazed at her reflection in the mottled mirror hanging above the derelict fire.

'Oh, wow,' she murmured. 'I look so different.'

'You look fan-bloody-tastic,' Chrissie corrected her. 'That purple eyeshadow really brings out the green of your eyes, and your lips look so lush I'm tempted to snog you myself. If Jakey boy doesn't go gaga when he sees you, he needs his flippin' head testing.'

Suddenly nervous, Leanne stepped back to get a full-length view. 'You don't think I'm showing too much cleavage, do you?' She tugged at the dress's low neckline.

'Behave!' Chrissie snorted. 'I'd forgotten you even *had* boobs, it's that long since I've seen any flesh below your chin.'

'I'm not that bad.'

'Yes you are, but at least you look decent tonight – for a change.'

'I'm not sure I feel comfortable.' Leanne frowned at her reflection.

'You make me laugh, you,' Chrissie said wearily. 'You've got absolutely no idea how gorgeous you are, have you? I would literally *die* for a figure like yours. And don't even get me started on your hair and your face. You're like some kind of exotic ballet dancer, and I'd hate your guts if you weren't my best mate.'

'No, you wouldn't,' Leanne chuckled, sitting down and reaching for her boots.

'Er, I don't think so!' Chrissie snatched them out of her hand and dropped them in disgust. 'They're absolutely minging.'

'I haven't got anything else,' Leanne protested. 'Only trainers and flip-flops.'

'Here . . .' Chrissie picked up her own shoes and passed them over. 'But don't scuff them, 'cos they cost me seventy quid. And that's with staff discount, so you can imagine how much they *really* cost.'

'I don't like heels,' Leanne complained as she slipped the stilettos on and tentatively stood up.

'They look a damn sight better than these clodhoppers,' Chrissie grumbled as she pulled Leanne's boots on and plodded heavily over to the armchair to get her coat. 'And don't you dare laugh, or I'll make you swap back.'

Leanne bit her lip. She loved her comfortable old boots, but as she watched Chrissie clumping around in them now, she had to admit that they'd had their day.

'Come on, then.' Chrissie made her way to the door. 'I'll walk you to the corner.'

'You don't have to,' Leanne said, slipping her jacket on and slotting her keys into her bag before following.

'Oh, but I do!' Chrissie grinned as she stepped out on to the landing. 'If you go arse over tit in front of lover-boy, I have *got* to be there.'

Leanne shoved her toward the stairs and followed her stiffly down, muttering, 'I don't know how you manage to walk around in these all day. I've only had them on for a minute and they're already killing me.'

'If you could see how good they make your arse look, you'd be begging me to let you keep them,' Chrissie countered.

Speedy came out of his room just as they reached the first-floor landing. He looked Leanne up and down with a sneer on his face, then shouldered past her, muttering, 'Fuckin' state of it.'

'She looks a damn sight better than *you*,' Chrissie yelled over the banister rail as he trotted down the stairs. 'And I'd get something for those spots before they turn into an extra head, if I was you!'

'And *you* wanna go easy on the burgers before your arse explodes!' Speedy shot back as he yanked the front door open and manhandled the bike out with its front wheel in the air, scraping the wallpaper in the process.

'Nasty little shit,' spat Chrissie. 'How do you put up with him?'

'I ignore him,' said Leanne, holding tightly on to the wobbly banister rail.

Mad Maggie was in the hallway when they reached the ground floor, staring at a scuff mark on the wall. Snapping her head round when she heard them, she gave Leanne an accusing look. 'Did *you* do this?'

'Of course not,' Leanne protested. 'It'll have been Speedy with that bike.'

'I'll thank you to remember that bicycles saved our lives in the war,' Maggie informed her haughtily, before marching into her room.

Chrissie looked at Leanne and burst out laughing. Shushing her, Leanne clutched at her arm and stumbled out on to the pavement.

'You're living in a total madhouse,' Chrissie spluttered as they made their way down the road.

'If *I* ever start acting like them, shoot me,' Leanne said, treading carefully as every tiny crack in the pavement threatened to send her flying.

'What do you mean *if*?' Chrissie quipped. Grinning when Leanne gave her a playful slap, she said, 'So what's the name of this restaurant Jake's taking you to?'

'He didn't say. Why?'

'I thought I might follow you, so I can keep an eye on you.'

'Don't even think about it!'

'Oh, go on, it'll be a laugh. I'll stay out of the way so he doesn't see me, obviously. And if you want to escape you can scratch your nose, then I'll ring you and pretend there's been an emergency.'

'I won't want to escape, and if you ring me I'll ignore it.'

'Only trying to help.'

'Being nosy, more like.'

There was no sign of Jake when they reached the corner of Leighton Avenue. Afraid that he may have already given up on her because she was late, Leanne took out her phone to check if he'd tried to call her.

A deep rumbling sound suddenly filled the air, and Chrissie's eyes widened when a black Audi A5 with full sports body-kit zipped around the corner and pulled up alongside them.

'Jesus wept! He must be absolutely minted,' she gasped when she saw Jake at the wheel.

'Oh, God, I can't do this,' Leanne whispered as the driver's side door opened.

'Yes, you can,' Chrissie hissed. 'Unless you're planning to do a runner in those heels?'

'I can't even walk in them, never mind run.'

'Well, shut up moaning, then.'

Leanne took a deep breath and forced a smile when Jake stepped out of the car. He was dressed casually in trousers and an open-necked shirt, but even in the dim light it was obvious that it was quality gear.

As he walked round to them, Chrissie's gaze dropped to his feet. 'Oh, my God, are they Ferragamos?'

'Pardon me?' He looked confused.

'Your shoes,' she explained. 'Sorry, I work in a shoe shop, can't help myself. They are, though, aren't they?'

'No idea?' Jake shrugged. 'I just tried them on and liked them; didn't think to check the label.'

When he turned to give Leanne a peck on the cheek, Chrissie mouthed, 'Min-ted!' to her friend.

Rearranging her face into a smile when they were both facing her again, she said, 'Oh my, what a beautiful couple you make. If I didn't know you, I'd swear Brad and Angelina were in town. I hope this restaurant you're taking her to isn't too flashy, Jake, or you're gonna have the paparazzi swarming all over you when you come out.'

'Don't tell her where we're going,' Leanne warned. 'She only wants to know so she can spy on us.'

'Grass!' Chrissie snorted. Then, sighing, she hitched the strap of her handbag over her shoulder, and said, 'Oh, well, if you're not going to let me have any fun, I might as well go home. Don't do anything I wouldn't,' she added, giving Leanne a quick hug. '*And I'd* so *do him!*' she whispered before letting her go.

Leanne waved her off before turning back to Jake.

'You look incredible,' he said, opening the passenger-side door and offering his hand to help her in.

'Thank you,' she replied shyly, thinking that he didn't look half bad himself. And his aftershave smelled divine.

Chrissie had just likened him to Brad Pitt, but Leanne thought he was more like Johnny Depp. Either way, he was one of the most handsome men she had ever met, and she had a feeling she was going to enjoy this non-date date.

6

The restaurant was situated on a little backstreet, a couple of minutes' walk from the city centre. The perfect gentleman, Jake held the door open when they got there, and then pulled out her chair for her before taking his own when the waiter had shown them to their table.

'Would you like something to drink before ordering?' the waiter asked, handing a menu to each of them.

Ordering a bottle of white wine, Jake opened his menu. 'Ben recommended the scallops, so I'll have them for starters,' he said, skipping straight to the main courses. 'Then I think I'll have a rib-eye steak and chips. What about you?'

It was a long time since Leanne had been to anywhere quite as posh as this and she felt suddenly self-conscious at the thought of eating in front of him. Nervous of ordering any-thing that required too much chewing, or – worse – that she was likely to spill down herself and ruin Tina's dress, she said, 'I'll have the tuna salad, please.'

'No starter?'

'No thanks.' Leanne closed the menu and pushed it aside. 'I'm actually not that hungry.'

It was a lie, because she hadn't eaten all day and the aromas that were drifting towards her from the surrounding tables were making her mouth water. But she could have fed herself for a week on the cost of one course, and she didn't want him to think she was taking advantage just because he'd offered to pay.

When the waiter had brought their wine and taken their food orders, Jake sat back in his seat and gazed at Leanne across the table.

'This is so weird.'

'Weird?' she repeated, shivering when the candlelight picked out the threads of gold in his eyes. 'How so?' She reached for her wine and took a sip.

'Us, sitting here, about to have dinner together,' he explained. 'I never thought I'd see you again, never mind get you to agree to come out with me. But here we are. I must say I'm still surprised you're not married, though. You're way too beautiful to be single. Or are you divorced?'

Leanne shook her head.

'No near misses?' Jake raised an eyebrow.

'Only one,' Leanne admitted. 'But it didn't work out so I called it off.'

'His loss, my gain.' Jake gave a slow smile. 'Anyone I'd know?'

'No.' Leanne shifted in her seat and gripped the stem of her glass a little tighter. 'He's from London originally. We met at a party and just sort of took it from there.'

'Love at first sight?'

'Kind of, I guess. At least, I thought so at the time.'

'So what happened?'

'The usual.' Leanne shrugged. 'We got engaged, moved in together, talked about starting a family. Then he screwed another woman in our bed, and I came home early and caught them. I'm sure you can guess the rest.' Pausing, she took another, much longer swig of her wine before throwing his question back at him: 'So what about you? How come *you're* not married?'

'Never really fancied it, to be honest,' Jake replied, giving her a piercing look as he added, 'Guess I must've been waiting for the right girl to come along.'

Unable to stop herself from asking the question that had been on her mind all day as the expensive wine began to loosen her tongue, Leanne said, 'And what about Sally? Are you really not seeing her, or did you just say that to get me to agree to come out with you?'

'I thought we'd cleared that up?' Jake frowned.

'We did, and I *do* believe you,' Leanne assured him. 'It was something Chrissie said.'

'Oh, yeah? And what was that?'

'Just that you probably wouldn't admit it if you *were* seeing Sally, in case it put me off.'

'Not my style,' Jake said coolly. 'I *would* have told you, and then I'd have split up with her and asked you out again when it was all over.'

'That's not good,' Leanne chided. 'Then I'd feel guilty for making you break up with your girlfriend.'

'Ah, but she's *not* my girlfriend, so there's nothing to feel guilty about, is there?'

Sitting forward now, Jake reached across the table for her hand and gazed deeply into her eyes. 'I don't think you realize how much I like you, Leanne. I know it's been a long time, but when I saw you last night it felt like fate had brought us back together, and I really think we could have something if we gave it a chance.'

Leanne bit her lip when the butterflies stirred in her stomach again. She had promised Chrissie that she wouldn't rush into anything, but it was so hard to maintain her reserve when Jake was looking at her like this.

'Your starter, sir.'

Seizing the opportunity to escape and pull herself together when the waiter interrupted them, Leanne slid her hand free and snatched her handbag up off the floor.

'I'm just going to the loo. Won't be a minute.'

As she stepped inside the ladies' her phone pinged and she saw two messages on the screen: the first from her mum, inviting her round for Sunday dinner; the other from Chrissie, asking how she was getting on. After replying to her mum's, telling her that she'd be there at three, she answered Chrissie's:

Restaurant lovely. Bit tipsy, so I'm in loo trying to sober up before food gets here.

Trust you to get pissed before the food's arrived. What you having?

Tuna Salad.

Instead of replying to this in writing, Chrissie rang. 'What do you mean you're having salad? You don't even *like* salad!'

'I know, but it was the cheapest thing on the menu,' Leanne told her, whispering in case the couple who were sitting at the table just outside the door overheard.

'I thought Jake was paying?'

'He is, but I don't want him to think I'm taking the piss.'

'Get a grip!' Chrissie scolded. 'He's obviously not short of a bob or two if that car's anything to go by, and if he wanted a cheap date he wouldn't have taken you to a restaurant, would he?'

'No, but—'

'But nothing,' Chrissie interrupted sharply. 'Tell him you've changed your mind. This might be the last good meal you'll be getting for a while, so you'd best fill your boots.'

'Thanks,' Leanne muttered, sobering at the reminder of the benefits sanction. 'I was trying to forget about that.'

'I'm not trying to put a damper on things,' Chrissie said, more softly. 'But you deserve to have a bit of fun after everything you've been through this year, so stop being daft and get back in there before Jake thinks you've climbed out of the window.'

Shaking her head when the phone went dead in her hand, Leanne smoothed her dress and fluffed her hair before heading back into the dining room.

Jake had finished his starter by then and was refilling their glasses.

'Nice place, isn't it?' he said as she sat down.

'Very,' she agreed.

'We'll have to come here again.' He handed her glass to her. 'Assuming there's going to *be* an again?'

'We'll see.' Leanne smiled and took a sip of wine.

'A flower for the lady . . . ?'

Glancing up at the sound of the voice, Leanne shook her head when she saw an old woman standing over her holding a basket of red roses.

'No, thank you.'

'We'll take a dozen,' Jake said at the same time.

'You don't have to do that,' Leanne protested.

Jake gave a mischievous grin and winked at her, before saying, loudly, 'It's the least I can do since you just made me the happiest man alive, my love.' Turning in his seat now, to include the other diners who were casting curious glances their way, he yelled, 'She said yes!'

'Oh, my God!' Leanne dropped her burning cheeks into her hands when people began to applaud. 'What are you *doing*?'

'Play along,' Jake whispered, still grinning. 'We might get a free meal out of it, if we're lucky.'

'You're terrible,' she whispered back, shaking her head in despair.

'Compliments of the management.' The waiter bustled over carrying a bottle of champagne in an ice bucket. 'It's been a while since we've had a proposal in here, and we hope you'll be very happy together.'

'Mate, I've loved this girl for twenty years, so I couldn't be any happier than I am right now,' Jake said.

When the waiter had returned to his post after shaking his hand, Jake turned to the rose seller. 'How much do I owe you, love?'

She told him the price and then waited until he reached into his pocket for his wallet before quickly leaning down and whispering into Leanne's ear. Straightening up when Jake held out two twenties, she snatched them from his hand and rushed away.

'What was that all about?' Jake laughed, standing the roses in the ice bucket.

'God knows,' Leanne said, watching as the woman weaved a path through the tables and hurried out of the door. 'Something about darkness and running.'

The waiter arrived just then with their main courses, so they forgot about the woman and her strange words and settled down to eat. Ice now completely broken, they chatted about their lives over dinner – and carried on for another hour over coffee.

After paying the bill, Jake asked the waiter for a card and

promised that he'd get in touch to book the place for their wedding reception as soon as a date had been set.

Still giggling about that as they made their way to the car, Leanne said, 'You're absolutely crazy! And I can't believe you kept it up for so long. Did you see the poor man's face when you told him to expect a hundred guests? I thought he was going to have a heart attack.'

'Probably counting all the tips he's hoping to make.' Jake grinned and pressed his key fob to unlock the car.

Thanking him when he took the roses from her and laid them in the boot, Leanne said, 'They are beautiful, but you shouldn't have bought them. They were way too expensive, and I haven't even got a vase to—'

The rest of the sentence was lost when Jake pushed her up against the side of the car and kissed her.

'Now *that* was worth waiting for,' he said huskily when he stopped. 'So when are we going to do this again?'

'I don't know?' Leanne said breathlessly, glad that he was still holding her, because her legs felt so weak she would probably have collapsed if he'd let go.

'How about tomorrow?' he suggested. 'I've got a few things to do in the morning, but I'll be free by twelve if you fancy going for lunch?'

'I'd like that,' Leanne said shyly, thrilled to think that she'd be seeing him again so soon.

7

Leanne had been ready and waiting and looking out of the window for ages when Jake's car turned the corner at dead on twelve the following day. She had intended to have him drop her off at the corner last night, but the wine had taken control of her mouth and she'd ended up giving him her address after leaving the restaurant. Desperate now to get to him before he climbed out of the car and caught a whiff of the stench coming from the broken drain, she snatched her handbag and jacket off the bed and rushed out of the bedsit.

Forced to wear the heels again, because Chrissie still had her boots, she'd decided that she might as well team them with the other dress of Tina's. It felt strange to wear such feminine, figure-hugging clothes after slobbing around in jeans and baggy T-shirts for so long, but she had to admit that it felt quite nice. And Jake obviously liked it, judging by the compliments he'd given her last night. She just hoped he wouldn't be too disappointed when Tina's clothes had been returned and she was reduced to wearing her own rags again.

Mad Maggie was prowling the hallway when Leanne reached the ground floor, looking even crazier than usual in a tartan dressing gown held together by a belt of knotted bin bags, an enormous pair of army boots, a woolly hat, and a pair of fingerless gloves.

'Where's my cat?' she demanded, glaring at Leanne.

'I didn't know you had one,' Leanne said politely, edging past her.

'If you've kidnapped him, I'll set my son on you.' Maggie jabbed her in the arm with a filthy fingernail. 'He's a champion boxer, you know.'

'Good for him,' Leanne muttered, rubbing the sore spot as she made a dash for the door.

'Something wrong?' Jake asked when she flew out of the house and leapt into the passenger seat.

'My crazy neighbour just accused me of kidnapping her imaginary cat,' Leanne explained, casting a nervous glance back at the house as she yanked her seat belt on. 'And she might follow me out and make a scene, so can we go please?'

'Aw, can't we stick around for a minute?' Jake asked. 'I love a good catfight.'

'Just move!' Leanne ordered.

'Anything you say, princess.' Jake grinned and set off. 'Sleep well?' he asked as they turned the corner.

'Great, thanks.' Leanne smiled. 'You?'

'Like a log. You must have worn me out with all that chatting last night.'

'Excuse me, but I think you'll find it was the other way round,' Leanne protested. 'I hardly got a word in edgeways.'

'If you say so.'

'I still can't believe you did that whole fake proposal thing,' Leanne chuckled. 'I don't think I've ever been so embarrassed.'

'Ah, you loved it,' Jake drawled.

'It *was* fun,' she conceded. 'But that flower woman was a bit freaky, wasn't she? I still haven't figured out what she was talking about.'

'Oh, yeah . . . what was it she said again?'

Frowning as she tried to remember the exact words, Leanne said, 'Something like: *When the darkness comes, run and don't look back.*'

'Probably warning you not to walk around on your own late at night,' Jake mused. 'Ben told me there's been a spate of muggings around here recently.'

'Three that I've heard of in the last couple of weeks,' said Leanne. 'And Chrissie saw some dodgy-looking blokes hanging about round the corner from mine when she went home the other night.'

'Well, you just make sure you don't go out after dark,' Jake said sternly. 'If you need anything, ring me and I'll bring it round for you.'

'I'm thirty-three,' Leanne reminded him amusedly. 'I think I can look after myself.'

'You're a woman,' Jake countered seriously. 'You can't take risks.'

Tickled that he was being so protective of her, because it was a long time since any man apart from her dad had given a toss, Leanne said, 'Don't worry. I never go out after dark unless I'm with Chrissie.'

'Well, I guess that face of hers is enough to send any potential muggers running for their lives,' Jake snorted. Following it with a wink to let her know he was joking, he said, 'You've got to admit, she is a bit scary, though.'

'She's lovely,' Leanne said loyally, smiling as they drove on.

As they passed her local shops a few seconds later, the smile evaporated when she spotted somebody who looked a lot like Dean going into the supermarket. Sure that she must be mistaken, because she'd heard that he and his tart had moved to Oldham, she twisted her head to take another look.

'Want me to stop?' Jake asked, thinking that she needed something from the shop.

'No, it's okay.' She faced the front again. 'I thought I saw someone I knew.'

'I've been doing that ever since I moved back,' said Jake. 'Doubt I'd actually recognize anyone, though, seeing as I was a kid the last time I saw most of them.'

'You recognized me,' she reminded him.

'Ah, but you're different,' he said. 'You know that saying: you never forget your first love?'

'I wasn't your first love.' Leanne blushed.

'You were,' he insisted. 'First and *only*.'

'Surely you've been in love since then?'

'Nope. Obviously, I've liked some girls more than others, but that's as far as it ever went. Guess I haven't been as lucky as you, eh? You loved your ex so much you were all set to get married.'

Leanne pursed her lips thoughtfully at this. She had genuinely believed that Dean was the love of her life, but his kisses had never affected her as strongly as Jake's had last night; and he'd never made her go weak at the knees just by looking into her eyes or smiling at her, like Jake did. So maybe his inability to keep his dick in his pants had been a blessing rather than a curse? If he hadn't cheated, she'd still be on course to marry him, and she had no doubt that it would have been the biggest mistake of her life.

Happy to realize that she was at long last getting over Dean, Leanne settled back and gazed out of the window as Jake drove out of town and into the suburbs on the south side of Manchester.

Surprised when he turned on to a tree-lined avenue some time later and came to a stop in front of a high gate, behind which she could see a sprawling Victorian house, she said, 'This doesn't look like a restaurant.'

'That's because it's not,' Jake replied, pressing his key fob to open the gate. 'I live here. I need to drop something off before we get going. Don't mind, do you?'

Leanne shook her head and gazed up at the house in awe as Jake drove in through the gate. Over dinner last night, he'd told her that he ran a security business; but he'd made it sound like a modest affair, so she hadn't imagined he could afford to live somewhere as grand as this.

Jake parked at the rear of the house and took a sports bag out of the boot before leading Leanne up to his apartment on the first floor.

'Go through.' He nodded towards a door after letting her in. 'I'll be with you soon as I've put this away.'

Leanne followed his directions and found herself in a spacious, open-plan lounge, into which sunlight was streaming through large windows at one end and a set of French doors at the other. Curious to know what lay behind those doors, she walked down to that end of the room.

'That's going to be great in summer,' Jake said, coming up behind her and wrapping his arms around her waist as she gazed out at a large balcony with wrought-iron railings and wicker garden furniture. 'I can see you now . . . lying on the sunlounger in your bikini; book in one hand, glass of wine in the other.'

'*Bikini?*' Leanne twisted her head and gave him a look that said *You must be kidding!* 'I haven't worn one of them since I was eighteen.'

'You're still beautiful enough to pull it off,' he murmured, lowering his head to plant a soft kiss on her lips.

Scared that she wouldn't have the strength to resist if he tried to take things any further, Leanne wriggled free after a few seconds and reminded him that they were supposed to be going out.

'Spoilsport,' he complained, giving her a knowing smile as he reached for her hand and led her back down to the car.

*

After eating lunch at a quaint little pub in Alderley Edge, Jake bought a couple of bottles of white wine from the bar, then he and Leanne set off for a stroll through the forest.

When they eventually came to a clearing overlooking a lake on which several tiny boats were bobbing around, they sat beneath a tree to drink their wine and enjoy the late afternoon sunshine.

'This is so peaceful,' Leanne said, resting on her elbows as Jake opened one of the bottles. 'It's easy to forget that places like this exist when you spend your life in the city.'

'Almost makes you wish you didn't have to leave, doesn't it?' Jake said, passing the bottle to her.

Leanne nodded her agreement and took a couple of sips before passing it back. Gazing wistfully down at the sparkling waters below, she said, 'If I could drive and had the money, I'd buy a camper van and drive round looking for places like this to park up at. Can you imagine waking up to this view every morning?'

'I wouldn't mind waking up to *this* one,' Jake said, resting his head on his hand and peering into her eyes. 'You know that pub's got rooms, don't you? How about we forget about driving home and stay for dinner, then book ourselves in for the night? We can get two rooms,' he added quickly when he saw a flicker of uncertainty in her eyes.

Leanne reached for the bottle and took another, longer drink. This would be her first time since Dean, but the sexual tension that had been passing between them all day was so strong, she knew it was futile to try and fight it.

Another swig of wine gave her the confidence to look him in the eye.

'One room will do.'

Jake gently brushed her hair off her face. 'Are you sure?'

'Positive,' she murmured, sliding her hand through his hair and pulling his face down to hers.

8

Jake was already awake when Leanne opened her eyes the next morning. Smiling when he held out his arm, she snuggled closer and breathed in deeply to inhale his musky scent.

They had spent the night making love to the backdrop of ghostly creaks in the corridor outside their room, and eerie screeches from the woods. Now, with dust motes dancing in the sunlight that was creeping in through the gap in the curtains, and the feel of Jake's strong arm enfolding her, she couldn't recall a time when she'd felt as contented.

Brought back to reality when Jake's phone suddenly started ringing, she reluctantly got up and went in search of a bathroom while he took the call.

He'd just finished that call when she returned, but his phone immediately began to ring again.

'Sorry about this,' he apologized. 'But it's business, so I need to take it. Why don't you go and order breakfast. I'll come down as soon as I'm done.'

'What would you like?' Leanne asked, wincing as she forced her swollen feet into Chrissie's shoes.

'Whatever you're having,' Jake said, still holding the ringing phone.

Leanne slipped her jacket on and reached for her handbag, then took one last wistful look around the room before leaving him to it.

The chubby landlady was behind the counter when Leanne walked into the low-ceilinged dining room. Glancing up, she gave a warm smile.

'Morning, lovie. Sleep well?'

'Great, thanks,' Leanne replied shyly, wondering if the woman had heard her and Jake having sex. She didn't usually make a lot of noise – well, she certainly hadn't with Dean, not even in the early days when it was supposed to have been at its very best; but she'd been so drunk by the time she and Jake had stumbled up the rickety old staircase and fallen into their room last night, she could have been screaming her head off for all she knew.

'Hubby not up yet?' the woman asked.

'Er, yeah, he's just taking a business call.' Leanne didn't correct her. 'Can I order breakfast?'

'Take a seat. I'll be with you in a tick.'

Leanne sat at the table by the window where she and Jake had eaten both lunch and dinner yesterday. It overlooked a winding stream that ran alongside the pub, and she smiled when she saw a duck float serenely past. While she waited, she decided to check her phone to see if she had any messages. She'd put it on silent last night, and she saw that she'd had a couple of missed calls from Chrissie. There were also a couple of messages, but Jake arrived before she had a chance to read them.

'I'm really sorry, but something's come up and I need to go back to town,' he said. 'You haven't ordered breakfast, have you?'

'No, she hasn't come over yet,' Leanne told him, shoving the phone into her pocket before standing up. 'Is everything okay?'

'Nothing I can't handle,' Jake said, taking out his wallet to settle the bill. 'Don't worry, I'll make it up to you.'

'There's nothing to make up for,' she insisted. 'I've had a great time.'

'Me too.' He gave her a conspiratorial smile.

*

All too soon, they had pulled up outside Leanne's house and, heart sinking at the thought of going inside, she leaned over and gave Jake a quick kiss before climbing out of the car.

'I'll give you a call when I'm done,' he told her through his open window. 'You might as well go back to bed while you've got the chance,' he added slyly. 'You must be wiped after all that *walking* yesterday.'

Grinning, because she knew exactly what he really meant, Leanne waved him off before heading inside.

'Leave it!' Mad Maggie barked, barrelling out of her room just as Leanne was closing the door.

Taken aback by her neighbour's bright orange lipstick and fluorescent-green pinstripe trouser suit, Leanne asked, 'Going somewhere nice?'

'Nosy is as nosy does,' the old woman snapped, pausing to pull on a pair of lace gloves which had clearly fed an army of moths during their lifetime, given how many holes were in them.

Leanne sighed and headed up the stairs, leaving Maggie to go on her secretive way. When she reached the top floor, she hesitated when she saw splinters of wood littering the thread-bare carpet outside her room and a man-sized footprint on her open front door. Thinking that Roger must have already sent his boys round to evict her, she ran inside to confront them.

The bedsit had been ransacked, and as she gazed around in dismay at the mess of clothes, CDs and books strewn all over the floor, she realized she had been burgled. The wardrobe door was hanging off its hinge, the dresser drawers had all been pulled out and tipped upside down, and her mattress was lying askew on the base of the bed.

Glass crunched underfoot as she walked further into the room, and tears welled in her eyes when she saw that she was standing on the framed photograph of her parents and her grandmother, taken just one week before her gran had died.

Chin wobbling as their smiling faces swam before her eyes, she tipped the glass out and laid the picture on the table before reaching into her pocket for her phone. It wasn't there, and she groaned when she realized that it must have fallen out of her pocket back at the pub when she'd jumped up from her seat. Hoping that Jake knew the name of the place so she could call and ask the landlady to look for it, she headed out to use the payphone on the corner instead.

Speedy was lounging against his doorframe when she reached the first floor, his phone in one hand, a half-eaten apple in the other. Instantly suspicious when he glanced up at her and smirked, Leanne marched the rest of the way down.

'It was you, wasn't it?'

'What you on about?'

'Don't act stupid, you know exactly what I mean,' she spat. 'You broke into my room, didn't you?'

'Fuck off!' he snorted, taking a bite of the apple. 'I ain't been nowhere near your poxy room.'

Unsure if she believed him, but unable to prove anything at this point, Leanne said, 'And I suppose you didn't hear anything, did you?'

'I did as it happens.' Speedy gave her a birds-eye view of the mashed fruit in his mouth. 'A fuck-load of banging. Thought you was having a fit or summat.'

'What time was that?' she asked, trying not to grimace as juice trickled down through the stubble on his chin.

'Dunno?' He shrugged. 'Three, four?'

'And you didn't think to come up and check on me?' Leanne frowned. 'What if I'd been getting attacked?'

'Nowt to do with me,' he said unconcernedly, dropping the

apple core and wiping his hand on his dirty jeans. 'You'd probably only have blamed me anyhow, knowing you.'

'Thanks for nothing,' she hissed. 'I'll just have to let the
police deal with it.'

Irritated when Speedy stepped in front of her as she tried to
walk past, she raised her chin and glared at him. 'Move!'

'Make me,' he snarled, shoving her so hard she lost her foot-
ing and fell back against the stairs.

'What the hell do you think you're doing?' she demanded,
jumping unsteadily back up to her feet.

'Giving you a taste of your own medicine,' he hissed, his
eyes glinting with malice as he walked up to her and shoved
his face into hers. 'You've treated me like shit ever since you
moved in, and I'm fuckin' sick of it.'

Leanne was scared, and his breath was turning her stomach,
but she forced herself to hold his gaze. 'Touch me again, and
I'll have you arrested for assault.'

'Go for it,' he challenged. 'But it won't get you nowhere, 'cos
it'll just be your word against mine.' Grinning now, he jabbed
her in the chest with his finger. 'What's up, gobby? Not gonna
fight back? Or haven't you got the bottle without your fat-twat
mate to protect you?'

'Pack it in!' Leanne yelped, using all her strength to hold
him off when he backed her up against the wall. 'I mean it,
Speedy, just stop this before it goes too far!'

'Know your trouble?' He placed his hands on the wall on

either side of her head and stared down into her eyes. 'You're such a stuck-up bitch, you think you can—'

He was grabbed from behind before he could finish what he was saying, and he let out a shocked squawk when he was lifted off his feet and slammed over the banister rail. Struggling to keep his balance when his attacker forced the top half of his body out over the stairs, he spluttered, 'What the *fuck*, man? I'm gonna fall! Pull me up!'

'Shut your mouth, or I'll drop you right now,' Jake snarled.

Speedy's face drained of colour when he saw the expression in Jake's eyes, and he held up his hands. 'All right, mate, calm down. Everything's cool. Me and her are friends – aren't we, Leanne?' He twisted his head and gave her a pleading look, begging her to back him up.

'She'd never be friends with a lowlife piece of shit like you,' spat Jake. 'And if I catch you so much as *looking* at her again, you're a dead man. Have you got that?'

'Okay, okay, I'm sorry!' Speedy squealed, beads of sweat breaking out on his spotty forehead when the banister creaked. 'I wouldn't have done nothing, I swear! I was just pissed off 'cos she accused me of turning over her gaff. But it weren't me – I swear it weren't.'

'I've been burgled,' Leanne explained when Jake flashed a questioning look her way.

'Do you think he did it?'

'I don't know,' she murmured. Then, feeling a little guilty

87

when she saw the panicked look in Speedy's eyes, she shook her head. 'Probably not.'

Hauling Speedy to his feet, Jake said, 'You're lucky she believes you. But if I ever find out it *was* you, I'll be coming back for you. And don't make the mistake of testing me, because I *never* make idle threats.'

Legs almost giving way when Jake suddenly released him, Speedy rushed into his room, slipping on the apple core as he went and falling heavily through the door.

'Thanks.' Leanne let out a shaky breath when his door slammed shut. 'I've never seen him like that before; I didn't know what he was going to do.'

'Don't worry, he won't come near you again,' Jake said with confidence. 'It's a good job your front door was open, or I wouldn't have caught him.'

'Maggie must have forgotten to close it when she went out,' Leanne said, turning to go upstairs.

'No wonder you were burgled if anyone can walk in off the street,' Jake chided as he followed her. 'You need to make sure it's locked at all times.'

'I do,' Leanne said truthfully. 'But Maggie's not all there, so she forgets sometimes.'

They had entered the bedsit by now, and Jake shook his head as he gazed around. 'Wow, what a mess. Is anything missing?'

'I don't know.' Leanne shrugged. 'I haven't had time to check. And I didn't really want to touch anything before the police get here.'

'Have you called them yet?'

'No. I was on my way to do it when I ran into Speedy.'

'I wouldn't bother,' Jake said flatly. 'They won't find whoever did it, so you might as well clean up and forget about it. Let me know if anything's missing, though, so I can replace it for you.'

'You don't have to do that,' Leanne argued.

'I *want* to,' Jake insisted. 'So just do as you're told and check. Okay?'

Leanne couldn't help but smile, but she shook her head at the same time, and said, 'Thanks, but there's really no need. I haven't got anything of value, so I won't have lost much even if they have taken anything.'

'You always were too proud for your own good,' Jake said, pulling her into his arms and walking her slowly back toward the bed. 'But I'll soon win you round to my way of thinking.'

'Oh, yeah?' Leanne squirmed when he kissed her neck. 'And what exactly *is* your way of thinking?'

'That it's a man's job to take care of his woman,' said Jake, reaching behind her and dragging the mattress back on to the base. 'And a woman's job to take care of her man,' he added as he pushed her down on to it.

'I thought you were supposed to be going somewhere,' she gasped when he lay on top of her.

'I am,' he murmured, dropping little kisses on to her neck. 'But I found your phone on the floor of the car and thought I'd best bring it round before I go.'

'Wait!' she spluttered as he worked his fingertips under the hem of the dress. 'The door's still—'

Jake's mouth covered hers before she could finish speaking, and she groaned when his hand slid up her thigh.

'Oh, my God!' Chrissie's shocked voice interrupted them. 'You could at least shut the door before you get down and dirty.'

Leanne gave a sheepish smile as Jake leapt back up to his feet. 'I tried to tell him, but we, er, got a bit carried away.'

'So I see.' Chrissie raised an eyebrow as she looked around.

'I've been burgled,' said Leanne, guessing that Chrissie thought they had made the mess because they had been over-come by passion.

'Seriously?' Chrissie frowned. 'When?'

'Sometime in the early hours, according to Speedy.'

'And where were you?' Chrissie asked, immediately follow-ing it with, 'Actually, don't bother answering that; I think I can guess. I suppose that explains why I couldn't get hold of you yesterday.'

'My phone was on silent,' Leanne admitted. 'I was going to call you when I got home, but then I found this and forgot.'

'Have you called the police yet?'

'No.'

'Why not?'

'Because they probably won't find whoever did it,' Leanne said, parroting Jake. 'Anyway, if it *was* Speedy, like I suspect, I doubt he'll dare come near me again now he's been warned off.'

'Oh, I see.' Chrissie flashed Jake a bemused look. 'Been playing the hero, have we?'

Jake shrugged as if it were no big deal and glanced at his watch. 'I'd best get going. Will you be okay till I get back, Lee?'

'She'll be fine now I'm here,' said Chrissie, taking her coat off and rolling up her sleeves.

'Aren't you supposed to be at work?' Leanne asked.

'Dylan had me up all night, and I was worried about you, so I pulled a sickie,' Chrissie said as she scooped up an armful of clothes off the floor and dumped them on the bed. Glancing up as she reached for the next lot, she said, 'Don't just stand there. Go and see lover-boy out, then get your arse back in here and help me.'

Glad that Chrissie had turned up – she'd have been nervous staying in the bedsit on her own – Leanne took Jake's hand and led him out.

'I wish I didn't have to go,' he said when they reached the landing. 'If anything happens – and I mean *anything* – ring me. I might not be able to get here straight away, but Ben's only round the corner and he could be here in two minutes.'

'Stop worrying.' Leanne looped her arms around his neck. 'It was a shock, but I'm okay now.'

'I won't apologize for caring,' Jake said, kissing her softly.

Leanne moaned and pressed her hips against his when he slid his tongue between her teeth. Wriggling free when she felt the stiffness in his pants, she whispered, 'Pack it in, or I'll never get anything done.'

'You and me are going to have some serious catching up to do when I get back,' Jake warned, giving a throaty little chuckle as he adjusted himself.

'Is that a threat?' she asked, smiling sexily.

'You bet it is,' he purred.

'Get moving,' she laughed, pushing him towards the stairs.

'You'll need this.' He pulled her phone out of his pocket and handed it to her. 'Oh, and pack a bag while I'm gone.'

'A bag?' She gave him a quizzical look.

'Yeah, you're moving in with me,' he said decisively. 'And don't bother arguing, because I won't have you staying here after this.'

'Don't be daft,' she spluttered. 'We've only been seeing each other for a couple of days.'

'So?'

'So, it's ridiculous to think about moving in with each other so soon. Anyway, this is my home, and I'm not letting a stupid break-in scare me out of it.'

'Why are you so stubborn?' Jake sighed.

'I'm not,' she argued. 'I just don't want you thinking I'm some pathetic little woman who needs looking after.'

'If I thought that, I wouldn't be here. But, come on . . . This place is the pits.'

'Maybe so, but it's all I can afford, so . . .' Tailing off when she remembered that she would soon be out on her ear if Roger decided not to wait for her benefits to be reinstated,

Leanne shrugged and folded her arms. 'It's honestly not that bad once you get used to it. And, like I said, it's my home.'

'Okay, what's the difference?' Jake demanded.

Thrown, Leanne frowned. 'Between what?'

'Between sharing a bed with me at that pub last night, or sharing *my* bed.'

'None, I suppose. But you could just as easily share mine.'

'With this smell hanging over us?' Jake pulled a face. 'Sorry, I didn't want to mention it, but what the hell *is* it?'

'The drain in the backyard,' Leanne said, dipping her face to hide her blushes. 'The landlord knows about it, so it'll get sorted soon.'

'Yeah, well, not soon enough for me,' Jake said softly, raising her chin with his finger. 'And you shouldn't be putting up with it, either. You're way too good for this dump.'

Leanne frowned. She was embarrassed enough about the smell without him pointing out that she was living in a hovel as well. As she'd already told him, it was too early in their relationship – if she could even call it that at this stage – for them to be thinking about living together, and she guessed he'd made the offer out of pity rather than a real desire to live with her. She liked him, a lot, but it had taken a long time to get back on her feet after Dean's betrayal, and she didn't know Jake well enough to jump into making that kind of commitment. That said, she couldn't deny that it would be nice to get a break from this place, if only for a couple of days.

'Okay, I'll make a deal with you,' she conceded. 'I'll stay at yours for the weekend. But then I'm coming home, and we'll alternate where we stay after the drain's fixed. Okay?'

'We'll see,' Jake said, flashing a victorious grin at her before strolling down the stairs.

Chrissie was sitting on the bed folding the clothes when Leanne returned. Giving her a mock-stern look, she said, 'And what do you have to say for yourself, you dirty little stop-out? I thought you were supposed to be coming home alone after dinner?'

'I did,' Leanne replied truthfully, unable to keep the grin off her face as she sat down and plucked a T-shirt off the pile. 'But then Jake took me out for lunch yesterday, and it was such a lovely place we thought we might as well stay for dinner. And then it got late, and they had rooms, so—'

'You thought you might as well stay the night and shag each other's brains out?' Chrissie finished for her, sure that Jake had probably planned it that way all along.

'It wasn't like that,' Leanne said, smiling coyly because that was *exactly* how it had been.

'Whatever!' Chrissie said dismissively. 'So, come on, then . . . spill. And I want details, baby.'

Leanne released a blissful sigh and crushed the T-shirt to her chest. 'Oh, Chrissie, it was fantastic. I wasn't sure how I'd feel after all this time, but Jake was really gentle, and he didn't try to rush me at all. It never felt as good as that with Dean,' she went on. 'Or anyone else, come to think of it. It was just . . . *amazing.*'

'Well, who'd'a thunk it?' Chrissie chuckled. 'No wonder he looked so pleased with himself just now. He must think all his Christmases have come at once.'

'He's not the only one,' Leanne admitted. 'I know it's fast and you probably think I'm an idiot, but I really like him.'

'I don't think you're an idiot at all,' Chrissie said softly. 'This is the happiest I've seen you in ages, and if that's his doing, good on him.'

'Does this mean we've got your blessing?'

'I wouldn't go quite *that* far,' Chrissie grunted. 'But he'll do for now, I suppose.'

Grinning, because that was the closest thing to the royal seal of approval in Chrissie-speak, Leanne said, 'Glad you think so, 'cos he asked me to marry him.'

'Say what?' Chrissie snapped her head up and peered at her through slitted eyes.

'I'm joking!' Leanne laughed. 'God, you're so easy.'

'Very funny,' Chrissie drawled, snatching the screwed up T-shirt out of her hand. 'If you're not going to help, go and put the kettle on. Some of us have got better things to do than sit around playing the fool.'

Doing as she'd been told, Leanne made a brew and then set about clearing up the broken glass and picking up the CDs and books while Chrissie dealt with the clothes. Chatting as they worked, she told Chrissie about Jake's fake proposal at the restaurant, and the rose seller's whispered warning.

'What do you think she meant by it?' Chrissie asked.

'No idea.' Leanne shrugged. 'But Jake thinks it probably had something to do with those muggings.'

'Maybe,' Chrissie mused, reaching into her handbag for her phone when it started ringing. 'All right, Mum. What's up?' Frowning as she listened to what her mum had to say, she said, 'Okay, I'll be there in five.'

'What's wrong?' Leanne asked when Chrissie cut the call and stood up. 'Is your mum okay?'

'I don't know.' Chrissie reached for her coat and quickly pulled it on. 'The doctor's just been round to see her, and he's sending her to hospital for some tests. But our Tina's gone AWOL, so I've got to look after Dylan.'

'Oh, no. I hope everything's all right.'

'Me too,' Chrissie replied worriedly. 'I keep telling her she's overdoing it, but she won't listen. If anything happens to her, I'll swing for our flaming Tina.'

'Nothing's going to happen,' Leanne said firmly. 'She's probably just a bit run-down.'

Chrissie nodded and looped her handbag over her shoulder. 'Hope so. Will you be okay on your own?'

'Course I will,' Leanne insisted, herding her out. 'Jake will be back soon, so stop worrying about me and go see to Dylan.'

When they reached the landing, Chrissie gave her a quick hug and promised to come back as soon as she could, then hurried down the stairs.

Going inside, Leanne took the bread knife out of the kitchen drawer before heading into the bedroom. She'd said she would be all right on her own, but it was a lie, and the silence her friend had left behind was already settling over her like a dead weight. Terrified that the burglar might return to finish what he'd started, and acutely aware that Speedy probably wanted to kill her for almost getting thrown over the banister, she cleaned up the rest of the mess as best she could, and then sat down on the armchair facing the door.

And there she stayed for the rest of the day; knife in hand, heart in throat.

*

Jake wasn't impressed to find the front door standing open again when he arrived at Leanne's at eight that evening. But he was even less impressed when he rushed up to the bedsit and found Leanne sitting in the pitch-dark with a knife in her hand.

'What's going on?' he asked, switching the light on and going over to her. 'Has something happened?'

'No, nothing's happened,' she assured him, shaking with relief to see him. 'I was just a bit nervous about the door being broken.'

'Where's Chrissie?' Jake asked as he removed the knife from her grasp and laid it on the table. 'I thought she was supposed to be staying with you?'

'Her mum got sent into hospital, so she had to go home to look after her sister's baby.'

'Why didn't you ring me? I'd have sent Ben round if I'd known she was going to abandon you.'

'She didn't abandon me, and I was fine, so there was no need to bother you,' Leanne lied. 'Anyway, you're here now, so I'll put the kettle on. What do you fancy – tea or coffee?'

'Neither.' Jake stood up and reached into his pocket for the lock he'd bought on the way over. 'Soon as I've fixed your door, we're leaving.'

*

In the car ten minutes later, Leanne took out her phone to let Chrissie know what was happening, just in case she was on her way back.

'Something wrong?' Jake asked when she let out a little groan.

'I've had a message from my mum,' she told him. 'I arranged to go round for dinner on Sunday, and she's reminding me to bring a card, 'cos it's my dad's birthday on Tuesday. I'd best tell her something's come up and I can't make it. *Unless ...*' She paused and gazed at Jake thoughtfully. 'I don't suppose you fancy coming with me, do you? Only it's been a while since I saw them, so I should probably make the effort.'

'I'd love to,' Jake agreed.

'*Really?*' Leanne was delighted. 'Great, I'll let her know. Oh, but I'd best warn you that my dad might be a bit funny with you. It's not personal; he's just a bit protective after all that stuff I went through with Dean.'

'I don't blame him,' said Jake. 'If I had a daughter and some

98

idiot treated her like that, I'd vet every lad who came within a mile of her for the rest of her life.'

Leanne smiled to herself as he drove on. Her mum would love Jake on sight, she was sure. And her dad, as wary as he would undoubtedly be to start with, would soon warm to him once he realized that Jake was nothing like her scumbag ex.

'Have you eaten yet?' Jake asked as he drove on. 'I haven't stopped all day, and I'm starving, so how about we drop your stuff off then go and grab a bite? There's a nice Italian place near mine. Or we could go Chinese, if you prefer?'

'Don't you ever eat at home?' Leanne asked.

'No,' Jake replied simply. 'I'm too busy.'

'Too lazy, more like,' Leanne teased. 'You must spend a fortune, eating out all the time.'

'What's money for if not to enjoy life?' Jake grinned.

'Well, I think it's scandalous,' Leanne said bossily. 'Stop at a shop and pick up some stuff; I'm cooking for you tonight.'

'Are you any good?' Jake asked doubtfully.

'Probably not up to the standards you're used to,' Leanne admitted. 'But I do a mean spag bol, even if I do say so myself.'

'Great.' Jake sighed as if he were thoroughly underwhelmed by the idea. Grinning when she gave him a mock-offended look, he said, 'I'm joking. I can't wait to taste your . . . *food.*'

Shivering when he gave her a sexy wink which told her that the food wasn't the only thing he intended to taste tonight, Leanne typed a quick reply to her mum, letting her know that she'd need to set an extra place for dinner on Sunday. After sending that message, and another to Chrissie, telling her that she'd be away for the weekend, Leanne switched the phone off and slipped it into her bag. Her troubles weren't going to disappear overnight, and she would definitely have to start looking for another place to live come Monday. But, for now, she just wanted to forget about the rest of the world and concentrate on enjoying some alone-time with Jake.

9

When Sunday afternoon came around, Brenda Riley stationed herself behind the net curtains at the living room window. She'd been there for a good fifteen minutes when a flashy car pulled up at her gate, and she craned her neck when the driver's-side door opened, impatient to see the mystery guest her daughter had said she would be bringing.

'I knew it!' she exclaimed when a handsome young man stepped out and walked around to open the passenger-side door. 'Norman, I was right; it *is* a man.' She flapped her hand at her husband, who was sitting behind her, studying the racing pages of his newspaper. 'Go and let them in while I fix my hair.'

'Don't go making a fuss of him,' Norman grunted, slapping the paper down on the arm of the couch and turning his wheelchair towards the door. 'He'll be another chancer like the last one, knowing her luck.'

'His car's a lot nicer,' Brenda said, as if that made him a worthier mate for their girl than Dean had turned out to be. 'And he opened her door for her, so he's obviously got good manners.'

'They all put on a show at the start,' Norman reminded her. 'But I'll get his measure soon enough. And if he's anything like the other bugger, he'll be going straight back out of here with my foot up his arse.'

Too busy checking her reflection in the mirror hanging over the fire to be bothered reminding her husband that his legs didn't work so his feet wouldn't be going near anyone's arse, Brenda shooed him on his way. It had taken her daughter a long time to get over what her ex had done to her, and Brenda had begun to fear that she might never trust anyone enough to risk starting a new relationship. Leanne was a stunningly beautiful young woman, but time wasn't on her side if she was ever going to settle down and start a family, so Brenda had been delighted to think there might be a new man on the scene. She just hoped that Norman wasn't going to give him too hard a time of it and send him running for the hills before they'd had a chance to get to know him properly.

Outside, Leanne was thinking pretty much the same thing as she and Jake walked up the path. Her father was sitting in the doorway, and from the guarded look on his face she instinctively knew that he wasn't going to give Jake an easy ride.

'Hi, Dad.' She leaned down and kissed him on the cheek when they reached him. 'This is Jake.'

'Nice to meet you, Mr Riley.' Jake extended his hand.

Ignoring it, Norman swivelled his chair around and wheeled himself into the living room just as his wife came bustling out.

'It's so lovely to see you,' Brenda gushed, pulling Leanne into a quick hug. 'We've missed you.'

'I've missed you, too,' said Leanne. Then, stepping back, she said, 'This is Jake. Jake, this is my mum, Brenda.'

Brenda gave him a beaming smile as she shook his hand. 'Come on in and make yourself comfortable, love. Dinner's almost ready. Hope you brought your appetites with you.'

Grinning when her mother went through to the kitchen after closing the front door, Leanne reached for Jake's hand and led him into the living room.

Norman had positioned himself in front of the window, and the sunshine pouring in behind his head made it impossible for Leanne to see the expression on his face when they entered the room.

'Why don't you go and give your mother a hand?' he said as she and Jake made to sit on the sofa.

Aware that he was ordering her out so that he could interrogate Jake, Leanne gave Jake a reassuring smile, and whispered, 'Don't worry, I won't be long.'

When she'd gone, Norman folded his hands in his lap and nodded for Jake to take a seat.

'So what's the score?' he asked when Jake perched on the edge of the sofa and rested his elbows on his knees. 'Are you and my girl seeing each other?'

'Yes, sir, we are.' Jake nodded. 'But I know she had a difficult time with her last boyfriend, so we're taking it slowly. She's very special.'

'You don't have to tell me that,' Norman grunted, unimpressed by the younger man's overly polite tone. 'She's worth a million of the last bastard. But while I've got you to myself, I'll tell *you* what I told *him*,' he went on, lowering his voice in case the women were earwigging. 'I might look like a decrepit old cripple, but I can still knock seven bells out of any man who tries to mess her around. You got that?'

Taking in the man's muscular tattooed arms and huge fists, and guessing that he must have been a bruiser in his youth – and was probably still more than capable of packing a mighty punch – Jake said, 'You don't have to worry, Mr Riley. I've known Leanne for a long time, and I care about her very deeply. Her ex was a fool for disrespecting her, but I would never do anything to hurt her.'

'Fool doesn't even come close to what *I* think of that prick,' Norman snarled. 'And if I ever catch him on the street, I'll . . .' He left the rest of the sentence hanging and took a long slow breath before sinking back in his chair. 'Okay, we'll say no more about it for now. If *she's* happy, *I'll* be happy. Just make sure it stays that way.'

'I will,' Jake promised, relieved that he seemed to have passed the test.

Leanne walked in at that moment, carrying two glasses of lager. Smiling when she saw that the men weren't beating their chests, she handed them each a glass and sat down next to Jake.

'The card,' Jake reminded her quietly.

'Oh, yeah, I nearly forgot.' Leanne reached into her handbag and took out an envelope. 'Happy birthday, Dad.'

Norman took a swig of his drink and wiped the froth off his mouth with the back of his hand before reaching for it.

'I know it's not till Tuesday,' Leanne said, watching as he ripped the seal, 'but I thought I'd best give it to you now, in case I don't see you on the actual day.'

Norman frowned when a second, smaller envelope fell on to his lap. 'What's this?'

'Open it and see.' Leanne grinned.

Frown deepening when he pulled a Manchester United season ticket out of the envelope, Norman said, 'Thanks, love, it's a lovely thought. But you can't afford this. Take it back and get a refund. The card's enough for me.'

'Jake got it, not me,' Leanne told him.

'I got it really cheap,' Jake said quickly, sensing that Norman, like his daughter, was probably too proud to accept big gestures. 'I know someone who works at the club.'

'Thanks, son; much appreciated.' Norman slotted the ticket back into the envelope and laid it down on the windowsill before picking up his lager. 'How's Mum getting on in there?' he asked Leanne after taking a swig.

'She's flapping,' Leanne told him quietly. 'She must think she's feeding the five thousand, judging by the amount of veg she's done. And what's with all that meat?'

'Don't ask me.' Norman shook his head in despair. 'I told

her not to overdo it, but it's like talking to a brick wall. *I* open my gob, *she* slams a brick in it to shut me up.'

'He's joking about the brick,' Leanne said to Jake. 'But he's right about her not listening. The kitchen's *her* domain, and God help anyone who dares to question what she does in there. Still, she's a great cook, so we can't complain, can we, Dad?'

'You're not wrong there, love.' Norman reached for the TV remote and switched the set on.

'How come *you* can't cook if your mum's so good?' Jake asked quietly.

'Hey, I'm not that bad,' Leanne protested. 'And I didn't hear you complaining about my spag bol last night.'

'I didn't want to offend you.'

'You're a braver man than me if you ate the muck *she* dishes up,' Norman muttered as he flipped through the channels.

'*Dad!*' Leanne gasped.

'Sorry, love, but it's true.' He was unrepentant. 'You might take after your mum in the looks department, but you definitely missed out on the cooking gene. And there's no point denying it, 'cos it sounds like the lad's already found that out for himself.'

'Don't you dare agree,' Leanne warned Jake, delighted that her dad had included him in the joke, because he'd have completely blanked him if he didn't like him.

'Wouldn't dream of it.' Jake grinned.

Brenda popped her head around the door. 'I'm ready to serve, if you'd like to come through and take your seats.'

'Why can't we eat off our knees like normal?' Norman grumbled, reluctant to miss the horse racing he'd just tuned into.

'Because it's common.' Brenda flashed him a warning look. 'Now come along before it goes cold.'

Muttering, 'Drop the posh voice and I might think about it,' when his wife withdrew her head, Norman raised his eyes at Leanne and Jake. 'Come on, you two; best not keep her lady-ship waiting.'

'Are they always like this?' Jake whispered as he and Leanne followed her father out of the room.

'*Always*,' she whispered back. 'Doing well for almost forty years together, aren't they?'

'They certainly are,' Jake agreed, winking at her as he quietly added: 'Hope we're like that when we've been together as long.'

Leanne couldn't keep the smile off her face as they took their seats at the cramped kitchen table.

And it was still there when the visit was over a couple of hours later and she climbed back into the car.

'Well, that went better than I expected,' she said, turning to wave goodbye to her parents, who had both come out on to the step to see them off. 'I think they really liked you.'

'You reckon?' Jake gave a doubtful smile as they set off.

'Your dad looked like he wanted to lamp me one, and I thought your mum was trying to kill me with all that food.'

'I know, bless her.' Leanne laughed. 'I'd probably be twenty stone by now if I was still living at home. I just hope you meant it when you said the lamb was delicious, because we'll be eating it for a week, the amount she put in that doggy bag.'

'Save me having to eat any more of *your* burnt offerings.'

'Oi, watch it, or I'll never cook for you again.'

'Can I have that in writing?'

'Don't worry, you can go back to your fancy restaurants when I go home tomorrow.' Leanne feigned indignation. 'I'm sure Maggie's imaginary cat will help me with the leftovers.'

'You're still going, then?'

'What do you mean?'

'You know what I mean.' Jake turned his head and glanced at her. 'We both know you're going to move in with me eventually, so why wait?'

Leanne bit her lip, unable to think of a suitable reply. She'd really enjoyed staying at his place, and wasn't looking forward to going back to her grotty bedsit. But it was ludicrous to think about moving in together.

Wasn't it?

They weren't teenagers in the grip of a crush that could die out as quickly as it had ignited; they were full-grown adults who had dated enough misfits between them to know that they weren't willing to settle for a meaningless fling. Leanne couldn't see herself wanting to break things off any time soon – and Jake clearly felt the same. So why was she still wary?

Because you thought Dean was perfect, and look how that turned out.

Taking her silence as a sign that she still wasn't ready to take the plunge, Jake said, 'Why don't you mull it over for a few days? And, don't worry, I won't be offended if you say no. Well, not much, anyway.' He grinned.

'Okay, I'll think about it,' Leanne agreed, wishing that she could talk it over with level-headed, straight-talking Chrissie. Left to her own devices, she was likely to do one of two things: let her heart rule her head and rush into something she may end up regretting; or, let her head rule her heart and risk losing the man who might just be 'the one'.

10

Leanne's road was blocked at both ends when Jake drove her home on Monday morning. Shocked by the sight of several police vehicles and an ambulance, her stomach lurched when she saw a paramedic pulling Mad Maggie out over the doorstep in a wheelchair.

'Oh, my God!' she gasped, fumbling with her seat belt. 'I wonder what's happened.'

'Wait,' Jake cautioned when she made to open the door. 'They're wearing whites, so whatever it is, it must be serious.'

'Whites?' Leanne was confused.

'The suits they wear when there's been a crime and they're gathering forensic evidence,' Jake explained.

'Oh, no,' Leanne murmured, covering her mouth with her hand as she stared out at the scene. 'I hope that burglar didn't come back and attack Maggie.'

'She didn't look like she had any blood on her,' Jake said, watching as a uniformed officer tied the end of a roll of a crime-scene tape to a lamp post two doors down from Leanne's house.

'I can't just sit here.' Leanne reached for the door handle again. 'I need to know what's going on.'

'Okay, but I'll come with you,' said Jake. 'Just let me park up.'

Legs shaking as she climbed out of the car a few seconds later, Leanne held tightly on to Jake's hand as they walked over to the officer who was now securing the other end of the tape to a lamp post on the opposite pavement.

'Excuse me, but that's my house,' she said. 'Has something happened? Only I've been away for the weekend, and I've just seen my neighbour being put in the back of the ambulance. Is she okay?'

'I can't tell you anything,' the copper replied. 'But if you live there we'll need to take your details, so go and speak to my colleague.' He nodded towards a policewoman who was sitting in the squad car parked behind the ambulance, then asked Jake, 'Do you live there, as well, sir?'

'No, he was just dropping me off,' Leanne blurted out, thinking it best to keep Jake out of this until she knew what was going on. He hadn't done anything wrong when he'd warned Speedy off the other day, but if something violent had taken place in the house, the police were bound to suspect him.

Turning back to Jake now, she pulled him aside, and whispered, 'You'd best go before they start asking questions.'

Nodding, Jake said, 'Okay, but ring me when you know what's happening, and I'll pick you up. I'd best hang on to your suitcase,' he added, remembering that it was still in the boot of his car. 'They won't let you into the house until they've finished, and you don't want to be lugging it around while you're waiting.'

Leanne thanked him and gave him a quick kiss before ducking under the tape.

A group of her neighbours were huddled together on the other side of the road. As Leanne passed, one of them stage-whispered, 'What's going on, love? Maggie hasn't flipped out again, has she?'

'No idea, I wasn't here,' Leanne said, continuing on her way.

The policewoman had been talking into her radio, but she abruptly stopped when she spotted Leanne heading her way and, jumping out of the car, tried to herd her back behind the tape, saying, 'This is a crime scene. Stay on that side of the cordon.'

When she explained that she lived in the house and had been sent over to give her details, Leanne was directed to take a seat in the back of the car. Gazing out through the window after climbing in, she shuddered when a white-suited man walked out carrying a clear plastic bag containing a large knife with dried blood on its blade.

'Has . . . has someone been hurt in there?' she asked the policewoman who had just climbed back into the driver's seat.

Ignoring her question, the woman said, 'Name, please?'

Leanne gave her name, and then asked, 'You don't think this could be connected to the burglary, do you?'

'Burglary?'

'Oh, sorry, you wouldn't know about it because I didn't report it. Nothing was stolen, you see, and I didn't want to waste your time.'

'When was this?'

'Friday night. I'd stayed out, and when I got back on Saturday morning my door had been kicked in. My neighbour, Speedy, told me he'd heard a load of banging up in my room at around three or four in the morning, but he reckons he didn't see anything.'

'You should have reported it,' the policewoman said, making a note of it.

'I know,' Leanne murmured guiltily. 'I just thought you had more important things to deal with. Sorry.'

'When you say Speedy, are you referring to Darren Humphries?'

'I don't know his real name,' Leanne admitted. 'We had a bit of a falling out not long after I moved in, and we haven't really spoken since.'

'Would you know if he's fallen out with anyone else recently?'

'I only ever see him in passing, to be honest, and I don't know any of his friends,' Leanne said, guessing that, whatever had happened, it must involve Speedy. Frowning now, as it occurred to her that Maggie might already have told the police about the altercation she'd had with Speedy the other night, she said, 'We, um, had a bit of a row a couple of days ago, actually. He'd left a bike in the hall and I tripped over it in the dark. It looked expensive, so I thought he might have stolen it, but he said it was his friend's.'

'I take it you didn't believe him?' The policewoman raised an eyebrow.

'Not really.' Leanne shook her head. 'He's not the most trustworthy of people.'

The policewoman made another note in her book, and then pushed her door open. Telling Leanne to wait there, she climbed out and walked over to speak with another officer.

Unable to hear what they were saying, Leanne gazed back at the ambulance. The doors were still open, and she could see Maggie sitting in the shadows at the back. Still in the wheelchair, with a blanket around her shoulders and a blank expression on her wrinkled face, the old woman looked so frail Leanne couldn't imagine how she could possibly have caused any harm to Speedy. He might be as skinny as a rake, but Leanne knew from bitter experience that he was far stronger than he looked, and the amphetamines he was addicted to had made him so paranoid he was always on edge, so she doubted the old woman could have caught him off guard. Anyway, the police would surely have handcuffed her if she were the one who'd caused that blood to be on the knife, so it was more likely that the real owner of the bike Speedy claimed was his friend's had found out where he lived and come to take it back.

'We'd like to ask you a few more questions, so I'm going to need you to come down to the station,' the policewoman said when she came back. 'It's a bit busy down there at the moment, so you might have to wait around for a while.'

'That's okay,' Leanne agreed. 'Is Maggie all right?'

'She wasn't hurt,' the woman assured her. 'She just had a bit of a funny turn after calling us, so we thought we'd best get her checked out.'

Leanne nodded and gazed back at the ambulance again. Catching one last glimpse of her elderly neighbour as a paramedic closed the doors, an uneasy feeling settled over her. Poor Maggie would probably end up getting sectioned if the funny turn was anything like the last few Leanne had witnessed. But while that might do *her* some good, considering how erratic her behaviour had been of late, Leanne didn't relish the thought of having to go back into the house on her own.

Jolted from her thoughts when the squad car's engine suddenly started, Leanne reached into her bag for her phone to let Jake know what was happening. Realizing that word must already be spreading that something had happened when she saw several increasingly frantic messages from Chrissie asking if she was okay, she sent a quick reply to let her know that she was fine before sending another to Jake, telling him that she'd call him as soon as the police had finished with her.

*

It was three hours before a detective was free to interview Leanne, and her head was pounding by the time it was over. Still shaken by what she'd learned, she was touched when she walked outside and saw Chrissie waiting for her on a bench.

'What are you doing here?' she asked, running over and giving her a hug. 'Aren't you supposed to be at work?'

'I was, but I couldn't settle for worrying about you,' said Chrissie. 'So I told my boss I had a migraine, and came here to wait for you.'

'You shouldn't have done that,' Leanne said, grateful that she had. 'You're going to get the sack if you carry on pulling sickies.'

'To be honest, I couldn't care less.' Chrissie sighed. 'I'm sick of being treated like a skivvy while the rest of them stand around filing their talons. Anyway, what's happened?' She changed the subject as, arm in arm, they set off in the direction of the bus stop. 'Have they told you anything?'

Leanne shook her head. 'Not in detail, no. But I think Speedy might have been murdered.'

'Are you serious?' Chrissie gaped at her.

'Well, he's definitely dead, and I doubt they'd have asked so many questions if they thought it was from natural causes.'

'What kind of questions?'

'Just about his activities, and people I might have seen him with. They asked about the burglary as well; wanted to know how Speedy reacted when I told him about it.'

'Do they think that had something to do with it?'

'No idea.' Leanne shrugged.

'This is crazy.' Chrissie shook her head in disbelief. 'I've never known anyone who was murdered before.'

'Me neither.' Leanne sighed and reached into her bag for change when their bus came around the corner. 'I know he was a nasty little shit, but still . . .'

'Are you okay?' Chrissie asked. 'You look shattered.'

'I'm just struggling to take it all in,' Leanne said as they boarded the bus. 'How did you hear about it, anyway?'

'Tina rang me.' Chrissie flashed her pass at the driver after Leanne had paid her fare. 'She passed yours on her way to the post office this morning, and rang me when she saw the police taping everything off. I started thinking all sorts when I couldn't get hold of you.'

'I was at still at Jake's when it happened,' Leanne said, flopping down on to the back seat. 'I didn't know anything about it till he dropped me off this morning.'

'Well, if it *was* murder, I hope they hurry up and catch whoever did it,' Chrissie said grimly as she sat down heavily beside her. 'And I don't think you should go back there until they do.'

Leanne hugged herself when a shiver coursed down her spine. 'What if it was me they were after and Speedy just got in the way?' she mused.

'Don't be ridiculous!' Chrissie snapped. 'I'm sorry to speak ill of the dead, God rest his miserable soul, but this is the kind of shit that happens when you live the kind of life he lived.'

'I know, and I keep telling myself I'm just being paranoid,'

Leanne said quietly. 'But don't you think it's a bit of a coincidence: me getting burgled, then him getting murdered a couple of days later?'

Aware that her friend was scared, Chrissie said, 'Why don't you come and stay at ours while you look for another place, babe? You'll have to top and tail with me, but it's got to be better than going back there while all this is going on.'

'Thanks,' Leanne said gratefully. 'But your mum's got enough on her plate with your Tina and the baby.'

'She won't mind,' Chrissie insisted. 'I'll ring her now, if you want?'

'No, don't.' Leanne touched her hand. 'Jake's already said I can stay at his, so I'll go there until I can get back into the house.'

'I take it things are going well between you, then?'

'Yeah, really good.' Leanne smiled for the first time in hours. 'Better than good, actually. He's asked me to move in with him.'

'What's his rush?' Chrissie asked. 'It's only been a few days.'

'Don't worry, I haven't said yes,' said Leanne, careful not to let the word *yet* slip out at the end. 'I said I'd think about it, but this probably isn't the best time to be making big decisions like that.'

'No, it isn't,' Chrissie agreed, getting up when their stop came into view.

Leanne pulled her collar up as they stepped off the bus and a blast of wind smacked her in the face.

'Let's take a quick look to see what's happening at your place, then go to mine,' Chrissie suggested, covering her hair with her handbag when it suddenly started raining. 'We can talk about you and lover-boy over a brew.'

'Okay,' Leanne agreed, shoving her hands into her pockets as they hurried across the road. 'He said he'll pick me up when I'm ready, so I'll ring him when we get there.'

When they turned the corner on to Leanne's road, they saw that the ambulances had gone, as had most of the police vehicles; but the crime-scene tape was still in place, and two uniformed officers were standing guard outside her front door. An Incident Response vehicle was parked directly opposite, behind which a transit van with blacked-out windows was sitting.

'I bet Speedy's in there.' Chrissie nodded at the van.

'God, I hope not,' Leanne muttered, superstitiously crossing herself.

At the sound of a car turning the corner behind them, they both turned to see who it was. Hoping it might be Jake, Leanne was disappointed to see that it was her landlord.

'I've been trying to get hold of you,' Roger said, emerging from the car and walking briskly over to her. 'Don't you ever check your phone?'

'I was at the police station so I had to switch it off,' she explained. 'What's up?'

'I've decided to put the house on the market, so you'll have to move out,' he told her bluntly.

119

'You can't do that,' Chrissie protested. 'You've got to give her proper notice, in writing.'

'I wasn't talking to you.' Roger flashed a dismissive look at her before turning back to Leanne. 'I know you won't be able to get in there today, obviously, but I'll need you out by the end of the week. And make sure you get everything out on time, because I've booked a skip, and anything that's left will be going in it.'

'Are you serious?' Leanne gasped. 'How the hell am I supposed to find somewhere else to live in five days?'

'I'm sure you'll manage if you start looking today,' Roger said unconcernedly. 'You're lucky I'm giving you that long, because I could evict you right now if I wanted to be a bastard about it. You're behind with your rent, don't forget.'

'So take her to court,' Chrissie challenged, her nostrils flaring with anger.

'Will you stay out of this?' Roger barked. 'It's got absolutely nothing to do with you.'

'Who the hell do you think you're talking to?' Chrissie shot back. 'I'm her mate, and if you think I'm going to stand here and let you . . .'

Shivering as the rain pelted down on her, Leanne gazed back at the house as Chrissie and Roger argued the toss. This was all happening too fast, and she couldn't take it in. Speedy was dead, and poor old Maggie was in hospital, unaware that she, like Leanne, was about to lose her home.

'Leanne . . . ?'

Snapped from her thoughts, Leanne turned to see Jake striding towards her. 'What are you doing here?' she asked. 'I thought you were going to wait for me to call you.'

'I was passing, so I thought I might as well check what was going on,' he told her. 'How did you get on with the police?'

Raised voices reached them before Leanne could tell him what she'd learned, and they both turned in time to see Chrissie whack Roger with her handbag.

'How *dare* you put your hands on me, you cheeky bastard!' she screeched. 'I'll have you done for assault.'

'What's going on?' Jake asked Leanne. 'That's not her boyfriend, is it?'

'No, it's my landlord,' she replied glumly. 'He's just told me he's selling up and I've got to be out by the end of the week, and she's not too happy about it.'

'Is that right?' Jake narrowed his eyes.

'Jake, leave it.' Leanne grabbed his arm to prevent him from going over. 'I didn't really want to have to tell you this, but I'm behind with my rent so he was going to evict me soon, anyway. And, if I'm honest, I don't fancy staying there now there's been a murder, so—'

'*Murder?*' Jake's eyebrows shot up. 'Christ, I knew it must be serious when I saw the white suits this morning, but I didn't expect that. Who was it?'

'Speedy.'

'Wow, poor guy. Have they any idea who did it?'

'Not as far as I know. But they're still investigating, so I don't suppose they'd tell me even if they did.'

'Can you believe the cheek of him?' Chrissie marched over with a furious look on her rain-drenched face. 'Trying to push me around like I'm some kind of dog, just because I'm a woman who can stand up for myself. Arrogant, misogynistic pig! I pity his poor wife, having to put up with a prat like him! And talk about *smelly* . . .' She pulled a face. 'I've been in pig sties that smell fresher than him!'

Seizing the opportunity to have a word with the man while Chrissie vented her indignation, Jake walked over to Roger's car.

'Oh God, I hope he doesn't kick off,' Leanne murmured, no longer listening to Chrissie as she watched Jake squat down to speak with Roger through the window.

'I hope he *does*,' Chrissie countered angrily. 'That prick could do with being brought down a peg or two.'

'Not with the police standing right there,' Leanne pointed out.

Relieved when Jake came back after a couple of minutes and Roger drove away unscathed, she said, 'What was that about?'

'Just letting him know that I'm not too impressed with the way he's treating you at a time like this,' said Jake. 'Don't worry, I kept my cool.'

'Thanks, but there was no need,' Leanne said resignedly. 'I don't blame him for wanting to sell up. I'd do the same in his shoes.'

Jake caught the note of desolation in her voice and peered down at her. 'Are you okay?'

'Yeah.' She nodded and forced a weak smile. 'Just got a bit of a headache.'

'It'll be the shock catching up with her,' Chrissie said to Jake. 'And standing here getting drenched can't be helping. We were about to go to mine for a brew, actually. You're welcome to come with us, if you want?'

'Thanks, but I've still got a few things to do,' Jake said. 'Probably best if I take her back to my place so she can get her head down for a while.'

'Yeah, she could probably do with a hot bath and an early night,' Chrissie agreed. 'She must be wiped.'

'Excuse me, but do *I* get a say in this?' Leanne interjected.

'Sorry,' Jake apologized, giving her a sheepish smile. 'What would *you* like to do?'

Leanne gazed over at the house again and shrugged. 'I'm obviously not getting back in there anytime soon, so I guess I haven't got much choice, have I? But would you mind if Chrissie came with me, only I don't really want to be on my own if you're going out again.'

'Fine by me,' Jake agreed. 'You up for that, Chrissie?'

'Absolutely!' she said without hesitation. 'But can we call in at mine on the way so I can change out of my work clothes?'

'As long as you're quick.' Jake glanced at his watch. 'I really need to be somewhere.'

'I'll be straight in and out,' Chrissie promised.

'Come on, then.' He jerked his head. 'I'm parked around the corner.'

11

Joan O'Brien felt like death warmed up. Her chest infection wasn't showing any signs of letting up despite the strong course of antibiotics she'd been prescribed, and she hadn't had a full night's sleep in ages, so she wasn't pleased to have been woken from her afternoon nap by somebody repeatedly ringing the front door bell.

Tutting when she peeped through the spyhole and saw who was standing on the step, she shuffled to the foot of the stairs, and yelled, 'Tina, it's for you! *TINA!*'

'No need to shout, I'm not deaf,' Tina grumbled, tying the belt of her dressing gown as she trotted down the stairs.

'No, but *I* will be if he don't pack in ringing that flaming bell!' Joan's brow creased in pain when another peal echoed through the hallway. 'I haven't had a minute's peace since you've been back.'

Ignoring her, Tina peered through the spyhole and muttered, 'What does *he* want?' when she saw her on-off lover, Eric Price, staring back at her.

'Try opening the door and you might find out,' Joan said, coughing into her hand as she made her way back to the living room.

Sticking two fingers up at her mother's back, Tina yanked the front door open.

'What are you doing here? I thought I told you to sling your hook?'

'Don't be like that.' Eric's voice was as pathetic as the imploring look in his watery eyes. 'I just need—'

'Viagra?' Tina arched an eyebrow and folded her arms.

Embarrassed, Eric shoved his hands into the pockets of his faded leather jacket. 'There's no need to be cruel about it. You know I've got problems.'

'Oh, you've got problems, all right, and not just in that department,' Tina sneered. 'I mean, come on . . . you look like a ninety-year-old garden gnome trying to be Elvis, and you seriously expect me to fancy you?'

'You said you didn't care about the age gap.'

'So, I lied. Anyway, you know the rules: no money, no honey.'

'You know I'd give it to you if I could, but it's not that easy. I've already drawn out more than—'

'Oh, for God's sake!' Tina snapped, losing patience and shoving Eric hard in his bony chest. 'I'm not interested, so just get lost!'

Jake pulled up at the gate at that moment, and Chrissie muttered, 'Bloody hell, that's all my mum needs,' when she saw her sister pushing the man up the path.

'Who is he?' Leanne asked.

'Eric Price,' Chrissie said as she yanked her seat belt off. 'He used to run the pub round the corner, and his wife's an absolute nutter who weighs about fifty stone, so our Tina should know better.'

'She's not seeing him, is she?' Leanne was horrified. 'He's ancient.'

'Her sugar daddies usually are,' Chrissie grunted, opening the door.

'Why can't you just get it through your thick head that I don't want you?' Tina's screeching voice filled the car. 'Your dick's as limp as wet lettuce, and your breath smells like dead fish, so why don't you do us all a favour and chuck yourself under a train!'

'Can't we talk about this?' Eric whined, stumbling backwards on to the pavement. 'You know I'd get you the money if I could, but my wife's already suspicious.'

'Do I look like I give a flying fuck what that fat cunt thinks?' spat Tina. 'You knew I needed it, and you promised you'd get it for me.'

'Pack it in!' Chrissie marched over and herded her sister back on to the path. 'Mum isn't well, and the neighbours are watching.'

'Get off me!' Tina snarled, struggling to get past so she could continue the argument.

'Inside – *NOW!*' Chrissie barked. 'And *you* piss off home to your wife,' she shot back at Eric. 'You should be ashamed of yourself, a man of your age, messing round with young girls.'

Furious with Chrissie for interfering, Tina yelled, 'This has got nothing to do with you, so keep your fuckin' nose out. Just 'cos you're too fat and ugly to get a bloke, you think you can—' The rest of the sentence died on her lips when she spotted Jake watching through his open car window. 'Who the hell is *that*?' she gasped.

'Leanne's boyfriend,' Chrissie told her sharply. 'So put your eyes back in their sockets before you make an even bigger fool of yourself than you already have.'

Tina wasn't about to take orders from her sister. Nimbly dodging her, she sashayed out on to the pavement with her lips pouted and her hips in full sway.

'Well, hello there,' she purred, extending her hand palm side down, as if expecting Jake to kiss it. 'I'm Tina – *her* younger, better-looking sister.' She jerked her head at Chrissie. 'And you are . . . ?'

Eyes narrowed as he took a drag on his cigarette, Jake gazed past her and called, 'You're not going to be long, are you, Chrissie?'

'Two ticks,' Chrissie replied smugly, delighted that he'd given her sister short shrift.

Mortified when she suddenly remembered that she was wearing Tina's blouse, Leanne sank down in her seat and zipped her jacket up to her throat.

'So how come I've never seen you before?' Tina asked flirtatiously, not giving a damn that Leanne was sitting right there as she rested her elbows on Jake's door and gave him a bird's-eye view of her cleavage. 'Do you live around here?'

Before he could answer, Chrissie popped her head back out of the house, and shouted, 'Tina, you'd best get your arse in here! Dylan's awake, and he's got hold of your Chanel bag!'

'You what?' Tina snapped her head around. 'That cost a ton. You'd better be joking!'

'I'm not,' Chrissie replied grimly. 'He's pulled everything out, and now he's trying to eat it.'

'Little shit, I'll kill him!' Tina squawked, pushing herself away from the car.

'What about me?' Eric asked as she rushed to the gate.

'Fuck off!' she snarled, shouldering past him and striding up the path.

'Okay, I'll get you the money,' he called after her.

'What a mug,' Jake muttered, flicking his cigarette butt into the gutter and closing his window. 'It's obvious she's using him.'

'Oh, he knows,' Leanne said as she watched the elderly man scuttle away. 'But he won't care as long as he can carry on seeing her. She's a very pretty girl.'

'If you like that kind of thing,' Jake said dismissively, glancing at his watch.

Conscious that he wanted to get moving, Leanne said, 'Give her five minutes, then I'll knock on.'

Jake nodded and sat back. 'So how are you feeling?' he asked.

'Still a bit shocked about Speedy,' she admitted. 'It's crazy to think he's been murdered. I know we didn't get on, but no one deserves that.'

'Well, you know what they say: live by the sword, die by the sword. He could have done all sorts that you don't know about.'

'I suppose so.' Leanne sighed. 'I just hope Maggie's okay. If *I'm* feeling like this when I wasn't even there, God only knows what's *she's* going through.'

'I'm sure she's being well looked after,' Jake said, reaching out to give her hand a reassuring squeeze.

Chrissie came out of the house just then and, leaving the front door ajar behind her, marched down the path with a scowl on her face.

'What's going on?' Leanne asked when she heard raised voices coming from inside.

'Our Tina and her fella are having a barney,' Chrissie said as she climbed back into the car.

'Eh?' Leanne was confused. 'But we just watched him leave.'

'Not *that* one, the one who was waiting for her in *my* bed,' Chrissie said indignantly. 'The cheeky bitch must have been at it with him when the other one turned up. I got the shock of my life when I walked into my room and found him lying there with his soldier in his hand. Ugh!' She gave an exaggerated shudder.

Leanne and Jake looked at each other and burst out laughing.

'I'm glad you two think it's funny, but I'm going to have to boil my bedding now in case I catch something,' huffed Chrissie. 'And that dressing gown she had on was mine an' all, so I'll be burning *that* when I get back.'

'Heads up,' Jake said when he spotted Eric coming back around the corner.

'Good!' spat Chrissie when she saw him. 'Let's hope the three of 'em kill each other so my mum can get a bit of peace.'

'Are you sure you don't want to stay in case it kicks off?' Leanne asked.

'What, and miss out on seeing this amazing flat you've been bragging about?' Chrissie snorted. 'No chance. Let's go.'

*

Half an hour later, after Jake had dropped them off and Leanne had shown Chrissie round the apartment, they opened a bottle of wine and carried it out on to the balcony. It had stopped raining by then, but the wind was still high, so they were both wearing their coats.

'Okay, I'm sold,' Chrissie said through chattering teeth. 'This place is the nuts, and Jake really *is* Mr Perfect. And *you*, lady, are the luckiest bitch that ever walked the face of the earth.'

'I am, aren't I?' Leanne agreed, shivering wildly but feeling warm inside.

'So have you made your mind up about moving in yet?'

'I don't know.' Leanne shrugged. 'What do *you* think I should do?'

'Hmmm, let me see,' Chrissie drawled, gazing up at the sky as if giving it real consideration. 'Go back to the ghetto and find another crappy little bedsit, or move in here and live a life of luxury with a gorgeous man who worships the ground you walk on . . . ? You'll have to give me a few minutes, 'cos it's a difficult one, this.'

'Talk about two-faced!' Leanne said amusedly as she uncapped the bottle and poured them each a glass of wine. 'You couldn't stand him a couple of days ago.'

'What can I say?' Chrissie shrugged. 'He's grown on me.'

'Told you you'd like him if you gave him a chance.'

'Yes, you did. And, for once, you were right.'

'It's still not very long, though, is it?' Leanne said as she sat back. 'I can't help thinking it's all happening a bit fast.'

'Ordinarily, I'd agree with you,' said Chrissie. 'But the way I see it, you haven't got too many options since Roger the Dodger's already given you your marching orders.'

'Don't remind me,' Leanne groaned, taking a swig of wine. 'I wonder if the police have finished with the house yet.'

'Doubt it, or they'd have let you know it was okay to go back,' said Chrissie. 'I'm just glad you weren't there last night.'

'Me too,' Leanne said quietly, shuddering at the thought of what she might have witnessed if she had been. 'I can't stop thinking about the burglary, and those blokes you saw hanging about round the corner from mine. What if it was them, and they were planning to do it that night, but called it off 'cos you saw them?'

'Who knows?' Chrissie shrugged. 'But, whoever it *was*, I honestly don't think they were after you. I've been thinking about it, and I reckon they were probably after Speedy all along.'

'But why would they trash my room if they were looking for Speedy?' Leanne asked. 'They must have known a woman lived there when they saw my stuff. And surely they would have checked the other flats once they realized they'd made a mistake?'

'They probably got disturbed and had to leg it, then decided to wait a couple of days before going back to finish the job, in case the police were sniffing around,' said Chrissie. 'Either way, the police must think it's connected, or they wouldn't have asked you all those questions about it.'

Leanne shivered as she mulled over what Chrissie had said. If she was right and Speedy *had* been the intended target all along, then a cold-blooded killer had been in her home. *A killer who was still on the loose.*

'I can't go back there,' she said decisively. 'I'm going to ring Jake and ask him if it's okay if I stay here while I look for somewhere else.'

'Thank God for that!' Chrissie said approvingly. 'Put it on loudspeaker so I can hear what he says.'

Sure that it must be a good omen when the sun suddenly broke through the clouds, Leanne was smiling as she reached for her phone and dialled Jake's number.

'Sorry for disturbing you,' she said when he answered. 'I just wanted to tell you that I've decided I'm not going back to the bedsit.'

'Are you kidding?' Jake replied delightedly. 'That's brilliant! You won't regret this, Lee. I knew you were the girl for me when I first laid eyes on you, and now I've got you, I'm going to make you the happiest woman alive.'

'You'd better,' Chrissie called out. 'Or you'll have me to deal with.'

'Am I on loudspeaker?' Jake asked.

'Er, yeah,' Leanne admitted sheepishly. 'Sorry.'

'Blame me,' Chrissie shouted. 'I wanted to hear your reaction when she told you.'

'No worries.' Jake laughed. 'Anyway, this calls for a celebration, so why don't I give Ben a ring and see if he fancies making up the numbers?'

'That'd be nice,' Leanne said.

'Okay, I'll book a table and we'll pick you up at eight,' Jake said.

'It's not fair,' Chrissie moaned, slumping in her seat when the call was finished. 'Why can't *I* find a man like him?'

'How about *him*?' Leanne whispered, smirking as she gave a surreptitious nod at the window of the neighbouring apartment.

'Oh, my God, is he even alive?' Chrissie spluttered when she spotted an old man watching them.

'Don't stare or he'll think he's in with a chance,' Leanne teased.

'Piss off!' Chrissie shuddered. 'I'm not that desperate.'

Laughing, Leanne reached for her glass and the bottle and stood up. 'Come on, let's go in and start rearranging stuff.'

'Are you crazy?' Chrissie protested as she followed her inside. 'This place is absolutely perfect as it is.'

'It is, isn't it?' Leanne agreed, gazing around after closing the French doors. *And I'm going to be living here,* she thought, unable to believe how much her fortunes had changed in the space of a few short hours.

12

Leanne and Chrissie had been ready and waiting for an hour when Jake and Ben arrived later that evening.

Rushing straight over to Leanne, Ben gave her a big hug. 'Jake's told me the good news, and I'm made up that you two have decided to make a go of it. He hasn't stopped talking about you all day.'

'All right, don't go overboard,' Jake scolded. 'You'll have her thinking I'm some kind of sap. This is Chrissie.'

'Ah, yes, of course.' Ben turned to Chrissie and politely reached for her hand to shake it. 'Really nice to see you again. You haven't changed a bit.'

'Do I know you?' she asked, thinking that he was the biggest geek she'd ever met as she took in his brown loafers and the blue checked shirt tucked into his green trousers.

'Not really,' Ben admitted. 'But I've seen you around.'

'So where are you taking us?' Leanne asked Jake when he put his arm around her.

'A nice little place not too far from here,' he said, planting a kiss on her lips.

'Oh, please don't start with the mushy stuff,' Chrissie groaned. 'At least let us eat first.'

Laughing softly, Jake jerked his chin up at Ben. 'See what I mean?'

'Excuse me?' Chrissie drew her head back. 'Am I missing something?'

'I was telling him on the way over that you've still got a mouth on you,' Jake explained.

'Oh, so first I'm bolshie, and now I've got a mouth on me,' Chrissie retorted mock-indignantly. 'Anything else you'd like to call me before we go?'

'No, I think that covers everything,' Jake quipped, winking to let her know he was joking. 'Shall we . . . ?' he said, ushering them towards the door.

*

When they arrived at the restaurant, they were shown to a booth table in the corner. Chrissie quickly slid on to the semi-circular seat and reached for a menu.

'Sorry if it looks like I'm being greedy,' she apologized, her mouth already watering as she scanned the dishes, 'but I haven't eaten since breakfast and I'm absolutely starving.'

'Me too,' Ben said as he shuffled up beside her. 'If you like chicken, you should try the Sicilian Pollo,' he suggested. 'Or, if you prefer fish, the sea bass in white wine and lemon sauce is incredible.'

'I might have known you'd eaten here before,' Leanne teased as she took her seat. 'Honestly, Chrissie, you'd think these two were made of money the amount of times they eat out.'

'You can't take it with you, so why not enjoy it?' Jake said as he sat next to her.

'Shall we get the sharing platter as a starter?' Ben suggested, already greedily perusing the menu.

'That's fine by me,' said Leanne.

'Me, too,' Chrissie agreed. 'As long as it's fast and filling.'

'It's filling, all right.' Ben grinned and patted his stomach. 'Even *I* struggle to get through it – and, believe me, *that* doesn't happen very often.'

Jake called the waiter over to give him their order, then placed his arm along the back of Leanne's seat. Shivering when he caressed her neck, she smiled and moved a little closer.

A phone started to ring, and they all looked at each other.

'Oops, sorry, that's mine,' Chrissie said, reaching into her handbag. 'Let me switch it off.' Hesitating when she took out the phone and saw her mum's name on the screen, she said, 'Actually, I need to get this. Won't be a sec.'

'It's me,' Tina blurted out when she answered. 'Where are you?'

'Out with friends,' said Chrissie. 'How come you're using Mum's phone? Is she okay?'

'No, she's on her way to hospital.'

'Why, what's happened?'

'I just came home to get changed and found her on the floor. The ambulance man said it might be her heart.'

'Right, I'm coming. Which hospital are they taking her to?'

'What's happened?' Leanne asked when Chrissie finished the call. 'Is it your mum?'

'She's collapsed,' said Chrissie, grabbing her coat and standing up. 'They think it's her heart. I'm really sorry, but I've got to go. Are there any taxi ranks round here?'

'I'll take you,' Jake offered.

'No, I don't want to ruin your night. I'll be fine in a cab. You stay and enjoy yourselves.'

'Don't be daft, we're coming with you,' Leanne insisted.

'No!' Chrissie said firmly. 'Thanks, but there's no point. I could be there for hours.'

'That doesn't matter,' Leanne argued. 'You're my best mate and I'm not letting you go on your own.'

'Why don't I go with you?' Ben suggested, rising to his feet. 'I'm sure these two will have a better time without me cramping their style. And I'd be getting a cab back later anyway, so we might as well kill two birds with one stone.'

'Fine, whatever,' Chrissie said. 'But we need to go now.'

'Take my motor.' Jake fished his keys out of his pocket and tossed them to Ben. 'Me and Leanne can walk back. It's not that far.'

'Are you sure?' Ben asked.

'Course he is, or he wouldn't have offered,' said Chrissie, pushing him in the direction of the door before leaning down to hug Leanne. 'I'll let you know what's happening as soon as *I* know,' she promised. Then, turning to Jake, she kissed him on the cheek, and said, 'Make sure she enjoys herself and doesn't spend all night worrying about me.'

'I've got this,' he assured her. 'You just go and see to your mum.'

*

When Ben pulled up outside the A and E department fifteen minutes later, Chrissie fumbled with her seat belt when she spotted Tina pacing up and down at the corner of the building sucking on a cigarette.

'Calm down, I'm sure everything will be fine,' Ben said, reaching over to unclip the belt for her. 'Go and let them know you're here. I'll park up and follow you in.'

'Thanks, but there's no need,' said Chrissie. 'My sister's over there, so I'll be okay.'

'If you're sure?'

'I'm positive.' Chrissie gave him a grateful smile. 'Thanks for the lift, but you might as well go back to the restaurant. You never know, they might not have finished the starter yet.'

She said goodbye and rushed over to Tina.

'What's happening? Where's Mum? Have they told you anything yet?'

'They've got her hooked up to some machines,' Tina said, dropping the cigarette and stamping it out before immediately lighting another. 'They're talking about keeping her in for the night, but they'd better not, 'cos I left Dylan with Mrs Ford, and I said it'd only be for a couple of hours.'

'Why don't you go and get him?' Chrissie suggested. 'It's not that late, and I'm sure Mum will be pleased to see him.'

'I can't,' Tina muttered, peering down at her phone when a message came on to the screen. 'I've made plans.'

'Well, you'd better *unmake* them if Mrs Ford is expecting you back,' said Chrissie. 'It must be serious if they want to keep Mum in.'

'I called the ambulance, what more do you want?' Tina said irritably. 'I have got a life, you know. Anyhow, *you're* here now, so she doesn't need me.'

'You selfish cow!' Chrissie gasped. 'Mum could be dying for all you know, and all you care about is your flaming social life!'

'Oh, wind your neck in.' Tina tossed her a scathing look. 'Don't expect *me* to drop everything just 'cos *you* haven't got anything better to do.'

'Don't you dare walk off!' Chrissie snapped when Tina started doing exactly that. 'I mean it, Tina, get back here right now or I'll never speak to you again!'

'That a promise?' Tina called back over her shoulder without slowing down.

Chrissie watched her for a moment, then threw up her hands in despair and marched toward the hospital door.

Still sitting in the car, Ben had just sent Jake a message to let him know that he'd dropped Chrissie off and would bring his car back first thing in the morning. About to head home, he hesitated when Chrissie's sister walked past. Frowning when he glanced over at Chrissie and saw her going into the hospital with a thunderous look on her face, he turned the car around and drove into the car park.

*

Chrissie was standing by the reception desk, agitatedly rapping her nails on the countertop. Jumping when Ben came up behind her and asked if there was any news, she said, 'The receptionist's just gone to find out where they've taken her. But why are you still here? I thought I told you to go.'

'I saw your sister leaving and thought you might need the company,' Ben said, looking around for empty seats as he spoke. Spotting one in the far corner, between a man whose bloody head was wrapped in a dirty tea towel and a small boy with a gaping cut on his leg, he said, 'Why don't you go and sit down till the receptionist comes back. I'll get us some coffee.'

Chrissie shook her head. 'Thanks, but I'd rather wait here. And thanks for checking on me,' she added gratefully, touched by his kindness. 'But you don't have to stay. I'm sure you've got better things to do than hang around here.'

'Not really.' Ben shrugged. Then, lowering his voice, he said, 'To be honest, I get a kick out of hospitals at night. I love all that *He's tachycardic, get me bloods and fifty mils of adrenalin, stat!* stuff.'

Smiling bemusedly at the American accent he'd affected, Chrissie said, 'You're a strange little man, aren't you?'

'What's strange about liking drama?' Ben replied with a deadpan expression. 'Truth be told, I always kind of fancied myself as a surgeon. But it'd have to be something like brain, or heart; none of that trivial stitch-'em-up-and-send-'em-packing nonsense. Give me life-and-death any day.'

'Strange, *and* a megalomaniac.' Chrissie chuckled.

'Well, at least I've cheered you up.' Ben grinned. 'So how about that coffee?'

'Go on then,' Chrissie agreed. 'White, with sugar.'

Watching as he went off in search of a drinks machine, Chrissie wondered if Leanne and Jake had sent him to keep an eye on her. If so, he was doing a pretty good job of making it seem like he didn't mind.

The receptionist came back to the desk just then, and informed Chrissie that her mother was in bay three.

'Is she okay?' Chrissie asked. 'Was it her heart?'

'You'll have to ask the nurses,' the woman said. 'Just go round that corner and press the buzzer.'

Thanking her, Chrissie said, 'My friend's gone to get coffee. When he comes back, can you tell him I've gone in and he should go home, please?'

*

Joan O'Brien was restless. She'd tried telling the paramedics that she was okay when she'd come round in the ambulance, but they'd insisted on fetching her in, so now she was flat on her back with pads stuck to her chest and wires trailing all over her body, when she could have been at home, watching telly with her feet up. And to make matters worse, the stupid doctor was trying to tell her that she'd have to stay in for a couple of nights at least, which was not what she'd wanted to hear.

Twisting her head at the sound of the curtain swishing back, she said, 'Oh, hello, love,' when Chrissie appeared. 'When did you get here?'

'Just now.' Chrissie pulled a chair up beside the bed and reached for her hand. 'How are you feeling?'

'There's nowt wrong with me,' Joan grumbled. 'Not that you'd know it, with this lot treating me like I'm on my flaming deathbed. I've a good mind to discharge myself.'

'You will not!' Chrissie said firmly. 'They don't do this stuff for fun, so you'll stay put and do as you're told.'

Joan gave a little snort, but Chrissie was confident that she wasn't going to try and make a break for it. Despite her protest-ations to the contrary, her mum was clearly too weak to go anywhere right now. And that scared her, because her mum was one of the strongest people she had ever known.

'Can you give our Tina a ring and let her know what's hap-pening?' Joan asked. 'She must be worried.'

'She already knows,' said Chrissie, trying not to let her

annoyance show in case it upset her mum as she added, 'She's only just left.'

'I didn't know she was here. Was Dylan with her?'

'No, she left him with Mrs Ford.'

'Thank God for that,' Joan muttered. 'I know he's not mine, and I probably shouldn't fuss, but I don't trust her to do right by him when I'm not there to keep an eye on things.'

Surprised to hear this, because it was the first time her mum had openly admitted that she disapproved of the way Tina was raising her child – or rather, the way she was leaving their mother to raise him – Chrissie bit her tongue to prevent her own damning thoughts from leaping out. Instead, she said, 'Will you please stop worrying about everyone else and think about yourself for a change, Mum? I've been telling you to stop overdoing it for ages, and now look what's happened.'

'And I've told you there's nowt wrong with me,' Joan insisted, fingering the pads on her chest. 'Least there wouldn't be if I didn't have all this rubbish stuck all over me. And do they have to have that thing on so loud?' She nodded at the monitor that was standing on the other side of the bed. 'Be a love and see if you can find the volume button.'

'I'm not messing with the machinery,' Chrissie protested. 'What if I press the wrong thing and give you a shock?'

'It might give me a kick-start so I can get out of here faster.'

Joan chuckled, but it quickly turned into a hacking cough. Concerned that her mum might choke to death when her eyes bulged and her skin turned from grey to puce, Chrissie yanked the curtain back.

'Can somebody help us in here, please?'

*

Ben's nerves were jangling like live wires by the time Chrissie came back out into the reception area. He'd drunk several coffees by then, and the subtitles scrolling across the bottom of the muted TV that was bolted to the wall were making him feel sick and jittery. Leaping to his feet when he realized Chrissie hadn't seen him, he stumbled over the legs of a drunk who had been causing an uproar but was now snoring loudly, and quickly followed her outside.

Shocked to see him, Chrissie said, 'I asked the receptionist to tell you to go home. Please don't tell me you've been here all this time?'

'I wanted to make sure you were okay,' Ben said, leading her over to the car. 'How's your mum?'

'Asleep, at last.' Chrissie's teeth started chattering as the icy morning air bit into her cheeks. 'They reckon she's got pneumonia.'

'Really? So it's not her heart, then?'

'They're not sure yet. Apparently it's one of the symptoms of pneumonia, so they're hoping it'll settle down once the antibiotics kick in.'

Climbing into the car when he'd unlocked the door, Chrissie

flopped into the passenger seat and covered a yawn with her hand.

'You look exhausted,' Ben said as he climbed behind the wheel.

'Absolutely knackered,' she admitted. 'What time is it?'

'Just gone three.'

'Seriously? God, I'm so sorry.'

'I'm fine,' Ben insisted, reversing out of the space and heading out on to the road. 'I don't feel sleepy at all, and it's actually been a bit of an eye-opener. I never realized accident and emergency units got so busy on weeknights; I thought the loonies usually waited till the weekend to make a nuisance of themselves. I've seen some pretty unusual sights tonight, I can tell you . . .'

Resting her head on the back of the seat as he rattled off the array of injuries and strange behaviours he'd witnessed, Chrissie studied his face from the corner of her eye. With his wild curls and terrible dress sense, he wasn't her usual type, but it was impossible not to like him. And she thought it was really cute the way his eyes crinkled at the corners when he smiled.

'Oops, sorry, forgot to ask your address,' Ben said suddenly. 'Almost took you back to my place by mistake.'

Chrissie sat up straighter and gazed out through the windscreen. 'Don't worry, you're going the right way. Turn left at the next lights and go over the roundabout, then take the second right on to Lansbury Road. I live halfway down; number seventy-nine.'

Ben followed her directions and, a few minutes later, eased to a stop outside her gate.

'Thanks again for waiting,' Chrissie said, grinning slyly as she added, 'I'd invite you in for a coffee, but I think you've had enough already.'

'Sorry,' Ben apologized sheepishly. 'I always get a bit hyper when I have too much caffeine. Hope I didn't make your ears bleed? I probably should have switched to hot chocolate after the second cup, but—'

'I was joking,' Chrissie cut him off, grinning. 'And you're welcome to come in if you want a drink?'

Ben glanced at the dashboard clock and shook his head. 'Best not. It's really late – or should that be early? I'm never quite sure.'

Laughing softly, Chrissie thanked him again and waved him off before making her way inside.

Tina wasn't in her bed when Chrissie reached their room, and Chrissie guessed that she must have picked Dylan up and gone to stay with a friend. Grateful for the chance to sleep without being disturbed by the baby crying or her sister snoring, she quickly undressed and got into bed.

13

Woken by the sound of the doorbell echoing in the hallway below the next morning, Chrissie peeled an eye open and peered at the clock. Dismayed to see that it was 8.45 and she was late for work, she winced when the next-door neighbour's furious voice bellowed: 'Tina . . . open this door right now! I know you're in there!'

Chrissie pulled the quilt up over her head, but she couldn't bring herself to ignore the woman, so after several more rings on the bell, she got up and padded down the stairs.

Dylan was screaming blue murder in his pram, and Mrs Ford looked as if she was on the verge of a nervous breakdown as she bounced the handle up and down in an effort to soothe him.

'Where is she?' the woman demanded, peering into the hall.

'I don't know,' Chrissie admitted. 'Here, let me take him.'

'This isn't on,' Mrs Ford bristled. 'I only agreed to watch him because she promised she'd be back in a couple of hours. And I wouldn't mind, but all she left me was one nappy and one bottle. Have you any idea how uncomfortable the poor little thing must be feeling right now?'

'I'm really sorry,' Chrissie apologized, pulling the pram in over the step. 'I'd have come for him last night if I'd known Tina wasn't coming back, but I didn't get home from the hospital till the early hours.'

Aware that she was blasting the wrong person, Mrs Ford said, 'Yes, well, I appreciate that, Christine. And I hope you don't think I'm annoyed with you, because I'm not. This is your sister's doing, not yours. She always was wilful, but she needs to remember that she's a mother now and she can't come and go as she pleases. It's not fair on the baby, *or* your poor mum.'

Chrissie nodded her agreement, but didn't say anything as she unstrapped Dylan and lifted him out. She hadn't paid him much attention since Tina had moved back in, but she was flooded with pity as she cuddled him now. Two years old, and he'd received more love and affection off his grandmother in the last few months than he'd ever had from his feckless excuse for a mother.

A little calmer now that the burden had been lifted from her shoulders, Mrs Ford asked, 'Any news on your mum, love?'

'She's got pneumonia,' said Chrissie, relieved that the cuddle seemed to be working and Dylan was starting to quieten down. 'They put her on an antibiotic drip last night, and they reckoned it should start working really fast, so I'm hoping she'll be home soon.'

'Well, that's good.' Mrs Ford smiled. 'Send her my regards when you see her, won't you? And I'm sorry for taking my frustrations out on you just now, but I—'

'There's really no need to apologize,' Chrissie interrupted, shifting Dylan on to her other arm when she felt liquid seeping out of his heavy nappy. 'Tina was out of order, dumping him on you like that, and I'll be having words with her when she gets home.'

'Yes, well, good luck with that,' said Mrs Ford.

Closing the door when she'd said goodbye, Chrissie gazed down at Dylan and sighed. He'd stopped crying and was resting his head on her shoulder, but his little chest was still heaving. She knew she was a poor substitute for his doting nana, but she was all he had right now, so she kissed him softly on the head and carried him into the living room.

After changing him and settling him on the settee with a bottle, Chrissie tried to call Tina, but it went straight to voicemail. Certain that the bitch had switched her phone off on purpose, Chrissie left a terse message telling her to get her arse home ASAP. That done, she rang work to let them know that she wouldn't be coming in today, then rang the hospital to ask how her mum was doing. Relieved to hear that she was responding well to the antibiotics, she asked the nurse to let her mum know that she would bring some stuff in for her as soon as she had a chance.

Dylan was asleep by the time she got off the phone, so Chrissie went upstairs to have a quick wash and get dressed.

151

The doorbell rang as she was coming back down, and she was surprised to find Ben on the step.

'Aren't you supposed to be at work?' she asked, leading him into the kitchen.

'I've already been,' he said. 'I actually went after I dropped you off last night. Or should that be this morning? Either way, I was too wired to sleep, so I thought I might as well catch up on some paperwork while my head was buzzing.'

'Have you been there all night?' Chrissie glanced over her shoulder as she reached into the cupboard for cups. Smiling slyly when he nodded, she said, 'I guess that explains why you're still wearing those disgusting trousers.'

'What's wrong with them?' Ben frowned and gazed down at himself.

'Would you like me to be nice, or honest?'

'How about both?'

Laughing softly, Chrissie said, 'Okay, I'm going to assume you're colour-blind, 'cos that's the only excuse for going out in public wearing puke-green pants. But *this* has got to stop right now!' She yanked his shirt out of his trousers. 'And don't even get me started on *them*.' She pulled a face and pointed at his shoes.

Before Ben could respond, the doorbell rang again. This time it was Leanne.

'You said you were going to text me and let me know what was happening,' she scolded, pulling Chrissie into a hug. 'I've been worrying all morning.'

'And night,' Jake added mock-wearily when he joined them after paying the taxi driver.

'Sorry,' Chrissie apologized, waving them into the hall. 'I didn't get home till gone three, and our Tina dumped the baby on next door, so I had to take him in when I got up. Poor thing was bawling his head off, but he's asleep now, thank God.'

She had led them into the kitchen by then, and Leanne exchanged a knowing look with Jake when she saw Ben finishing off the brews Chrissie had started. He was wearing the same clothes he'd been wearing the previous night, but his shirt was now hanging loose instead of being neatly tucked inside his trousers.

'Ben's just called round to ask if there was any news on my mum,' Chrissie said pointedly when she caught the exchange. 'Isn't that kind of him?'

'*Very,*' Leanne replied facetiously.

'All right, mate.' Jake clapped Ben on the back. 'Good night, was it?'

'Very good, actually,' Ben said innocently as he took two more cups out of the cupboard.

'Okay, you two, pack it in,' Chrissie said wearily. 'He's been at work all night, so just grow up and quit with the innuendos.'

Still smirking, Leanne and Jake took a seat at the tiny table.

'How's your mum?' Leanne asked. 'Was it her heart, like they thought?'

'No, it's pneumonia,' said Chrissie, perching on a stool so Ben could take the third chair. 'I can't believe they didn't pick up on it when the GP sent her in for those tests the other day. They're just lucky she didn't die last night, or I'd be suing the arse off them right now.'

'It's a good job your Tina was here to call the ambulance,' Leanne said, smiling at Ben when he carried their teas over. 'Is she still in bed?'

'Probably, but not her own,' Chrissie snorted. 'She took off as soon as I turned up at the hospital and I haven't seen her since. I've already had to take the day off work to look after Dylan, and there's no way I can take tomorrow off as well, so she's got till six, then I'm calling social services.'

'You don't mean that.' Leanne frowned.

'Don't I?' Chrissie shot back. Then, sighing, she rolled her eyes. 'Course I don't; my mum would never forgive me. And it's not his fault, bless him. He didn't ask to get lumbered with a waste of space like her.'

'Is that him waking up?' Leanne asked when she heard a muffled whimper coming from the next room.

Muttering, 'Great! He's only been asleep five minutes,' Chrissie dragged herself to her feet and went to check on him.

'She looks really stressed out,' Leanne said quietly when she'd gone. 'I think I'd better stay with her till Tina gets back. You don't mind if we give lunch a miss, do you, Jake?'

'Of course not,' he assured her, reaching for his tea. 'I've got plenty to be getting on with, so I'll have this then get going. You going to the office, Ben?'

Stifling a yawn, Ben shook his head. 'I went in after I dropped

Chrissie off last night, so I should probably go home and get my head down for a couple of hours.'

Leanne and Jake exchanged another secretive smile, both still convinced that Ben was lying and had actually spent the night here. Sure that she'd get the truth out of Chrissie when they were alone, Leanne showed the men out as soon as they had finished their drinks, then popped her head around the living room door.

'How's he doing?'

'He'll be okay,' Chrissie whispered, gently patting Dylan's back. 'Probably just missing his nana.'

When the boy's eyes closed after a moment, and the snuffling quietened, Chrissie motioned Leanne back into the kitchen.

'You look knackered,' Leanne said, watching as Chrissie carried the cups to the sink and rinsed them out. 'Anything you'd like to tell me?'

'Like what?' asked Chrissie, switching the kettle on to make a fresh brew.

'About you and Ben.'

'I've already told you, nothing happened.'

'Well you looked pretty cosy when me and Jake got here. You all flustered; Ben with his shirt hanging out like he'd got dressed in a hurry.'

'I'd just pulled it out when you got here, actually.'

'You dirty mare!'

'Behave! I'm talking about his shirt, not his soldier.'

'Joking aside, you could do worse,' said Leanne. 'He seems really nice.'

'He is,' Chrissie agreed. 'And I could have kissed him when I came out after seeing my mum last night and found him waiting for me. But he's not my type, and I'm not his, so there's no point trying to push us together.'

'We'll see,' Leanne murmured, sure that Chrissie was *exactly* Ben's type. Why else would he have spent the night in that hospital waiting room, and then come round here first thing to check on her, if he didn't fancy her?

'So, how was your first night with Jake as an official couple?' Chrissie asked when she carried their drinks to the table. 'Still think it was the right decision?'

'Yes,' Leanne said without hesitation. 'I honestly do.'

'Well, at least one of us is getting laid at last,' Chrissie teased. 'Just let me know when I need to start shopping for a hat.'

'What was that?' Leanne said, hearing a noise in the hall. 'Dylan hasn't got up again, has he?'

Chrissie listened for a moment, and shrugged when she heard nothing. 'Probably just the post. Anyway, tell me about the meal. I was gutted I missed it. Was it good?'

*

Out in the hall, Tina hesitated at the sound of Chrissie's voice in the kitchen. She'd hitched a ride after leaving the hospital last night, and the lads who'd picked her up had invited her back to their place for a party. Never one to turn down the offer of free drugs, she'd forgotten about the man she was supposed to be meeting and had spent the night snorting coke and having sex with the lads instead. But if she'd thought they were going to let her stick around to sleep it off this morning, she was sadly mistaken. The bastards had turfed her out at first light, and she'd been forced to make her own way home, even though she hadn't known where she was.

Back now, her head pounding and her legs aching from the long walk, she'd already crept past Mrs Ford's to avoid having to pick up Dylan and have him pester the fuck out of her, so there was no way she was hanging around down here to take shit off her sister.

She started to creep up the stairs, but forgot about the creaky one in the middle, and winced when the kitchen door flew open.

'Don't start,' she muttered sickly when Chrissie walked out. 'I'm not feeling well, so I'm going for a lie-down.'

'Ah, you poor thing,' Chrissie said sweetly. 'Hard night, was it?'

'A bit,' Tina replied warily, wondering why her sister was being nice to her for a change.

'Well, you're home now, so you can have a rest,' said Chrissie, taking her coat off the hook behind the door and slipping it on. 'Dylan's in the front room, but he's only just dropped off so try not to wake him when you carry him up.'

'Why's he here?' Tina frowned. 'I left him with Mrs F.'

'She brought him back,' said Chrissie. 'And she wasn't best pleased, so I'd stay out of her way, if I was you.'

'Can't you take him out with you?' Tina moaned. 'My head's killing me.'

'No, I can't,' Chrissie snapped, dropping the act. 'You're his mother, not me, and it's about time you started acting like it.'

'I might have known you were just being sarky,' Tina sneered. 'You're such a bitch. You can see I'm not well.'

'Self-inflicted,' Chrissie said unsympathetically, recognizing the signs of a drug comedown. 'Move,' she said then, marching up the stairs and pushing Tina aside. 'I need to get my bag.'

Tina waited until Chrissie had gone into the bedroom, and then darted back down the stairs.

'Tina . . . ?' Chrissie rushed back out on to the landing when she heard the door opening and closing. 'Don't you dare sneak out!'

Furious to see that her sister had disappeared by the time she ran outside, Chrissie kicked the gate before making her way back into the house.

'See what I mean?' she complained. 'She doesn't give a toss about anybody but herself.'

'No point getting upset about it,' Leanne counselled, rising from her seat when Dylan started to cry. 'Sit down and finish your brew; I'll see to him. And I can watch him later if you need to go and see your mum.'

Chrissie nodded and breathed out slowly to release the anger. 'Thanks, you're a lifesaver.'

'You'd do the same for me,' said Leanne, pushing her gently into her seat.

14

Three weeks had passed since Ben had driven Chrissie to the hospital to see her mum, and he hadn't been able to stop thinking about her. She was on his mind from the moment he woke in the morning until he climbed into bed each night. She still had that same sharp tongue that had earned her a reputation as being a tough nut when they were kids, but he'd seen humour behind the spikiness, and he liked that she was direct without being nasty. She was also rather attractive, he thought; with curves in all the right places and a smile that lit up her face in a way they never did with skinnier, more image-conscious girls. Sadly, she'd made it quite clear that she didn't fancy him, so nothing was ever going to develop between them. But he was hoping that they could at least be friends. If he ever saw her again.

Jake had been busy in the weeks following the aborted meal, and Ben hadn't seen much of him. So when he was woken early one morning by an out-of-the-blue phone call from his friend, he immediately thought the worst.

'What's up?' he asked worriedly when he answered. 'It's not Chrissie's mum, is it?'

'Chrissie's mum?' Jake repeated, amused. 'Man, you *must* have it bad if she was the first thing you thought of.'

'You're not usually up this early, so I thought something must be wrong,' Ben muttered, feeling foolish. 'She was really ill, last I heard, so I just thought you might have heard something.'

'Well I haven't, so I'm guessing nothing's changed,' said Jake. 'Anyway, never mind her, do you want to hear my news?'

Ben sat up and pushed his wayward curls out of his eyes. 'Go on,' he said.

'I've just bought a house,' Jake announced.

'Seriously?'

'Yep. I've been toying with the idea of investing in property for a while, and this place came up, so I figured it was time to take the leap.'

'Wow, that's great, I'm really pleased for you. Where is it?'

'Round the corner from you,' said Jake. 'It's Leanne's old place.'

'Where that bloke got murdered?' Ben spluttered, wondering if his friend had lost his mind. 'You are joking, aren't you?'

'Why would I joke about something like that?'

'Because someone got *murdered* in there,' Ben repeated slowly. 'No one's going to want to live there after that, and they definitely wouldn't be crazy enough to buy it if you're thinking of selling it on.'

'Which is exactly why I got it so cheap,' said Jake. 'I had a word with the owner the day it happened and told him I was interested. We met up yesterday to discuss it, and he almost bit my hand off when I made him an offer.'

'I thought you said it was a wreck,' Ben reminded him. 'What if the bank refuses to give you a mortgage?'

'I'm paying cash, so that's not an issue,' Jake said unconcernedly. 'And the owner's agreed to take care of the major repairs, so it'll be set for new tenants as soon as that's out of the way and you've given it a lick of paint.'

'*Me?*' Ben replied incredulously. 'Are you forgetting I've got a business of my own to run?'

'Mate, I'm not being funny, but we both know it's on its arse,' said Jake. 'I know you're strapped, so I'm trying to do you a favour here. And it won't be a one-off, 'cos I'm intending to buy a lot more places in the future. So, are you in, or what?'

Ben didn't know what to say. He'd known that Jake was doing all right for himself, but he'd had no idea that his friend had enough ready cash lying around to buy a house outright. Ben's business, on the other hand, was in serious trouble. Unlike Jake, who had flitted from one get-rich-quick scheme to another after leaving school, Ben had gone to college and studied to become an accountant – the most secure of all careers, he'd thought, given that money made the world go round. Unfortunately, the recession had put paid to most of the smaller businesses he'd handled when he first set out, and as larger companies tended to hire in-house accountants, he was now down to just a handful of clients. And the way *their* fortunes were going, he reckoned that most of them would be throwing in the towel before too long.

'Mate, I need an answer,' Jake cut into his thoughts. 'Are you in, or do I need to look for someone else?'

'Okay, I'll do it,' Ben agreed, wondering as he said it if he was going to be fit enough to paint a three-storey house by himself after spending the last few years getting fat behind a desk.

'Good man,' said Jake. 'Now get your arse out of bed, 'cos I've just pulled up outside yours. We're going to see the house.'

'What, *now*?' Ben frowned. 'What about the police?'

'They finished with it a while ago,' Jake assured him. 'And I've only got an hour, so get moving.'

'Okay, give me five,' said Ben, shoving the quilt off his legs.

*

A piece of crime-scene tape was still tied to the lamp post when they arrived at the house ten minutes later, and Ben shivered when he climbed out of the car and heard it flapping in the wind.

'This is creepy,' he muttered, casting a nervous glance at the downstairs window. 'They reckon the old woman who lived in there found the body and called the police. Can you imagine if it had been Leanne who found it? Or, God forbid, that she'd been here when it happened and got in the way.'

'Well, she wasn't, and she's not coming back, so shut up about it,' Jake said, unlocking the door and pushing it open.

'Bloody hell, that's rank,' Ben complained, holding his nose when a foul odour hit him in the face. 'Are you sure the body isn't still here?'

'It's a blocked drain,' said Jake, stepping into the dark hall-way and feeling his way along the wall for a light switch.

Ben felt uneasy as he followed his friend inside. It was too quiet, and it felt wrong to be going into someone else's home when they weren't around.

Jake had found the switch, but it didn't work, so he blindly started slotting keys into the lock on Maggie's door.

Ben winced when the door popped open after a few attempts and daylight hit his eyes. When he glanced inside the room and saw that it was crammed full of rubbish, he mur-mured, 'Wow! Talk about a hoarder's paradise.'

'Leanne reckons the old girl is off her nut,' Jake said, forcing his way past several stacks of ancient, yellowed newspapers that were almost as tall as he was.

A glass-fronted cabinet full of china figurines caught his eye, and he kicked a path through the clothes that were strewn all over the floor to get to it.

'These are all Royal Doulton,' he said when he'd checked them out. 'Bet they're worth a fortune.'

'You can't steal the woman's belongings,' Ben chided from the doorway. 'She's already lost her home – unless you're plan-ning to let her move back in after you've done it up?'

'No chance!' Jake straightened up and wiped his hands on his trousers. 'Benefit tenants are too much hassle; I'm only taking professionals.'

After looking around the other rooms, each of which was as cluttered as the first, Jake moved on up to the first floor.

Speedy's door was standing open, and a sickly taste flooded Ben's mouth when he spotted a pool of dried blood on the lino in the hallway.

'Don't worry, that'll be gone by the time you start working on it,' Jake assured him as he stepped over it and walked into the flat.

Staying put on the landing, Ben jumped when he heard a bang coming from the floor above. '*Jake . . .*' he called through the door in a loud whisper. 'I think someone's upstairs! *JAKE!*'

'What's up?' Jake asked distractedly, his gaze fixed on the bundle of letters he was sifting through as he came out into the hall. 'Have you seen this lot? There's a ton of final demands here, and loads of court summons. Cheeky fucker!' he spluttered when he saw a familiar name on one of the letters. 'Look at this' – he held it out to show Ben – 'it's addressed to Leanne. And so's this one. He must have been nicking her post.'

'Just shut up about the bloody post and listen, will you?' Ben hissed. 'I think somebody's up there.'

'They'd better not be,' Jake said gruffly. 'That's Leanne's place, and her stuff's still in there.'

'What are you *doing*?' Ben squawked when Jake set off up the stairs, taking them two at a time. Groaning when he got no answer, he pulled his keys out of his pocket to use as a weapon and reluctantly followed. He had never had a fight in his life, and would rather be anywhere else than here right now. But Jake was his best mate, and he wasn't about to run out on him.

Jake was in the tiny kitchenette when Ben joined him. 'There's your killer,' he chuckled, pointing to a pigeon perched on top of the ancient boiler. 'It must have got in through the hole in the roof.'

Ducking when the bird suddenly took flight, narrowly missing his head as it flew into the bedroom, Ben said, 'It's trying to get out, poor thing.'

'Here . . .' Jake snatched a tea towel off the ledge and tossed it to him. Pulling a face when Ben put it over his head, he said, 'What *are* you doing?'

'Covering my head so it can't crap on me.'

'Get it off, you idiot! It's to throw over the bird, so you can hold it down while I whack its brains out.'

'Don't be so cruel!' Ben protested. 'I'll catch it and let it out.'

'Go on, then, Doctor Doolittle,' Jake challenged. 'Let's see you.'

'Okay, but make sure it doesn't fly out again.' Ben held the tea towel out in front of himself and tiptoed into the front room, where the bird was now perched on the back of the armchair.

'Don't break anything,' Jake warned when Ben knocked his

knee against the coffee table. 'I don't want Leanne to know we've been here.'

'Don't you think she'll guess when you tell her you've bought the place?' Ben pointed out as he edged around the table to creep up on the bird.

'I'm not going to tell her just yet,' said Jake. 'I want to surprise her when it's ready.'

'Quick!' Ben chucked the tea towel over the bird and grasped his struggling captive with both hands. 'Get the window!'

Jake rushed over to the window and pushed it open. Tutting when the handle came off in his hand, he tossed it on to the chair.

'And you still want to buy this dump?' Ben asked, wiping his hands on the tea towel after releasing the bird. 'No wonder that bloke was so keen to get rid; it's going to need an absolute fortune spending on it.'

'Don't you worry about that,' Jake said unconcernedly as he walked out on to the landing and set off down the stairs. 'It'll be worth a bomb by the time I've finished with it.'

Relieved to be getting out of there, Ben followed Jake down to the first floor and, pressing himself up against the banister rail as they passed Speedy's door, rushed down the rest of the stairs and out on to the pavement.

'Right, I'd best get moving,' Jake said, glancing at his watch as he headed to the car. 'Do you want dropping at yours, or would you rather go to Chrissie's?'

'Why would I want to go there?' Ben frowned to cover his blushes. 'She's yours and Leanne's friend, not mine.'

'Whatever you say,' Jake drawled, smiling to himself as he climbed behind the wheel. It was obvious that Ben had the hots for Chrissie, but the wuss was too shy to admit it, much less do anything about it.

15

Chrissie had been furious with Tina for doing a runner the morning after their mum was taken into hospital, but her anger had slowly changed to concern when several weeks went by with no word from her sister. As inconsiderate as Tina was, she had always let their mum know if she planned to stay out for the night, so it worried Chrissie that she hadn't phoned or messaged to say that she was okay, or even to check on Dylan. Scared that she might have had an accident or been arrested, Chrissie rang the police and the hospitals, but there was no record of Tina being taken in by either.

Unlike Leanne, who had talked about trying for a baby with Dean before she'd realized he was a worthless, lying cheat, Chrissie had never harboured the desire to have children of her own, so it hadn't come naturally to look after Dylan. And it was particularly hard since she was also looking after her mum, who had been pretty much bedridden since coming home from the hospital after suffering a series of mini-strokes. But as difficult as it had been, she and Dylan had gradually begun to get used to each other, and she'd known she had it cracked when he stopped crying over every little thing and started coming to her for cuddles.

Within the space of a month, Chrissie had weaned Dylan off the bottle, taught him how to use a potty, and got him sleeping right through the night. And she'd now enrolled him in a nursery, which had freed her up to go back to work – for which she would be eternally grateful to her boss, Lisa, who had been amazingly supportive once she knew the situation and had told Chrissie to take as much time off as she needed.

Now that everything was stable, Chrissie wasn't about to let Tina walk in and mess it all up again. So when the bell rang one morning as she was getting ready to go to work, and she opened the door to find her sister on the step, she wasn't impressed.

'Sorry for coming round so early,' Tina muttered, rubbing her nose on her sleeve. 'I tried my key, but it didn't work.'

'That's because I changed the locks,' Chrissie informed her. 'What do you want?'

'Where's mum?' Tina ducked her head to peer into the hall. 'I need to see her.'

'She's dead,' Chrissie said bluntly.

'*What* . . . ?' Tina looked as if she'd been whacked in the face with a shovel. '*How?* She was all right last time I saw her.'

Unmoved by the tears that had sprung into her sister's eyes, Chrissie said, 'Don't pretend you care. If you gave a shit, you'd have come home ages ago. In fact, you wouldn't have gone in the first place.'

'I didn't know she was that ill or I would never have left,' Tina snivelled. 'I only went 'cos I knew you didn't want me here.'

'Don't you dare try and blame this on me!' Chrissie retorted furiously. 'All I did was tell you to look after your own son, and you took that as a—'

'Who is it, Chrissie?' Their mum's voice floated down from the top of the stairs. 'If it's them Jovies again, tell 'em to piss off.'

Tina's jaw dropped, and she gaped at Chrissie in disbelief. 'You said she was *dead*! How could you be so wicked?'

'*Me* wicked?' Chrissie shot back indignantly. 'I've been looking after your son for a month and you haven't so much as called to ask how he's doing. What kind of monster does that make *you*?'

'I've called loads of times,' Tina lied. 'But you never answer.'

'Don't even try it,' Chrissie sneered. 'And don't think you're walking in here like you've done nothing wrong, 'cos it's not happening.'

'*MUUUUM* . . .' Tina yelled. 'Tell her to let me in. I need to see you and Dylan.'

'Get lost!' Chrissie pushed Tina away when she tried to force her way in. 'You made your choice when you took off, so go back to wherever you've been staying and leave us in peace!'

'I can't,' Tina whined. 'The house got raided this morning and I'll get nicked if I go back.'

'Good!' Chrissie said coldly. 'Prison's the best place for a scumbag like you. Look at the bloody state of you . . . You're filthy, and you're obviously on drugs.'

'It's not my fault I'm in a bad way. They stopped my benefits.'

'Yeah, because *I* told them to.'

'Why would you do that?' Tina gasped.

'Because it was meant for Dylan, not you,' said Chrissie. 'How else was I supposed to feed him and buy nappies while you were gone?'

'You're working, you can afford it,' Tina argued.

Their mum had made her way down the stairs by now. Still under the weather, and too tired for a scene, she touched Chrissie's arm. 'Let her in, love.'

'Are you kidding?' Chrissie spluttered. 'Why would you let her step one foot in here after everything she's done?'

'She's my daughter,' Joan said wearily. 'And Dylan's her son, so she's got a right to see him.'

'I'm sorry, Mum.' Tina squeezed past Chrissie and threw herself into Joan's arms. 'I didn't mean to stay away for so long. I've been dying to come home, but I couldn't face *her*.'

'Don't start slagging our Chrissie off, 'cos that boy would be in care now if it wasn't for her,' Joan said clippily. 'And get off me – you stink.'

'It's not my fault,' Tina sniffled. 'I've been sleeping rough.'

'Go and have a bath.' Joan flapped a hand towards the stairs. 'We'll talk when you come down.'

Disgusted that her sister had wormed her way back in so easily, Chrissie threw up her hands in despair and snatched her coat off the hook.

'Where are you going?' Joan asked.

'Work,' said Chrissie. '*She* can take Dylan to nursery – if she sticks around long enough. And you'd best hide your purse before she robs you blind,' she added as she yanked the door open. 'She's obviously rattling for a fix.'

She marched out, slamming the door behind her. Ringing Leanne as she headed for the bus stop, she said, 'Guess who's just turned up? Yeah, I know, a *month*! Cheeky bitch! And you should see the state of her! Talk about dirty. The house reeks and she's only been back five minutes. I can't believe my mum's willing to take her in after everything she's done.'

'You knew she'd come home sooner or later, so there's no point letting it get to you,' Leanne said sleepily.

'I know,' Chrissie muttered, quickening her pace when her bus came into view. 'But it pisses me off that she always gets her own way. Anyhow, I wanted to ask if it'd be all right if I stop at yours tonight? I'll be up for murder if I have to see that bitch's face again today.'

'Course you can,' Leanne agreed. 'Jake went out first thing and I'm not sure when he'll be back, but I'm sure he won't mind.'

'Thanks,' Chrissie said gratefully, sticking her hand out for the bus. 'I'll pick up a bottle of wine after work.'

'No need,' said Leanne. 'We stocked up the other day.'

'Get you, Lady Muck.' Chrissie chuckled as she boarded the bus and flashed her pass at the driver. 'Wish I could find a rich man to keep *me* in the lap of luxury.'

'Hey, I do my share,' Leanne protested.

'Oh, I know,' Chrissie drawled. 'It must be *so* tiring following the cleaner round to make sure she hasn't missed a bit. I pity you, I really do.'

'Piss off!' Leanne laughed.

Chrissie felt a lot lighter of heart after saying goodbye to Leanne, and she sighed as she sank on to a seat and gazed out of the window. When the bus passed the end of Ben's road a few minutes later, she twisted her head around when she saw him walking to his car in a pair of paint-splattered overalls. She hadn't seen him since he'd called round the morning after her mum was taken into hospital, and she was sure he'd lost weight. It suited him, she thought, smiling as the bus continued on its way. Now all he had to do was get a decent haircut and learn how to dress properly, and he might actually be presentable.

*

After chucking his work bag into the boot of his car, Ben went back into the house to get the tins of paint he'd left in the hall. He'd started working on Leanne's old house a couple of days earlier, and it wasn't as hard as he'd thought it would be. He was actually quite enjoying the work, although he still thought that Jake was insane for buying the place; in his opinion, it was an absolute money pit. Still, it was Jake's house and he seemed happy enough to throw cash at it, so who was Ben to complain?

There had been no one around when Ben had gone inside, so he was surprised to find Sally Walker on the step when he came out again.

'Are you Ben?' she asked.

'Er, yeah,' he replied warily, wondering how she knew, given that she had flat out ignored him in school and, apart from that one time when he'd picked Jake up outside hers, they hadn't clapped eyes on each other since. 'Can I help you?'

'I'm trying to get hold of Jake, but he never answers his phone,' she said. 'I know you're his friend, so I was hoping you might know where I can find him.'

Aware that Jake regretted the night he'd spent with her and would not welcome her turning up out of the blue, Ben said, 'He's probably at home. With his girlfriend,' he added pointedly.

Guessing that he'd added that last bit to warn her off, Sally raised her chin. 'I really need to speak to him, but if you won't tell me where he is, will you at least call him for me?'

'I'm actually on my way out.' Ben reached back to pull the door shut. 'But I'll let him know you're looking for him when I see him.'

'I'm pregnant, and he's the father,' Sally blurted out. 'So *now* will you ring him?'

Ben gazed down at her for several long moments. Then, sighing, pushed the door open again and waved her inside.

16

Jake had just arrived at a property auction in Oldham when his phone rang. He'd meant what he said about Leanne's old house being the first in a string of properties he intended to invest in, and he'd added a one-bed terraced house and a run-down flat above a Chinese takeaway to his portfolio since then. Today, he was after a three-bedroom ex-council semi that he'd seen listed on the auction website. It had been repossessed, so the guide price was well below the average for its size and location. And it was in fairly good repair, from what he had seen in the pictures, so he was confident that he'd be able to put tenants straight in.

Eager to get inside, he answered the call as he parked up.

'Where are you?' Ben blurted out.

'Oldham,' Jake told him. 'Why, what's up?'

'You need to get over here ASAP,' Ben said quietly. 'We've got a problem.'

Jake glanced at the dashboard clock. 'It'll have to wait, mate. The auction starts in fifteen.'

'This can't wait,' Ben insisted. 'Sally's here.'

'You what?' Jake frowned. 'What does *she* want?'

There was a pause, and Jake heard muffled voices before Sally came on the line.

'Jake, it's me. Don't hang up, we need to talk.'

'I've already told you, I'm not interested,' he said coldly.

'Don't flatter yourself,' she replied scornfully. 'I'm not trying to get back with you. I just thought you should know that I'm pregnant, and you're the father.'

'Bullshit!'

'It's the truth. But if you're not willing to discuss it with me, maybe I should talk to your *girlfriend*?'

'Put Ben on,' Jake ordered.

'Sorry, mate,' Ben apologized when Sally passed the phone back to him. 'She snatched it off me.'

'Never mind that. Is she for real?'

'Sounds like it.'

'*Shit!*' Jake slammed his hand down on the steering wheel. 'Right, keep her there till I get back,' he said, restarting the engine and reversing quickly out of the parking space. 'And don't tell her anything. If she finds out where I live and goes looking for Leanne, I'm fucked!'

*

Sally was sitting on Ben's couch with a glass of juice in her hand when Jake arrived forty minutes later. She'd forgotten how handsome he was in the flesh, and her stomach did a little flip at the sight of him.

'Sorry for snapping at you on the phone,' she apologized, giving him a tentative smile. 'But I had to make you take me seriously.'

'And *are* you being serious?' he demanded. 'Or is this just some sick joke to trick me into seeing you again?'

'I knew you wouldn't believe me, so I brought these.' Sally put the glass down and pulled three used pregnancy tester sticks out of her handbag. 'Check for yourself; they're all positive.'

Jake peered at the writing in the small windows, and shrugged when he saw that they all read: *6-7 weeks pregnant*.

'That doesn't mean anything. You could have got them out of a bin, for all I know.'

'I thought you might say that.' Sally reached into her bag and brandished an unopened tester. 'I'll do it in front of you, if you like?'

Doubting that she'd be willing to do that if she was lying, Jake did a quick mental calculation. He'd been with Leanne for six weeks, and they'd got together the day after he'd made the mistake of sleeping with Sally, so the dates definitely corresponded. But that still didn't mean it was his.

'All right, so maybe you *are* pregnant,' he conceded. 'But it could be anyone's.'

'It's *yours*,' Sally insisted. 'I hadn't slept with anyone in ages before I got with you, and I haven't been with anyone since.'

Jake gave her a disbelieving look. 'You don't seriously expect me to buy that, do you?'

'It is *yours*,' Sally repeated adamantly, tears beginning to glisten in her eyes.

Jake instinctively knew that she was telling the truth, and he looped his hands together behind his head as his cosy world threatened to come crashing down around him. Dropping them after a moment, he said, 'Okay, let's say it *is* mine, what do you expect me to do about it?'

'The baby's going to need a father as well as a mother,' Sally started. 'So I thought you might—'

'Whatever you're about to say, forget it,' Jake interrupted sharply. 'I'll pay for an abortion, but that's as far as I'm willing to go.'

Sally shook her head and shoved the unopened tester into her bag. 'I'm not getting rid of it.'

'Suit yourself.' Jake shrugged. 'But if you go ahead with it, you're on your own.'

Chin quivering, Sally gazed up at him. 'Why are you being so horrible about this? It's not just *my* fault I got pregnant. You were there, too.'

'I was off my head, or I wouldn't have gone anywhere near you,' Jake shot back cruelly. 'I mean, come on ... *seriously*? Look at you. You're a mess.'

'Mate, there's no need for that,' Ben said quietly, feeling sorry for Sally when he saw the hurt in her eyes. She might not be a patch on Leanne, but she wasn't a monster by any means, and in the forty minutes he'd spent making small talk with her while they were waiting for Jake, he'd sensed that she wasn't as tough as she made out.

'It's all right, he can think what he likes.' Sally proudly rose to her feet. 'But I guarantee he won't be laughing by the time I've finished with him.' She turned to Jake now, and said, 'This isn't over. As soon as the baby's born, I'll be taking you to court for maintenance.'

'Good luck with proving I'm the father,' he scoffed. 'I'll just deny I ever slept with you.'

'I'm sure the judge will order you to take a DNA test when he sees the photos of you naked in my bed,' she shot back. 'And they're date-stamped, so it won't take a genius to figure out that they were taken exactly nine months before the baby was born.'

Furious to hear that she'd taken pictures of him without his knowledge, Jake seized her by the arms and shook her roughly. 'Where are they?'

'You're hurting me!' she cried, struggling to break free.

'If you think this is pain, you ain't seen nothing,' he spat, slamming her up against the wall. 'If you don't give me those pictures, I'll *kill* you!'

'Pack it in!' Ben yelled, rushing over and dragging Jake off her. 'She's pregnant, you idiot! What the hell's got into you?'

Jake held up his hands and backed off, but the anger was still burning brightly in his eyes.

'You seem to forget that I'm not the one who's desperate to keep this a secret,' said Sally, visibly shaking as she backed toward the door. 'I don't care who knows, and if you ever threaten me like that again, I'll tell everyone!'

'Just go!' Ben shouted, holding on to Jake when he made to lunge for her again. 'I'll talk to him.'

Jake turned to the wall when Sally darted out and smashed his fist into it.

'Get a grip and stop acting like a maniac,' Ben scolded. 'You want her to keep her mouth shut, and then you go and do something stupid like *that*? Well done, mate. Talk about shooting yourself in the foot.'

'What was I supposed to do? If Leanne hears about this, I'm fucked.'

'I know you love Leanne, but if this baby *is* yours, are you seriously telling me you'd turn your back on it – like your dad did to you?'

Jake clenched his teeth at the reminder of his father. His life had been difficult enough before his dad had decided to uproot the family and move to Liverpool, but it had totally hit the skids when the bastard had fucked off with some tart, never to be seen again. Left to fend for himself when his mum turned to the bottle, Jake had gone off the rails and ended up in young offenders' – where he'd learned hard and fast that only the strongest and most ruthless survived. It was a lesson that had stayed with him as he fought his way up in the world, and now that he finally had everything he'd ever wanted, there was no way he was about to let Sally ruin it with this unplanned, unwanted baby.

'You don't know Leanne like I do,' he said. 'It took her a year to get over the last bloke who screwed her over. She'd never forgive me for this.'

'You didn't cheat on her,' Ben reminded him. 'You weren't even with her when you slept with Sally, and I'm sure she'd understand if you explained it to her.'

'It won't make any difference,' Jake argued. 'You saw what she was like when Sally rang me that morning. It took both of us to convince her that nothing was going on, and she *still* asked me a few more times, so I've had my chance.'

'Well, if you're not going to come clean, you'd best pray that Sally doesn't tell anyone.'

'How am I supposed to stop her? You heard her. She's got nothing to lose if people find out.'

'Maybe not,' Ben said thoughtfully. 'But I saw the way she looked at you when you walked in just now, and I reckon she still fancies you. If you can convince her that she's in with a chance, it might buy you some time. And if I was you, I'd start by apologizing before she reports you for threatening to kill her.'

Jake closed his eyes and breathed in deeply. He wished he'd never clapped eyes on Sally in the first place, and would have been more than happy if he never had to see her again. But Ben was right. If he was to stand any chance of putting a lid on this, he had to speak to her.

17

Sally was still shaking as she made her way home. In her entire life, nobody had ever spoken to her the way Jake had, and she truly believed he would have beaten her up if Ben hadn't intervened. She could still feel the imprint of his fingers on her arms and cheeks, and she just knew there would be bruises when she looked.

She'd known that he wouldn't be happy to hear about the baby, but she hadn't expected him to react so violently. And the look in his eyes when he'd threatened to kill her had chilled her to the bone. But he was wrong if he thought he was going to bully her into keeping her mouth shut. She hadn't conceived this baby by herself, and he was going to take responsibility for the part he'd played whether he liked it or not. She didn't know if he had already been living with his girlfriend when they'd slept together, or if he'd got with her in the six weeks since. But, either way, it was clear that he desperately didn't want her to find out about the baby. And Sally was going to use that to her advantage. She just wasn't sure quite *how* yet.

Still mulling everything over as she approached her house, her stomach lurched when her phone rang and Jake's name appeared on the screen. Determined not to let him think he'd cowed her, she answered it sharply.

'I'm warning you now, if you're ringing to threaten me again, I'm going to record it and play it to the police.'

'I'm not going to threaten you,' Jake assured her. 'I only want to apologize for going off on you like that. It was out of order, and I'm sorry if I scared you.'

'*If?*' Sally repeated incredulously. 'I was absolutely terrified! You had no right to push me around like that.'

'I know, and I'm really sorry,' Jake said again. 'It was a shock to hear about the baby, that's all. But I've calmed down now and I think we need to talk, so can we meet up?'

'How do I know you won't go for me again?' Sally asked, turning her back to the house when she saw her mum peering out at her through the living room window. They'd had an argument before she went round to Ben's place this morning, and she wasn't in the mood for another one after the stress of fighting with Jake.

'Look, I'm not going to lie, I'd rather this wasn't happening,' Jake admitted. 'But it is, so we need to work something out that suits us both.'

Sally bit her lip. He'd been horrible to her at Ben's, and she'd been genuinely scared when he'd attacked her. But he sounded sincere right now, and the softness of his tone reminded her of how nice he'd been when they had spent the night together.

'Okay, I'll meet you,' she agreed. 'But I'm not taking any chances after what happened earlier, so it'll have to be some-where public.'

'Fine by me,' said Jake. 'Just let me know where and when.'

Sally told him that she would get back to him when she'd had a chance to think about it. After saying goodbye, she made her way inside the house. The atmosphere still felt chilly and she was in no mood for another row, so she decided to take refuge in her room. But she'd only taken a few steps up the stairs when the living room door opened and her mum marched out into the hall.

'Well?' Betty Walker folded her arms and stared up at her daughter.

'Well what?'

'Don't play games with me. Did you make an appointment at the clinic like I told you to?'

'No. And I'm not going to, so there's no point nagging me about it.'

'Oh, for God's sake!' Betty snapped. 'I told you this morn-ing me and Dad are too old for your nonsense. And *that*,' – she nodded at Sally's stomach – 'is the last straw.'

'*That* is your grandchild,' Sally reminded her tartly. 'And I don't see why you're being so funny about it. It's not like I did it on purpose to piss you off.'

'Are you sure about that?' Betty raised an eyebrow. 'I wouldn't put it past you.'

'Have you heard yourself?'

'I can hear myself perfectly well, thank you. But I'm not sure *you* can. You seem to think this is some kind of joke, but it's time you realized that we can't keep picking up the pieces every time you do something stupid. This is your mess, and you need to deal with it. We've stood by you through thick and thin, but enough is enough.'

'Stood by me?' Sally gave her mother an incredulous look. 'What, by having a go at me, and making my life an absolute misery? Don't make me laugh!'

'This "poor me" routine is starting to wear thin,' Betty said coolly. 'When you moved back in after your last boyfriend chucked you out, I told you not to expect a free ride. Dad's retired now, and you're a grown woman, so it's time you started contributing. We can't afford to keep you, never mind you *and* a child.'

'Don't worry, no one's expecting you to pay for it,' Sally retorted bitterly. 'I've already told the dad that he's got to give me maintenance, and he's agreed, so I don't need your money.'

'Well, that's something, I suppose,' Betty sniffed, only slightly mollified. 'Although, I still don't know why you're so determined to keep this one. I know you, and you'll be bored with it in no time.'

Furious with her mother for throwing her previous pregnancies in her face, Sally gave her a dirty look before stomping up the stairs.

'You can't bury your head in the sand for ever,' Betty called after her. 'If you go ahead with this, it'll be the biggest mistake of your life, you mark my words.'

Sally slammed the door and threw herself down on the bed. It had been as much of a shock for her as it had been for Jake when she'd realized she was pregnant. Unbeknown to her mum – who seemed to think she was a complete moron – she *had* toyed with the idea of booking herself in for an abortion. She'd done it before without regret, so it would have been easy to do it again. But something felt different about this one. Maybe it was the realization that she wasn't getting any younger, and that the later she left it, the more likely she was to have a baby with disabilities; or the fact that – and this had been a hard one to admit – the men she tended to attract these days weren't as good-looking as the ones she'd had her pick of in the past, so she was likely to end up with an ugly baby if she didn't keep Jake's child. Whatever the reason, she hadn't been able to go through with it – and nothing her mother or anyone else said would make her change her mind.

Subconsciously stroking her stomach, Sally reached for her phone and pulled up the photos she'd taken of Jake when he'd fallen asleep after making love to her that night. He'd made no secret of the fact that he wished it hadn't happened, but as she gazed at his handsome face, she knew that she would do it again in a heartbeat.

A tap came at the door, and she quickly closed the phone and sat up when her dad walked in.

'You okay, love?' Ron Walker asked, sitting on the edge of the bed.

Sally nodded and drew her knees up to her chest. This man had spoiled her rotten from the day she was born, and he could still be relied on to slip her a twenty here or a tenner there when her mum's back was turned. But as she looked at him now, taking in the stoop of his once broad shoulders and the lines criss-crossing his face, she felt a little tug of sadness in the pit of her stomach.

'I know you and Mum don't always see eye to eye,' Ron said quietly. 'But she's only trying to help. You do know that, don't you?'

Sally gave a sulky little shrug and rested her chin on her knees. She hated when her dad sided with her mum; it made her feel like they were ganging up on her.

'We know you're under a lot of pressure,' Ron went on, gently stroking her back as he spoke. 'And we're doing our best to support you, even if you think we're not. But we really need you to think about what you're doing before it's too late. Babies are hard work, and we're not going to be around for ever to help you out.'

'Don't start banging on about dying, or I'll go out again,' Sally warned. 'I hate it when you do this.'

'I know it makes you uncomfortable, but we think it's important to talk about these things,' Ron persisted.

'You mean *Mum* does.'

'No, we *both* do. Because we love you, and we need to know you'll be okay when we're gone.'

'I'm perfectly capable of looking after myself,' Sally insisted. 'And the dad's going to help me with the baby, so you've got nothing to worry about.'

'Are you sure about that?' Ron gave her a doubtful look. 'I'm not being funny, love, but you haven't exactly had the best of luck with fellas in the past. The last one couldn't break it off fast enough when he heard you were expecting.'

'*I* finished with *him*, actually,' Sally lied, blushing furiously at the reminder of the unceremonious way her ex had dumped her by text after she'd told him she was pregnant. 'But this one's different. He loves me, and he's going to look after us.'

'Well, I hope you're right, and he's not just stringing you along till he gets fed up of you,' said Ron, catching himself in time to stop '*like the rest of them*' from coming out. 'But you still need to think this through before you make a concrete decision, because a baby won't make a man stick around if he decides he wants out.'

'I've had enough of this,' Sally snapped, angry that he seemed to think that no man could possibly love her enough to stand by her.

'Don't run away, love,' Ron pleaded when she jumped up from the bed and snatched her handbag off the floor. 'We need to talk.'

'Save your breath,' Sally muttered, heading for the door. 'I'm having this baby, and that's the end of it.'

Betty had been standing out on the landing with her ear pressed against the door. Sally had always been a daddy's girl, and Betty had hoped that she might listen to Ron. But the stubborn mare was clearly determined to do the exact opposite of whatever they suggested.

'Where are you going?' she asked when Sally came out of her room with a thunderous look on her face.

'Out,' Sally threw back over her shoulder as she flounced down the stairs.

Losing patience, Betty leaned over the banister rail. 'This has gone far enough, Sally Ann Walker. You either make that appointment, or I'll make it for you! And if I have to, I'll drag you to the clinic by your bloody hair. Do you hear me?'

Sally walked out without answering, slamming the door behind her. As she set off down the road, she pulled out her phone and dialled Jake's number.

'If you're still up for that chat, meet me at the cafe on the high street in an hour.'

*

The cafe was heaving when Jake arrived, and it took a few seconds before he located Sally at a table in the corner. She was staring down into her cup, and her shoulders were slumped as if she had the weight of the world bearing down on her. With her matted extensions and the black smudges around her eyes, Jake thought she looked like a neglected doll that had been dragged out from the back of the cupboard.

'Sorry I'm late, I got held up,' he said when he reached her. 'Can I get you a coffee?'

'Tea.' Sally pushed her cup across the greasy tabletop. 'The coffee tastes like piss in here.'

When Jake brought the drinks back a couple of minutes later, she waited until he'd taken his seat before saying, 'Go on, then.'

'Go on what?' He gave her a questioning look.

'You said you wanted to talk, so talk.'

Jake was irritated by her snappy tone, but he reminded himself why he was here and forced a contrite smile.

'I wanted to apologize again about what happened earlier. It wasn't like me to go off like that – and if it's any consolation, Ben gave me a right bollocking after you'd gone.'

'That's because he's a decent man who knows how to treat women with respect,' Sally sniped. 'You should try taking a leaf out of his book sometime.'

'Okay, point taken.' Jake held up his hands. 'I was a bastard, but it'll never happen again, so can we just forget about it and start over?'

Sally reached for her cup and took a sip of tea before answering. She quite liked making Jake grovel, but she needed a favour, so she couldn't afford to push it too far.

'Did you mean what you said earlier about doing right by the baby?' she asked.

'If it's mine,' said Jake, letting her know that he still wasn't completely convinced. 'Why?'

191

'I'm in a bit of a tricky situation,' Sally explained. 'My mum and dad aren't too happy about me being pregnant. I told them you were going to help, but I don't think they believed me.'

'You didn't tell them I'm the dad, did you?' Jake frowned.

'No.' Sally shook her head. 'I haven't told anyone.'

'So what's the problem?'

'They've made it clear that they don't want a baby in the house, so I'm going to need a place of my own,' said Sally. 'I called in at the estate agent's on the way here, but the deposits they're asking for are outrageous, so I was wondering if you might be able to help me out?'

Jake took a sip of his tea and gazed at her over the rim of his cup. How times had changed. Back in the day, Sally Walker's parents had been loaded, and she'd looked down her nose at the poor kids like Jake. Now he had money and she was on her uppers, and he couldn't deny that it gave him a certain level of satisfaction.

'Okay, I'll help you,' he said after a moment. 'But not with a deposit.'

'But that's all I need.' Sally frowned. 'And it's for *your* baby, don't forget.'

Jake sat forward and rested his elbows on the table. 'I've just bought a house, and I'm doing it up to get it ready for tenants,' he said. 'But if you need a place, you might as well move in there.'

'Are you serious?' Sally narrowed her eyes, waiting for the catch.

'Absolutely,' said Jake. 'It's split into three flats, and I reckon the ground-floor one would be perfect for you. You'd have the backyard to yourself, and you wouldn't have to worry about lugging a pram up the stairs.'

'I'm not sharing a house,' Sally protested. 'What if one of the other tenants is a paedophile and they take a liking to the baby? No, I'm sorry, I can't do it. You'll either have to help me out with a deposit, or ...' She paused, and then shrugged, before adding, 'I'll go back to my original plan and take you to court.'

Jake kept his expression neutral as he studied her. Not only had she thrown his offer in his face, she was now threatening him with court again – and that pissed him off big time, considering the effort he was making to be nice. If they hadn't been surrounded by people right now, he would happily have throttled her. But she had him over a barrel, and she knew it.

'Okay, fine,' he said after a moment. 'If you want it, it's yours.'

Sally hadn't expected him to give in so easily, and suspicion flashed in her eyes. 'You're giving me a house?'

'No, I'm not *giving* it to you,' Jake corrected her. 'But you can live there until you find somewhere more suitable. And I won't put any other tenants in until you've gone. What do you think?'

'You're not expecting me to pay rent, are you?' Sally asked. 'Only I haven't got much money, and it's going to cost me a fortune to get stuff for the baby.'

'You'll have to claim housing benefit,' said Jake. 'It's not about the money, I just can't risk anyone finding out that I'm letting you live there rent free, so we'll do this by the book.'

'Anyone' being your girlfriend, no doubt, thought Sally.

'I'll pay the bills and give you an allowance for the baby,' Jake went on. 'But there's a condition. No one, and I mean *no* one, not even your family, can ever know that I'm the father.'

'Ben already knows,' Sally reminded him. 'What if he tells someone?'

'He'd never betray me,' Jake said with certainty. 'So, do we have a deal?'

Sally took another sip of tea and mulled it over. She'd lived with several boyfriends in the past, but it had always been their place so she was the one who'd had to leave and go running home to her parents when the relationship came to an end. Now, for the first time ever, she'd be able to do whatever she liked without having to ask someone else's permission, follow their rules, or pretend that she enjoyed having sex with them. And she wouldn't have to worry about money, because Jake was going to take care of everything. It was better than she could ever have hoped for, and she was sure that she could get a whole lot more than he was offering now if she played her cards right.

'Where is it?' she asked. 'And when can I move in?'

'It's not too far from here,' Jake said evasively. 'And it should be ready in a couple of weeks.'

'What if I don't like it?' Sally asked, hedging her bets in case it was disgusting.

'Then you'll have to stay where you are until we find something else,' Jake said, glancing at his watch. 'Look, I have to get moving. I'll try to speed things up at the house so you're not waiting too long. And, here . . .' He pulled a wad of notes out of his wallet and handed them to her. 'Take this to tide you over in the meantime.'

Sally looked at the money and then gaped at him. 'These are all fifties.'

'I know.' He smiled. 'So are we all right now?'

'I suppose so,' she agreed, quickly stuffing the money into her handbag before he changed his mind. 'As long as you don't start messing me around.'

'I won't,' he assured her. 'As long as *you* stick to your side of the bargain and keep your mouth shut.'

'My lips are sealed,' Sally promised, already mentally spending the money on a trip to the salon to get her hair and nails sorted out. And maybe she'd get a spray tan and a facial while she was at it.

Jake pushed his chair back. 'I'll ring you when the house is ready. Take care.'

'You, too,' said Sally, smiling to herself as she watched him leave. He could deny it as much as he liked, but there was definitely a spark between them. Girlfriend or no girlfriend, that man would soon be hers.

18

Leanne and Chrissie were sharing a bottle of wine in the living room when Jake got home that evening.

'Do you have to?' Chrissie complained when he leaned over and planted a kiss on her friend's lips.

'Ignore her, she's just jealous,' Leanne said tipsily, resting her cheek on the back of his hand. 'Mmmm, you smell nice.'

'It'll be the soap from the pub toilets,' Jake told her.

'You've been to the pub without me?' She gave him a mock-sulky look.

'It was business, so you'd have been bored stiff,' he said, slipping his jacket off and lighting a cigarette. 'Anyway, it looks like you've had enough already,' he added as he looked around for an ashtray. This was one of the drawbacks of living with a non-smoker – Leanne was constantly moving and washing his ashtrays, and never remembered to put them back where she'd taken them from.

'I keep meaning to ask what it is that you actually do,' Chrissie said curiously. 'I know you've started dabbling in property, but what's the security business about? Do you fit burglar alarms, or is it one of those outfits that hire out teams of bouncers, and what have you?'

'A bit of everything,' Jake said cagily, pulling his mobile out of his pocket when it began to ring.

'Proper little man of mystery, isn't he?' Chrissie whispered when he excused himself and went into the kitchen to take his call in private. 'If I didn't know better, I'd swear he was some kind of spy. The name's Pearsh . . . Jake Pearsh.'

'Stop it!' Leanne laughed, reaching for the wine to refill their glasses.

'Sorry about this, but I've got to go out again,' Jake apologized when he came back into the room.

'Do you have to?' Leanne moaned. 'I haven't seen you all day.'

'Can't be helped, I'm afraid.' Jake slipped his jacket on.

'Oh, I meant to tell you, Chrissie's staying tonight. That's okay, isn't it?'

'Course it is.'

'When will you be home?' Leanne asked, getting up.

'Not sure.' He shrugged and headed for the door. 'I've been trying to set something up with this guy for months but he's really hard to pin down, so I can't afford to miss this opportunity.'

'Okay,' Leanne said resignedly, following him out into the hall. 'Me and Chrissie will just have to amuse ourselves. We'll probably watch some films, have a few drinks . . . go out on the balcony and moon the pervy old man next door.'

'You will not!' Jake gave her a mock-stern look as he pulled her forcefully into his arms. 'No one sees that body except me. Got it?'

'Spoilsport,' she chuckled, wrapping her arms around his neck.

In the living room, Chrissie made a gagging sound when she heard them kissing again. Finishing her drink, she'd refilled both of their glasses by the time Leanne came in with a dreamy look on her face.

'Can't you keep your flaming hands off him?'

'No.' Leanne grinned and flopped down on to the couch. 'He's been working so hard lately, I've hardly seen him, so I've got to take whatever I can get.'

'Don't you mind him taking off like that without telling you where he's going?'

'It's business, so why would I worry about it?' Leanne asked, reaching for her glass. 'It's not like he's going out clubbing and picking up women, is it?'

'I'm sorry, but if I had a man who looked like him, I'd want to know exactly *who* he was seeing and *where*,' said Chrissie. 'And then I'd probably follow him to make sure he was telling the truth.'

'I used to check up on Dean, but it didn't stop him cheating on me, did it?' Leanne reminded her. 'Anyway, it's different with Jake. He's loved me for ever, so why would he play around?'

'He'd be an idiot if he ever did,' said Chrissie. ''Cos he ain't gonna find another woman as good as you in a hurry, and that's a fact.'

Touched, because she knew Chrissie genuinely meant it, Leanne leaned over to pick up the house phone when it started ringing.

'Hi, Leanne, it's Ben. Sorry for disturbing you, but I've been trying to reach Jake and his phone keeps going to voicemail. Is he there, by any chance?'

'He was, but he's had to go out again. Can I help?'

'No, it's okay; I was only checking in because I noticed I'd missed a couple of calls off him earlier. No worries. I'll try him again in a bit. Everything all right with you?'

'Everything's fine,' Leanne said, smiling slyly as she added, 'Chrissie's here. I'll pass you over so you can say hello.'

'Well, hello there, stranger,' Chrissie greeted him playfully. 'How you doing?'

'Good, thanks,' Ben replied shyly. He hadn't seen her in ages, and the sound of her voice made his stomach feel a little weird. 'So, um, how's it going at your end? Is your mum feeling any better?'

'She's getting there,' said Chrissie. Then, changing the subject, because she knew that he was likely to ask if there had been any word from her sister, and she didn't even want to *think* about that bitch, she said, 'I saw you outside yours this morning. You look like a proper little Bob the Builder in your overalls. I didn't realize you were working on one of Jake's places till Leanne told me this afternoon. How's it going?'

'I, um . . . yeah, it's coming along fine,' Ben replied evasively. 'Sorry, but I've got another call coming through, so I'm going to have to go.'

'Oh, okay. It was nice to speak to you. Take it easy.'

Smiling when Chrissie handed the phone back to her, Leanne said, '*Such* a nice man.'

'Yes, he is,' Chrissie agreed. 'But if you'd heard how desperate he was to get off the phone, you'd know he isn't interested, so please stop trying to matchmake.'

'Don't be daft, of course he's interested,' Leanne argued. 'He fancies the arse off you. It's obvious.'

'He might have done once, but I reckon I've put him right off,' said Chrissie. 'The way he clammed up when I told him I'd seen him outside his place this morning, anyone would think I was some kind of crazy stalker. And then he lied about another call coming through, just so he could get off the phone.'

'You don't know that.'

'Yes, I do, but hey-ho . . .' Chrissie sighed. 'I don't even like him that way, so who cares if he's gone off me?'

Leanne drew her head back and gazed at Chrissie through narrowed eyes. 'You *do* like him.'

'Shut up and pass me the wine,' Chrissie ordered.

*

Ben was annoyed with himself for reacting badly when Chrissie had mentioned seeing him this morning, but he'd panicked, scared that if she'd seen him she might also have seen Sally. And, God forbid, Jake, because Leanne was sure to be suspicious if she heard that those two had been in the same place at the same time.

Jumping when his phone rang, he was relieved to see that it was Jake, and not Leanne ringing to demand to know what was going on.

'What took you so long?' Jake said when he answered. 'I've been trying to get hold of you since this afternoon.'

'Sorry, I didn't realize till I got home and saw your missed calls,' Ben apologized. 'The signal's really bad in that house.'

'Yeah, well, it's the house I wanted to talk to you about,' said Jake. 'I've got a tenant lined up, so I need you to get a move on.'

'That was quick. I didn't even know you'd started advertising yet.'

'I haven't. Sally's taking it.'

'Are you serious?' Ben frowned. 'Don't you think Leanne might have something to say about that?'

'If she finds out – which she won't – I'll tell her the letting agent is handling the tenancies and I didn't know,' said Jake. 'But Sally needs a place for her and the baby, and I need her where I can keep an eye on her, so it makes sense to do it this way.'

'Sounds a bit risky to me, mate.'

'Sally's not stupid; she knows she'll gain more from this if she plays by my rules.'

'I hope you're right,' Ben said doubtfully. 'But you'd best know that I just spoke to Chrissie, and she said she saw me outside mine this morning.'

'So?'

'So I don't know if that was before or *after* Sally turned up.'

'Makes no odds either way,' Jake said, unconcerned. 'If you were outside, I wasn't there yet, so she can't read anything into it. Anyway, I've got a meeting so I'll have to get off. I'll pop round tomorrow to see how you're getting on.'

Ben sighed when the phone went dead in his hand. In his opinion, Jake was playing with fire, letting Sally move into the house. But it sounded like a done deal, so there was no point trying to talk him out of it.

19

Sally had to wait three tortuously long weeks before she heard from Jake again. Though she'd been seriously tempted to ring him to ask what was going on, she had managed to resist the urge, scared that he might think she was being pushy and call the deal off.

She still hadn't told a soul that he was the father of her baby, and she hadn't told anyone about the house either – not even her parents, who had no clue that she was getting ready to leave home again. Although, she doubted they'd have tried to dissuade her if they *had* known, given the hints they both kept dropping about everybody needing to tighten their belts.

When, at last, Jake did call and arranged to pick her up on the corner that evening, she made an extra special effort with her appearance; brushing her new platinum extensions until they shone, carefully applying false lashes, and dressing in the skin-tight jeans, leather bomber jacket and high-heeled boots she'd bought with the money he'd given her. She looked a million dollars, and thought for sure that Jake would regret dumping her when he saw her. So she was disappointed when he barely glanced at her as she climbed into his car.

Consoling herself with the knowledge that she'd have plenty of opportunities to work on him in the future, she settled back in her seat to enjoy the ride, her stomach already bubbling with excitement to see the house that would soon be hers.

The fantasy house she'd created in her mind while she'd been waiting for this day was detached, with a large living room, a dining room with patio doors leading on to a huge back garden, and an amazing kitchen with state-of-the-art equipment. Upstairs, there were three bedrooms, of which the master was en-suite, of course; and a family bathroom, complete with walk-in power shower and spa bath.

That was the fantasy, but the reality couldn't have been more different, and her heart sank into her sexy boots when, ten minutes after setting off, Jake pulled up outside a mid-terrace house on a scruffy road in the heart of Old Trafford.

'Why have you brought me here?' she asked, hoping against hope that he would tell her he was only calling in on a friend before continuing on to the real house.

'This is it,' said Jake, taking off his seat belt and climbing out. 'Come on, I haven't got long.'

'Didn't someone get murdered round here a few weeks back?' Sally asked, reluctantly following him out.

'No idea,' he lied, unlocking the front door and ushering her in.

Sally clutched her handbag to her stomach as Jake unlocked

the door to the ground-floor flat and led her inside. It was a lot smaller than she'd been expecting, but the neutral colour scheme made it seem a little roomier. And the carpets and furniture were obviously brand new, which was a definite plus, because she'd been dreading the thought of having to use someone else's cast-offs.

After showing her around the flat and giving her a quick tour of the rest of the house, Jake led her back down the stairs.

'So what do you think?'

Sally had already decided that she was going to take it, because anything was better than staying at her parents' place now she'd set her heart on leaving. But she didn't want to appear too eager, so she pursed her lips and gazed around as if she wasn't sure.

'It's a bit dark, isn't it? And it'll be really creepy living down here on my own with all those empty rooms up there.'

'Well, you're the one who insisted you didn't want to share, so there's nothing I can do about that,' Jake reminded her bluntly. 'Anyway, you won't be on your own once the baby comes. When's it due, by the way?'

Delighted that he was taking an interest, Sally smiled and placed a hand on her still-flat stomach. 'May. But they reckon it can be a couple of weeks either way, so it's not definite.'

'Let me know when it's born so I can get a DNA test lined up,' said Jake. Then, glancing at his watch, he said, 'Have you decided yet? Only I need to get moving.'

Irritated that he still thought she was lying about him being the father, Sally folded her arms. 'I suppose it'll do – for now. When can I move in?'

'Whenever you like.' Jake handed her a set of keys. 'I'll pop round sometime next week with the tenancy agreement. And I'll give you a copy so you can start your claim for housing benefit.'

Sally nodded and slipped the keys into her handbag. Then, giving Jake a sheepish look, she said, 'I don't suppose you'd be able to help me bring my things over, would you? My parents aren't talking to me at the moment, so I can't ask them. And I can't afford to hire a van.'

'Have you spent all that money I gave you already?' Jake asked. Sighing when she admitted that she had, he said, 'Okay, I'll get Ben to do it.'

'*Ben?*' she whined. 'Why can't *you* do it?'

'Because I don't want anyone to see us together and jump to conclusions,' said Jake. 'Anyway, his car's an estate, so he'll get more in.'

Sally had really wanted Jake to help her, because it would have given them more time together. But she supposed this would give her an opportunity to quiz Ben. He knew Jake better than anyone, and it was obvious from the way he'd kept eyeing her tits when they'd been waiting for Jake in his flat that day that he fancied her, so it shouldn't be too difficult to worm the name of Jake's mystery girlfriend out of him. And once she knew who she was up against, she'd do whatever it took to eliminate the bitch from Jake's life.

'All right, I suppose it's okay if Ben does it,' she conceded. 'Can you ask him to come round in an hour? I've already packed most of my stuff, so I should be ready by then.'

'An hour?' Jake raised an eyebrow as he ushered her out. 'That's a bit short notice, isn't it?'

'No point hanging around when you know what you want,' Sally said, giving him a secretive little smile before walking over to the car.

*

Ben had spent the day working on another of Jake's flats. It was a particularly dirty job, and he was covered from head to toe in dust by the time he left, so he wasn't amused when Jake rang him as he was driving home and announced that he'd volunteered him to help Sally move.

Annoyed with himself for never being able to say no to Jake, Ben sighed when he pulled up outside Sally's house later that evening and saw her waiting for him on the step. He still thought Jake was off his head for letting her move into his house, and he desperately hoped that Leanne never found out about it, because he really liked her and would hate for her to think that he had willingly betrayed her. His mum had always said he was too nice for his own good and that people would take advantage of him if he didn't put his foot down, and he was starting to think that she might be right.

Sally gave Ben a sweet smile when he climbed out of the car. 'Thanks so much for doing this.'

'It's okay,' he mumbled, opening the boot. 'If you want to start bringing your stuff out, I'll pack it in for you.'

'Actually, I was going to ask if you wouldn't mind getting it for me?' Sally wheedled. 'The doctor told me not to do any heavy lifting, because the first twelve weeks are the most risky.'

Ben sighed as he watched her cradle her non-existent bump. She was taking the piss, but he was too much of a gentleman to refuse, so he reluctantly followed her into the hallway. Unnerved when he spotted her parents watching from the kitchen table where they were both seated, he asked, 'Where is it?'

'In my room.' Sally pointed up the stairs. 'Second on the left.'

Ben went up a couple of steps, but hesitated when Sally stayed put. 'Aren't you coming?'

'You don't need me getting in your way,' she said, waving him on with a flick of her hand. 'It's all packed, so you just have to carry it down.'

A little miffed at being treated like a joey, Ben continued on up to her room, where he was greeted by a heap of bulging bin bags, a massive suitcase, at least thirty handbags, and almost as many shoe boxes. Eager to get this over with as fast as possible, he pushed his irritation to one side and, picking up as many of the bags as he could manage in one go, carefully made his way back down the stairs.

Ron Walker had come out of the kitchen and was standing at the foot of the stairs.

'I take it you're the dad?' he asked.

'No, I'm, er, helping out,' Ben replied politely. 'And I'm actually in a bit of a rush, so if I could just . . .' He nodded at the front door, indicating that he wanted to get past.

'You know she only told us she was leaving half an hour ago?' Ron didn't budge. 'And I can't say I'm too happy about it, to be honest. Our Sally's not as tough as she makes out, and we're sick of having to pick up the pieces when blokes let her down. So if you've got any doubts, you'd be as well to speak up before this goes any further.'

'With respect, Mr Walker, this really isn't my business,' Ben mumbled guiltily, all too aware that the man thought he was lying about not being the baby's father. 'I'm sorry if you're upset about what's happening, but you really need to speak to Sally about it, not me.'

'It's not easy, letting go of your child,' Ron went on. 'Especially when you haven't got a clue where they're going.'

Ben saw the question in the other man's eyes and knew that he was asking for the address. But it wasn't his place to give out that kind of information, so he said, 'I'm really sorry, but I've arranged to see my mum tonight, and I'm going to be late if I don't get a move on.'

Ron gazed at him for a few more seconds. Then, sighing, he held out his hand. 'Give 'em here.'

Ben gratefully passed the bags to him and scuttled back up the stairs for more.

Sally came outside as the men finished loading the car.

Waiting until Ben had closed the boot and climbed in behind the wheel, Ron pulled her to one side.

'Are you sure about this, love? It's not too late to change your mind, you know.'

'I'm going, and there's no point trying to talk me out of it,' Sally said firmly. 'I know you and Mum think I can't manage without you, but I'll be fine.'

'You said that last time,' Ron reminded her. '*And* the time before that. But it always ends the same way, and it breaks my heart when you come home in tatters.'

'This is different. Anyway, I'm a big girl now, and you've got to stop mollycoddling me.'

'And what if me laddo abandons you?' Ron jerked his head in the direction of the car. 'You might think he's better than the others, but how well do you really know him?'

Sally drew her head back and gave a bemused smile. 'You can't seriously think that me and *him* . . . ? Come on, Dad, give me *some* credit. I'm not that desperate!'

'Well, if you'd tell us who it is, we wouldn't have to guess, would we?' Ron raised a greying eyebrow.

Sally shook her head. 'Sorry, I can't. Not yet, anyway,' she added, partly to get him off her back, and partly because she hoped that when she and Jake were a couple – and they *would* be, one day, she was determined – she would be able to tell not only them but the rest of the world, too.

'Have it your own way,' Ron sighed, sensing that she wasn't going to budge. 'But do me a favour and give your mum a ring when you get to wherever you're going. You know she'll only fret if she doesn't hear from you.'

Promising that she would, Sally reached up and kissed him on the cheek before climbing into the car.

Ben glanced in the rear-view mirror as he pulled away from the kerb and felt genuinely sorry for Ron Walker when he saw the plaintive expression on the man's face. So he wasn't impressed when Sally immediately started to complain.

'God, they are *so* annoying. Anyone would think I was a child, the way they treat me. Why can't they accept that I'm a grown woman and let me get on with my life without sticking their noses in?'

'You should think yourself lucky they care,' Ben chided. 'Plenty of parents don't give a toss about their kids. And it sounds like they've helped you out a lot in the past.'

Reminding herself that she was supposed to be acting sweet in order to get Ben on her side, Sally murmured, 'I know, and they're not that bad really. I'm just a bit stressed out with everything.' Sighing, she glanced over at her belongings as they drove on. 'I didn't realize I had so much stuff. Hope I can get it all in without straining myself.'

'I'll take it in for you,' Ben offered. 'But I won't be able to stay long, so you'll have to do the rest by yourself.'

'Thank you,' Sally said gratefully, resting her hands on her stomach. 'I suppose I'll have to get used to doing a *lot* of things on my own from now on, won't I?'

Ben glanced at her out of the corner of his eye. This was the second time he'd been alone with her, and she didn't seem anywhere near as hard-faced as people made out. If the circumstances had been different, he might even have cancelled the plans he'd made to take his mum out this evening and stayed to help her put her stuff away. But he couldn't shake the feeling that he was being disloyal to Leanne, and that didn't sit comfortably with him.

20

Tina was curled up on the couch, watching TV and trying her hardest to ignore Dylan, who was messing about in the corner. She'd been home for three weeks, and Chrissie had barely spoken two words to her in all that time, so when her sister walked into the room and gave her a dirty look, she braced herself for an argument.

'Have you seen what he's doing?' Chrissie rushed over to Dylan and took away the ashtray he was playing with. 'He's eating the bloody dimps.'

'You're in my way,' Tina complained, craning her neck to see the TV when Chrissie scooped Dylan off the floor and stood in front of her.

'You are one bone-idle little bitch!' Chrissie hissed, wiping the ash off Dylan's mouth before depositing him in his play-pen. 'He could have choked, for all you care.'

'Yeah, yeah, tell someone who's interested,' Tina drawled.

Nostrils flaring, Chrissie snatched her keys off the mantel-piece and marched out, slamming the door behind her.

'Oh, thanks a fucking lot!' Tina yelled when Dylan immediately started bawling. 'And *you* shut the fuck up before I give you something to cry about, you little shit!'

'Don't talk to him like that,' her mum scolded, shuffling into the room and lifting Dylan out of the pen with her good arm.

'I don't feel well, and he's giving me a headache,' Tina moaned.

'Don't blame him. All he wants is a bit of attention, but you've hardly spent two minutes with him since you came back.'

'Don't start.'

'You can cut that attitude right now, lady,' Joan barked, flopping into the armchair and giving Tina a fierce look. 'I might have had a stroke, but I can still wipe the floor with you, and don't you forget it!'

Satisfied that her daughter knew who was boss when Tina didn't reply, Joan turned her attention to Dylan, bouncing him up and down on her knee.

'I think he's hungry,' she said when he carried on griping. 'What time did he have his tea?'

'Dunno.' Tina shrugged. 'I thought you'd fed him.'

'I've been in bed,' Joan reminded her, glancing at the clock as she spoke. 'It's half seven. Don't you think you'd better get him something?'

Tina gave an exaggerated sigh and, reluctantly getting up, stomped her way to the kitchen, coming back a few seconds later with a packet of crisps.

'That's not food,' Joan said when Tina tossed them to her. 'You need to cook him something.'

'There's nothing in,' Tina muttered, falling on to the couch.

'So go to the chippy.'

'With what? I'm skint.'

'For God's sake, you're bloody useless, you!' Joan reached into her cardigan pocket for her purse. Taking out a fiver, she chucked it at Tina. 'Get him some chips and a little sausage out of that. And you can pick my meds up while you're out.' She shuffled to the edge of her seat and reached for the prescription slip that was slotted behind the clock. 'Our Chrissie was supposed to get it on her way home from work, but she forgot to take it with her this morning.'

'Chemist'll be shut by now,' Tina sniffed, in no mood for running errands.

'The one on Stretford Road stops open till nine,' Joan reminded her. 'And make sure they've got everything in before you give them the script, 'cos I need them painkillers tonight. Come on . . . get moving.'

'What if they haven't got them?' Tina asked as she lazily sat up and reached for her shoes.

'You'll have to go to the all-night one in town instead. And take him with you.' Joan nodded down at Dylan.

'Do I have to?' Tina pulled a face.

'Yes, you bloody do,' Joan snapped. 'Our Chrissie's gone to her works' do, and I'm not up to looking after him by myself. The fresh air'll do him good. And if you get his chips before you go to the chemist, he might drop off, with any luck. I don't know what's up with him since you came back, but our Chrissie had him sleeping right through while you were gone.'

Irritated to have Super Nanny's achievements thrown in her face again, Tina snatched the child off her mother's knee and, marching out into the hall, shoved him roughly into the buggy. He'd been annoying the hell out of her since she came home, and her mum repulsed her, limping around like some kind of retard with her useless arm dangling at her side and drool spilling out of the wonky side of her mouth. As for lard-arse Chrissie . . . Their mum was always banging on about what an amazing job she'd done with Dylan in Tina's absence, but Tina couldn't see any change. He was still a whiney little shit, and Tina couldn't bear for him to touch her because she never knew where his filthy little hands had been. Twice this week she'd caught him with them down his pants after crapping himself, so Chrissie's claim that she'd toilet-trained him was a blatant lie.

If she'd had anywhere else to go, Tina would happily have walked away from the lot of them and never looked back. But the squat where she'd been staying the last time she took off had been boarded up after it got raided by the drug squad, so that wasn't an option; and she'd lost touch with her regular fuck-buddies, none of whom had been answering her calls since she came home. Not even faithful old Eric, who'd have done anything for the merest sniff of her pussy in the past.

At the thought of Eric, she pushed her lips out as she

dragged the buggy out over the step and set off down the road. He might be ignoring her calls, but he wouldn't find it so easy to ignore her if she turned up at his house. No doubt his beached-whale wife would kick off, but Tina wasn't scared of her. Eric was, though, so he'd be bound to bung Tina a few quid to get rid of her.

Planning to call round there after she'd done her chores, Tina nipped into the newsagent's to buy ten cigarettes with the money her mum had given her, and a packet of Jelly Tots for Dylan in lieu of the chips she could no longer afford. Shoving the sweets into Dylan's hand when she came out, she lit up and took a deep drag before setting off for the pharmacy.

The route took her past Leanne's old house, and when she turned the corner and saw light spilling out through the open front door, she quickened her step, curious to know who was in there. She'd overheard Chrissie telling their mum that Leanne had moved in with her hunky boyfriend and wasn't planning to come back here, so she guessed it must be a new tenant. Or maybe it was the police? As far as she knew, they still hadn't caught whoever had murdered that bloke in there, so maybe they'd come back to look for more evidence?

Tina had no sooner drawn level with the door than a woman stepped out, and her hackles rose when the bitch glanced into the buggy before giving her a disapproving look.

'Got a problem?' she demanded.

'Yeah, *you*,' the woman replied coolly. 'You should be

ashamed of yourself, bringing a child out at this time of night without a coat. Poor thing must be freezing.'

Tina reached into the tray beneath the buggy and yanked out the little woolly blanket her mum had knitted. 'There!' She tossed it over Dylan's legs. 'Happy now, you nosy cow?'

The woman gave a scornful look and dismissed Tina with a waft of her hand. 'Off you go, dear. I've got better things to do than trade insults with a skank like you.'

Tina wanted to slap her, but the woman had a tough glint in her eye and Tina had a feeling she'd come off worst if they got into a fight, so she swallowed her pride and pushed the buggy on. But she hadn't gone more than a few yards when she heard a man say: 'Right, I think that's everything. I'll ring Jake when I get a chance; let him know you're in.'

Ears pricking up at the mention of that name, because it was too much of a coincidence for there to be two men called Jake connected to that house, Tina went round to the front of the pram and, squatting down, pretended to tuck the blanket around Dylan's legs while she eavesdropped.

'You've been fantastic,' the woman replied, in a far sweeter tone than the one she'd used on Tina. 'I could never have managed it without your help.'

'No problem,' the man said. Then – sounding a little embarrassed, Tina thought – he added, 'Look, I know this is an awkward situation, and you probably think Jake doesn't care about the baby. But he's a good man, and I know he'll look after you if you stick to the agreement.'

'Don't worry, I'm not stupid,' the woman said. 'If I was going to tell anyone, don't you think my parents would know by now?'

'Yes, well, it's none of my business,' said the man. 'I just wanted you to know that Jake will do his bit, so you won't have to face this on your own. And, um, I'm only round the corner if you have any problems with the house and can't get hold of him.'

'Thank you, that's really sweet,' the woman said gratefully. 'I wish . . .' Tailing off without finishing the sentence, she sighed. 'Sorry, I shouldn't be putting this on you. Like you said, it's mine and Jake's business, not yours. Anyway, thanks again for everything you've done tonight, and feel free to pop in for a coffee if you're ever passing.'

When the man had climbed into his car and driven away, and the woman had gone back into the house, Tina stood up with a sly smile on her lips. Well, well . . . So not only was Jake screwing around behind Leanne's back, he was having a secret baby with his bit on the side. Chrissie would be furious when she found out that her friend's perfect boyfriend wasn't so perfect after all. But Tina wasn't about to waste a perfectly good opportunity like this by telling *her*. Not when she could go straight to the man himself. She just had to find him first – which might prove a little difficult since she had no idea where he lived. There was no way she could ask her sister without raising suspicion. But the fat man had said he only lived round the corner, so if Tina could find him, she'd be halfway there.

Excited by the thought of seeing hunky Jake again and letting him know that she'd discovered his dirty secret, Tina
walked quickly on to the pharmacy. Relieved that it was still
open and she wouldn't have to waste time trekking into town,
she picked up her mum's tablets and rushed home.

*

After leaving Sally, Ben went straight home and jumped into
the shower. He'd just got out and was drying himself when
Jake turned up.

'How did it go? Did you get it all moved?'

'I think so,' Ben said, rubbing his hair with a towel. 'But if
she's left anything behind, *you* can go for it, 'cos I've done my
bit.'

'What you being so narky for?' Jake frowned as he took a
seat on the couch. 'There wasn't that much, was there?'

'It's not about how much there was; I just can't face her parents again. Her mum was dead upset and her dad's convinced
I'm the father of her baby.'

'Don't worry about it,' Jake said, unconcerned.

'It's all right for you,' Ben replied irritably. 'You don't live
around here, so you don't have to worry about bumping into
them.'

'The baby won't look anything like you, so her folks will
realize it's not yours as soon as they see it,' Jake reassured him.

'That's *if* they ever see it,' Ben corrected him. 'She only told
them she was moving out half an hour before I got there, and

220

she still hadn't told them where she was going when we left. Her dad practically asked me outright for the address, and I had to give him the swerve. I felt like a right bastard.'

'Ah, well, at least that proves we can trust her.'

'There's no *we* about it, mate. This is your mess, not mine.'

'You're the one who told me to keep her sweet,' Jake reminded him. 'If I'd had my way, she'd have got rid of it weeks ago.'

'Fine, blame me if it makes you feel better,' Ben snapped. 'But leave me out of it in future. Now, if you don't mind, I need to get dressed.'

'No one's stopping you.' Jake tossed a cigarette to him before lighting one for himself. 'Hurry up, though, 'cos we're going to see that flat I told you about.'

'No can do.' Ben clutched at the towel that was looped around his waist as he leaned over to get a light. 'I'm taking my mum out.'

'Can't you put it off till tomorrow?'

'No, I can't. She's been looking forward to seeing that new Julia Roberts film for ages. Or was it Sandra Bullock? I always get those two mixed up. Anyway, never mind who's in it. I've promised to take her, and I'm not letting her down.'

'Mate, you really need to find a woman,' Jake scoffed. 'People are going to start talking if they find out the only action you ever get is taking your ma out on dates.'

'I happen to enjoy my mum's company. And I don't give a toss what anyone thinks about it.'

'Good for you. But I bet you'd have a damn sight more fun if you were going with Chrissie instead.'

'How many times do I have to tell you, she's *not* interested.'

'Okay, mummy's boy, keep your hair on,' Jake teased, grinning as he stood up at last. 'Enjoy your date.'

'Ha bloody ha,' Ben drawled, taking a deep pull on his smoke.

'I'll pick you up first thing,' Jake said as he headed for the door. 'And make sure you're ready, 'cos I've got a lot on tomorrow.'

Ben waved his agreement and went into the bedroom, leaving Jake to see himself out. Trotting down the stairs, Jake glanced at his watch. He'd told Leanne he would be late tonight, but he figured he might as well go straight home and surprise her now that Ben had bailed on him. And maybe he'd stop off on the way and pick up a bottle of something nice to celebrate getting the Sally situation under control. It had been a bit dicey for a while there, but now that things were back on track he could crack on with building his empire without having to worry about anyone throwing a spanner into the works.

21

Dylan had been asleep by the time Tina got home, so her mum had agreed to watch him for a bit, leaving Tina free to head back out and look for the fat man's car.

She'd thought she would easily recognize it, but it soon became apparent that old bangers were the norm for that area, and it was impossible to pick his out from the rest.

Cold and footsore after forty minutes of fruitless searching, she decided to call it a night and try again in the morning. But she soon forgot her discomfort when she turned a corner and spotted a *very* recognizable car parked outside a house.

Glancing quickly around for a hiding place when the door suddenly opened and Jake strolled out of the house, she pulled her hood up over her head and darted into the mouth of an alleyway on the opposite side of the road. Unable to believe her luck, she had to think fast as she watched Jake climb into the car. Bracing herself when he pulled away from the kerb and started heading her way, she waited until the very last second, and then lurched out of the alley and ran in front of him.

Screeching to a halt, Jake leapt out of the car.

'Are you on a fucking death wish, you stupid bitch? I could have hit you!'

'I'm sorry, but I've got to get away before he catches up with me,' Tina cried, glancing fearfully over her shoulder. 'Can – can you give me a lift? *Please*, I'm begging you!'

She'd managed to force out some tears by then, and her chin was quivering wildly as she clutched at Jake's arm. Silently congratulating herself on a brilliant performance when he told her to get in the car, she had to force herself not to grin as she quickly clambered into the passenger side.

'Thank you so much,' she whimpered, sliding down low in her seat. 'I didn't think I was going to get away this time.'

'Just tell me where you want dropping off,' Jake said coolly.

'Anywhere.' Tina wiped her nose on the back of her hand. 'As long as it's away from *him*.'

When he set off, Tina bit her lip and looked him over from the corner of her eye. He was even more handsome than she remembered, and his aftershave smelled amazing. But she didn't have time to sit here admiring him. She had to make her move before he decided he'd taken her far enough and kicked her out.

Taking the plunge when they'd left the backstreets and were heading towards the main road, she said, 'You don't recognize me, do you?'

Jake glanced round at her and shook his head. 'Should I?'

'I'm Chrissie's sister,' she said, waiting a beat to let that sink in before adding: 'I met you when you gave her a lift home that day. You were with your girlfriend. Or at least I *thought* she was your girlfriend, but I heard you're with someone else now.'

'What are you talking about?' Jake frowned. 'I'm still with Leanne.'

'*Really?*' Tina affected surprise. 'I'm sure I heard you were with some blonde girl now, and you're supposed to be having a baby.'

Jake slammed his brakes on and swerved over to the kerb. Ignoring the angry honking from the driver who'd had to brake to avoid slamming into the back of him, he twisted round in his seat. 'Where did you hear that shit?'

Tina's heart was racing. She'd known there was a chance that the blonde and the fat man had been talking about a different Jake, but the anger in *this* Jake's eyes told her that her suspicions had been spot on.

'It doesn't matter who told me,' she said slyly. 'But I'm guessing by your reaction that Leanne doesn't know. And I'm betting you'd like it to stay that way. Am I right?'

Jake narrowed his eyes. 'Is that supposed to be some kind of threat?'

'Why would I threaten you?' Tina feigned innocence. 'Your girlfriend is my sister's best mate, so we're practically family.'

Jake breathed in slowly, then jerked his chin at the door. 'Get out.'

'Aw, don't be like that,' Tina wheedled, giving him a seductive look as she reached out to stroke his thigh. 'I'm not going to grass you up or anything. I like you, and I reckon you like me, too, 'cos I remember the way you looked at me when we met that day. You could hardly keep your eyes off my tits. And if you play your cards right, you might just get to – *aagghh*!' Squealing with pain when Jake seized her by the wrist, she contorted her body to ease the pressure. 'Pack it in, man! That really hurts!'

'That was your one and only warning,' Jake hissed, tossing her hand aside after a moment. 'If I hear you've been talking shit about me to your sister or anyone else, you won't know what's hit you. Now fuck off back to whatever hole you crawled out of.'

'What, so *you* can go crawling up that blonde slag's hole behind Leanne's back again?' Tina sniped. 'Yeah, you'd like that, wouldn't you? Well, guess what . . . I don't take orders from the likes of you and, soon as I get home, I'm going to get our Chrissie to set Leanne straight.'

'You really think they'd believe a word *you* said?' Jake sneered.

'We'll soon find out, won't we?'

Tina reached for the door handle, but Jake activated the child lock before she could get to it.

'Oh, it's like that, is it?' She turned back to him. 'Suppose you're gonna beat me up now, are you? Well, go on then, *do* it. But I'm still gonna tell. *Unless* . . .' She paused and pursed her lips. 'You could always pay me off.'

Jake stared at her without answering. He didn't know how

she'd found out about Sally and the baby, but she had, so now he was going to have to do something to stop her from telling Leanne. The way he saw it, he had two options: bung her the money she was asking for, and hope that would be the end of it; or drive her to a deserted quarry and bury her. And, right now, he was leaning towards the latter.

Taking his silence as a sign that he was considering her suggestion, Tina said, 'What's it to be, Jakey boy? I know you're minted, 'cos this car must've cost a bomb, and that Rolex don't look like a snide, so it's not like you can't afford to give me a bit of spends, is it?'

When he still didn't answer, Tina flopped back in her seat and, pushing her sleeve up, rubbed her sore wrist.

'Fine, don't talk to me, then. But we can't just sit here all night, so you'd best hurry up and decide what you're going to do.'

A couple were walking slowly past the car, and Jake frowned when the woman stared in at him while the man checked out the motor. Tina, however, waved at them and made sure they got a good look at her face before turning back to Jake.

'Can't do anything to me now, can you?' she declared victoriously. 'Not now there's witnesses who've seen us together.'

'Shut your mouth,' Jake snarled.

They sat in silence for several tense minutes, and Tina started fidgeting in her seat.

'God, this is daft,' she said after a while. 'I know we got off on the wrong foot, but it doesn't have to be like this. I reckon we could be friends, me and you.'

'And why would I want to be friends with a blackmailer?' Jake raised an eyebrow.

'I wasn't trying to blackmail you,' she protested. 'Well, not really. Truth is, I'm kind of desperate right now, so when I saw my chance I went for it. Can't blame a girl for trying, can you?'

'Desperate for what?' Jake stared pointedly at the track marks he'd spotted on her arm when she pushed her sleeve up. 'Smack, crack, or both?'

Blushing, Tina yanked her sleeve down. 'I'm not a junkie, if that's what you're thinking. My ex used to force me to take it, but I've been trying really hard to get off it. It's just not that easy with my mum and Chrissie having a go at me all the time. I'd do one if I could afford it, but my benefits got stopped when Chrissie grassed me up to the dole, so I'm stuck in this shithole. That's why I thought ...' Pausing, she released a defeated sigh. 'Well, you already know what I thought. I was going to sting you for a pile of dosh, then get the hell out of here.'

Jake gazed at her and noticed for the first time the gaunt-ness of her cheeks and the deep hollows around her eyes. He'd remembered her as soon as she'd said who she was, but he would never have recognized her the way she looked now. Her lifestyle was clearly taking its toll on her looks.

'Is that what you really want?' he asked.

'God, yeah!' Tina replied without hesitation. 'Why?' She gazed at him with hope in her eyes. 'You gonna help me?'

'Maybe,' Jake said, smiling as he restarted the engine and eased the car out on to the road.

*

Chrissie had a dreamy smile on her lips as she climbed out of the taxi later that night. She'd been to a leaving party for one of the girls from work, and they had ended up going on to a club afterwards. It wasn't Chrissie's usual scene, and she'd tried to get out of going, but her workmates had dragged her along. And she had to admit that it hadn't turned out to be as bad as she'd thought it would be. In fact, she'd had a really nice time, thanks to the brother of one of the girls, who had already been at the club when they got there.

Blond, tall, and skinny, Gary was the complete opposite of any of the men Chrissie had dated in the past, and his bushy beard would ordinarily have turned her right off. But he'd been charming and funny, and she couldn't deny that she'd been flattered that he'd chosen to sit with her instead of going after any of the younger, slimmer, prettier women who'd been there.

They had swapped numbers before she called it a night, and Gary had promised that he would call her to arrange a date. Chrissie wasn't holding her breath about that, because she had no doubt that he'd have turned his attention to some other girl as soon as she left the club. But it had been a massive ego boost all the same, and she couldn't wait to ring Leanne in the morning and tell her all about it.

No longer smiling when she let herself into the house and heard wails coming from the living room, she frowned when she walked into the room and saw her mum on the couch with a bawling, wriggling Dylan in her arms.

'Thank God you're back,' Joan cried. 'He's been at it for hours and I've tried everything, but I can't settle him.'

'Give him here.' Chrissie threw her jacket over the armchair and plucked Dylan out of her mum's arms. 'Where's our Tina? If she's in bed leaving you to deal with this, I'll—'

'She's out,' Joan interrupted, sagging against the cushion with relief. 'She said she'd only be an hour, but it's been ages now. And she's not answering her phone.'

'Why the hell did you let her go out in the first place?' Chrissie demanded as she patted Dylan's back. 'You know what she's like. She can't be trusted.'

'I'd sent her to pick my meds up,' Joan admitted. 'And Dyl was fast asleep when she got home, so when she asked me to watch him for an hour, I didn't see any harm in it.'

'That's exactly *why* she asked, because she knew you wouldn't say no,' Chrissie chided. 'You can't keep giving in to her like this, Mum. You've got to toughen up before you end up having another stroke.'

'I know.' Joan sighed. 'But she hasn't been out in a while, and she was only nipping round to her mate's for a brew.'

'What mate?' Chrissie frowned at her mother over Dylan's

shoulder. 'She hasn't bloody got any. And I thought *you* had more sense. She'll be after drugs.'

'All right, stop going on about it,' Joan said irritably. 'She took me for a mug, but it won't happen again.'

Chrissie gazed at her mum and sighed when she saw how pale and exhausted she looked. 'Why don't you get yourself off to bed,' she suggested. 'I'll look after Dylan. And don't worry about our Tina,' she added darkly. '*I'll* deal with her.'

'Thanks, love.' Joan hauled herself off the couch and squeezed Chrissie's arm gratefully before making her way out into the hall.

Dylan had stopped crying by then, and his swollen eyes were beginning to droop as he sniffled into Chrissie's shoulder. Stroking his damp hair, she said, 'Let's get you to bed as well, eh, little man?'

'Can I sleep wiv you?' Dylan asked, the words coming out in little sobs.

Chrissie squeezed her eyes shut. He was a restless sleeper, and she'd be black and blue come the morning from him tossing and turning. But she supposed it was better than the alternative: both her *and* her mum being kept awake by him crying because she'd made him sleep in the cot he was fast growing out of.

'All right,' she agreed. 'But only for tonight, and then you're back in your own bed. And you'll have to be a big boy and go to the toilet first. Okay?'

When Dylan nodded and wrapped his little arms around

her neck, Chrissie kissed his clammy cheek and carried him up the stairs. She loved him dearly, but she could happily have throttled his feckless mother for once again forcing her to give up her sleep for him.

22

'Annie Kiss Kiss . . . Annie Kiss Kiss . . .'

Chrissie jerked awake when she heard Dylan calling her and felt him tugging on her hand. The room was still dark when she peeled an eye open, but a faint sliver of daylight was showing at the top edge of the curtains, and a glance at the clock on the bedside table told her that it was 7.30 a.m.

Raising the quilt, she murmured, 'Get back in, sweetie. It's too early to get up yet.'

'Nana cold,' Dylan said as he clambered up and wriggled in beside her. 'Want brek-brek, but she won't get up.'

Chrissie's instincts bristled, and she felt as if someone had poured a bucket of ice water down her back.

'Wait there,' she said, climbing quickly out of the bed and tucking the quilt around him. 'I won't be a minute. Keep it warm for me.'

Her heart began to pound in her chest when she approached her mum's door. Mum was a life-long snorer, and Chrissie would usually have been able to hear her by now. But the only sound she could hear was the dripping of the bathroom tap.

'Mum . . . ?' she whispered, forcing herself to push the door open and go into the room. 'Are you asleep?'

Even as the words left her mouth, she instinctively knew that she wouldn't get a reply, but she prayed that she was wrong. The heating wasn't set to come on for another hour and the room was icy, so that would be why her mum had felt cold to Dylan.

Or maybe it's because she's dead . . .

Shaking her head to clear the unwelcome thought, Chrissie went over to the bed and gazed down at her mother in the dim light leaking in from the hall. She was lying on her back with her head turned to one side, eyes closed, mouth open – the way she always slept. But the quilt wasn't rising and falling, and the silence was becoming more deafening by the second.

Shaking with dread, Chrissie reached out and tentatively touched her mother's exposed shoulder – her cold, unmoving shoulder.

'Oh, no . . .' she murmured. 'Please, no, you can't be. Come on, Mum . . . wake up. *Please* . . .'

'Nana 'wake now?'

Jumping when she heard Dylan's voice, Chrissie turned to see him peering in at her from the doorway. It was all she could do to hold herself together, and her voice sounded high and squeaky to her own ears as she told him to be a good boy and go back to bed.

'She gon' get my toast now?' Dylan rubbed his eyes with a tiny fist.

Furiously blinking back the tears that were flooding her eyes, Chrissie shook her head and walked over to him. 'No, baby, she's too tired, so let's leave her in peace, eh? I'll make your breakfast.' She took his hand and led him out on to the landing, pulling her mum's door shut behind her.

When Dylan was settled on the couch with a plate of toast on his knee and his favourite cartoons on TV, Chrissie went into the kitchen to make some calls. She tried her sister first, but when it went to voicemail for the fourth time, she reluctantly left a message.

'Tina, it's me. I know you're probably blanking my calls because you think I'm going to have a go at you for staying out, but you need to ring me as soon as you get this. I can't tell you over the phone, but it's urgent, so please ring me. Or, better still, come home. *Please!*'

That done, she dialled 999.

'Ambulance – I think,' she said when the operator asked which service. 'It's my mum. I just – I just went into her room and f-found her, and I don't know what I'm supposed to do.'

Unable to hold back the tears any longer, she sobbed as she gave the operator the details she needed. Then, cutting the call when it was done, she covered her face with a tea towel so that Dylan wouldn't hear her as she bawled her eyes out.

The pain was sharper than anything she'd ever felt in her life before. Her mum . . . her funny, beautiful, sometimes crabby, always supportive mum was gone – and she'd ripped Chrissie's heart right out of her chest and taken it along with her.

23

'Oh, darling, I'm so sorry,' Leanne cried, her own eyes swimming with tears when she and Jake arrived at Chrissie's house half an hour later. 'Come here . . .' She pulled her friend into her arms and hugged her tightly.

Chrissie had only just managed to pull herself together for Dylan's sake, and she didn't want Leanne setting her off again, so she quickly extracted herself from the embrace.

'I'm fine,' she said, filling the kettle and switching it on to make them a brew.

'Has anyone been yet?' Leanne asked.

'No.' Chrissie shook her head. 'I wasn't sure who I was supposed to contact, so I rang the emergency services. They said they'd have to pick her up and take her to the hospital because it was unexpected, so they're going to send someone over. They didn't say how long they'd be, but I don't suppose they class it as urgent if the person's already . . .'

Dead.

Unable to say the word, Chrissie took a deep breath before

continuing. 'Anyway, they'll get here when they get here. So, what are we all having? Tea or coffee?'

'You don't have to put on a brave face for us,' Leanne said softly, guessing that Chrissie was trying to do exactly that. 'Why don't you sit down and let me make the tea?'

'Thanks, but I need to stay busy,' Chrissie insisted. 'You can check on Dylan for me, though, if you don't mind? He's in the front room. Here, take this to him.' She poured a glass of milk and passed it over.

'Does he know what's happened?' Leanne asked quietly.

'Not yet.' Chrissie shook her head. 'He found her and woke me up to tell me she was cold and wouldn't get up to make his breakfast. He thinks she's still sleeping, but it won't be long before he realizes something's wrong.'

'Poor little mite, it's going to break his heart.'

'Mmmm.' Chrissie nodded her agreement and quickly turned to take cups out of the cupboard before the fresh tears that were welling in her eyes spilled over.

'Would you like me to leave and give you two some space to talk?' Jake asked from the doorway.

'No, stay.' Chrissie sniffed the tears back and turned to face him. 'Unless you'd *rather* go, obviously, in which case don't feel like you've got to hang around. I know it's not easy for men to deal with women at the best of times, but when they're cry-ing . . .' She gave a mock grimace. 'I'm sure you'd rather be a million miles away.'

The doorbell rang at that moment, and Jake went off to answer it while Leanne went to see to Dylan.

'It's your neighbour,' he said quietly when he returned a few seconds later. 'What do you want me to tell her?'

'It's okay, I'll speak to her,' said Chrissie. 'She's probably guessed that something's wrong, 'cos the walls are like paper in these houses.'

She headed for the door now, but hesitated before going out. 'Thanks for coming over, Jake. It means a lot to have you both here.'

'That's what mates are for,' he replied softly. 'Now go see to your neighbour; I'll finish the brews.'

Chrissie nodded and went to see Mrs Ford. She'd given Jake some stick in the past, but she couldn't fault him for how happy he'd made Leanne, and she truly was grateful that they were both here to help her through this.

Unlike her waste-of-space sister, who still hadn't called back or replied to any of the texts Chrissie had sent since leaving the voicemail.

The messages had all been marked as read when Chrissie had checked shortly before Jake and Leanne arrived, so she knew that Tina had seen them and must have realized something was badly wrong. But her lack of response highlighted how little the selfish whore cared about anything or anyone apart from herself.

It was a frosty morning, and Mrs Ford was shivering as she waited on the doorstep. 'Is everything all right, love?' she asked, wrapping her cardigan tight around her bony frame when Chrissie opened the door. 'I don't like to pry, but I thought I heard someone crying when I was making my morning cuppa. And then when I saw your friends rushing in looking all upset, I knew something must be wrong. It's not the little one, is it?'

'No, it's my mum,' Chrissie told her quietly. 'She, um, passed away in her sleep last night.'

'Oh, no . . .' Mrs Ford's face crumpled. 'I'm so very sorry, love. Is there anything I can do?'

Feeling tearful again when she saw the genuine compassion in the older woman's eyes, Chrissie shook her head and swallowed the lump that was forming in her throat.

'Thanks, but there's honestly nothing anyone can do until the ambulance gets here.'

'Well, you know where I am, my love.' Mrs Ford reached out and patted her arm. 'Call me if you need me. Anytime, day or night.'

Chrissie thanked her again and was about to go inside when Ben's car pulled into the avenue. Waiting for him to park up as Mrs Ford made her way back into her own house, shaking her head sadly with every step, Chrissie smiled at Ben when he came up the path.

'What are you doing here?'

'Jake phoned and told me what's happened,' Ben explained. 'I hope you don't mind me coming round uninvited, but I needed to make sure you were okay.'

'I'm fine,' Chrissie told him, reaching into her dressing gown pocket for a tissue to wipe her nose. 'And you're always welcome, so of course I don't mind you coming round.' She waved him inside now and nodded at the kitchen door. 'Jake's in there. I'm just going to check on Leanne and Dylan. Won't be a sec.'

Jake was leaning against the sink drinking the tea he'd made and smoking a cigarette. 'Good to see you, mate,' he said quietly, flicking his ash down the plughole. 'Awful news, isn't it?'

'Terrible,' Ben agreed, giving him one of the quick hugs that men reserve for times such as this. 'How's she holding up?'

'Pretty well, considering,' said Jake, lowering his voice. 'On the way over, Leanne told me this'll be the third funeral she's had to arrange in the last few years. Apparently, her dad died on holiday in Spain, and her mum went to pieces, so Chrissie had to fly over and arrange to have his body brought home. Then her fiancé got knifed to death in a car-jacking a few months later.'

'*Seriously?*' Ben frowned. 'I had no idea she'd been engaged. Wow, that must have been traumatic.'

'And now this.' Jake sighed. 'Doesn't seem fair, does it?'

'It's absolutely tragic,' Ben murmured, shaking his head. To lose one parent was bad enough, but to then lose her lover and her mother in such a short space of time was brutal.

'I could swing for that bloody Tina,' Leanne muttered, walking into the kitchen. 'She went AWOL last night, and Chrissie's been trying to get hold of her all morning, but she's still not answering her phone. I know she doesn't actually know what's happened, but *I* knew something was up as soon as I heard Chrissie's voice, 'cos any idiot could tell she'd been crying, so Tina *must* have picked up on it when she heard the voicemail.'

'If Chrissie knows where she is, I could go and pick her up,' Ben offered.

'Believe me, if Chrissie knew, I'd have dragged Tina back by her hair by now,' Leanne said angrily. Then, tempering her tone, she said, 'Hi, by the way,' and leaned down to give Ben a peck on the cheek.

'At least she's got you.' Jake put his arm around her waist when she went over to him.

'It's not the same, though, is it?' Leanne rested her head on his chest. 'You need family around you at a time like this.'

'I've got all the family I need right here,' Chrissie said with forced brightness as she walked in with Dylan on her hip.

Dylan caught Ben's eye and shyly hid his face before peeping round Chrissie's shoulder and giving a little grin.

'Ah, bless him,' Leanne said when she saw what he was doing. 'I think he likes you, Ben.'

'You're honoured,' said Chrissie. 'He doesn't usually take to men – do you, bud?' She tickled Dylan's tummy, but he was more interested in playing peek-a-boo, so she handed him to Leanne before opening the fridge and taking out a pack of ham and some cheese slices. 'I'm making him a butty. Anyone else want one?'

'How about me and Jake take him to McDonald's for a bit?'

Leanne suggested after giving him a cuddle. 'We'll get him some food, and he can play in the ball pit.'

Guessing that Leanne was offering to take him out so that he wouldn't have to witness his beloved grandmother being taken away, Chrissie put the food back into the fridge.

'Thanks, babe, that's a great idea. I'll just give him a quick wash and get him dressed.'

Ben stood up when Chrissie had left the room. 'I'd best get out of the way. Can you tell her I said goodbye, and let me know how she gets on?'

'You can't go,' Leanne said quietly. 'She shouldn't be on her own at a time like this. I'd stay myself, but Dylan doesn't know either of you, so he'd freak out if you tried to take him, and we need to get him out of here before they . . .' she glanced at the staircase before whispering, 'come for the body.'

'Oh, sorry, I wasn't thinking,' said Ben. 'But don't you think she'd rather have someone she knows a bit better with her?'

'You'll do fine,' Leanne said with certainty. 'But can you give us a ring when the coast's clear, so we know when it's safe to bring Dylan home?'

Promising that he would, Ben sat back down.

Ten minutes later, when she'd dressed herself and Dylan, and Jake and Leanne had taken the child out, Chrissie flopped on to the chair facing Ben's at the kitchen table.

'Are you okay?' he asked.

'Not really,' she admitted, giving him a sad smile. 'The house feels way too quiet. I don't know what to do with myself.'

Jumping when her phone started ringing, she leapt to her feet and snatched it up off the ledge where she'd left it.

'Tina, is that you?'

'No, it's me,' an unfamiliar voice replied. 'Don't tell me you've forgotten me already? And there was me thinking I'd made a big impression on you last night. Guess I'm not as irresistible as I thought, huh?'

'Sorry,' Chrissie murmured, turning her back to Ben when she realized it was Gary, her workmate's brother. 'It's, um, not a very good time.'

'It's too early, isn't it?' Gary said apologetically. 'I knew I should have messaged first to make sure you weren't at work, but I was thinking about you, so I thought I'd take a chance. Shall I call you back at lunchtime?'

'I'm not at work,' Chrissie told him, remembering as she said it that she hadn't let her boss know she wouldn't be coming in today. 'Look, I really can't talk right now,' she went on. 'Let me call you when things are a little calmer.'

'Sure, no problem,' Gary agreed. 'I hope I haven't—'

Chrissie cut the call before he could finish. As flattering as it was that he'd called when she genuinely hadn't expected him to, she'd lost whatever enthusiasm she'd felt last night for the proposed date, and knew that she wouldn't be calling him anytime soon.

She turned to Ben now and glanced at the clock on the wall behind his head.

'I thought the ambulance would have been here by now.'

'I'm sure they won't be too much longer,' Ben said reassuringly.

'Hope not,' she muttered. 'All this waiting is making me feel jittery.'

'Come and sit down,' Ben suggested. 'You've spent the morning running round after everyone else, so why don't I make you a fresh cup of tea while you take a break?'

'I'll do it,' Chrissie said, scooping the empty cups off the table and carrying them to the sink. 'I need to keep myself occupied, or I'll end up . . .' Unable to continue speaking as the tears she'd been trying so desperately to contain began to escape, she dropped her face into her hands.

Ben got up and gently guided her to her seat. 'Come on, you need to rest while you've got the chance.'

When Chrissie suddenly turned and buried her face in his shirt, he patted her back in a soothing gesture – praying that she couldn't hear how fast his heart was beating. It was so inappropriate to feel this way at a time like this, but the scent of her hair and the feel of her body pressed against his was making him light-headed.

'I'm so sorry,' Chrissie apologized when she'd managed to pull herself together after a couple of minutes. 'I've made a mess of your shirt.'

'Don't worry about it,' Ben said, shivering when cold air replaced the heat her body had generated.

'I must look a sight,' Chrissie murmured self-consciously as she pulled a soggy tissue out of her sleeve and blew her nose.

'Don't be daft, you're beautiful,' Ben blurted out. Immediately blushing, he mumbled, 'I, erm . . . Sorry, I shouldn't have said that. Right, that brew . . .'

'It can wait,' Chrissie said quietly.

'Sorry?' Ben was confused.

'I said it can wait,' she repeated, reaching for his hand.

Taken aback when she kissed him, Ben couldn't breathe for several seconds. Blinking rapidly when she stopped, he gasped, 'Oh, wow, that was . . . *Wow!* Where did *that* come from?'

Cheeks flaming as it occurred to her that she'd misinterpreted his kindness and crossed a line, Chrissie turned and fled from the room.

'Chrissie, wait!' Ben went after her and grabbed her by the arm before she could run up the stairs. 'I didn't say I didn't like it,' he said softly, tilting his head to peer up at her down-turned face. 'I didn't expect it, that's all. Please don't be embarrassed, because we both know it would never have happened if you weren't grieving, so let's just pretend it never happened, eh? And it goes without saying that I won't tell anyone, if that's what you're worried about.'

Chrissie gazed up at him with despair in her eyes. 'You are *such* a massive idiot, Ben Smith, or Jones – or whatever the hell your surname is. You've got no idea how nice you are, have you?'

'It's Maitland,' Ben told her, a tiny grin curling his lips as he added, 'And I don't know about the second bit, but I've been called the first so many times, I guess it must be true.'

Chrissie smiled, but it was replaced by a look of sheer panic when the doorbell rang.

'Oh, God, that must be them.'

'Are you ready?'

'*No!* I haven't said goodbye yet.'

'Go and do it now. They can wait.'

Chrissie squeezed her eyes shut and nodded. 'Thanks. I'll try not to be too long.'

Chrissie made her way up the stairs as Ben went out to speak with the ambulance crew. She paused and took a deep breath before entering her mum's bedroom. This would be the last time she ever saw her face, because her mum had always insisted that she wanted a closed casket when the time came.

'*I've never understood this fascination with gawping at dead people,*' she'd told Chrissie once when they had been watching the footage of some American celebrity's funeral on TV. '*It's downright bloody creepy, if you ask me. When my time comes, I want my coffin closed and double-bolted, 'cos there's no way I'm having people traipse past making sarky comments about me hair.*'

With that memory in mind, Chrissie glanced at her mum's hair now as she approached the bed. Like Chrissie's own hair, her mum's had been a dark shade of red when she was younger, but the colour had faded as she'd aged. She'd tried home-dyeing it for a while, but it had become too time-consuming after she got ill, and she'd refused to let anyone else do it for her, so it was now a messy blend of dark and light greys.

It felt like straw when Chrissie stroked it and, knowing that her mum would be mortified if she let the ambulance crew take her like that, she rushed into her own room to get a bottle of leave-in conditioner.

Aware that she didn't have much time when she heard the men talking quietly in the hall below, she returned to her mum and sat on the bed beside her.

'Well, I guess this is it,' she murmured as she sprayed conditioner on to her mum's hair and gently massaged it in. 'I couldn't let you go without making you look decent, 'cos I know you'd never forgive me. And I thought I might as well grab the chance to tell you how much I love you while I'm at it,' she went on sadly. 'You always told me to belt up and stop being so soft whenever I tried in the past, but you knew, didn't you? I *did* love you, and I always will, 'cos you're the best mum in the world. I just wanted you to know that.'

She paused and swiped at a rogue tear that was trickling down her cheek before continuing.

'Anyway, I expect Dad'll be waiting, so I'd best let you go. Give him a big hug from me when you see him. Good night, God bless.'

She leaned over now and kissed her mum's cold cheek for the last time, before going out on to the landing to let the crew know she was ready.

24

The funeral service was short and sweet – exactly as Joan no-fuss, no-nonsense O'Brien would have wanted it to be. When it was over, Chrissie stood outside the crematorium doors and thanked the mourners who had come along to pay their last respects. There weren't many; just a couple of distant relatives who Chrissie had only vaguely recognized because it was so long since she'd seen them, a few neighbours, and a handful of her mum's old bingo buddies. When at last she was done, she made her way to the funeral car, in which Leanne, Jake and Ben were already seated.

'Sorry about that,' she apologized as she climbed in. 'I tried to keep it short, but they kept hugging me and telling me how proud my mum was of me.'

'She was,' said Leanne. 'It's all she ever talked about when-ever I came round. *Our Chrissie's done this, our Chrissie's doing that.* She thought the world of you, and I could picture her standing there watching the service, saying, *My lass organized this. Isn't she clever?*'

'You don't think it was too quick, do you?' Chrissie asked. 'I know she'd have hated anything airy-fairy, but I wouldn't want her to think I rushed it to get it over with.'

'Babe, it was perfect,' Leanne said sincerely. 'Honestly, she'd have loved it. Especially when the vicar got her name wrong.'

Chrissie managed a grin at this. 'Oh, I know, that was awful, wasn't it? Mum would have torn him off a strip for that, and no messing. I don't even know where that came from. Margaret sounds nothing like Joan. Still, at least he had the grace to apologize.' She paused now and smiled at the three of them before saying, 'You lot have been amazing, by the way. Thank you so much for supporting me through this.'

'We love you,' Leanne said simply. 'So of course we were going to be here for you. Always have been, always will be,' she added. 'Same as you've always been there for me.'

'Oh, here we go.' Chrissie gave Jake a mock-weary look. 'Always has to turn it mushy, doesn't she?'

'Shut it, you!' Leanne gave her a playful dig in the ribs.

'What do you girls want to do?' Jake asked, resting his arm along the back of the seat and stroking Leanne's hair. 'I've got a few hours before I have to head off, so we could go out for something to eat, if anyone's hungry? My treat.'

'I'm okay, thanks,' Chrissie said, glancing at her watch. 'I think I'd best go straight home. Mrs Ford's daughter was an angel for offering to look after Dylan so her mum could come to the funeral, but I don't want them to think I'm taking the piss.'

'We could always pick him up and take him with us?' Ben suggested.

'Might have known you'd say that.' Chrissie smiled. 'Proper taken to him, haven't you?'

'He's a smart little fella,' Ben said fondly. 'And his auntie's pretty cool, too,' he added, giving her a shy grin.

Chrissie settled in her seat with a secretive smile playing on her lips as the chauffeur drove them out through the crematorium gates. She and Ben had grown quite close this last week, and she wasn't sure she'd have coped without him. He'd been an enormous help; running her around whenever she'd needed to go anywhere, and bringing food in when she'd been too tired or emotional to cook. He'd also spent hours looking after Dylan, who adored him, giving Chrissie time alone to grieve.

True to his word, he hadn't breathed a word to Jake about the kiss; and neither he nor Chrissie had had the courage to speak about it for several days after it had happened. But Chrissie hadn't been able to get it out of her mind so, last night, after she'd put Dylan to bed and she and Ben were sharing a glass of wine, she'd finally taken the plunge.

'Are we going to talk about it, or is it going to be the elephant in the room for the rest of our lives?' she'd asked.

'What do you mean?' Ben had replied shyly, his sudden inability to look her in the eye letting her know that he knew exactly what she meant.

'The kiss,' she'd said bluntly. 'I know you think I only did it because I was in a state over my mum, but you're wrong. I like you, and I thought it was mutual, but I should never have put you in that position, and I'm really sorry if I embarrassed you. I'm just glad it hasn't affected our friendship, because that would have awful.'

'Are you serious?' he'd asked.

'About which bit?'

'About liking me?'

'Of course. I thought you knew.'

'I honestly didn't.'

'I'm obviously more subtle than I thought.' Chrissie had laughed. 'Still, at least we've aired it now, and we both know where we stand, so there's no need for either of us to feel awk—'

Ben had kissed her before she could continue, and this time neither of them had pulled away. They had spent the rest of the night cuddling on the sofa, and Chrissie had fallen asleep in his arms – the pair of them still fully clothed.

Things had been a little hectic this morning, so they hadn't had a chance to talk in any depth, but they *had* agreed that, out of respect for her mum, this probably wasn't the best day to come out as a couple.

They hadn't needed to say a word about any of this to Leanne, because she'd already guessed that something had changed between them. All day she'd been watching them exchange surreptitious glances when they'd thought nobody was looking, and they were sitting comfortably close now, she thought. She knew they'd been spending a lot of time together this week, and if that had broken down the barriers which had been keeping them apart, then she was delighted. Chrissie hadn't had a serious relationship with any man since her fiancé had been murdered, and she deserved happiness. It seemed this most unhappy of occasions might have been the prod they had both needed to bring it about.

When they reached the house a short time later, Chrissie led her friends inside and took a quick look around.

'Anything?' Leanne asked.

Chrissie shook her head.

'She was hoping Tina might have turned up while we were out,' Leanne explained when Jake gave her a questioning look. 'She read Chrissie's last message, so she knows the funeral was scheduled for today.'

'I actually don't know if I'm more annoyed or worried,' Chrissie said, hanging her coat on a chair before reaching for the kettle. 'As bad as she is, she's just lost her mum, for God's sake. How could she not want to say goodbye?'

'Because she's selfish,' Leanne said bluntly as she took a seat at the table.

'I wish that *was* all it was,' Chrissie murmured, leaning against the sink and folding her arms. 'But I've got a niggling feeling something might be wrong.'

'Like what?'

'I'm not sure, it's just a feeling. I know she's probably been hiding out in some squat getting off her nut, but she did love Mum, so I can't understand why she hasn't phoned or texted.'

'I'm not being funny, but she was gone for a whole month last time, and she didn't get in touch once,' Leanne reminded her.

'I know, but this is different,' Chrissie argued. 'No one can be cold enough to ignore their own mother's funeral – not even our Tina.'

'So what do you want to do?' Leanne asked when she saw the worry in Chrissie's eyes.

'I don't know.' Chrissie shrugged. 'I haven't called the police yet, but maybe I should?'

'Is there really any point?' Jake asked. 'Like you said, this isn't the first time she's taken off, so I can't see the police taking it too seriously. And she must still have her phone if she's seen your messages, so she'd have let someone know by now if she was in trouble.'

'I guess so,' Chrissie conceded, unable to argue with his logic. Then, with finality, she said, 'No, you're right. She's being a selfish cow, and I'm wasting my time worrying about her. Dylan's the only one I should be thinking about now. Tina can screw up her own life as much as she likes, but I won't have her messing that boy's head up again. From now on, it's just me and him.'

'And Ben,' said Leanne. Laughing when both Chrissie and Ben blushed, she said, 'Oh, come on . . . you can't seriously think we didn't notice that something's going on. It's obvious.'

'Okay, fine, we've been talking,' Chrissie admitted. 'But it's early days and we're taking it slowly, so don't go on about it.'

'Good for you!' Jake clapped his friend on the back. 'I thought you were never going to get the balls to ask her out.'

'He didn't.' Chrissie gave Ben a coy smile. 'I practically had to throw myself at him.'

'That's my girl,' Leanne said approvingly. 'I suppose this means we're an official foursome now?'

'Don't try to rush us,' Chrissie chided. 'We're not all like you two, you know. Some of us like to get to know each other properly before we leap into Romeo and Juliet territory. Anyway, enough about that,' she went on matter-of-factly. 'Jake hasn't got long, so finish making those brews while I go and get Dylan, Ben. Then we can decide where we're going to eat.'

'I guess we know who'll be wearing the trousers in this relationship,' Jake teased when his friend stood up to do as he'd been told without argument.

'Shut it, you!' Chrissie grinned.

PART TWO

25

Leanne stared at the stick in her hand and bit her lip as she waited for the words to appear. When they did, her heart skipped several beats.

3–4 weeks pregnant.

A quick flick through her memory bank told her the exact night she must have conceived. She hadn't seen as much of Jake as she'd have liked since he'd decided to go into the property business. He was out most days searching for new flats and houses to add to his portfolio, and stayed out late most nights dealing with his security business. She was often asleep by the time he got home, but she'd made an effort to wait up for him that particular night – and the result was in her hand right now.

And her belly.

She placed her free hand on her stomach and closed her eyes to picture the little life that had been secretly growing inside her for the last three and a half weeks. It would only be a tiny squiggle at the moment, but in her mind's eye it was a fully formed, perfect bundle of joy, with its mother's black hair and its father's brown eyes.

No, not it, *she*.

Telling herself to stop being so ridiculous, that it was impossible to know the sex at this early stage, Leanne went into the bedroom and, picking up her mobile phone, pulled Jake's number up on to the screen. Immediately changing her mind, because she wanted to see his expression when he heard the news, she decided to wait until he came home for dinner.

Too excited to sit around doing nothing for the rest of the day, she thought she might ring Chrissie and see if she fancied a catch-up. Chrissie had been busy working and taking care of Dylan since her mum's funeral, and any spare time she had was spent with Ben, so – as with Jake – Leanne hadn't seen much of her lately. They still spoke on the phone when they got the chance, but it wasn't the same as actually spending time together, and Leanne missed her.

As beautiful as this apartment undoubtedly was, Leanne often felt lonely. And she also got quite bored, but since Jake had vetoed the idea of her looking for work, insisting that it was his job to take care of her, she'd taken to reading in order to keep from going completely stir crazy.

It wasn't quite the life Leanne had imagined when she'd agreed to move in with Jake, but it felt ungrateful to complain when he was working himself to the bone to keep her in the lap of luxury. She only wished she could make him understand that she didn't need the extravagant gifts he brought her whenever he'd been out of town: the flowers, the chocolates, the clothes, the jewellery. While most women would have cut off their right arm to have what she had, Leanne would have been happy to still be scrimping and scraping in the bedsit if it meant she got to spend more time with Jake.

Still, as much as she'd have liked him to stay home more often, she would never dream of trying to make him do so, because she'd realized that his thirst for success ran far deeper than the need to make money. It was his way of getting one over on all the people who had tormented him as a child and the teachers who had told him he would amount to nothing. Most of all, it was a massive fuck-you to the father who had walked away as if he no longer existed.

Leanne hoped that, when he learned he was about to become a father to a child of his own, Jake might realize that he didn't have to try so hard to prove himself. This child deserved to have two hands-on parents, not a stay-at-home mummy and a workaholic daddy who popped in now and then with expensive presents.

Chrissie's phone went to voicemail, but Leanne decided it was probably just as well. Jake should be the first to know about the baby, and she wasn't sure she trusted herself not to blurt it out if she saw Chrissie. She still needed a break from this place, though, so she decided to take a walk into town. It was unusually warm for early May; the perfect day for sunbathing on the balcony with a book and glass of wine, in fact – exactly as Jake had envisioned the first time he'd brought her here. But there was no way she'd be able to relax out there knowing that the pervy old neighbour was probably spying on her. Anyway, the walk would do her good, she decided. And she'd be able to nip into the supermarket while she was out, to pick up something special for dinner.

*

Jake was tired when he arrived home later that evening. He'd had a hectic day, rushing from one side of Manchester to the other; picking things up here and dropping them off there, and dealing with a couple of tenancy issues in between. And he had more of the same lined up for tomorrow, so all he wanted to do was jump into the shower and then eat dinner before hitting the sack.

Leanne had other ideas.

Dressed up for the first time in ages, she was wearing the tight-fitting purple dress that Jake loved because he said it brought out the emerald in her eyes, and she'd coiled her long hair up loosely, leaving a couple of tendrils down to frame her face.

'Wow,' he said, pulling her into his arms when he saw her. 'You look amazing. What's the occasion?'

'I thought it was about time I made an effort,' she said, looping her arms around his neck. 'Don't want you losing interest in me now, do I?'

'That'd never happen,' he promised, kissing her softly.

'Even if I got fat?' She gazed up at him with a mysterious smile on her lips.

'Even if you were morbidly obese,' he said, clearly not picking up on the hint. 'What are you cooking?' he asked then, letting her go so he could take off his jacket.

'Spinach tagliatelle.'

'*Spinach?*' He pulled a face.

'It's very good for you,' she said. 'Full of iron.' Another hint.

'So's steak,' Jake countered. 'And I could do with a big, juicy rib-eye right now, so how's about we leave your stuff for another day and I take you out instead?'

'I'd rather stay in,' Leanne insisted, taking his jacket out of his hand and slinging it over the back of a chair before pushing him towards the sofa. 'Sit down and put your feet up while I get you a drink.'

'Fine,' Jake surrendered, flopping down and kicking his shoes off. 'But make it a large one.'

'I hope that means you're not going out again tonight?' Leanne asked.

'Nope.' He yawned. 'I need a break.'

'About time!' she said approvingly as she rushed into the kitchen to pour him a whisky.

Dropping a handful of ice into the glass, she carried it in to him and placed it on the table. 'Just going to check on dinner; won't be a sec.'

Jake sat forward to reach for the glass, but hesitated when he saw a white stick sitting next to it on the table. It took a couple of seconds before it clicked, and he snapped his head around.

'Surprise,' Leanne said, smiling at him from the kitchen doorway.

'Is this what I think it is?' he asked.

She bit her lip and nodded.

Jake gazed down at the stick for several long moments, a frown creasing his brow, and Leanne's smile slipped as it occurred to her that he might not be quite as thrilled by the idea of having a baby as she was.

'Are you okay?' she asked.

'Okay?' he repeated, standing up and walking over to her. 'I'm absolutely fucking delighted!'

'God, you scared me for a minute there!' she gasped when he picked her up and swung her around. 'I couldn't tell if you were happy or horrified.'

'I was shocked,' he said. 'Still am,' he went on, drawing his head back to peer into her eyes. 'Are we really . . . ?'

'Going to have a baby?' she finished for him when he left the rest unsaid. 'Yes, we really are.'

'When?' He gently placed her on her feet. 'How far gone are you?'

'Almost a month,' she said, amused when he guided her to the couch and sat her down as if she were made of china. 'I'm pretty sure it happened the night I waited up for you.'

'Ah . . .' Jake gave a knowing smile. 'That night. I remember it well.'

'I bet you do,' Leanne teased, recalling the lust in his eyes when he'd walked in and found her sprawled on the rug in front of the fire wearing nothing but a basque, stockings, and his favourite red lipstick.

'God, this is unreal,' he said, staring at her with wonder in his eyes. 'I'm going to be a dad.'

'Yes, you are,' she confirmed, her eyes glowing with joy when he placed his hand on her stomach. 'And I hope you meant what you said about not caring if I get fat, 'cos it's *so* gonna happen.'

'I wouldn't care if you were twenty stone,' Jake said, hugging her tightly. 'You'd still be the most beautiful woman in the world. Does anyone else know?' he asked then. 'Have you told Chrissie, or your mum and dad?'

'No, I wanted to tell you first. And I think we should keep it to ourselves for now. I know you'll probably think I'm being superstitious, but they reckon you shouldn't tell anyone till you've passed the twelve-week mark. It's supposed to be unlucky, and I don't want to risk anything going wrong.'

'Then we won't tell a soul,' Jake promised as he pulled her into his arms.

Happier than she'd felt in a while, Leanne wriggled free after a couple of minutes.

'Where are you going?' Jake asked, holding on to her hand when she tried to stand up.

'To get dinner,' she reminded him.

'Sorry, but I'm not eating that green shit.' He pulled her

back down. 'If you insist on staying in, I'm going to order a pizza. Then we're going to crack a bottle of bubbly and celebrate in style. If you're allowed to drink, that is? I don't want to put the baby at risk.'

'I'm sure one glass won't hurt,' Leanne said, loving him more than ever because it was obvious that he was going to be a caring, protective father.

26

Sally woke in a cold sweat, her heart still pounding with fear after dreaming that she was being chased down a pitch-dark alley by a hooded gang. Reaching out to switch the bedside lamp on, she felt a wet patch on the sheet beneath her and shoved the quilt off her legs in disgust. She thought she must have pissed herself in her sleep, but the agonizing pain that suddenly tore through her stomach told her otherwise.

Panicking, because she'd never gone full-term with a pregnancy before, she grabbed her mobile phone off the nightstand.

'Ben, it's me,' she blurted out when her call was answered after several rings. 'I think I'm in labour! Can you call Jake and tell him to come round? Tell him it's urgent!'

'I'll, er, see what I can do,' Ben replied guardedly.

'Ben, *please*!' she squealed, her voice rising in pitch as another stab of pain ripped into her. 'I can't do this on my own! If you won't ring him, I'll do it myself. I mean it!'

'All right, give me ten minutes.'

'*Hurry!*' Sally was almost screaming by now. 'It really hurts, and I'm scared!'

*

'What's up?' Chrissie pushed herself up on to her elbows and squinted at Ben in the darkness when he climbed out of bed. 'Was that a woman? It sounded like someone screaming.'

Thinking on his feet as he quickly pulled his trousers on, Ben said, 'It was one of Jake's tenants. She's got a leak and she's freaking out about the electrics, so I'm going to have to go over and see if I can sort it.'

'Okay,' Chrissie murmured, lying down again and tugging the quilt up around her throat. 'Try not to be too long.'

'I'll be as quick as I can,' he promised, leaning down to kiss her on the cheek after pulling his jumper on.

As he quietly let himself out of the house and climbed into his car, Ben felt sick with guilt. Chrissie was one of the most honest people he'd ever met and he hated having to lie to her. But as much as he would have liked to, he couldn't bring himself to ignore Sally at a time like this.

Furious with Jake for laying this on him, he rang him as he drove away from Chrissie's house.

''S'up?' Jake asked sleepily when he answered. 'And it'd better be important, 'cos I've only had a couple of hours.'

'Ah, poor you, you must be knackered,' Ben replied sarcastically. 'Not like me. I don't mind getting woken up in the middle of the night, me. Especially when I've been working all day, and it's got bog-all to do with me in the first place!'

'All right, mate, you don't have to shout. What's up with you, anyhow? Are you drunk, or something?'

'No, I'm not fucking drunk, I'm fucking fuming!'

There was a rustle of material, followed by a door clicking shut, and then Jake hissed, 'What the hell is your problem?'

'*You* are,' Ben said. 'I just had to lie to Chrissie and tell her there's a leak in one of your flats to cover for you. Have you any idea how pissed off she'd be if she knew where I was really going?'

'What you on about?'

'I'm on my way to Sally's. Remember her, do you? The one who's having your kid? And when I say having it, I mean having it *right now*, so you'd best get your arse over there.'

'It's three in the fucking morning,' Jake protested. 'What am I supposed to tell Leanne?'

'The same thing I had to tell Chrissie.'

'She knows I hired you to deal with the maintenance of my properties, so she's not going to believe that.'

'Well, you'd best think of something, and quick, 'cos Sally's threatening to ring you herself if you don't go round,' Ben warned. 'And the way she was screaming, I wouldn't test her if I was you.'

'Shit!' Jake muttered. 'I can't deal with this right now.'

'And you think I can?' Ben countered angrily. 'I'm driving around at stupid o'clock, feeling guilty for lying to Chrissie –

and God only knows what I'm going to be faced with when I get to Sally's. And it's not even my flaming kid!'

'All right, I'll try to think of something,' Jake conceded. 'Don't let her do anything stupid.'

Ben tutted when Jake cut the call, and then sighed when, almost immediately, his phone began to ring and he saw *Tenant 48* on the screen – the name he had Sally listed under in case Chrissie ever got hold of his phone. After folding his own failing company a couple of months ago, he'd taken on the role of maintenance manager for Jake's properties, so Chrissie thought nothing of the tenants having his number – and him theirs. But it was yet more lies, and Ben resented Jake for putting him in this position.

Pushing Chrissie out of his mind when he answered the call and heard Sally crying out in pain, he said, 'I'm pulling up outside yours. Can you open the door, or should I let myself in?'

'Let yourself in,' she gasped. 'And *hurry*!'

Ben took a moment to brace himself before entering the house. He was the squeamish type, and couldn't even bear to watch women giving birth on TV, never mind in real life. Hell, he couldn't even stomach the fictitious midwife drama that Chrissie liked to watch, so he didn't know how he was going to cope if Sally was as far on as she sounded.

Sally was lying on top of her bed, her face contorted in pain, her knees pulled up to her chest. Against his better judgement, Ben let his gaze slip to the space between her legs, and the room went into a spin when he spotted the gore-covered top of what he presumed was the baby's head poking out.

'Where's Jake?' Sally panted when the contraction subsided. 'Did you ring him?'

'Yeah, he said he'll try to come over,' Ben mumbled queasily.

'What do you mean, "try"?'

'He's coming,' Ben quickly corrected himself, hoping that Jake wouldn't let him down. 'It might take a while, though, 'cos he's got further to come than me.'

'How long?' Sally demanded. 'Where's he coming from?'

'The, um, other side of Manchester,' Ben said, flinching when Sally let out another low growl that escalated into a scream. 'Is – is there anything I can do?' he asked, forcing himself to move closer to the bed.

'It's coming!' she screeched, clutching at his hand. 'It's coming and I can't stop it!'

Almost throwing up when blood spurted out on to the sheet beneath her, Ben put his free hand on the wall to steady himself. 'I think we need an ambulance,' he croaked, wincing as her grip threatened to crush his fingers.

'I want Jake!' Sally cried. 'Call him again! He promised he'd be here! I need him!'

Thinking that the loss of blood must be making her delirious, because there was no way Jake would have promised to be present at the birth of a child he'd never even wanted, Ben tugged his phone out of his pocket and dialled 999.

'I'll get out of the way and leave you to it,' Ben said when the ambulance arrived five minutes later.

'You can't leave me!' Sally cried.

'We need to take her in,' one of the paramedics said when they realized she was haemorrhaging. 'You can come with her, if you like?' he added to Ben.

Ben didn't want to go anywhere but home to bed and Chrissie. But Sally was panicking, and he felt sorry for her, so he reluctantly agreed to follow behind them in his car.

As they set off, he tried to call Jake again, and guessed – *hoped* – that his friend must already be on his way when he didn't answer.

When they reached the hospital, Sally was rushed to the maternity ward in a wheelchair. Terrified and screaming with pain, she held on tightly to Ben's hand as he walked alongside her.

Unable to break free without hurting her, Ben hoped that she might let go of her own accord when they transferred her on to a bed in the birthing suite and placed her feet in stirrups. But she didn't.

Everything happened so quickly after that, Ben didn't get a chance to explain that he wasn't actually the father when one of the nurses gave him a reassuring smile, and said, 'Don't worry, Daddy; won't be long now.'

Still trapped in Sally's vice-like grip, he watched, transfixed, as she gave one last almighty push.

'It's a boy!' The midwife beamed at Ben as he stared down

at the bloody, squirming creature that had just slithered out of Sally's body. 'Would you like to cut the cord?'

Unable to speak, he was vaguely aware of shaking his head as the room began to swim around him.

*

Still feeling shaky when he came round sometime later, Ben gratefully accepted a cup of sweet tea from one of the nurses before following her to the side room they had moved Sally and the baby into after he'd fainted.

Sally was lying on her side, gazing at the now-clean baby sleeping in a Plexiglas cot beside her.

'Isn't he beautiful,' she purred, smiling proudly up at Ben when he entered the room.

He stared down at the child, and swallowed loudly when he saw that it was a miniature replica of Jake.

'He's a bonny little chap,' he managed after a moment.

'I don't suppose Jake's here yet?'

'Not yet, no.' Ben shook his head, his gaze still riveted on the child. 'He must have got held up, and I can't get a signal in here so I can't call him.'

'Will you try again when you leave?' Sally asked. 'Let him know that Jack's here, and we're both fine?'

'Jack?' Ben raised an eyebrow.

'Suits him, doesn't it?' Sally smiled. 'If he'd been a girl, it would have been Jackie. Jake wasn't too keen; he thought it was too close and people might put two and two together. But I like it, so he's got no choice.'

Frowning, Ben perched on the bedside chair. 'You and Jake have talked about names?'

'Of course,' said Sally.

Ben was confused. Jake had always maintained that he wanted nothing to do with Sally or the baby, and Ben had thought that Sally must be delirious when she'd said that Jake had promised to be present at the birth. But now it seemed that they had discussed names, as well.

'Am I missing something here?' he asked, peering into Sally's tired eyes. 'Is something going on between you and Jake?'

Sally dipped her gaze as her cheeks reddened. 'No, of course not. He comes round to drop my money off, and sometimes stays for a brew, and we chat about the baby. That's all.'

'You said he'd promised to be at the birth?'

'Did I?' She frowned as if she couldn't remember. Then, shrugging, said, 'It was probably wishful thinking. At least I had you, though, eh?' She gave Ben a grateful smile. 'Sorry I freaked out. Are you feeling better now?'

'I'm fine,' he said quietly. 'Just never seen anything quite so . . .'

'Gross?' She raised an amused eyebrow.

'A bit,' he admitted. 'But it was kind of amazing, as well. Awe-inspiring, actually,' he added as he gazed over at the sleeping child. 'To witness his arrival into the world, hear him take his first breath, his first cry.'

'Are you sure you heard that?' Sally teased. 'I thought you were already on the floor by then?'

'I heard it,' Ben murmured, thinking that it really ought to have been Jake. 'Anyway, I'd best go and let you get some rest. I didn't realize it was so late.'

'Thanks for being here,' Sally said as he stood up. 'And don't forget to tell Jake.'

'I won't,' Ben promised. 'And, um, well done,' he added, taking one last peek at the baby.

*

It was already light when Ben walked out of the hospital. Exhausted, and still feeling peculiar after witnessing the birth of his friend's child, he paused to light a cigarette before trying Jake's phone again.

Unsurprised when it went straight to voicemail, he waited for the beep. Then, choosing his words carefully in case Leanne should hear the message, he said, 'It's me again; just letting you know that I stopped that leak. But it's only a temporary fix, so you might want to take a look at the *boy*-ler.' He placed heavy emphasis on the word, hoping that his friend would pick up on it and understand that he now had a son.

Sucking deeply on the cigarette as he walked slowly to his car, Ben replayed the conversation he'd had with Sally. Although she'd denied it, her expression when he'd asked if there was something going on between her and Jake had contradicted her words. But Jake was crazy about Leanne, and this whole situation had arisen out of his desperation to keep her from finding out about the baby, so why would he start seeing Sally again and put everything at risk? It didn't make sense.

Still trying to figure out what had changed, and how he'd failed to notice, Ben made a decision as he climbed into the car and started the engine. This shit had to stop, and it had to stop now! His and Chrissie's relationship was becoming serious enough that they had been talking about Ben selling his flat and moving in with her and Dylan, and there was no way he was going to put that in jeopardy by continuing to play go-between for Jake and Sally. From now on, Jake could deal with this by himself.

27

Jake had switched his phone off and gone back to bed after speaking to Ben. He wasn't worried about Sally opening her mouth; she enjoyed the money he gave her far too much to risk losing it. And she wouldn't risk losing the chance to see him, albeit at his leisure and on his terms.

It had been Ben's idea to make her think she was in with a chance of getting back with him in order to keep her sweet, and it had worked, because she practically melted at Jake's feet whenever he called round there. And, the best part was, he hadn't even needed to do anything other than give her a promising smile every now and then, and drop the odd compliment.

When she'd first told him she was pregnant, he'd insisted that he wanted to get a DNA test done as soon as it was born. But he'd had time to think about it since then, and he'd decided that it might not be such a good idea after all. If she ever tried to blow him up, he fully intended to deny it, so the last thing he needed was for her to have actual proof.

But it wouldn't come to that, he was sure. He might have

more to lose than Sally did, but she knew which side her bread was buttered on. And if there was one thing he knew about Sally and her kind, it was that money spoke louder than anything – even so-called love. And, luckily for him, he could afford to feed her greed.

Ben, however, was another matter. As much as Jake appreciated all the help his friend had given him over the years, Ben's bleeding-heart approach to life was fast becoming an irritation. His loyalty had never been in question before he'd got with Chrissie, and Jake had known that he would never bleat a word to Leanne about Sally. Now, however, he wasn't so sure that he could trust Ben not to spill his guts to Chrissie. And that was worrying, because there was no way she would keep something like this to herself.

With that on his mind as he got dressed the following morning, Jake decided to call Ben and arrange a catch-up. They hadn't had seen much of each other lately; Jake had been working long hours, and Ben had been spending all of his free time with Chrissie and the boy. But he was sure they could both spare half an hour.

Leanne was still sleeping by the time Jake was ready to leave the apartment, so he left some money on the bedside table alongside a note telling her to treat herself to a new dress because he was taking her out tonight, before quietly letting himself out and making his way down to the residents' car park.

As he climbed into his car, he switched his phone on and

activated the Bluetooth. Listening to Ben's voicemail message as he pulled out on to the road, he immediately got the pointed remark about him needing to see the *boy*-ler, but he didn't bat an eyelid. As far as he was concerned, the kid was Sally's, not his, and – despite her obvious desire to the contrary – that was never going to change.

*

Leanne sighed when she woke a few hours later and saw Jake's note and the money. It was a week since she'd told him about the baby, and he'd promised to cut down on his working hours and spend more time with her. Nothing had changed as yet, but she still had eight months to go, so she could hardly expect him to drop everything right now, she supposed.

She got up and made herself a coffee, then went into the living room. Sunlight was streaming in through the blinds, and she smiled when she opened the French doors and heard the sound of children's laughter coming from the park beyond the boundary fence. She hadn't actually visited the park since moving in here, but she thought she might take a walk through it before heading into town to look for a dress. She wanted to see if there was an actual play area, or if the kids were left to run riot – as they were in the so-called parks near her old home.

These were the kind of things she needed to know before the baby arrived, she reasoned: the safest play areas, the best nurseries and schools, etc. And she supposed she really ought to register with a GP while she was out. She'd had no need of a doctor until now, so it hadn't even crossed her mind; but this was her first pregnancy and she wanted everything to go as well as it possibly could.

She had a spring in her step when she walked down the long driveway a short time later and pressed the button on the gate-post to open the pedestrian section. It was a pity there wasn't a gate leading into the park through the fence at the back of the house, because that would have cut a good few minutes off her walk, but the weather was nice enough that she didn't really mind.

*

'Excuse me, love . . .'

Leanne had just reached the copse at the end of the avenue, to the right of which a dirt-track ran alongside the wall of the large house at the end of the row, leading to the park. Hesitating when she heard the voice, she looked round and saw a man smiling out at her from the driver's seat of a transit van that was partially concealed by a canopy of thick bushes and low-hanging trees.

'You wouldn't 'appen to know if there's any garages round here, would ya?' he asked in a thick Liverpudlian accent. 'Only me satnav brought us down this dead end, and I got stuck trying to reverse out, and now me engine's packed in.'

'Sorry, I wouldn't know,' Leanne said truthfully. 'Have you tried the AA?'

'Can't, me phone's dead,' the man said, sighing as he ran a hand through his thick blond hair. 'This is all I need, this,' he muttered, gazing past her as if expecting to find a solution in the windows of the houses behind her. 'I'm s'posed to be at a job in ten minutes, and I can't even let 'em know I'm not gonna make it.'

For a split second, Leanne considered offering him the use of her phone. But she quickly decided against it and, instead, gave him a sympathetic smile.

'Sorry I couldn't help. Hope you get it sorted.'

As she continued on her way, she heard the side door of the van slide open. Seconds later, a strong arm clamped around her stomach, knocking the wind out of her as the ground fell away beneath her feet.

'Get off me!' she gasped as the man half-carried, half-dragged her to the van. 'What are you *doing*? *HEL*—'

Covering her mouth with his hand when she started screaming for help, the man slammed her head into the side of the van. 'Shut it, or you're dead!' he hissed, tearing her handbag off her shoulder as he shoved her roughly into the back of the van.

Crying out in pain when she landed heavily on a pile of tools, Leanne clutched at her stomach as the door slid shut, plunging her into pitch-darkness. Terrified when the van's engine suddenly fired to life and the floor vibrated beneath her, she groped her way to the door and tugged on the handle with all her might. It wouldn't budge, and she was thrown violently against the panel that separated the back of the van from the cab when the vehicle began to move.

'Let me out!' she screamed, banging her fists on the panel. 'You can't do this! Somebody will have seen and phoned the police!'

Blasted by loud music when a section of the panel suddenly opened, her breath caught in her throat when a woman's face appeared.

'Shut your fuckin' mouth, or I'll shut it for ya,' the woman warned in an accent as thick as the man's.

A squeak of terror escaped Leanne's lips when the woman grabbed her by the hair, and her body went rigid when she felt the point of a knife digging into the soft flesh beneath her chin.

'Please don't,' she whimpered, praying that the van wouldn't hit any bumps or potholes.

'Keep it zipped an' everything'll be okay,' the woman hissed, her cold stare boring into Leanne's eyes.

'Okay, okay,' Leanne gabbled, holding up her hands. 'I'll be quiet, I promise.'

'Good girl. Now sit back and enjoy the ride.' The woman gave her a forceful shove. 'But be warned,' she added ominously, pointing the knife at Leanne's face. 'Make any noise, and I'll be climbin' in to keep you company.'

When the panel slid shut again, Leanne bit down hard on her knuckles to keep from crying out. Where were they taking her – and, more importantly, what were they going to do with her when they got there? She'd heard about couples who kidnapped women and held them hostage to use as sex slaves, but the victims were usually foreign or vulnerable in some way. She'd never dreamed it would happen to her, and certainly not in broad daylight.

Clinging on to a strap that was hanging from the wall as the van continued on its way, Leanne tried to keep track of the direction they were taking. It felt like they had taken two lefts and one right turn, in which case they must now be on the main road. If they took a left at the end, they'd be heading towards open countryside, whereas a right would lead them straight to the motorway.

Liverpool! The word flew into her mind when they took a right. *They're Scouse, so they must be taking me to Liverpool!*

Leanne wanted to scream and kick the sides of the van to attract attention, but she had no doubt that the woman would carry through with her threat and climb into the back, so she forced herself to stay quiet, helpless to do anything except wait until they reached their destination. Once they were there, she would . . .

What? she asked herself. *What exactly* will *you do, Leanne? Scream and risk getting stabbed? Or try to fight the pair of them off – and risk getting battered* and *stabbed?*

With tears streaming down her cheeks, she squeezed her eyes shut as the van picked up speed, and prayed like she'd never prayed before.

*

After a busy morning, Jake decided to call Ben and ask if he fancied meeting up for a lunchtime pint. But as he pulled up his friend's number, his phone started ringing. He smiled when he saw that it was Leanne.

'Hello, darlin'. Missing me?'

'She sure is,' an all-too-familiar voice replied mockingly, making his blood run cold. 'You wanna hear the fuss she's makin'. Anyone'd think her throat was gettin' cut.'

'If you hurt her, I swear to God I'll—'

'*What?*' the sneering voice cut him dead. 'What you gonna do, JP? You seem to forget you ain't runnin' these streets no more.'

Jake breathed in deeply before asking, 'What do you want, Alex?'

'Ahhh, he remembers me,' Alex Delaney drawled with mock pleasure. 'And there was me thinkin' he'd forgot his old muckers, seein' as we haven't heard from him in so long. What's it been, JP? A year?'

'Something like that.'

'Well, I reckon it's time for a reunion. You know where I am, so why don't you come on over and join the party? And don't forget to bring my shit with you, or I guarantee you won't see your bird again. Not alive, anyhow.'

'And *I* guarantee *you'll* never take another breath if you harm one hair on her head,' Jake warned. 'And you should know me well enough to know that I *never* make idle threats.'

'Have you heard this divvy, makin' out like he's the fuckin'

Godfather?' Alex sneered. '*I'm gonna make him an offer he can't refuse*,' he said, adopting the muffled tone of Marlon Brando's Don Corleone.

At the sound of laughter in the background, a white-hot rage began to burn in Jake's gut.

'I'll be there in an hour,' he snarled.

Alex Delaney had been one of his best mates when he'd lived in Liverpool, and he knew exactly how the cunt operated. That's why he knew he'd have to tread very carefully if he hoped to get Leanne out of there unscathed. Like Jake, Alex was a good-looking lad who had little problem charming the knickers off any bird he fancied. But there was one huge difference between them. Whereas Jake could take a knock-back on the chin – as rarely as that had ever happened – Alex couldn't take no for an answer. And the more his victims protested, the rougher he'd get – and the more he'd enjoy it.

Forcing the unwelcome images out of his mind, Jake scrolled through the contacts list on his phone until he found the number he wanted. Alex didn't have the bottle to face him one on one, so he would undoubtedly have his crew there as backup. But if he thought Jake was going to walk into that on his own, he was an idiot.

28

Rampage – the nightclub Jake had once owned a slice of – occupied the ground floor of a vast, almost derelict warehouse tucked away on a dingy backstreet half a mile from Liverpool's revamped city centre. Surrounded by the rubble of former factories and cotton mills, it was a forlorn reminder of the long-gone era of industrial boom.

When Jake drove in through the rusted gates, he saw Alex's clapped-out transit van parked in the yard at the rear of the building, alongside a jeep that belonged to the twins, Paddy and Tommy Makin, and a rusted BMW that he didn't recognize. His souped-up Audi A5 looked like a Ferrari in comparison, and he made sure not to park it too close to any of the wrecks. If they couldn't take care of their own shit, they sure as hell wouldn't be bothered about his.

A fortified steel door was the only way in at the rear of the club, and this led directly into an ancient goods lift. Jake heard the lock being automatically released as he approached it, and knew that Alex must have been watching him on CCTV.

Stepping into the lift, he gazed out through the metal bars as it clanked and groaned its way down into the bowels of the building. Grimacing when he spotted a rat washing itself in a hole in the slime-coated wall, he was reminded why this place was on its knees: because no self-respecting clubber would choose to come to a dive like this when they could opt for one of the upmarket nightclubs on the main drag instead.

That was why he'd refused to even think about spending money on the dump when he'd been involved in it – *and* why he'd turned a blind eye to the criminals, drug-dealers, prostitutes and pimps who used it as a hang-out. As long as they had customers, they could explain the money that went through the tills – his share of which Jake had used to start his legit security business after moving back to Manchester.

When the lift came to a juddering halt, Jake stepped out and peered down the dimly lit corridor off which a warren of damp chambers branched. The office was at the far end, its door standing ajar, and Jake heard the twins' slurred voices coming from inside. Alex would have brought them in as backup because they were a pair of muscle-bound meatheads, but he'd obviously forgotten how useless they were when they got stoned – as they clearly were right now.

Jake strolled down the corridor and pushed the door open. He was hit in the face by a blanket of smoke coming from the fat spliff that the twins, who were dwarfing the shabby leather couch on the right of the cramped room, were passing between themselves. Jake wafted it away and looked around. A man he'd never seen before was sitting at the desk facing the door, staring at the screen of a laptop that was sitting open on the desk. With his clean-shaven head, diamonds in his earlobes, and thick gold chains around his neck and both wrists, Jake pegged him for a wide-boy dealer.

'Is this all you've got?' he asked, turning his attention to Alex, who was sitting on the corner of the desk.

'It's enough,' Alex said, unconcerned, his gaze travelling slowly down to Jake's shoes before coming up to rest on his face. 'Looks like you've been doing all right for yourself.'

'Can't complain,' said Jake.

Instantly dropping the calm facade, Alex jumped up and kicked the door shut. 'I should fuckin' think so, seeing as it's *my* money you're living it up on, you robbin' cunt! Thought you was proper smart, waltzin' off with all that coke, didn't you?'

'Get a grip,' Jake snorted. 'I only took what was mine, and you know it. It's not my fault you shoved your share up your fucking nose.'

Alex narrowed his eyes nastily and pressed his forehead up against Jake's. 'Who d'ya think you're talking to, dickhead?'

'There's four dickheads in here, but I ain't one of them,' Jake drawled, holding his ex-friend's gaze. 'Now back the fuck off before someone gets hurt.'

'See, that's your problem right there,' Alex sneered, backing up a step and lighting a cigarette. 'You always thought you was the boss, but you forget who let you into this crew in the first place. If I hadn't give you a leg-up after you got loose from nick, you'd be face down in a sewer right now, never mind standing here like some kind of fuckin' Armani mannequin.'

Out of the corner of his eye, Jake saw the man who was sitting behind the desk reach into the drawer and take out a hefty brass knuckleduster. Guessing that he was about to get a kicking when the man got up and walked over to flank Alex, he flashed a quick look at the twins. Relieved to see them still seated on the sofa, both wearing inane grins as if they thought they were watching a film, he slid the gun he was carrying out of his waistband.

'Tell your goon to take a seat, or this won't end well,' he warned.

'You reckon?' A slow smile lifted Alex's lip.

'Well, I'm the one who's packing, so I'd say so, yeah,' said Jake. Then, parroting Alex, he said, 'See, that's your problem right there . . . you don't think before you act, you just jump right into things without planning ahead.'

'Oh, I planned,' Alex said almost proudly, narrowing his eyes as smoke swirled up from his nostrils. 'First I tracked you down, then I watched you, and then I nabbed your bird – who you haven't even asked about since you got here, by the way.' He turned his head and grinned at the thug who was smacking the knuckleduster into the palm of his hand. 'Must be love, eh?'

Jake lurched forward and shoved the gun up against Alex's throat. 'Where is she, you cocky twat?'

Alex gave the slightest jerk of his head to knuckleduster. 'Show him.'

The man reached across and turned the laptop around. Jake stared at the image on the screen and gritted his teeth when he saw Leanne sitting on a straight-backed chair in the middle of an empty room. Her ankles were bound to the legs of the chair by what looked like rope, and her hands were behind her, no doubt also bound. Even from a distance and without the benefit of sound, it was clear to Jake that she was crying, and he was so maddened by the sight it took every ounce of his willpower not to squeeze the trigger.

Alex had been studying Jake's expression with a malicious glint in his eyes. Grinning when Jake dropped his hand after several moments, he snatched the gun before slapping his cheek in a mock-friendly gesture.

'Good lad; knew you'd see sense once you realized who's in charge.' He pushed his chest out now and walked slowly around Jake, cracking his knuckles as he went. 'You know I could have whacked you ages ago, if I'd wanted to?' he said – as if, Jake thought, he expected Jake to be grateful that he hadn't. 'But I'm smarter than that.' He jabbed a fingertip into his temple. 'You're not the only one who's got a brain, see. I've been planning this for a while.'

'Good for you,' said Jake.

'Oh, it *will* be,' Alex sneered. 'Soon as I get what's mine. You might have thought you'd got away with shafting me, but I was only biding my time. And now *your* time's up, matey.'

Bemused by his ex-friend's hard-man posture, when they both knew that Jake would have kicked the living shit out of him by now if Leanne weren't being used as bait, Jake said, 'Spit it out, man. What you after?'

'*That*, for starters.' Alex nodded at the four CCTV screens set into the wall behind the desk, on the third of which Jake's car was pictured.

Jake pulled the keys out of his pocket and tossed them over. 'Have it.'

'Ta.' Alex gave a victorious smile as he pocketed them. 'Now I'll have the rest.'

'Rest of what?'

'*Every*thing.' Alex pushed his smirking face into Jake's. 'I know you're still shifting gear, so I'll have that for starters.'

'I thought the motor was for starters?'

'Do *not* fuck with me,' Alex warned, baring his teeth as he waved the gun under Jake's nose. 'You might have got away with treating me like a muppet back in the day, but *I'm* in control now, and you'll do as you're fuckin' told or *she'll* be sleeping in a box under my fuckin' bed from now on.' He jerked his head at the laptop. 'And just in case you think I'm messing, watch!' He pulled his mobile out of his pocket.

Unable to do anything else, Jake stared at the laptop as Alex made a call, letting it ring twice before cutting it off. Almost immediately, Alex's sister, Sylvie, appeared on the screen behind Leanne. With a quick glance at the camera, as if to make sure she was in shot, she threw an arm around Leanne's neck and, pulling her head right back, sank her teeth into Leanne's cheek.

'Fuck me!' Alex chuckled, mock-wincing as he watched. 'She a mad cunt, her. Wouldn't leave your bird with her for too long, if I was you, JP. Never know what might happen.'

Jake's stomach churned as Leanne thrashed around, her mouth opened wide in a scream they couldn't hear. Releasing her after a moment, Sylvie walked around to the front of the chair and kicked her in the stomach, so hard the chair toppled over.

'All right, enough!' Jake barked when Sylvie drew her foot back to kick out again. 'Take whatever you want, just call her off and bring Leanne to me.'

'Now we're talking!' Alex grinned and pressed redial on his phone.

Still staring at the screen, Jake saw a look of disappointment cross Sylvie's grainy face when her phone flashed. She and Alex had clearly worked this system out in advance: first call, give Leanne some welly; second, back off. *Third . . .*

Jake wasn't about to let it get that far.

'Sit down!' Alex ordered, shoving Jake roughly towards the desk before yanking a sheet of paper out of the ancient printer that was sitting on top of the filing cabinet. 'I know what a slippery cunt you are, so I want this in writing.' He slapped the paper down on the desk and flicked a biro at Jake. 'I, Jake Pearce . . .' he dictated.

'You're not serious?' Jake almost laughed out loud.

RUN

'Do as you're fuckin' told!' Alex yelled, smashing the gun into the side of his head. 'Or I swear to God I'll do you, and then I'll rip your bird in half with my fuckin' dick!'

29

Leanne's face was ashen as Jake helped her out of the goods lift half an hour later. With a firm arm around her waist to keep her legs from buckling, he walked her out through the gates and down the road away from the warehouse.

'I can't do this,' she moaned, clutching at his arm with one hand and cradling her stomach with the other. 'I need to sit down.'

'Just a little further,' Jake urged, his gaze flicking every which way as they walked on.

When they turned the corner, Leanne pulled up short when she saw two black Range Rovers parked up with their engines running. 'It's them!' she squealed, her legs almost giving way with terror when four muscular men dressed in black climbed out. 'They're going to kill us!'

'No, they're not, these guys work for me,' Jake reassured her as he led her to the first vehicle and helped her on to the passenger seat. 'Try to relax. Pete'll take you home.'

'Where are you going?' She clutched at his hand. 'You can't go back in there! Please, Jake, they'll kill you!'

'I won't be long,' he promised, holding firmly on to her wrist to slide his hand free of her grasp.

'Don't go!' she pleaded, tears streaming down her cheeks.

'Listen . . .' Jake cupped her bruised cheek gently in his hand and gazed into her eyes. 'If I let them get away with this, they'll only do it again, and I can't let them hurt you. Do you understand?'

'What are you going to do?'

'Whatever it takes to get the message across. Now relax. I've got this, and I'll be home soon. Okay?'

Leanne could do nothing but nod her agreement, though her heart was pounding so loudly she couldn't hear anything else as Jake closed the door. Looking through the window when the driver set off, she shivered when she saw Jake and his security guards walk stealthily around the corner. Covering her mouth with her hand when she noticed that one of them was carrying a petrol can, she squeezed her eyes shut and prayed that they weren't going to do anything stupid.

*

Leanne was silent on the journey home. She'd felt so happy and secure when she'd set out this morning, but in the space of a few hours her whole world had been turned upside down.

She and Jake had been living together for several months

and she had seen no evidence of the supposed drug dealing that the vicious bitch who'd bitten and kicked her had said he was involved in. The woman had also claimed that Jake had stolen thousands of pounds off her brother before doing a runner, and that he was supposed to have spent time in prison – none of which he'd told Leanne about.

The ache in her stomach had turned into stabbing pains by the time they reached the apartment, and her cheek was throbbing painfully. All she wanted to do was go inside and lock the door on the world, so she wasn't happy when the driver informed her that Jake had told him to stay with her until he returned. She didn't want this stranger in her home; his very presence was a reminder that Jake wasn't the man she'd thought him to be. But, more than that, she needed time alone to put her jumbled thoughts into order.

'Okay, I'll stay in the car,' the man agreed when she told him that she'd rather he didn't come inside. 'But if anything happens, come to the window. I can be up there in seconds.'

Unnerved that he seemed to think it would be easy to get through the heavy security door, Leanne hobbled up to the apartment. After letting herself in, she went into the bedroom and sat tentatively down on the bed when another pain rippled through her stomach. Placing both hands over it, she rocked herself until it passed, then stood up to go to the bathroom. Panicking when she saw blood on the duvet cover, she looked around for her handbag to get her mobile, but remembered that the man had taken it from her when he'd shoved her into the van. Tears streaming down her cheeks as it occurred to her that she might be losing the baby, she stumbled into the living room to use the landline instead.

30

Chrissie and Ben were sitting in the corridor outside Leanne's room when Jake arrived at the hospital later that afternoon.

'Where is she?' he asked, his eyes dark with concern.

'In there.' Chrissie jerked her head towards the room behind them. 'The doctor's with her.'

Jake glanced at the door, but the blind had been pulled down so he couldn't see through. 'Have they said anything?' he asked. 'About the baby?'

Chrissie shook her head sadly. 'I'm sorry. She'd already lost it by the time we got here.'

Ben stood up and gave Jake an awkward hug. 'So sorry, mate. But she's in the best place and they'll take good care of her, so try not to worry too much. Do you want a coffee while we're waiting?'

Jake nodded and flopped down on to a chair as Ben went off in search of a drinks machine. Resting his elbows on his knees, he dropped his head into his hands.

'She'll be okay,' Chrissie said quietly. 'They've got the bleeding under control now. They are a bit concerned about the bruises, though,' she added pointedly. 'She's got a massive one on her stomach, and what looks like a bite mark on her cheek.'

He'd said he was at work when Ben had called to tell him Leanne was in hospital, and didn't, therefore, know what had happened to her.

Frowning when he sensed a hint of accusation in her tone, Jake said, 'I hope you don't think *I* did it?'

'No, of course not,' Chrissie replied, her words contradicting the suspicion in her eyes. 'Leanne told us she got jumped in the park. I just think it's a bit odd that something like that could happen in broad daylight and nobody was around to help her. Every time I've been at yours in the daytime, we always hear kids in the park.'

'It wasn't me,' Jake said flatly. 'I love that girl, and I would *never* hurt her.'

Chrissie held his gaze for several seconds, then patted his hand. 'Okay, I believe you. And I'm sorry if it sounded like I was blaming you, but . . .'

She tailed off when the door to Leanne's room opened, and Jake quickly stood up when the doctor came out.

'How is she?' he asked. 'I'm the dad,' he explained when the woman drew her head back. 'I was at work when I heard. Is there any chance it's still—'

'I'm afraid not,' the doctor interrupted kindly.

Jake breathed in deeply and ran his hands through his hair.

Then, nodding, he said, 'Thanks. I appreciate your honesty. So what now?'

'I'm assuming your friends have told you what happened to your wife?'

'That she got jumped in the park? Yeah, they told me.'

'I've spoken to Leanne about reporting it to the police, but she says she needs time to think about it,' the doctor said quietly. 'I'd urge you to persuade her, if you can, because this was a serious assault.'

'I'll talk to her,' Jake agreed. 'Can I see her now?'

'Yes, but make it quick; she'll be going to theatre for a D and C shortly.'

'What the hell's a D and C?' Jake asked Chrissie when the doctor went off to see another patient.

'They're going to scrape her womb,' she explained. 'They need to make sure it's all gone, otherwise she might get infected.'

Jake blew out a loud breath and shook his head. 'This shouldn't be happening. I was supposed to protect her.'

'It's not your fault,' Chrissie said firmly. 'You were working, so there was nothing you could have done.'

'I should have been with her,' Jake countered guiltily. 'She only told me about the baby last week, and I promised to take some time off.'

'You weren't to know something like this was going to happen,' Chrissie pointed out. 'Anyway, Leanne knows how important your work is, so she probably wouldn't have wanted you to. Not yet, anyway.'

Jake gave her a sad smile. 'I know you're right, but I can't help the way I feel.'

Ben came back just then carrying three lidded Styrofoam cups of coffee. 'Is everything all right?' he asked when he saw the glum expressions on their faces.

'The doc just came out,' Jake told him. 'They'll be taking her to theatre soon, so I need to see her. Will you two wait out here for a minute?'

'Actually, we should probably get going,' Chrissie said, glancing at the clock on the wall. 'Mrs Ford picked Dylan up from nursery, and I said we'd try not to be too long. Give Leanne our love, and tell her I'll come and see her in the morning.'

Nodding, Jake thanked them and watched as they walked away, Ben still carrying all three cups. Then, taking a deep breath, he made his way into Leanne's room.

She was lying there, staring up at the ceiling with tears trickling down her cheeks. Pulling a chair up beside the bed, he sat down and took her hand in his.

'Don't cry, sweetheart.'

'What do you expect?' she croaked without looking at him, her hand unresponsive to his squeezes. 'I've lost my b—' The word caught in her throat, and she swallowed deeply, before continuing. 'They're saying I might have internal injuries, and if it's bad, I might have to have a hysterectomy.'

'It won't come to that,' Jake said with a confidence that wasn't reflected in his eyes. 'And we can try for another baby whenever you're ready.'

'Just like that?' Leanne's voice was as hollow as the expression on her face. 'As if this one was . . . *what*? Some kind of practice run?'

'Of course not,' Jake murmured. 'I wanted it as much as you did, and it's killing me to see you like this, knowing it's my fault.'

Leanne slid her hand free and looked him coldly in the eye.

'Please don't look at me like that,' he begged.

'Why not? Like you said, it's *your* fault. Those *friends* of yours,' she spat the word out, 'told me all about the drugs, and you spending time in prison.'

'They're no friends of mine, and you can't believe a word they say,' Jake retorted angrily. 'They're the criminals, not me. Why do you think I cut ties with them and moved back to Manchester?'

'If you've done nothing wrong, why did you agree to sign everything over to them?'

'To stop them from hurting *you*. But don't worry, I got the paper off them.'

'How?' Leanne demanded. 'What happened after you sent me home, Jake?'

Jake pursed his lips and inhaled deeply through his nose. Then, exhaling loudly, he said, 'If you really want to know, I forced them to hand it over.'

'*How?*' Leanne asked again.

'The details aren't important.'

'They are to me.'

'Okay, we beat them up,' Jake admitted. Frowning when she flashed him a disapproving look, he reached for her hand again. 'Come on, Lee, what was I *supposed* to do? Look what they did to you. I couldn't let them get away with that. And they'd have done it again the next time they ran out of money if I hadn't taught them a lesson.'

'So you and your thugs beat them up, and I'm supposed to believe that's the end of it?'

'I guarantee they will *never* come after you again,' Jake said adamantly. 'And when you come home, I'm going to make sure you never have to worry about anything from this day on.'

Leanne closed her eyes for a second, then, sighing wearily, stared up at the ceiling again. 'I'm tired. I think you should go now.'

'Please don't blame me,' Jake implored. 'If I'd had any inkling they were going to pull a stunt like this, I wouldn't have let them get within a mile of you.'

'If you'd been honest with me in the first place, I might have been prepared,' countered Leanne. 'Now will you please go? I need to think about what I'm going to say to the police.'

'The police?' Jake's frown deepened.

Nostrils flaring as she struggled to contain the tears, Leanne said, 'The doctor reckons I shouldn't let the *muggers* get away with killing my baby. If I had my way, I'd tell them exactly who did it,' she went on angrily. 'But I can't, can I? Not until I know what part *you* really played in it all.'

'I swear to God it had nothing to do with me,' Jake insisted. 'They're just bitter because I made a success of my life.'

'They knew too much about you for it all to be lies,' Leanne snapped. 'And that made me realize that *I* don't really know you at all.'

Aware that he wasn't getting anywhere by fobbing her off, Jake held up his hands. 'Okay, if you want the truth, I'll tell you everything. Some of what they said is right: I *did* deal drugs, but not for long. It was after I got out of prison. I'd already lost touch with my old man, and my mum was shacked up with some bloke I couldn't stand, so I had nowhere to go. I'd shared a cell with Alex, and he'd told me to get in touch if I ever needed a place to stay, so I kipped on his sofa for a few months. He was mates with the guy who owned that club, and when he heard it was getting sold off he asked me if I wanted to buy into it with him. It was a bargain, so it seemed like a good idea, but I knew I'd made a mistake when Alex started using the place to shift powders. That's why I called it a day. I'd saved enough by then, so I came back here and started the security business. And I've been legit ever since – I swear.'

A frown creased Leanne's brow as she listened to his version of events. It sounded plausible, and she was sure she would have known if he'd been involved in anything illegal while she'd been with him. But he'd still lied to her, and that had placed her in a vulnerable position, resulting in her losing their baby.

'I know you're disappointed in me,' Jake said, stroking her hair. 'But the only reason I didn't tell you about my past was because I was ashamed. I'm not that person now – you know that.'

'I don't know *what* I know any more,' Leanne said wearily. 'You need to go home.'

'Okay, I'll go,' Jake relented. 'But call me as soon as you're ready to talk. I'll be waiting.'

Leanne nodded, and then closed her eyes. Leaning over, Jake kissed her softly on the lips before backing out of the room.

31

Leanne was discharged from the hospital a couple of days later, and Jake pushed her down to the car in a wheelchair.

Sitting stiffly in the passenger seat when he joined her after returning the chair, she said, 'Take me to Chrissie's.'

'But I've got everything ready for you at home,' he argued, his disappointment clear in his eyes. 'And I've lined Ben up to take care of the businesses for a couple of weeks so I can spend some time with you. I've missed you.'

'I'm not ready,' she said. 'I need a break.'

'From me?'

'From *every*thing.'

'Don't cut me out,' Jake pleaded. 'I love you, and I know you still love me.'

'Of course I do,' Leanne replied quietly. 'But I don't feel safe going back there just yet.'

'I won't leave your side,' Jake promised. 'Nobody will get near you.'

'I can't face it,' she said with finality. 'Anyway, you need to work.'

'Sod work,' he said. 'How about a holiday? We can go wherever you like. As long as it's somewhere warm,' he added with a hopeful grin. 'I don't do snow.'

'I don't need a holiday,' she murmured. 'I need some time on my own.'

Jake could tell that she wasn't going to change her mind, so he flapped his hands in a gesture of surrender. 'Okay, fine, I'll take you to Chrissie's. If that's what you really want.'

She nodded, relieved that he wasn't going to try and talk her round.

*

Chrissie was only too happy to take Leanne in. She and Ben had recently redecorated her old bedroom for Dylan, but she ordered Ben to move Dylan's fold-down bed into their room so Leanne could stay.

'I'll go back to my place,' Ben offered. 'Give you two some space.'

'You don't have to do that,' Leanne said guiltily. 'If it's a problem, I can stay on my mum and dad's sofa.'

'You're going nowhere,' Chrissie said bossily. 'Ben doesn't mind – do you, Ben?'

'Of course not,' he agreed, giving Leanne a conspiratorial grin as he added, 'It'll give me a chance to get some proper sleep without *her* snoring down my ear.'

Aware that he was teasing, Chrissie gave him a playful shove and sent him upstairs to get the bedroom ready.

'Are you sure this is okay?' Leanne asked.

'Positive,' Chrissie said, sitting beside her. 'You need looking after.'

Perched on the armchair facing them, Jake felt like a spare part as he watched the girls share a hug. Leanne's place was at home with him, but he supposed it was understandable that she'd be nervous after everything that had happened.

Glancing at him, Chrissie sensed that he was struggling and quickly stood up. 'I'm going to check on Ben,' she said diplomatically.

Gazing over at Jake when they were alone, Leanne said, 'I know you're not happy about this, but I need a bit of time.'

'I know.' He sighed. 'And I don't blame you. I'm just hoping it won't be for too long.'

'Me too,' she murmured, unable to give him anything better than that. 'I do still love you,' she assured him when she saw the look of defeat in his eyes. 'But it hurts to know you've been lying to me.'

'I haven't,' Jake insisted, coming over and squatting down in front of her. Placing his hands on her knees, he said, 'The only reason I didn't tell you everything was because I didn't think the past was important. I probably should have,' he went on resignedly. 'And I promise I'll never keep anything from you again. I know it's going to take time to regain your trust, so I won't pester you. But promise me you'll call me if you need anything.'

Leanne nodded her agreement, and Jake kissed her on the cheek then made his way out into the hall, calling goodbye to Chrissie and Ben before letting himself out.

When, shortly after, Ben also left, Chrissie took a bottle of wine out of the fridge and carried it and a couple of glasses into the living room.

'Isn't it a bit early for that?' Leanne asked. 'You've got to pick Dylan up from nursery in a couple of hours.'

'Ben's going to get him and take him to McDonald's, then back to his place for a bit,' said Chrissie, passing a glass to her after pouring their drinks. 'So . . . do you want to talk, or would you rather watch some old films?'

Leanne dipped her gaze and took a sip of wine. It was obvious that Chrissie hadn't believed her story about getting mugged in the park, but she couldn't tell her the truth. If she knew what had really happened, Chrissie would pressurize her into calling the police. As upset as she still was with Jake, and as raw as the pain of losing her baby still was, Leanne didn't want Jake to get into trouble for whatever he'd done to her attackers after sending her home that day, so it was safer to keep her mouth shut.

'Old films, please,' she said.

Nodding, Chrissie reached for the TV remote and switched the set on.

*

Feeling a lot more relaxed when Ben called round to drop a very sleepy Dylan off later that evening, Leanne decided to have an early night. She hadn't slept properly during her time in hospital for fear of Jake's enemies finding out where she was and coming after her again, so she was absolutely exhausted. Soothed by the sound of Chrissie's soft voice as her friend read Dylan a bedtime story in the next room, she quickly fell asleep.

32

After a week at Chrissie's, Leanne was slowly beginning to feel like her old self again. It had been great to spend time with her friend, and she'd enjoyed watching Dylan run around. Under the loving care of his Annie Kiss Kiss – as he still called Chrissie – he'd blossomed into a secure, happy little boy, and it was lovely to see him thriving. Although it did upset her at times when she watched him play with his toy cars, eat the tuna pasta he seemed to want for dinner every day, or even just lie on the sofa watching cartoons, because it was a sharp reminder that she would never get to see her own child do any of those things. Clinging to the knowledge that her injuries hadn't robbed her of the chance to be a mother in the future, she made a conscious effort to stop thinking about what might have been and, instead, concentrate on working through her issues with Jake.

The day after she'd arrived at Chrissie's, she'd seen a report on the local news about a blaze at an old warehouse in Liverpool in which three bodies had – so far – been found. She'd

been in too much shock that day to take notice of her sur-
roundings, so she couldn't say for sure that the ruined building
they showed, which had still been blazing at the time of filming, was the place where she'd been held prisoner. Surely it
would be too much of a coincidence for it to be unrelated?

Jake had denied that he was behind it when she'd confronted
him on the phone later that evening, but her instincts told her
that he was lying. Ashamed to admit that she'd have been glad
if it was her attackers who'd died because they deserved it after
killing her baby, she resolved to accept Jake's word and try not
to dwell on it. But it wasn't so easy to forget that it was his fault
it had happened in the first place. And the longer they were
apart, the more she began to fear that their relationship might
never get back to where it had been before the attack.

That was what she was thinking about as she made herself a
cup of coffee shortly after Chrissie had left for work at the
beginning of the second week. Tired of going over the same
old ground, she carried her drink into the living room and
switched the TV on, hoping to forget her own problems for an
hour by watching other people air their dirty laundry on the
Jeremy Kyle Show. But Jeremy hadn't even introduced his first
guest before the phone rang, and when Leanne heard her
mother's frantic voice, her own woes evaporated in an instant.

'Oh, love, thank God you're there!' her mum cried. 'I've
been trying your mobile all night, but it seems to be switched
off. I found Chrissie's number in an old address book and
thought I'd give her a ring to see if she knew where you were.'

'I lost my phone,' Leanne lied. 'What's wrong?'

'It's your dad,' her mum replied shakily. 'He's in intensive care.'

'*What?*' Leanne felt as if she'd been punched in the gut. '*Why?*'

'He went to the pub last night to meet up with some of his old mates from the 'leccy board,' her mum explained. 'And someone jumped him on that wasteland by the canal on his way home. They left him for dead, love. He's in a terrible state, and they're not sure if he's going to make it.'

'Where are you?' Leanne asked, slamming the cup down and leaping to her feet. 'I'll be there as soon as I can.'

Remembering that she didn't have money to take a cab or even a bus to the hospital, Leanne rang Jake after speaking with her mother.

'Where are you?'

'Longsight,' he told her, concern coming into his voice when he heard the panic in hers. 'What's wrong? Has something happened?'

'My dad's in intensive care and I need to go to him, but I've got no money,' she cried, her eyes swimming with tears. 'Can you pick me up?'

'Of course I can,' Jake agreed without hesitation. 'I'll be there in ten minutes.'

*

Half an hour later, Leanne jumped out of Jake's car at the hospital's main entrance and ran inside, leaving him to go and find a parking space. Making her way up in the lift to the ICU, she grabbed the first nurse she saw.

'My mum told me that my dad was brought in last night. His name's Norman Riley.'

'Come with me,' the nurse said quietly.

Fearing the worst when she saw sympathy in the woman's eyes, Leanne's legs felt like jelly as she followed her to a room at the other end of the small ward.

Her dad was lying in the bed with a tube down his throat and an IV line in one of his tattooed arms. Several sensor pads were stuck to his chest, their wires connecting him to a beeping ECG monitor that was standing beside the bed. Gasping in horror when her gaze came to rest on his battered, swollen face, Leanne covered her mouth with both hands.

'Oh, love, don't cry.' Her mum rose from her seat on the other side of the bed and came round to hold her. 'They say he can probably still hear us, so we've got to try and stay positive.'

'How could anyone *do* this to him?' Leanne whispered, unable to find anything positive to say as she took in his injuries. 'He was in a wheelchair, for God's sake. It's pure evil!'

'The police think he was probably followed from the pub,' Brenda murmured, gazing down sadly at her husband. 'They're going to try and track his movements from CCTV footage of the area, see if they can spot anything unusual.'

'I hope they find the bastards and throw away the key,' Leanne hissed, making an effort to pull herself together.

A small tap came at the door, and Brenda managed a tiny smile when she saw that it was Jake.

'Oh, hello, love. I didn't realize you were here. Come in.'

'Jake drove me over,' Leanne said, pulling a tissue out of her pocket and blowing her nose. Looking at him now, she said, 'Thanks so much for getting me here so fast, but you don't have to stay if you need to get back to work?'

'I'm not leaving you,' he said firmly, pulling her into his arms.

Relieved, because she hadn't wanted him to go, Leanne rested her head on his chest.

'Do they know who did it?' Jake asked Brenda.

'Not yet. But the police are checking CCTV footage, so I'm praying they'll pick something up from that.'

'I'll get my lads to ask around,' said Jake. 'I'm sure we'll find someone who knows something.'

Stiffening at the reminder of his security guards, Leanne muttered, 'No! I don't want you getting involved in this. Let the police deal with it.'

'I won't do anything you don't want me to,' he assured her. 'But the offer's there if you change your mind.'

Nodding, Leanne looked at her dad for several long moments before turning to her mum. She looked so sad and lost, it was heartbreaking.

'How long have you been here?' she asked.

'Since about four this morning,' said Brenda. 'Some blokes who were going fishing found him, and I got a lift off the coppers who came to tell me.'

'Why don't you go home for a bit?' Leanne suggested. 'We'll stay with Dad, and I can ring you if there's any change.'

'I'm staying,' Brenda said flatly. 'I promised to stand by him for better or worse, and I'm not going to break my vows for the sake of a bit of sleep.'

'Okay,' Leanne conceded, all too aware that nothing would change her mum's mind once it was made up. 'Have you eaten anything yet?'

'I'm not hungry.'

'How about a drink, then?'

'Fine.' Brenda sighed. 'If it makes you feel better, I'll have a hot chocolate.'

Telling her that she'd be back in a minute, Leanne took Jake's hand, and they went to look for a drinks machine. As they reached the doors at the end of the ward, two nurses jumped up from behind the desk and ran past them, and Leanne's stomach flipped with dread when she realized they were heading towards her dad's room.

'What's happening?' she cried, rushing after them. 'Is he okay? *Mum . . . ?*'

Unable to speak, Brenda clutched at Leanne's arm and pulled her out of the way as one of the nurses pressed a red button on the wall behind the bed, adding a second alarm to the one already sounding from the monitor.

Ushered out of the room when the resus team arrived a few seconds later, Leanne and her mum paced the floor while Jake took a seat; Leanne chewing on her nails, Brenda mouthing silent prayers.

The door was shut, so they couldn't see what was happening. But after an agonizing ten-minute wait, it finally opened, and one of the nurses walked out.

'I'm so sorry, Mrs Riley,' she said. 'Your husband went into cardiac arrest and we weren't able to resuscitate him.'

'*Noooo . . .*' Brenda wailed, her face crumpling as she tried to shove the nurse back into the room. 'You didn't try hard enough! Go in and try again! You can't leave him like that!'

The nurse looked at Jake and Leanne and gave the slightest shake of her head.

'Mum, don't,' Leanne sobbed, putting her arms around her mother. 'There's nothing they can do.'

As they cried in each other's arms, Jake wrapped his own arms around them both and nodded to the nurse over the tops of their heads. 'Thanks, love. We know you did your best.'

*

When they finally left the hospital several hours later, Leanne didn't want to leave her mum, and Jake didn't want to leave Leanne, so they cuddled up together on her mum's sofa after driving back to the bungalow.

Aware that Brenda was going to need help to register the death and arrange the funeral, they got up early the following morning to talk about arrangements. Leanne said that she wanted to stay with her mum at least until they'd got the funeral over with, so Jake agreed to pick her stuff up from Chrissie's. But as he was about to head over there, Brenda's sister, Gloria, arrived.

No longer needing them, as Gloria had buried three husbands and knew exactly what to do, Brenda thanked Leanne and Jake for helping her, then insisted that they go home and get some rest.

As they got into the car, Jake asked whether she wanted him to drop her at Chrissie's, but she shook her head.

'I want to go home,' she said. 'If that's okay?'

'Do you even need to ask?' he replied, unable to keep the grin off his lips as he started the engine.

When they got to the apartment, Leanne gazed around in amazement. There were vases of flowers on every surface, some in full bloom, while others were beginning to wilt, which told her they'd been there for a while.

'I got them when you were discharged from hospital,' Jake told her, explaining why they were past their best. 'I thought it might cheer you up when you got home, but you decided to go to Chrissie's, so they were kind of wasted.'

'I'm sorry,' Leanne murmured guiltily. 'I had no idea you'd gone to all this trouble.'

'Hey, forget it,' Jake said softly as he pulled her into his arms. 'You're home now; that's all that matters.'

Unable to resist a sudden urge to kiss him as she gazed into his soft brown eyes, Leanne felt the last of her resistance melt away when he locked his lips on to hers and carried her into the bedroom.

After they'd made love, Jake ran a bath for her and told her to relax while he made breakfast. As she soaked in the water, listening to Jake pottering around in the kitchen, Leanne knew that coming home had been the right decision. She'd been blaming Jake for what had happened, but those thugs who had kidnapped her were part of his past, not his present, and it wasn't fair to judge him as if he still belonged to that world when he'd made the conscious decision to remove himself from it.

He'd been so gentle last night, holding her as she cried for her father, and she loved him all the more for the kindness he'd displayed towards her grieving mum.

And so, it seemed, did her mum, who – unaware of what had happened, because Leanne had decided not to tell her about the baby – had called Leanne into the kitchen before they left and told her that Jake was 'a keeper'.

She'd been spot on, and Leanne had decided there and then that it was time to stop punishing him for things he'd had no control over.

33

The next few weeks were difficult, as Leanne and her mum waited for the police to release her father's body for burial. They still hadn't caught his attacker – or, more likely, *attackers*, since Norman had been quite capable of defending himself against one man, even in his wheelchair.

Jake didn't leave Leanne's side for the whole of that time, and she was grateful for his strength as her own frequently deserted her.

When at last the day of the funeral came around – which Jake had instead on paying for, and at which he, along with some of the workmates Norman had been drinking with the night he was attacked, carried the coffin – Jake escorted Leanne, her mum and her Aunt Gloria to Norman's local after the service to join the other mourners in a buffet lunch, which he'd also paid for.

Chrissie and Ben were already there when they arrived, and Chrissie smiled when she saw Leanne and Jake's hands locked together.

'I'm so glad you've sorted things out,' she said as she gave Leanne a hug. 'Me and Ben were starting to get a bit worried for a while there; thought we were never going to get rid of you.'

Grateful to her friend for lifting her spirits on this gloomiest of days, Leanne smiled, and said, 'Shut it, or I'll come home with you tonight.'

'You will not,' Jake interjected, looping an arm around her shoulder when Chrissie had let go. 'I've only just got you back, and I'm not letting you out of my sights again.'

'Yeah, well, you'd best make sure you look after her properly this time,' Chrissie warned, only half joking. 'Any more non-sense and you'll have me to deal with.'

Amused, Jake grinned and shook his head when Chrissie linked an arm through Leanne's and guided her towards a table, leaving him and Ben to get drinks for them all.

'I'm surprised you're still hanging in there, kiddo,' he teased, clapping Ben on the back. 'Thought she'd have eaten you up and spat you out by now.'

'She's not that tough when you get to know her,' Ben said loyally, shoving his hands into his pockets as they made their way to the bar. 'We're actually really happy.'

'Good for you,' said Jake. 'I mean it,' he added sincerely when Ben raised an eyebrow as if waiting for a sarcastic follow-up. 'You deserve it.'

Ben cast a quick look around, then murmured, 'I bumped

into Sally the other day, and she asked me to tell you to call in. She had the lad with her.'

'Not now.' Jake frowned.

Before Ben could say anything else, Brenda walked past, and Jake reached out and put a hand on her arm. Asking her if he could have a quick word, he told Ben to get the drinks in before steering her out through the doors and into the pub garden.

'Where's Jake,' Leanne asked when Ben carried their drinks to the table a few minutes later.

'He's talking to your mum,' Ben told her as he squeezed in beside Chrissie. 'I think they went outside.'

'Bless him.' Leanne sighed. 'He's been so good to her this week. She thinks the world of him. And my dad quite liked him, too.'

'That says a lot.' Chrissie smiled. 'He wasn't one for bullshit, your dad; proper straight-talker.'

'He was, wasn't he?' Leanne said softly, her eyes misting up all over again at the thought of her lovely father.

'Too much so, at times,' Chrissie said drily. 'Remember when we were fifteen and everyone was getting into tying hoodies round their waists and wearing their baseball caps the wrong way round? I thought I looked dead cool in mine, but your dad took one look at me and asked if I'd turned lesbian. "Not that there's owt wrong with it if you have, love," she added in an imitation of Norman Riley's gruff voice. '"But I can't say I'm too keen on the butch look you've gone for!"'

'He was a right one!' Leanne laughed. 'I remember back-combing my hair one time when we were going to The Ritz. I thought I looked really sexy, but he said I looked like I'd been dragged through a hedge then pushed back in for more.'

'Sounds like a character,' said Ben.

'Oh, he was!' both women said in unison.

A sudden hush fell over the crowded pub, and all eyes turned towards the bar, where Jake was helping Brenda to stand on a chair.

'I, um, just wanted to thank you all for coming along today,' she addressed the room nervously, adopting the posh voice that she saved for special occasions – and which Norman had always teased her about. 'I'm sure you can imagine how diffi-cult these last few weeks have been for myself and Leanne. Where is she, by the way?' She glanced around and raised a hand to wave Leanne over when she spotted her. 'Come here, love; this involves you, too.'

'Right, where was I?' she continued when Leanne was standing beside her. 'Oh, yes ... thank you all for coming today. Norman would have been blown away to see so many people paying their respects.'

'Norman!' a man in the crowd called out, raising his beer glass in a toast.

'Norman!' the rest echoed.

'He was a good man,' Brenda went on. 'And I was proud to stand by his side for forty years, because I couldn't have asked for a better husband. If you were his friend, he'd give you the shirt off his back, but if you wronged him, or – God forbid – hurt me or our girl, he'd be your very worst enemy.'

'You're not wrong there,' someone chuckled.

Brenda gave the speaker an approving smile, then continued: 'I only ever saw the best of him, and he brought out the best in me. And we were – *are* – both so very proud of our beautiful daughter.' She gazed lovingly down at Leanne now, who had to sniff back her tears as she reached up to squeeze her mum's hand. 'You were always a daddy's girl, and I know he'll have been watching over you these last few weeks, making sure that Jake's looking after you as well as your dad always looked after me. I also know he'd be very happy to . . .' Tailing off at this, she cast a quick glance at Jake, before saying, 'No, I won't ruin it. Over to you, love.'

Jake stepped forward and gave a sheepish smile at the crowd before saying, 'This isn't quite how I planned it, but Brenda insisted, so, I, um, couldn't exactly refuse, could I? Thing is . . .' He turned to Leanne now and peered into her bewildered eyes. 'I was gearing myself up to talk to your dad when . . . you know.' He smiled sadly. 'Anyway, I decided to ask Brenda instead, and she's given me her blessing, so . . .' He paused and swallowed nervously before pulling a little box out of his pocket. 'Leanne Riley' – he dropped to one knee – 'will you marry me?'

Unable to speak as tears spilled down her cheeks, Leanne covered her mouth with her hands and nodded.

'Is that a yes?' He grinned.

'Yes!' she cried, dropping to her own knees and throwing her arms around him.

'To my girl and my soon-to-be son-in-law!' Brenda beamed, raising her glass. 'And to my Norman,' she added, raising her eyes to the ceiling.

Back at the table, Chrissie raised her glass along with everyone else, but there was a hint of concern in her eyes. Seeing it, Ben leaned towards her, and whispered, 'You okay?'

'Yeah, I'm fine,' she whispered back. 'Just think it was a bit inappropriate to do something like that at a time like this.'

'To be fair, he did say Brenda insisted,' Ben reminded her. 'And Leanne seems happy enough, which can't be a bad thing if it takes her mind off grieving for a while.'

'Yeah, you're right,' Chrissie agreed. 'She's been through hell lately, and I should be happy for her. Jake loves the bones of her, and you can't ask for better than that, can you?'

Ben shook his head in agreement and took a sip of his pint, but a tiny frown was creasing his brow at the thought of how *un*happy Leanne would be if she ever found out about Sally and Jake's son. And how mad Chrissie was going to be with *him* if *she* ever found out. It didn't bear thinking about.

'Can you believe that?' Leanne gasped, rushing over to them. 'I had no idea!'

'Let me see it.' Chrissie held out her hand. Raising an approving eyebrow when she saw the huge diamond sparkling on Leanne's third finger, she murmured, '*Wow!* That's some serious rockage.'

'Isn't it gorgeous?' Leanne said proudly. 'And to think he chose it himself, in secret. He just amazes me.'

'Not as much as you amaze me,' Jake purred, coming up behind her and wrapping his arms around her. 'I've waited twenty years for this. It would have killed me if you'd said no.'

'As if!' She grinned. 'But you could have given me a hint. I've never been so shocked.'

'What, and ruin the surprise?' Jake scoffed. 'No chance. Oh, and, on the subject of surprises . . .' He let go of her and reached into his inside pocket. 'Remember that holiday I promised you?' He took out two tickets. 'How does a fortnight in Vegas sound?'

'Are you kidding?' Leanne gasped. 'I've always wanted to go there. My dad went there before he married my mum, and he used to talk about it all the time when I was a kid. How did you know?'

'A little bird told me.' Jake winked at Chrissie.

'Did I?' She frowned, unable to remember talking to him about that.

'Okay, maybe not directly,' Jake admitted. 'I overheard the pair of you having a conversation about it once, and the idea stuck.'

'When do we go?' Leanne asked, already excited.

'In two days,' said Jake. 'And don't worry,' he added when a flicker of doubt passed through her eyes. 'Your mum's fine with it. She thinks it'll do you good to get away for a while.'

'I agree,' said Chrissie. 'You've been through a lot this month, so a bit of sunshine will do you the world of good.'

'Sod the sunshine!' Leanne laughed. 'I'll be in the casino.'

Grinning as Leanne and Chrissie huddled together to discuss the upcoming holiday, Jake said thanks to several of Norman's old mates who came over to give him congratulatory slaps on the back and handshakes. As Chrissie had said, it had been a rough month for Leanne, but he'd never seen her as happy – or as beautiful – as she looked right now. And, if he had anything to do with it, she would stay that way for ever.

34

Left in charge of Jake's businesses while his friend was away, Ben had been leaving the house early each morning. After dealing with whatever maintenance needed doing on Jake's various properties, he had to meet with the guys from the security teams, to take whatever money they'd collected the previous night and sort out who was needed where that night.

The property side of things was no problem, but Ben wasn't so keen on the security side. The bouncers, doormen, or whatever they liked to call themselves, intimidated him. Not only were they all huge and extremely muscle-bound, which was the complete opposite of his own pudgy physique, they all looked at him as if he were some kind of bug they wanted to squash. He knew they wouldn't actually do anything and risk losing their jobs – Jake paid them too well for that – but it unnerved him all the same, and he couldn't wait for Jake to come home and take over the reins.

On the Saturday before Jake and Leanne were due home, Ben had received a call from the tenant of Jake's latest acquisition: a two-bedroom semi in Oldham. It was much further afield than his other properties, so Ben had to set off earlier than usual.

Chrissie was still sleeping when he was ready to leave. He didn't wake her, because she'd been doing overtime at the shop all week and had been rushed off her feet, so he knew she needed the rest. Tiptoeing out, he peeked in on Dylan, who was also sleeping, then quietly let himself out of the house.

It was dark outside, and quite cold, so he let the engine run for a few minutes after igniting it. Blowing on his hands to warm them as he waited, his thoughts drifted to Chrissie. After Jake's impromptu proposal at the wake, Ben had done a lot of thinking about his and Chrissie's relationship. He'd told Jake that they were very happy, and it was true. Chrissie was everything he could ever have hoped for in a woman: sexy, smart, strong, independent, and absolutely fantastic in bed. He'd baulked a little at her bossiness in the early days, when she had announced that he needed a complete overhaul and had chucked out all of his favourite corduroy trousers and replaced them with several pairs of jeans. But he supposed they weren't too bad once he'd got used to them. And he'd got used to his new haircut now, too – also by order of Chrissie. No longer floppy and out of control, his curls were neatly cropped and, admittedly, much easier to handle.

Bossiness aside, Chrissie really was the perfect woman. Ben had been seriously toying with the idea of making an honest woman of her, though he hadn't summoned up the courage to actually ask her yet. Or buy a ring. But he needed to do it soon, preferably before Jake and Leanne came home. Unlike Leanne, who hadn't minded the public proposal, Chrissie would die of embarrassment if Ben were to launch something like that on her while they were in company, so his proposal would have to be extremely low-key.

Telling himself that he needed to stop wasting time and get on with it, he resolved to call in at a jeweller's at some point during the day and start looking at rings. Although, God only knew how he was going to find out her ring size without alerting her as to his intentions.

Mulling that particular problem over as he set off, he didn't notice the shadowy figure lurking in the bushes two doors down.

*

Dylan had woken at the sound of Ben's car starting up, and he'd climbed out of bed and gone to the window to watch him drive away. About to return to the warmth of his quilt when the tail lights disappeared around the corner, he hesitated when he saw a woman dart out from the shadows of a clump of bushes and head quickly towards the house.

When she reached the gate, she looked up and gave a little wave when she saw him watching her. She said something, but Dylan couldn't hear her, so he pushed the window open an inch.

'Hey, Dyl,' she whispered. 'It's me . . . Mummy. Be a good lad and let me in, eh?'

Scared because he didn't know who she was and didn't like the look of her, Dylan quickly pulled the window shut again and ran into his aunt's room.

'Annie Kiss-Kiss,' he whispered, shaking her shoulder. 'There's a horrible lady outside.'

'Ugh?' Chrissie peeled an eye open and peered at him. ''S'up, love?'

'Horrible lady,' he repeated, pointing out into the hall. 'She says she's my mummy and telled me to open the door.'

'You what?' Instantly awake, Chrissie jerked into a sitting position and shoved the quilt off her legs.

'Come look,' Dylan said, taking her hand and tugging her into his bedroom.

Chrissie gazed out through his window and frowned when she saw the figure on the step below. At first she didn't recognize her, but when the woman looked up, her heart lurched in her chest and she quickly stepped back.

'Don't like her,' Dylan whispered, his eyes wide as he clung on to Chrissie's hand. 'She ugly.'

'Yes, she is,' Chrissie muttered. Then, pursing her lips, she said, 'Go back to bed, sweetie; I'll go and get rid of her. But don't come down,' she added firmly as she tucked him in. 'Okay?'

''Kay.' He nodded, peering up at her over the edge of the quilt.

*

Tina had assumed that Dylan was coming down to answer the door when he'd pulled the window shut, so it was a surprise to find herself face to face with Chrissie now.

'All right?' she said, her teeth chattering wildly as she forced a friendly grin.

Unable to disguise her shock, Chrissie took a moment to answer. 'What the hell have you done to yourself?' she managed at last, taking in Tina's sunken cheeks, her spot-ravaged complexion and missing front tooth. 'You look terrible.'

'Yeah, nice to see you, too,' Tina replied sharply, as if it wasn't the reaction she'd expected.

Stiffening, Chrissie folded her arms. 'What do you want, Tina?'

'Where's Mum?' Tina asked, gazing past Chrissie and into the hall. 'Is she still in bed? Do I have to shout and wake her up to get you to move?'

'You'll have a job,' said Chrissie. 'She's dead.'

Not about to fall for that trick again, Tina gave a knowing smirk. 'Yeah, right! Did you forget you've already pulled that one? *Muuum* . . .' She yelled now. 'Tell our Chrissie to let me in!'

'Shut up before you wake all the neighbours!' Chrissie hissed, grabbing Tina by the lapels of her jacket and yanking her over the step. Wrinkling her nose in disgust when she got a blast of BO as Tina stumbled into the hallway, she closed the door and pushed her into the kitchen.

'Stop pushing me,' Tina complained, glaring at her. 'I haven't come to see *you*. Well, actually, I have,' she immediately corrected herself, a sly little smile making her eyes glint. 'But we'll get to that later. I wanna see Mum first. And Dylan.'

'You're not seeing either of them,' Chrissie retorted frostily. 'Dylan doesn't know you, and I'm not letting you scare him any more than you already have. And you know full well that Mum's dead, 'cos I know you read my texts, so you can quit play-acting.'

A flicker of uncertainty replaced Tina's smirk as she gazed into her sister's eyes. 'Are you serious?' she asked. Frowning when Chrissie released an exasperated sigh, she mumbled, 'Jeezus, I had no idea. *Honestly.*'

'You saw the texts I sent you,' Chrissie repeated, unmoved by Tina's performance.

'I *didn't*,' Tina insisted. 'I swear to God. I haven't had my phone since I left.'

'I should have guessed,' Chrissie snorted. 'Sell it for smack, did you? Or is it crack these days?' she added with a sneer of disgust. 'Certainly *looks* like it.'

Tina flopped down on to a chair at the table and shook her head. 'I can't believe it.'

'Well, it's true, so get used to it,' Chrissie said bluntly. 'And now you know, you can bugger off back to whatever squat you've been hiding out in, and leave me and Dylan in peace.'

'He's my son, not yours.' Tina glared up at her.

'Maybe so, but I'm his legal guardian,' Chrissie informed her. 'And if I say you can't see him, you can't see him.'

'You can't do that,' Tina protested. 'I've got rights.'

'Do me a favour,' Chrissie scoffed. 'You gave up any rights you had when you abandoned him – *again*. But never mind him.' She folded her arms. 'What are you doing sneaking round here at this time in the morning? Planning to break in, were you?'

'I didn't want anyone to see me,' Tina admitted. 'But I wasn't going to rob nothing. I only wanted to see Mum. *And* you,' she added grudgingly.

'Ah, have you missed me?' Chrissie's voice was dripping with sarcasm.

'Fuck off!' Tina hissed. 'I just want to know where that mate of yours lives.'

'Which mate?' Chrissie screwed up her face in confusion.

'Leanne, obviously,' said Tina. 'Jake hasn't been round in ages, and I can't get hold of him, so now I'm gonna tell his precious girlfriend all about him – see how he likes that!'

Chrissie's heart thudded painfully in her chest as she picked up on the spite behind her sister's words. 'What are you talking about?' she demanded.

'I warned him,' Tina said, almost as if she were talking to herself. 'Don't fuck me about and your secret will be safe with me, I said. All's I wanted was a bit of respect, but the cunt proper took the piss. "I'll give you your own place and as much gear as you need,"' she went on in a mimicking voice. '"All you have to do is keep your gob shut and hand over half of whatever you make from your punters, and we'll be sweet." Lying bastard!'

Chrissie's head was reeling, and she sat down heavily on the chair facing her sister's. 'What are you saying?'

Tina jumped as if she'd forgotten that Chrissie was there. Chewing on her bottom lip nervously as it occurred to her that she'd already said too much, her gaze flicked everywhere but at Chrissie as she plucked the sleeve of her jacket with bitten-down nails.

'*Tina!*' Chrissie said sharply, slapping the palm of her hand down on the tabletop to get her attention. 'Start talking, or I swear to God I'm gonna slap you into next week!'

'Forget it,' Tina muttered, shuffling forward on her seat. 'I shouldn't even be here.'

'No, you shouldn't,' Chrissie agreed. 'But now you *are* here, you're not leaving till I know exactly what's been going on – even if I have to beat it out of you.'

'I can't,' Tina said, jumping to her feet. 'He'll kill me.'

Pre-empting her, Chrissie ran to the door before she could get to it, and pushed her into the chair.

'Now stay there and don't move!' she ordered, pointing a warning finger at her sister's face. 'I'm going to make a brew, then you're going to tell me everything. And I mean *every-thing*,' she reiterated firmly, determined to find out exactly what was going on.

35

Sally wasn't happy. Baby Jack was almost six weeks old, but Jake still hadn't been round to see him. And Ben was no help. As guilty as he clearly felt whenever he popped round to see how she was getting on, he refused to discuss Jake, beyond telling her that his friend was busy working and would come round as soon as he got a chance, so she was none the wiser as to when she was going to see Jake again.

He was still paying her allowance into her account each month, and she'd noticed that he had increased it by a couple of hundred pounds after Jack was born. But the money wasn't as important to her as he obviously thought it was. All she really wanted was for him to see his son and fall in love with him, the way she had – and then, hopefully, fall in love with her as well.

That was what this had all been about, after all, and if she'd known it was going to be like this, she would have thought twice about leaving the comfort of her parents' house to live here on her own. In agreeing to come here, she had sentenced herself to a life of mind-numbing loneliness, sitting in the flat day after day, with no family or friends to confide in, waiting for Jake to pay one of his sporadic visits. And then there were the sleepless nights to contend with, as she lay in bed with her heart in her throat, thinking that every little creak was the murderer who'd killed the old tenant from upstairs, come back to do the same to her.

And, yes, she now knew that this *was* the house where it had happened. Just as she also knew that Jake's girlfriend, whose name she now knew was Leanne, used to live on the top floor.

She'd been hurt when she'd learned these facts from one of the neighbours shortly after bringing Jack home. Not only because it meant that Jake must have known about the murder when he'd persuaded her to move in – which in turn meant that he'd lied when she'd asked him outright – but also because Jake obviously thought that precious little *Leanne* was too good to live in a dump like this. Why else would he have whisked her off to live with him as if *she* were some kind of princess, leaving Sally – the mother of his first-born child – to slum it like a great big nobody?

That last bit pissed Sally off more than anything, and the longer Jake stayed away, the more determined she was to have it out with him when he deigned to show his face.

In a dark mood today, thanks to Jack keeping her awake for half the night crying, she decided that enough was enough. She would give Jake a week, and if he hadn't been in touch by then, she was going to tell her mum and dad everything. If Jake wasn't interested by now, she reasoned, then she might as well give up trying and go home. At least she'd have support there, and would be able to sleep without worrying about getting hacked to death in her own bed. And, despite what her mum had said when she'd first learned that Sally was pregnant, Sally knew that she would be a doting grandmother, which meant that Sally would be able to pawn Jack off on her whenever he got too annoying.

But she'd still give Jake a chance, she decided. She hadn't forgotten all those times when he'd called round unexpectedly and had given her that sexy smile of his as he let his gaze slide up and down her body; or the tingle that had ricocheted inside her when his fingers had lingered over hers as she'd handed him his cup of tea or glass of wine. He'd made her believe that there was a possibility of something developing between them in the future, and that was his saving grace.

But she was still only giving him a week to get his arse round here, and then one more to make up his mind who he wanted: Sally and his son, or his other bitch. And if he didn't make the right choice, it was game over.

At the exact moment she made that decision, the doorbell rang. Heart leaping at the thought that it might be Jake – that he'd somehow sensed that she was thinking about him, and felt compelled to come and see her at long last – she quickly scooped Jack out of his bouncing chair and carried him to the door.

Disappointed to find a fat woman on the doorstep, she

raised an eyebrow. 'Can I help you?' she asked, thinking as she said it that *this* might be why Jake hasn't been round yet: because she'd been as fat as this heifer the last time he'd seen her.

Chrissie's gaze dropped to the baby in Sally's arms, and her lips tightened when she saw his beautiful, unmistakable little face.

'So it's true, then,' she stated rather than asked.

'Excuse me?' Sally frowned. Then, eyes widening in realization, she gasped, 'Oh, my God! Please don't tell me *you're* Leanne?'

'No, I'm not,' Chrissie snapped, offended by the look of scorn that had come over Sally's face as she looked her up and down. 'But I *am* her best mate, and I think you and me need a little chat.'

Sally bit her lip. She had no clue how this woman had found out about her and Jake, but she had, so Sally had no choice but to deal with it. And if *she* knew, did Leanne also know, she wondered. She kind of hoped so, because that would force Jake to make his decision sooner rather than later.

'You'd better come in,' she said at last, her stomach fluttering with excitement at the thought that she might be about to achieve her heart's desire.

*

Ben had called in at four different jewellery shops after doing his chores, but he was absolutely clueless as to what kind of ring Chrissie would actually like. The vast array of stones, with their varying cuts, clarities, carats – and whatever else each assistant had spouted on about while trying to entice him to part with his money – had boggled his mind.

After finally settling on a ruby and diamond ring, he'd put down a deposit and had promised to call as soon as he knew the size he wanted.

Aware that he would have to confess his intentions to Leanne if he were to stand any chance of getting it right, he decided that he would have a quiet word with her when she and Jake got home.

With his friend on his mind, Ben made a detour to Sally's place before going home. The baby wasn't his responsibility, and he knew it probably wasn't wise to keep going round there, but he couldn't deny that he'd formed a slight attachment to the little fella after watching him come into the world. And he also couldn't deny that he felt sorry for Sally. Jake might not have intended for any of this to happen, but it had, and he was every bit as responsible for that as Sally was. While Ben understood his friend's reluctance to get involved with the child, especially so in light of Leanne losing her baby, none of that was Sally's fault – and it definitely wasn't baby Jack's.

Parking up outside Sally's house now, he leaned into the back and picked up the Glo-Worm he'd bought after leaving the last jewellery shop. Sure that Jack would love it, he was smiling as he reached out to ring the bell. But the smile evaporated in an instant when the door suddenly opened and he saw Chrissie standing there.

'Wh-what are you doing here?' he asked, his face draining of colour.

'I could ask you the same thing,' she said, her gaze dipping to the toy in his hand before coming to rest on his face. A range of emotions from disbelief to disappointment to disgust flitted through her eyes before she spoke again. 'You *knew*,' she spat, her voice as accusing as it was cold.

'Let me explain,' Ben mumbled, holding out his hand. 'Please, Chrissie . . . it's not what it looks like.'

'Save it for someone who cares!' she yelled, slapping it aside. 'You and me are finished. And don't bother trying to let yourself in when you come for your shit, 'cos I'm going to dump everything on the path and change the locks!'

Calling her name again when she shoulder-barged him out of the way and stalked off down the road, Ben's shoulders slumped when she stuck up two fingers in reply.

'Sorry about that,' Sally apologized from the doorway. 'If I'd known she was your girlfriend, I'd have sent you a text to warn you she was here. But I had no idea.'

'It's not your fault,' Ben replied glumly. 'It's mine for keeping secrets from her. I should never have got involved in this in the first place.'

'You and me both.' Sally sighed. 'She's just told me about Jake getting engaged. Is it true?'

'Yeah.' Ben nodded.

'I wish you'd told me,' Sally murmured. 'If I'd known, I wouldn't have kept on hoping for so long.'

It was a lie, and they both knew it. She wasn't the kind of woman to let a little thing like an engagement ring put her off; Ben knew that she would think nothing of stealing Jake away from Leanne if she got the chance.

At the thought of Leanne, he squeezed his eyes shut and ran a hand through his hair. In two days she and Jake would be home, and she'd be expecting to get together with Chrissie to start planning the wedding. But now that the truth was out the only thing they'd be planning would be Jake's funeral, if the fury in Chrissie's eyes was anything to go by.

'How did she know?' he murmured. 'About you, I mean.'

'She reckons her sister told her,' said Sally, shrugging as she added, 'It's probably just as well. It was bound to come out sooner or later, wasn't it?'

Filled with dread at the thought of what was about to come, Ben's shoulders sank even lower. Taking pity on him, Sally said, 'Why don't you come in and have a brew? You look like you could do with one.'

'No, I need to go home,' Ben said quietly. 'Here.' He held out the Glo-Worm. 'It's for Jack, but I've got a feeling I won't be seeing him again, so you'd best give it to him.'

'That's a shame,' Sally said, giving him a sad smile as she took the toy. 'I know he's too young to know anyone properly, but I'm sure he's starting to recognize you – he gets all gurgly whenever you come round.'

Feeling sick at the thought of the child wondering why the fat man with the funny hair had deserted him just like his daddy had, Ben muttered a guilty apology before rushing back to his car.

In his flat a few minutes later, he flopped into an armchair and dropped his face into his hands as the realization that he'd lost the best thing that had ever happened to him hit home with the force of a sledgehammer. He had no clue how Chrissie's sister had found out about Sally, but now Chrissie was aware that he had known about the baby and had been keeping it from her, she would never forgive him. Even if she were willing to hear him out long enough for him to explain that Jake had sworn him to secrecy, and that he'd gone along with it in order to save Leanne from getting her heart broken, she definitely wouldn't understand why Ben had taken it upon himself to keep going round there to visit the child. And if, God forbid, she ever found out that he had been present at the actual birth, after lying and telling her that he was doing maintenance work, he'd be lucky if she didn't *kill* him, never mind speak to him again.

As much as he hated Jake for putting him in this position, Ben knew that he had to warn him before he came home and walked into World War Three. If nothing else, it would give Jake a chance to confess everything to Leanne before she heard it from Chrissie. And she, in turn, would have a couple of days to get her head around it.

Not caring that making a mobile phone call to America was

probably going to cost an arm and a leg, Ben dialled Jake's number. Tutting when an automated message immediately informed him that the recipient was unable to accept his call, he cut it off and tapped a fingernail against his front teeth. Relieved to know that Chrissie wouldn't be able to contact Leanne, and truly doubting that she'd tell her something as enormous as this by text, he decided to send a quick one to Jake, telling him to call as soon as his phone was back on. And, just in case Jake responded in his usual I'll-reply-when-I-can-be-bothered way, he wrote *URGENT!!!* at the end of it.

That was all he could do for now, so he resolved not to think about Jake any more, and deal with his own problems instead. Namely: Chrissie.

He knew her well enough to know that she wouldn't take kindly to him turning up there tonight. But if he didn't at least try, she'd think he didn't care. And, right now, he didn't know which was the worse of those options. Go round and get his head bitten off, chewed up and spat back at him; or leave her to cool off for a day or two and then crawl to her on his hands and knees and beg for forgiveness. Either way, he was going to get it in the neck – and rightfully so.

Deciding that he deserved whatever she had to throw at him, and he'd have to be a man and take it on the chin if he was to stand any chance of getting back with her, he bit the bullet and dialled her number.

'Chrissie, it's me,' he blurted out when, to his amazement, she answered. 'Please don't hang up, we need to talk.'

'I've got nothing to say to you,' she replied icily. 'And the only reason I answered was so that I could tell you never to call me again. I trusted you, but that goes to show what a fool I am.'

'You're not a fool,' Ben interjected when she paused for breath.

'Shut up!' she snapped. 'I don't even want to hear your pathetic voice. I just want you to get it into your thick head that we're over. And now I'm going to block you so you can't call me again. Goodbye.'

With that, she was gone, leaving Ben in no doubt that she had meant every bitter word. Cursing Jake as tears spilled from his eyes, he hurled his phone across the room and dropped his face into his hands, his heart breaking for the love he'd found and then lost again, all within the space of six short, incredible, irreplaceable months.

36

Leanne was relaxed, if a little exhausted, as she and Jake left the airport and climbed into a taxi. The Vegas trip had been her first ever international holiday, and it had been magical. She'd felt as if her dad was right there with her as she played the slot machines, strolled hand in hand with Jake along the Strip at night taking in the bright lights, and sat through some amazing cabaret shows. But she'd known that her dad wouldn't have stayed around to see the action in the suite Jake had booked them into. That would have been way too much for him to handle. Hell, it had been almost too much for *her* at times. Their separation, as brief as it had been, had certainly put the spark back into their love life – and then some.

When they arrived at the apartment, Jake dropped their suitcases in the bedroom and opened the French doors to air the place out.

'I think I'll take a quick shower,' Leanne said, unbuttoning her blouse. 'I feel all sticky from the flight. Fancy joining me?' she added with a mischievous grin.

'I'd love to,' he said, glancing at his watch. 'But I think I'd best go see the lads first; make sure everything's okay.'

'I guess that's the holiday officially over, then?' Leanne sighed. 'I'm joking,' she said when he gave her a guilty look. 'Honestly, it's fine. I knew you'd be itching to check on things, so go.'

'As long as you don't mind?' Jake pulled her into his arms and gave her a sexy grin. 'Put that red basque on when you get out of the shower, and we'll do that thing again when I get home.'

'I don't think so!' she protested, slapping his arm. 'Not in broad daylight, anyway.'

'Spoilsport,' he chuckled, kissing her on the cheek before letting her go. 'I'll try not to be too long.'

Leanne nodded and waved goodbye over her shoulder as she made her way into the bathroom. If she knew him, he'd be out for hours. But that was okay. Unlike Jake, who'd had no problem sleeping on the flight and had stepped off the plane as fresh as a daisy, she hadn't slept a wink, so this would give her a chance to get her head down for a few undisturbed hours.

*

Jake's first port of call was the office from where he ran his security business. Situated above a launderette in Longsight, it was actually a poky flat, the front room of which he used as the reception-cum-meeting room, while the bedroom was his private office.

It had been all he could afford when he'd first set up in Manchester but, lately, he'd been thinking about relocating to somewhere better. Not only because it would look more professional – which would inevitably bring in more clients in need of top-class, reputable security – but also because he'd decided to get serious with the property side of things.

The run-down flats and houses he picked up at auction to rent out or sell on at a slight profit had been a good starting point, but it was time to expand into the higher end of the market, where the real money was made. And if he hoped to stand a chance of making his mark amongst the established city-centre developers, he needed a base as flash as theirs to operate from – preferably on the Quays, which was fast becoming Manchester's equivalent of London's Canary Wharf in terms of big business.

He'd allowed himself to become a little complacent before the holiday, and had been happy to let the businesses coast along in the middle lane. But the break had revitalized his ambitious streak and he was now ready to move up into the next league.

Ben was sitting behind the desk in the front room when Jake walked in, a deep frown on his face as he pored over a pile of paperwork.

'Oi, oi!' Jake said, creeping up on him and making him jump.

'Bloody idiot!' Ben croaked, his eyes bugging. 'You almost gave me a heart attack!'

Taking in the deep hollows beneath his friend's usually

bright eyes, Jake said, 'What's up with you? You look terrible. It's not been that hard, has it?'

'Didn't you get my message?' Ben asked.

'No, my phone's been off,' said Jake, reaching into his pocket for it. The moment he switched it on, numerous message and missed-call notifications filled the screen. Scrolling through them, he shrugged. 'Which one? There's loads.'

'The one marked urgent,' said Ben. Then, flapping his hand dismissively, he said, 'Forget it, you're here now, so I can tell you.'

'Tell me what?' Jake frowned, sensing from Ben's nervous expression that he wasn't going to like what he was about to hear. 'I hope you haven't screwed anything up, mate? Everything was running smoothly when I left, and I don't need any problems fucking my day up.'

'Sorry, but this is going to fuck up more than your day,' Ben said ominously. 'It's bad, man. *Really* bad.'

*

Leanne was feeling a little brighter after her shower. No longer sleepy, she rooted through her handbag for her phone as she towel-dried her hair. She'd call her mum first, she decided, and make sure she was okay. Then she'd call Chrissie, who would probably be at work, and leave a message to let her know that she was home.

Her mum wasn't in, so Leanne left a message on the answering machine, telling her that she would call round to see her in the morning. Pleasantly surprised when she then rang Chrissie and it didn't go to voicemail, she said, 'Hello, you! I'm back!'

'Where are you?' Chrissie asked, not sounding as pleased as Leanne would have expected. 'Is Jake with you?'

'I'm at home, and no, he's not,' Leanne replied warily. 'What's up, babe? You don't sound too good. Is everything all right?'

'No, it's not,' Chrissie said flatly. 'Can you come over?'

'What, now?' Leanne frowned. 'I've not long come out of the shower and I haven't even unpacked yet. Can't you tell me on the phone?'

'No, I need to see you,' Chrissie insisted.

Feeling suddenly apprehensive, Leanne said, 'Babe, you're scaring me. Please, tell me what's going on. It's not Dylan, is it?'

Sighing at her end, Chrissie said, 'No, he's fine. This has got nothing to do with him.' She paused for a moment, then said, 'I didn't want to tell you like this, but you need to know, and it's probably better that you hear it before Jake comes home, so you can decide what you're going to do.'

'Do about what?' Leanne's mouth had gone bone-dry. 'For God's sake, Chrissie, *tell* me!'

'Jake's been seeing Sally Walker behind your back,' Chrissie blurted out. 'He bought your old house, and he's been letting her live there . . . with their baby.'

'*What* . . . ?' Leanne's head was spinning, and her stomach felt as if it had fallen through the floor.

'I'm so sorry, Lee, but it's true,' Chrissie said regretfully. 'I went round there after I found out, and she told me every-thing. And I saw the baby,' she added quietly. 'He's the absolute spit of Jake. There's no doubt whatsoever that he's the father.'

*

Jake ran a red light and almost knocked a pedestrian over in his haste to get back to the apartment after Ben told him what had happened in his absence.

He'd tried to call Leanne, but her phone was switched off. He was praying that she simply hadn't got round to turning it on yet, rather than having turned it off because Chrissie had already got to her and she didn't want to speak to him.

He had no clue what he was going to say to Leanne when he got home; all he knew was that he had to act fast if he was to stand any chance of minimizing the damage this revelation was going to cause.

One thing was for sure: Sally Walker was dead when he got his hands on her. The bitch had been sitting pretty for months, taking advantage of his good nature – *and* the handsome allowance he'd given her. Well, those days were over, she'd made sure of that; and she was going to rue the day she decided to cross him.

As was that other back-stabbing, big-mouthed whore, Tina!

Jake leapt out of his car when he got home and ran all the way up to the apartment.

'Leanne?' he called nervously, walking into the bedroom. 'Are you sleeping?'

She wasn't in there, and the bed was still made. A wet towel was lying on the floor by her side of the bed. Picking it up, he dropped it into the laundry basket before heading into the living room.

'Leanne . . . ?'

She wasn't in there, and she wasn't in the kitchen or out on the balcony either, although the French doors were open. Frowning, because it wasn't like Leanne to go out and leave the apartment unsecured, Jake ran his hands through his hair.

A sudden breeze coming in through the open doors lifted a piece of paper he hadn't noticed up off the dining table and sent it floating to the floor. Hoping that Leanne might have nipped out to the shop, leaving the note in case he got back before her, Jake reached for it when it landed beneath a chair.

His hand froze when he noticed the engagement ring lying a few inches from it, and he squeezed his eyes shut and moaned, '*Noooo . . .*' when his gaze landed on the note.

I know everything, you bastard!

37

Chrissie's expression was as hard as flint when she answered the door an hour later, and her rigid posture as she stood in the doorway, stiff-backed, arms folded tightly over her chest, told Jake that she wasn't about to invite him in.

'Took you long enough, didn't it?' she sneered.

'I want to see Leanne,' he replied evenly.

'Well, she's not here,' Chrissie snapped. 'And she doesn't want to see you, so there's no point looking for her.'

Jake narrowed his eyes. 'I bet you're fucking loving this, aren't you?'

'Are you for real?' Chrissie snorted, her own eyes sparking with anger. 'I love that girl like she was my own sister, so, *no*, I'm not *loving* it! You've broken her heart, you two-timing bastard, and I'll never forgive you for that, so get lost!'

She went to slam the door in his face, but Jake shoved it so hard it sent her reeling back against the wall.

'Get out!' she yelped when he walked in and kicked the

door shut behind him. 'You're not welcome here, and if you don't leave right now I'll call the police!'

Ignoring her, Jake pushed Chrissie out of the way and stalked into the living room, calling, 'Leanne . . . ? Where are you? I know you're here, and I need to talk to you.'

'I've just told you she's not here,' Chrissie repeated angrily as she followed him. 'And you're wasting your breath if you think she's going to listen to any more of your lies. If you were half the man you claim to be,' she went on scathingly, 'you'd do the decent thing and leave her alone. You've hurt that girl more than anyone's ever hurt her before, and you should be ashamed of yourself!'

'Shut your mouth!' Jake hissed, trying to push past her again to go out into the hall.

'Don't tell me what to do in my own house,' she yelled, grabbing his arm to prevent him from getting out of the room. 'You might think you're some kind of hotshot out there, but in here you're nothing but a lowlife piece of shit!'

'And you're nothing but a poisonous fat slag!' Jake sneered, his eyes glinting maliciously as he bared his teeth at her. 'Your pathetic attempt to keep us apart didn't work the last time,' he went on quietly. 'And it ain't gonna work now.'

'What are you talking about?' Chrissie gasped, reaching out to steady herself when her knee hit the side of the sofa. 'You sound like a mad man.'

'Maybe that's because I *am* mad,' he said, walking after her when she backed away. 'Mad that I didn't see what *you* were up to from the start. You never liked me, and I could tell you were jealous when I took Leanne away from you. But, *tough*! 'Cos I love her, and she loves me, and when we sort this out, I'll do whatever it takes to make sure *you* never come between us again!'

'You're crazy!' Chrissie stuttered, still trying to distance herself. 'I've never tried to come between you. Christ, I was happy when she got with you, 'cos *she* was happy – and she deserved it after all the shit she'd been through. You can blame me as much as you want,' she went on as she edged around the coffee table. 'But this is *your* fault, not mine. You're the one who had a fling with Sally and lied to Leanne for months, not me.'

'I never had a fucking fling,' spat Jake. 'And this *is* your fault, 'cos Leanne would be none the wiser if you hadn't opened your big trap. Bet you were buzzing when that slag of a sister of yours turned up and spilled the beans, weren't you? See it as your big chance to get Leanne away from me and have her all to yourself, did you?'

'Leanne knows all about what you did to Tina, as well,' said Chrissie. 'The drugs you've been giving her, the blokes you've been pimping her out to – *every*thing.'

'She wouldn't believe a word that came out of that whore's mouth,' Jake sneered.

'Well, *I* did,' said Chrissie. 'And I'm sure the police will, too!'

Lunging at her when she snatched up the phone, Jake wrenched it out of her hand and, gripping her by the throat, forced her down on to the sofa.

'You've been nothing but trouble since the day I clapped eyes on your ugly face,' he spat, causing her to flinch as his nose grazed hers. 'Think I've forgotten all those times you took the piss out of me when I was a kid? All the dirty looks you gave me, and the sly comments you made whenever I walked past? And don't think I didn't know it was you who egged Leanne on to turn me down that time. Just 'cos no lad would touch *you* with a bargepole, you had to make damn sure your little friend couldn't have any fun, didn't you?'

'*Fun?*' Chrissie's croaked, struggling to pull his hand off her. 'With *you*? Don't make me laugh! You were the biggest loser walking!'

'Brave words,' Jake hissed, his eyes flashing a warning. 'But I'd zip it, if I was you. Unless you want to end up going the same way as her dad.'

'*What?*' Chrissie's eyes bugged with shock.

'You heard me,' Jake snarled, tightening his grip. 'Thought you'd won when you got Leanne to stay here, didn't you? All week you had her, and you pecked at her head the whole time, chipping away at her bit by bit, trying to make her think she'd be better off without me. But I knew she'd turn to me when she needed a shoulder to cry on, and I was right. Daddy dies, and she comes running straight to me. But you couldn't stand that, could you? That's why you couldn't wait to tell her about Sally.'

'Get off her!' Leanne cried, running into the room at that exact moment with tears streaming from her swollen, raw eyes.

'Let her go!' She tugged on the back of his jacket. '*Please*, Jake . . . she can't breathe!'

Releasing Chrissie, Jake turned to Leanne and held out his hands.

'Baby, we need to talk. But not here. She's already tried to poison you against me, but we can sort this out, I know we can.'

'No, we can't,' Leanne replied shakily. 'It's over, and nothing you say or do is going to change my mind, so just go. *Please*.'

'No.' He shook his head. 'Not without you. You're my life.'

'This isn't your choice,' she cried. 'It's *mine*, and I don't want you any more, so forget you ever met me and go and be with Sally and your son.'

'It's not my kid,' Jake said through clenched teeth.

'Jake, I've *seen* him,' Leanne sobbed. 'He's the image of you, so there's no point denying it. And I've seen the pictures of . . .' She paused and swallowed deeply as a sickly taste flooded her mouth. 'You and *her*, together in bed,' she managed at last. 'Or are you going to tell me they're fakes, as well?'

'She took them before me and you got together,' said Jake.

'At least you've admitted it at last.' Leanne gave a humourless laugh. 'All those times I asked you to tell me the truth, and you stood there and lied to my face. God, I'm so stupid.'

'How could I tell you after the way you reacted when she rang me?' Jake asked. 'Come on, Lee, this isn't all my fault. Let's go home and talk about it.'

'No.' Leanne shook her head. 'If it was just that, there might have been a way to get past it. But there's all the other stuff, too. Those people in Liverpool . . . And *Tina*.' Her eyes flashing with disgust now, she said, 'If what she told Chrissie is true, I think you're absolutely despicable.'

'That's not all he's done,' Chrissie said, slipping her phone into her pocket after sending the text she'd typed while Jake's back was turned. 'Ask him what he just said about your dad.'

'My dad?' A deep frown creased Leanne's brow. 'What about him?'

'Are you going to tell her, or shall I?' Chrissie glared at Jake.

'You fucking *bitch*!' he snarled, spinning round and punching her square in the mouth, knocking her flat on her back.

'JAKE, NO!' Leanne screamed, frozen to the spot in horror when he aimed a kick at her friend's ribs. '*JAAAKKKEEE!*'

*

Ben's face was pouring with sweat as he screeched his car to a halt outside Chrissie's house. Luckily, he'd gone home after Jake ran out of the office, so he hadn't had far to come when Chrissie's text came through a few minutes ago, reading: *Come quick! Jake's going off his head!*

Reaching for the monkey-wrench he kept under his seat, he leapt out of the car without bothering to close the door, and ran towards the gate.

Mrs Ford poked her head outside as he approached. 'Whatever's going on in there?' she asked, her eyes wide with concern. 'What's all the screaming about?'

'It's okay,' Ben lied, flapping his hand at her to go inside. 'Chrissie's seen a mouse, that's all.'

He could – probably *should* – have told her to ring the police, he thought as he fumbled his key into the lock. But he didn't know what was going on yet, and he hoped that he might be able to get Jake to calm down without needing to involve the authorities.

The screams grew louder as the door popped open. Silently thanking God that Chrissie hadn't followed through with her threat to change the locks, Ben followed the sound into the living room.

'JAKE! *STOP!*' he roared when he saw what was happening. 'I mean it, man! Back the fuck off!'

'Oh, for fuck's sake!' Jake said, his chest heaving as he turned around. A sneer came on to his face when he saw the wrench in Ben's hand, and he opened his arms wide. 'Come on, then, fat boy . . . bring it on – if you've got the bollocks!'

'Fuck off out of here, or I will,' said Ben, his gaze flicking down to Chrissie, who was curled in a ball, clutching at her ribs. 'I mean it, Jake. Go now, before this gets any worse!'

Narrowing his eyes when Ben re-established his grip on the wrench and started moving towards him with a determined expression on his sweaty face, Jake reached into his pocket and slid his gun out.

'I wouldn't come any closer, if I was you,' he warned, pointing it at Ben's face.

'Oh, God!' Leanne squawked, holding herself up on the

back of the couch as her legs threatened to give way. 'Jake, put it away, I'm begging you. This has gone far enough.'

'No, it hasn't,' he replied coolly, his stare still fixed on Ben.

'Mate, don't be stupid,' Ben said, as calmly as he could manage. 'Mrs Ford's already called the police,' he went on, praying as he said it that she'd ignored him and done exactly that. 'They could be here any minute.'

Leanne's heart leapt into her throat. If the police arrived and caught Jake with the gun, somebody was going to end up getting badly hurt, or even killed. But if she could get him out of here before it went any further, she'd be able to talk him down, she was sure.

She took a hesitant step forward and held out her hand. 'This has got nothing to do with Ben and Chrissie, Jake; it's between you and me. You said you wanted to talk, so let's talk. It's not too late.'

'Not here,' he muttered.

'Okay, we'll go home,' she suggested, desperate to get him away from her friends. 'Jake, *please*,' she urged when he didn't move. 'We've got to go *now*!'

He turned his gaze to her and pursed his lips, giving it some thought. Then he asked, 'Will you hear me out; give me a chance to explain?'

'Yes,' she agreed, nodding to emphasize the word. 'I promise.'

Jake released a heavy sigh, as if a weight had been lifted from his shoulders. Then, turning to Ben, he smashed the side of the gun into his face.

Crying out in pain when his nose exploded, Ben collapsed into a heap and held his hands over his face as blood poured through his fingers and soaked the carpet beneath him. Squatting down, Jake grabbed him by the hair and yanked his head back.

'Say one fucking word about this to the police, and I'll come in the middle of the night and kill the whole fucking lot of you,' he snarled. 'And don't test me on that, 'cos you know I'll do it.'

With that, he got up and, taking Leanne by the arm, steered her out through the door.

38

Leanne was terrified when Jake bundled her into his car and drove her away from Chrissie's house. She'd never seen him so angry, and she certainly hadn't known that he possessed a gun. But, then, it appeared that there were a *lot* of things she hadn't known about him, so she couldn't work out why she was so surprised. She only hoped that he'd have calmed down enough to be reasonable by the time they got home and sat down to talk.

He still wasn't going to get the result he wanted, though. As she'd told him, she *would* hear him out. But as she'd also said, nothing he said was going to change her mind.

Even if she'd been able to forgive him for attacking Chrissie and lying about sleeping with Sally, there was no way back for them now Leanne knew about the baby. It had been hard enough losing her own, without knowing that he had another child with someone else. That was just too heartbreaking.

'Where are we going?' she asked, speaking for the first time since they'd set off when she realized they were heading in the wrong direction.

'Somewhere safe where we can talk,' Jake muttered.

'But I thought we were going home?'

'I'm not *that* stupid.'

Jake turned and glanced at her, and Leanne shivered when she saw the expression in his eyes. He was one of the most handsome men she had ever met, and his soft brown eyes usually made her stomach flip because they reflected nothing but love and gentleness. But there was an alien light in them right now that she could only describe as evil.

'Put this on,' he said suddenly, reaching into his pocket and pulling out the engagement ring she'd left at the apartment.

'*No!*' She shied away from it and folded her arms as if to hide her hands. 'I told you, we're over.'

'No, you said you'd hear me out,' Jake reminded her angrily. 'So put the fucking ring on!'

Afraid that he might crash the car and kill them both if he flipped out again, Leanne reached out shakily and took the ring from him. It felt like a dead weight when she slid it on to her finger, and she couldn't believe that, only a few short hours ago, she hadn't been able to stop admiring it and everything it symbolized. The happy life she'd thought they were embarking on after the trials of the previous few weeks; the perfect future in their perfect apartment, with her perfect husband-to-be.

There had been times, when she'd been alone in bed waiting

for him to come home from work, when she'd thought it was all too good to be true. And now she knew why.

*

When Jake pulled into a narrow alleyway some time later, Leanne gazed out through the window and frowned when she saw the barbed wire coiled along the tops of the walls on either side. She shivered when the moon disappeared behind a thick bank of clouds, plunging them into inky darkness. Rain began to spatter the windscreen as the car tyres bounced slowly over the cobbles, and the sudden swish of the automatic wipers made her jump.

Hugging herself, she gazed up at the rear windows of the derelict row of shops to her left and the uninhabited terraced houses to the right. Most were concealed behind metal sheeting or smashed, and they were all as dark as the alleyway, which told her that there was no one around to help her.

Jake eased to a stop alongside a padlocked gate halfway along the alley and cut the engine before jumping out and walking quickly around to her side. An icy blast of wind whipped her cheeks when he opened her door, and her legs felt like jelly as she unhooked her seat belt and climbed out.

'Don't even think about it,' he warned, gripping her tightly by the arm when he caught her casting a glance back down the alley in search of an escape route. 'I don't want to hurt you, but I will if I have to.'

'You already are,' she replied shakily, wincing at the pain of his fingertips digging into her flesh.

He let go after a moment, and she rubbed at the sore spot as he turned and slotted a key into the padlock. The gate opened on to a rubble-filled yard at the rear of an empty shop unit, and he waved for her to go in ahead of him.

'I can't,' she croaked, taking a stumbling step back. 'It's too dark. There could be rats.'

A squeal of fear escaped her lips when Jake seized her by the wrist and hauled her into the yard, and tears flooded her eyes when her ankle twisted painfully as he marched her across the debris. He stopped at the steel back door and unlocked it with a mortice key before shoving her into a tiny, pitch-dark hall-way. A steep flight of stairs faced them, at the top of which was another door.

The hallway reeked of mildew and rotten food, but when they reached the top of the stairs and he opened the door, an even fouler smell hit her in the face. Covering her nose with her hand, she stumbled over the threshold into the flat above the empty shop unit.

The front room was dark, but the moon had emerged from behind the clouds and tiny pinpricks of light were leaking in through the holes in the metal covering the window. As her eyes began to adjust, she was able to make out the outlines of a sofa, a single bed, a cluttered coffee table, and what appeared to be an upturned cardboard box holding a portable TV.

Behind her, he locked the door and then slid his hand along

the wall in search of the light switch. Squinting in the unexpected brightness, she inhaled sharply when her gaze landed on the origin of the putrid smell.

'Oh, my God!' she cried, staring in disbelief at Tina's battered body sprawled on the floor between the sofa and the window. 'What the hell did you do to her, Jake? Is she . . .'

'Dead?' he finished for her. 'I'd say so, judging by the stench she's giving off. Not that she was too bothered about hygiene when she was alive,' he went on, a glint of disgust flaring in his eyes as he gazed down at the body. 'And to think she actually thought I'd be interested in a skank like her. What a joke!'

'I don't understand.' Leanne stared at him as if she'd never seen him before. 'What did she do to deserve this?'

'She couldn't keep her big mouth shut,' Jake said, gazing coolly back at her. 'And the other one's lucky she was out when I called round before coming for you, or she'd have got the same.'

'*Sally?* Why?'

'The pair of them have been blackmailing me for months,' Jake explained, giving her a little shove now, sending her heavily down on to the sofa. 'And I went along with it because I didn't want *you* to find out. See, that's how much you mean to me,' he went on, his gaze intense as he sat beside her and peered into her eyes. 'I'd do anything to keep you happy. And you were, weren't you?'

'Yes, but it wasn't real,' Leanne murmured sickly. 'It's all based on lies, and you must have known I'd find out about the baby eventually. You couldn't keep it secret for ever.'

'Why not?' he asked. 'Sally would never have told anyone if *she'd* kept her big mouth shut.' He aimed a kick at Tina's lifeless body. 'Filthy crackhead whore! I should have known she couldn't be trusted.'

Leanne's heart was beating so hard it felt like it was going to explode as she stared at Jake. He actually believed that everything would have been all right if only she hadn't heard about Sally and the baby. But sooner or later, something bad would have happened. It already *had*, when she'd been used as bait to lure him to Liverpool. He'd insisted that her kidnappers had targeted him out of bitterness because he'd cut ties with them and made a success of his life. But maybe that woman had been telling the truth when she'd said that Jake had ripped her brother off. And what had he *really* done when he'd gone back to them after sending her home that day? He'd already proved that he was capable of killing somebody in cold blood – the evidence of that was lying right there. So had he killed those people, too, and set fire to the warehouse in order to get rid of their bodies?

When Jake entwined his fingers through hers, she gripped the cushion she was sitting on with her free hand and, drawing on every ounce of willpower she possessed, forced herself to gaze into his eyes as if she was sad that it had come to this.

'What are we going to do?' she whispered.

'I don't know,' Jake replied quietly. 'Go away somewhere? It'd have to be abroad, though.'

Astonished that he actually believed she'd be willing to move abroad with him, knowing what she now knew, Leanne forced herself to give him a tiny smile.

'Maybe,' she said. 'Or maybe we could stay and try to sort this mess out?'

'How?' Jake narrowed his eyes.

Unsure if she'd roused his suspicions, or if he genuinely thought she was trying to find a way out of this, Leanne shrugged. 'I don't know. We need to think this through carefully before we make any decisions. Chrissie's my best mate, and Ben's yours, so I'm sure they'll forgive you once they realize I'm okay. Nobody knows about . . .' Unable to say Tina's name, she nodded in the direction of the body. 'Do they?'

'No.' Jake shook his head. 'Only you.'

'Well, that's one good thing,' Leanne muttered, feeling sick all over again. 'Chrissie knows what she's like, so she won't think anything of it if she never goes home. And that's the only bad thing you've actually done, so if we can get rid of the body, everything will go back to normal.'

'It won't, though, will it?' Jake said flatly. ''Cos you'll never be able to forgive me for what happened with Sally.'

'I'm not saying it'll be easy,' Leanne replied carefully, knowing that he would never fall for it if she suddenly declared that she could forget the pain he'd caused her. 'It might take a long time before I really get over it, and you'll just have to accept that I might never forgive you completely. But that little boy is innocent, and I'd have to be some kind of monster to hold any of this against him. *Or* his mother.'

Jake stared into her eyes, as if weighing up whether or not he believed her. After several moments, he opened his mouth to speak, but the sound of a brick knocking against another in the yard below made him snap his head around.

'What was that?'

'I don't know,' Leanne squeaked, shrinking away from him when he yanked the gun out of his pocket.

Jumping up, Jake rushed over to the window and, straddling Tina's body, peered out through a hole in the metal sheeting.

'It's the police,' he hissed when he saw several shadowy figures moving through the pitch-dark yard below. 'How the *fuck* did they find out about this place?'

'I don't know, but it's over now,' Leanne said, her legs shaking wildly as she stood up and backed towards the door.

A bright light suddenly flared, causing Jake to wince as it hit him in the eyes.

'Armed police . . .' a voice boomed from below. 'Come out with your hands in the air.'

'It isn't over until I say it is!' Jake snarled, lunging at Leanne and dragging her back into the room. 'I'll shoot the first cunt who comes through that door.'

'Please, Jake, do as they say,' Leanne pleaded when he threw her down on to the sofa. 'If you love me half as much as you say you do, stop this now and let me go. I promise I won't tell them anything. We'll – we'll say we stopped off here to pick up your rent on our way home and found Tina like this. She was a prostitute, so one of her punters could have done it. There's nothing to prove it was you.'

'Shut up,' Jake hissed, pacing in a tight circle.

'We haven't got time for this,' Leanne sobbed. 'If you don't give up, they're going to force their way in and shoot us both. Hide the gun and tell them you don't know what they're talking about if they ask where it is. I'll back you up, I swear!'

Jake stopped pacing and ran his hands through his hair. Then, exhaling loudly, he walked over to Tina's body and dragged it away from the wall before pulling the edge of the carpet away from the rotten skirting board. Yanking at the floorboard beneath until a piece came away in his hands, he dropped the gun down into the hole and shoved the wood into the gap before replacing the carpet. Then, after rolling Tina over to cover it, he went back to Leanne and pulled her to her feet.

'You're the only girl I've ever loved,' he said, his eyes boring into hers as the vibration of a battering ram being smashed into the steel door shook the floor beneath their feet. 'Everything I've done I did for you, because I wanted to make you happy. But if you betray me now, I swear to God I'll kill you.'

'I won't,' Leanne whimpered, afraid that she might wet herself as the thunderous hammering continued down below.

'Swear on our baby's soul,' Jake demanded.

Fresh tears spilled down Leanne's cheeks, but she forced herself to hold his gaze. 'I swear on our baby's soul.'

Satisfied that she would never have said it if she didn't mean it, Jake pulled the mortice key out of his pocket and unlocked the door just as the battering ram broke through and footsteps began to pound up the stairs.

'Don't shoot!' he shouted, raising his hands into the air. 'We're coming out.'

39

Leanne was completely drained by the time a police officer dropped her off at Chrissie's house later that night. Acutely aware that Jake was in the same building, maybe on the other side of the wall listening to every word she was saying, it had taken three long hours to give her statement. The police officers had assured her that he couldn't hear her, but she'd been terrified all the same, and it had been a struggle to speak up when they had asked her to.

That part was over now, and they had told her that they would be holding Jake for twenty-four hours at the very least, so she didn't have to worry about him coming after her tonight.

But what about tomorrow?

If they didn't have enough evidence to charge him, they would have to let him go, and what would happen then? He would know she'd betrayed him, and he'd already warned her that he would kill her if she did that. Even if they *did* charge him, she still wouldn't be safe, because they had told her that she'd be called to testify against him at the trial.

She couldn't believe that she had been so completely and utterly taken in by Jake. How had she lived with him these last few months and not seen any hint of the dangerous criminal that lurked behind his Mr Nice Guy facade? She wasn't stupid by any means, and nor was she a silly little girl who was so blinded by love that she refused to see the signs that were staring her in the face. But she genuinely hadn't noticed anything amiss about him. And that was scary.

Chrissie opened the door before Leanne had a chance to ring the bell. 'Are you all right?' she asked, pulling her into a hug. 'I was so worried about you.'

Chrissie's eyes were red and swollen. Guessing that the police must have told her about Tina, Leanne said, 'I'm okay. What about *you*?'

Chrissie shook her head and pulled a tissue out of her cardigan pocket to wipe her nose. 'I might not have liked our Tina very much, but I wouldn't have wished something like this on her. They couldn't tell me much; just that it looks like she was murdered, and not an overdose, or something. They said they're going to try and trace her punters, but I told them not to bother, 'cos I know it was Jake. It was, wasn't it?'

Leanne nodded. 'I'm so sorry, babe. She was already dead when we got there.'

Chrissie released an anguished breath. Then sadly, she said, 'She looked terrible when I saw her the other day; the worst I've ever seen her. If Jake hadn't killed her, she'd probably have killed herself before long. At least she's got my mum to take her in hand now, eh?'

Leanne gave her a sympathetic smile. She'd never been particularly religious herself, but it obviously gave Chrissie comfort to believe that her mum and Tina had been reunited in God's care.

'Anyway, there's no point standing here all night,' Chrissie said wearily. 'I left Ben pouring us all a stiff drink, so let's go and sit down, then you can tell us what happened at the station.'

Leanne nodded and followed her friend into the living room. Thanking Ben when he handed her a glass of brandy, she sagged down on to the sofa and swallowed the drink in one.

'God, I needed that.'

Chrissie sat down beside her and flapped a hand at Ben to refill her glass.

Leanne gazed at Chrissie's face, and then over at Ben's, and felt sick with guilt when she saw the livid bruises on their cheeks and around their eyes.

'I'm so sorry for getting you both involved in this,' she murmured. 'It would never have happened if I hadn't reacted so badly to finding out about Sally and the baby.'

'You can pack that in right now,' Chrissie scolded. 'This is *his* doing, not yours.'

'You've done absolutely nothing wrong,' Ben agreed, his swollen nose making his words sound muffled. 'Anyway, if anyone should be apologizing, it's *me*. I've known about the baby from the start, but I was too much of a wuss to tell you.'

'You're not a wuss,' Chrissie countered. 'You're just too loyal for your own good.'

'Yeah, well, it was misguided where he's concerned,' Ben said miserably. 'I felt sorry for him when we were kids, and I guess I kind of took it upon myself to look out for him because I knew no one else cared. But I'll never make that mistake again, believe me. He took me for a mug, and I'm ashamed that I went along with his lies for so long. But I'm completely done with him now. From here on in, it's just you, me and Dylan.'

'And Leanne,' said Chrissie.

'Of course,' he agreed. 'That goes without saying.'

Chrissie turned back to Leanne. 'What did the police say? They're not going to give him bail, are they?'

'Not if they can help it,' said Leanne. 'The detective who took my statement said he's determined to take this to trial. If he can make it happen, he reckons Jake will get at least twenty years.'

'God willing,' Ben said bitterly, taking a swig of his drink.

'But what if he doesn't?' Chrissie asked.

'I don't know?' Leanne admitted, shivering when a wave of apprehension passed over her. 'If Jake finds out what I told them . . .' She paused and breathed in deeply before continuing: 'He said he'd kill me if I betrayed him, and made me swear on our baby's soul that I wouldn't. I'll never forgive myself for that.'

'You had no choice, so don't feel guilty,' Chrissie said softly. 'They're only words, and God and the baby know you didn't mean them.'

Leanne nodded and blinked back the tears that were stinging her eyes.

'So what happens now?' Chrissie asked. 'Please tell me you're not going back to the apartment?'

'Only to pick up my stuff.'

'Okay, Ben will take you so you can get everything out in one go. And then you're coming to stay here with us.'

'Thanks, but I need to get away for a bit,' said Leanne. 'At least until I know if it's going to court. I don't want to be around if they let him out. Even if they keep him in, I don't trust him. He's got all those thugs working for him, so what's to stop him from sending them after me?'

'I can't see that happening,' Chrissie said. 'They'd have to be really stupid to get involved, knowing what he's accused of.'

'I don't know about that,' Ben said ominously. 'I had the . . . shall we say *pleasure* of working with them while Jake was away, and I wouldn't put anything past them. *Or* him.'

'So where will you go?' Chrissie's eyes were dark with concern as she peered at Leanne. 'You will phone me, won't you?'

'Of course I will.' Leanne reached over and squeezed her hand. 'But if it does go to trial, I might have to go into hiding, because they've told me I'll be called as a witness. They'll probably call you, too,' she added guiltily. 'I told them what you said about Jake insinuating that he'd killed my dad. Sorry.'

'Don't worry about me, I'll gladly testify against the bas-tard,' Chrissie said vehemently.

'Me too,' added Ben. Then, turning to Leanne, he said, 'I don't suppose this'll be of any help, but my cousin got married a few months back. It was actually his stag party we were at the night you and Jake met up.'

'What's your point?' Chrissie asked impatiently.

'He inherited his mum's house,' Ben explained. 'But he doesn't live in it, because him and his wife emigrated to New Zealand a couple of weeks after the wedding. It's in Bury, which isn't so far from here that Leanne would feel cut off; and it's still fully furnished, 'cos our Scott couldn't bring himself to get rid of his mum's stuff. Best of all, Jake knows absolutely nothing about it.'

'Wow,' Chrissie murmured. 'That sounds perfect. What do you think, Leanne?'

'It's definitely worth considering,' Leanne said thoughtfully. 'Would you be able to contact your cousin to ask if it'd be okay for me to stay there, Ben?'

'I don't need to. He left his keys with me so I could keep an eye on the place.'

'And Jake definitely doesn't know about it?' Chrissie asked. 'There's no chance your cousin could have told him about it at the stag do?'

'No chance.' Ben shook his head. 'His mum was still alive at that time, so it wasn't an issue. Anyway, Jake was far too busy copping off with Sally to be bothered talking to any of my mates that night. To be honest, I don't even know why I invited him in the first place. It wasn't like he knew any of them. I only asked him because thought I *should*, 'cos he hadn't been back in Manchester long, and I was his only mate. More fool me, eh?'

'You're no more of a fool than me,' said Chrissie. 'I got taken in by him as well. And he must be good, 'cos it takes a lot to pull the wool over *my* eyes.'

'I'm the biggest fool of us all, 'cos I let myself fall for him hook, line and sinker, even though my instincts told me at the start that he was lying about Sally,' Leanne said wearily. 'If only I'd listened to them, none of this would have happened.'

'Well, the sooner you get your stuff out of his place, the sooner you'll be able to start picking yourself up,' said Chrissie, glancing at the clock as she spoke. 'Why don't you go now? I'll make up the spare bed for you while you're gone. Then, tomorrow morning, we can drive over to Bury to take a look at that house.'

'Sounds good to me,' Leanne said, rising wearily to her feet. 'New day, fresh start, and all that.'

'For all of us,' Chrissie said as they walked out into the hall. 'We've just got to keep our fingers crossed that Jake doesn't worm his way out of this.'

'He won't, not if that detective's got anything to do with it,' said Leanne. 'And if I have to face him in court to make sure he pays for what he did to my dad and your Tina, then I will. But after that, I never want to see him again for as long as I live.'

Epilogue

Ice cracked underfoot as Jake walked quickly along the road. Winter had hit early and hard that year, and the freezing wind was battering everything in its path. His padded jacket and gloves were protecting him from the worst of it, and he'd pulled his woollen hat down low and his collar up high to conceal his face. But that last precaution hadn't really been necessary, because no lights were showing in any of the windows of the houses he was passing, which told him that the residents were all dead to the world, oblivious to what was about to happen.

He couldn't wait to see the look on her face when she realized he'd found her. He wished he could prolong the agony and really make her suffer. But he couldn't afford to indulge himself. He'd been on the run for two days now after arranging for his boys to hijack the van taking him to court, and the police would be going all out to find him, so this had to be an in-and-out job; no wasting time, no messing around.

The house he was looking for was conveniently situated at

the end of the terraced row, and the adjoining hovel had recently been vandalized, judging by the broken glass littering the pavement beneath its boarded-up window. The front door was hanging off its hinges, and Jake picked up the acrid scent of stale smoke as he approached. A glance inside as he passed revealed heaps of bin bags stacked against the fire-scorched walls, and he sneered when he saw the blood-caked syringes that had spilled out of the one nearest to the door.

Oh, she must love it round here, he thought smugly. *Reduced to living alongside dirty scummy junkies. Serves her right, that does; serves her fucking right.*

A narrow alleyway separated the block from the windowless side wall of a derelict tyre warehouse. Confident that he hadn't been spotted, Jake made his way to the gate at the rear of the house. It was locked, and jagged shards of glass were embedded along the top of the wall that enclosed the backyard. But he wasn't about to let a little thing like that deter him. He'd come prepared.

The towel-wrapped hammer made a dull thudding noise as he quickly flattened a section of the glass. When he'd made a wide enough gap to safely climb over, he stepped into the shadows and waited to see if the noise had roused anybody. No lights came on, so he hauled himself over the wall and dropped quietly down into the pitch-dark yard.

Metal bars protected the windows here, but no such measures had been taken to secure the door. It didn't even have a mortice lock, which would have made his task more difficult, just a flimsy old Yale that gave little resistance when he gently pushed the door. Easing the hammer forks between the door and the frame, he gave a couple of tugs, and almost fell inside when it easily popped open.

An alarm rang out as soon as he stepped into the kitchen. Aware that somebody might hear it and come to investigate, he rushed through the hall and darted up the stairs.

As Jake had guessed, Leanne was in the front bedroom, and he smiled when he pushed open the door and saw her lying there; her beautiful face bathed in the faint orange glow from the street lamp outside the window. Her hair was fanned out on the pillow, and he could hear her breathing softly as he walked quietly over to the bed. She looked surprisingly relaxed, he thought. In her shoes, he'd have been sleeping upright with one eye open and a machete in each hand. But the bitch obviously thought she'd got away with it and he wouldn't bother coming after her.

More fool her.

The alarm hadn't roused her, but she must have sensed his presence because her eyes suddenly snapped open and a whimper of terror escaped her lips when she saw him standing over her.

'How . . . how did you find me?' she croaked, shrinking back when she saw the hammer in his hand.

'It's amazing how fast people spill their guts when you're torturing someone they love,' he said, leaning over her and staring down into her eyes.

'What do you want?' she cried, flinching when his hot breath peppered her cheeks.

'You fucked me over, so now I'm going to fuck you up,' he said matter-of-factly. 'Just like I *warned* you I would.'

'I didn't say anything,' Leanne spluttered. 'I swear I didn't. I – I—'

'Shut your lying mouth!' Jake seized her by the throat and forced her head down into the pillow. 'I know *exactly* what you said, you back-stabbing bitch. Did you really think they wouldn't let me read your statement?'

'Jake, please don't do this,' she whimpered. 'Just go. I promise I won't tell them you were here.'

'And why would I believe a word you say?' he sneered. 'You've already proved you can't be trusted. And to think I would have done anything for you. *Anything*,' he repeated through gritted teeth. 'I treated you like a fucking queen, and you repaid me by trying to get me banged up for fucking life.'

Leanne's eyes were bulging from the pressure of his grip. 'The police will be on their way,' she gasped, clawing at his hands with her nails in her desperation to get him off. 'The alarm goes straight through to the s-station.'

'Is that right?' He smiled coldly. 'Best get on with it then, hadn't I?'

He straightened up and raised the hammer above his head with both hands, his gaze never leaving hers. But just as he was about to bring it down, his eyes widened, and Leanne screamed in horror when blood sprayed over her face and soaked the duvet cover.

Jake dropped the hammer and clawed at the handle of the knife that was embedded in his neck, but the blade was in too deep.

Shaking wildly, her hands curled into fists, Brenda Riley stood over him when he fell to the floor and glared down at him as he thrashed weakly at her feet.

'My Norman was right about you – you *are* a cocky little shit!' she snarled. 'You might have got away with what you did to him, but you will *not* take my girl away from me.'

'Oh, Mum!' Leanne sobbed, scrambling out of the bed and running to her mother as the sound of approaching sirens filled the air. 'Thank God you were here!'

'Well, I wasn't going to leave you on your own with *him* on the loose, was I?' Brenda said, hugging her tightly as blue lights began to strobe their faces.

'Police!' a voice called out loudly from the hallway below a few seconds later.

'Up here,' Brenda yelled. 'But you'd best fetch a body bag,' she added coolly. 'This bastard might have given *you* lot the slip, but I was buggered if he was getting past me.'